BEST FRIENDS

Books by Consuelo Baehr

REPORT FROM THE HEART

BEST FRIENDS

BEST FRIENDS

Consuelo Baehr

DELACORTE PRESS/NEW YORK

Published by
Delacorte Press
1 Dag Hammarskjold Plaza
New York, N.Y. 10017

Manufactured in the United States of America

First printing

Designed by Terry Antonicelli

Library of Congress Cataloging in Publication Data

Baehr, Consuelo
  Best friends.

  I. Title.
PZ4.B1423Be   [PS3552.A326]   80-15067
ISBN: 0-440-00841-7

For my Uncle Charlie, with love

The world, or life, or death, or things present, or things to come; all are yours. (1 Cor. 3:22)

Prologue
Late Fall 1956

IT WAS UNLIKELY THAT THEY SHOULD EVER meet. One was too rich, one too poor, and the third learned early to live by her wits. The fragile coincidence that brought them together simultaneously sealed their destinies. Had they known, Sara and Miranda would probably not have changed anything. Natalie, on the other hand, would have been scornful.

They came together at St. Mildred's Academy for girls, a small convent school favored by the rich for its shabby gentility and by the middle class for its endorsement by the rich. The school was situated between a racetrack and an insane asylum. It was conservative in every way and promised, among other things, to teach its charges womanly deportment and classical Latin.

Such things were still important in 1956. Mr. Eisenhower had been reelected by the largest majority in American history. The Edsel was advertised as performing fine, riding well, and handling good. The number one song ecstatically told the world that ". . . my baby rocks me with a steady roll." *Too Much Too Soon* by Diana Barrymore and *Peyton Place* by Grace Metalious were best-sellers, giving fair warning that public innocence was hanging by a thread.

Sara arrived at the school in late October wearing a dress that was far too short. Walking to the library to wait out the first afternoon, she was horrified to feel air on her thighs. If she walked normally, the skirt flounced out and revealed her underpants. If she walked slowly, it looked as if she had to go to the bathroom. Her coat was no better. It was too short to be a coat and too long to be a jacket. Too thin for winter and too ugly for spring. She made small fists in her pockets. There was nothing else she could do.

The sudden concern for appearances was no coincidence. Sitting at the other end of the long library table engrossed in a book was a girl whose every accessory showed great care. Her blond hair, precisely cut to end midway between her ears and shoulders, was held by a silver barrette. She wore a heart-shaped ring on her smallest finger which struck Sara as an extraordinary place to wear a ring. Tiny burgundy initials were embroidered on her uniform jumper. When the girl looked up briefly and saw she was not alone, she jumped and Sara laughed.

"I'm sorry. Really. I didn't mean to scare you on purpose." The girl continued to stare. "Laughing is a reflex, you know. Like blinking—or sneezing." The girl said nothing. "Your heart stops every time you sneeze. If you couldn't stop sneezing, you'd die right off." The girl lowered her eyes as if she had seen something embarrassing. "A woman back home killed her husband like that once."

Silence. Large blue eyes flickered with interest and finally looked up. "How?"

"She shook sneezing powder all over him. It took seventy-three sneezes before he croaked right at her feet. His heart just blew out like a fuse."

"Did that really happen?"

"Nope. I made it up."

"Just now?"

"It was a story I wrote last year at my other school. A magazine almost bought it, but they said it wasn't a real mystery because the killer was never caught."

"Why'd she kill her husband?"

"He was old and mean."

"Why'd she marry him?"

"Money. Her mother made her do it."

"Did she get the money?"

"Yup."

"Was she happy after that?"

"Yup. Went to live in Paris, France."

The girl began laughing. She laughed so hard she began to hiccough, which made her laugh more. After a while she returned to her book and Sara watched her hand with the pinky ring and wondered how she could hide her exposed legs until bedtime. She wanted the girl to like her.

She had attended the school three years before when she was nine. Her father had had a nervous breakdown and her mother had returned to work. "Your dad's gone off the track," her aunt Gloria had said matter-of-factly. What track? Why, the track of life. That was a poetic way of saying he was crazy, and she had used the phrase many times since to explain the unexplainable.

Aunt Gloria was rich, or at least richer than her parents, and had pressed her sister into letting her provide Sara with a fancy education at a proper school in the Maryland horse country. She assumed Sara would spend much of her day on horseback, an idea that appealed to her sense of wholesomeness. Sara never had the heart to tell her no horse ever set hoof on the grounds.

"Are you new?" This time Sara was startled.

"I was here once before. I won't be staying long."

"That's what everyone says," said the girl.

"You just wait," answered Sara hotly.

"Okay, okay. I didn't mean to get you all worked up," said the girl. "How come you left your other school?"

"My dad's gone off the track."

"You mean crazy?" The girl was fascinated.

"Yes."

"How? I mean how does he act?"

"Different." She had not meant to blurt it out and was disappointed in herself. "He acts very different . . . mostly at his office. He begins to move desks around and he rearranges things."

"Are you sure he's crazy? That doesn't sound so bad to me. Just moving a few desks."

"We have to put him away anyway," said Sara, wishing she had more exciting details to tell the girl. "He *asks* us to. He comes home and says to my mother, 'Dora, I began to move the desks again, it's time to go back.' " Sara assumed the air of someone at the mercy of an antic world. "This time he arranged some people, too. He locked Mr. Eton, the sales manager, in a supply closet overnight." Sara was quiet, remembering how her father had looked that last day. "Wanna play checkers?" she had asked him, and he nodded vaguely. When she jumped one of his men, he had begun to cry.

"I'm sorry," said the girl. Sara nodded and tried to hold back the tears that were spilling down her cheeks.

"I bet you think I bawl all the time, don't you?" she asked.

"No. Honest."

"I'm not crying about my dad, either."

"Why *are* you crying?"

"My mother's gone and this dress is too short. I think my behind shows when I walk, and I won't get my new uniforms for two weeks."

"What if you borrowed one of mine?"

"Do you think I could?" Relief flooded her small, oval face.

"Sure. Stand up and let's see how tall you are."

"Now don't be surprised by my long legs," she said uncertainly, rooted to her chair. "It's from all those years of dancing and acrobatics . . . made my legs grow too fast."

"What kind of dancing?"

"All kinds. Tap, apache . . . you name it."

The girl began to smile. "Did you make that story up at your other school, too?"

"Nope," said Sara calmly. "I made it up right here."

"Come on, stand up now. We have to go to chapel for rosary and you can sit next to me. My name's Natalie. Natalie Davidson."

Sara rose and stuck out her small white hand. "Sara Rafferty." The knot in her heart began to unravel.

The feeling was not to last. Coming toward them, leading a line of girls who had just come in from a game of softball, was a small, thin nun with a sharp, pointed face that barely filled out her wimple. It was Sister Francisca, the day nun in charge of the older girls.

"I see you're back with us, Sara," she said without expression, "a bigger girl now. We'll see how much growing you've done." It was a reprimand and Sara felt uneasy. Some people like you and others don't, she thought and moved closer to Natalie. "All right, girls," said the nun, "form a line. You, Sara, come to the front."

Miraculously, Natalie stayed by Sara's side, and they marched side by side into the shiny, varnished pews, ready to face Jesus. After rosary, drowsy from the chanting, they splashed cold water on their faces and went to the refectory for dinner. Sara was relieved when Natalie bribed Denise Wilson, a tall, wiry girl, with the promise of her tapioca pudding so she could sit with Sara. When dinner was over and they sat in the darkened library waiting to see a film about Thomas Edison, Sara got the courage to ask Natalie a question that had been with her all afternoon.

"Are you rich?" she said as naturally as she could.

"Yes," answered Natalie simply. "Very."

Georgia Bancroft was crying. Tears were so regular at St. Mildred's that the four girls playing crazy eights hardly glanced up. They knew the difference between real tears, which were rare, and rich girls' tears, which were gulping, quiet, and usually shed over trivial annoyances. Girls that could tolerate and speak glibly (sometimes boastfully) of their parents' sexual escapades, declines or advances of fortune, and split-ups in the family, went to pieces over a misplaced sweater or an unsuccessful haircut.

Natalie never cried. She considered tears inexcusable, a sign of emotion gone awry; and emotions made her nervous. One other good reason for not crying was that it infuriated her stepmother.

She had not cried when her mother divorced her father and ran off with a golf pro or when her cat died. She had not cried when she fell off a horse and broke her leg and it had to be set without pain-killers in the wilds of Wyoming where she and her father and stepmother were on a riding vacation.

Celine, her stepmother, was convinced that Natalie's deadpan expression and indifference to everything was a form of criticism. Criticism of Celine. And it was.

When Natalie was eleven, Celine in a fit of annoyance insisted that Natalie see a psychiatrist. The first four sessions were spent in stony silence with Natalie sitting primly, staring at the doctor's framed diplomas and pictures of scrawny children in Little League uniforms. The doctor remained unruffled by the silence, and out of sheer boredom Natalie decided to report something insignificant. Yes . . . she would tell him about her thighs. Their slight roundness bothered her, and sometimes she felt that while she might diet herself to nothingness, her lower body would survive and grow on its own.

The next visit she confided her fears that her thighs would grow to unmanageable proportions, and the doctor, who asked to be called Rufus, assured her that such fears were unfounded and could be neutralized. Her thighs were fixable.

"It's love for your daddy trapped in there," he said with perfect seriousness. Natalie assumed he meant something horrid and began to dislike Rufus intensely.

In subsequent visits Rufus began to knead the flesh above her knees between his strong fingers and talked to her quietly and firmly as he did so. "Natalie, we're taking all the daddy love out of your thighs and spreading it throughout your body. Also, and this is important, you can let some of the love out and express it. You won't use it up." He paused to let the idea sink in, which it did, leaving Natalie uncomfortable. The dislike now turned to hatred. Express love? She was certain that people wanted to be loved because they were afraid of *not* being loved. It was a sort of blackmail. What's more, most people, including Celine and all the girls at school and practically everyone she'd ever met, wanted her to think well of them which mostly she did not.

"You're creating love all the time," Rufus continued, "just like you make red blood cells or anything else your body needs."

The idea, though bizarre, might be plausible. What concerned her, however, was not the discovery that she did not express love, but that he could dig something out of her like a ripe potato. What else might he dig up, and what if he dug something up that she didn't want known?

After that session Natalie casually described to Celine what took place during her therapy. "It's not all head stuff, you know. He does physical things, too."

"Physical things?"

"Yes. Massage. He says he's taking the daddy love out of my thighs and spreading it out in my body."

Celine's jaw dropped and she clasped and unclasped her hands several times. Rufus had been her idea and now she would have to find a way to quietly dump him. After that conversation Natalie made it a point to behave more cheerfully and snuffled noisily every time she watched Lassie on television. In a quiet moment she suggested to her stepmother that she might benefit from the companionship of other girls. Perhaps it would do now to be in boarding school. Celine readily agreed and after some inquiries chose St. Mildred's as suitably far to circumvent frequent trips home.

Natalie adjusted quickly and well to the school. She made a game of the rules and deprivations, using them to hone those traits in herself which she valued most: self-control and the manipulation of those around her. It made her feel safer. She could get people to do almost anything if she pretended not to care what they did.

The girls at St. Mildred's were cliquish, snobbish, quick to ostracize, slow to accept. After some initial jockeying for power each girl grudgingly accepted whatever position fell to her. Nancy Jordan was an heiress to fast food money, and though her accent was Brooklyn, she had enough flair and social know-how to be included not only during the week, but for weekends as well, a sign of true belonging. Sally Watkins, a shoe manufacturer's daughter, was grateful to be taken up by Rita Ford whose fortune had come via Wall Street.

The sole break in the chain was Natalie who allied herself with no one and dipped into all groups. Given her high recognition name and well-publicized sportsman father, she could have taken any position she chose. She was more than beautiful; she was a prototype of what every other girl would opt to be—tall and graceful and well-proportioned. Her hair was both silky and plentiful and hung straight down, controlled and golden. Her eyes were turquoise rather than blue, and startling in their clearness.

Everyone had waited for Natalie to make her move but it never came. She was not interested in close alliances or in the protection of a clique. She didn't need them. She managed to make the others unhappy with their own looks and slightly disappointed with the friends available to them.

Given these circumstances, Natalie was able to orchestrate Sara's downfall swiftly and easily. Her reasons for doing so were simple. Sara was an irritant. The girl's behavior was the opposite of her own. Natalie, attracted by indifference and detachment, while Sara was determined to tap dance her way into everyone's heart. Instead of merely freezing Sara out of her life, Natalie decided to rid her of those self-debasing traits once and for all. It would be for Sara's own good.

Having made up her mind, she gathered the A group around the library table one afternoon and began by letting her eyes rest for an instant on each girl. Rufus had said that eye contact was a powerful communication tool, and Natalie was gratified to watch them all smile back uncertainly. They would believe everything she told them.

She began by saying that Sara did not belong at the school because she lacked the proper background and the proper manners to feel comfortable among them. Their eyes widened with interest. They were slightly disappointed that they hadn't come to this conclusion on their own.

"You can see how she eats," Natalie continued in a businesslike voice. "She's so . . . so . . . fond of her food." The girls couldn't remember anything specific but nodded gravely. "Of course, her pathetic efforts to be one of us are all wrong. She laughs too loud. She snorts. There's no sense of . . . of privacy. We must teach her to contain her emotions."

She paused for it all to sink in. "As a matter of fact she could even be . . ." Natalie stopped abruptly, surprised at what she had been about to say. She had been about to say that Sara might be crazy like her father, and she shuddered at the immediate havoc this would cause. She hadn't planned to tell them that. She had set a limit on how far she would go because she wanted to be able to rescue Sara at any time.

She took a deep breath and let it out slowly to give her words added import. "Well, as long as she's here, it's up to us to point out to her what she's doing wrong. We can correct her when she needs it and leave her to think things over the rest of the time."

They carried it further than Natalie had intended. Given their frustrations, it was a relief for the A group to suddenly have someone on which to settle their hostility. They despised Sara. They despised her quick, intelligent eyes and her humor which they assumed was a clumsy attempt at acceptance. She personified things about themselves that had not worked out and frightened them. Her hair frizzed up around her face. Her eyes were too far apart and too wide. She looked perpetually surprised. Worst of all she was earnest.

The slights at first were passive. Sara's questions weren't answered. If she called a name, the girl didn't look up. If she sat next to someone during a film, the girl moved elsewhere. More aggressive acts followed. Her toilet articles were missing, and when she arrived at breakfast, remarks about her uncombed hair and unbrushed teeth would hiss across the table. After that came notes—one sentence messages found among her things, including one which left her throat dry and her knees weak. "We know you touch yourself down there." What did it mean?

Sara was mystified and yearned to ask Natalie why these things were happening to her. But each time she approached Natalie, a distant look came over her face as if she didn't know who Sara was.

One day, however, almost miraculously, Natalie stayed behind when the others went to early morning mass and sat with Sara at the library table. Hope sprang up in her heart that everything would be resolved. Perhaps Natalie had even stayed back on purpose to have some private time with her.

After five minutes the proper moment presented itself for Sara to speak. Natalie had been writing furiously and suddenly her pen went dry. She shook it violently but to no avail. It made indentations, but no ink came out.

"Here, take mine," offered Sara quickly. "I've got two."

"I couldn't do that," said Natalie politely.

"Why not?"

"Because I have no intention of being buddies. It would be misleading of me to accept your pen."

"Oh hell's bells, Natalie, take the old pen. Nobody's asking for your precious friendship." Sara threw the pen across the table. It bounced on Natalie's fingers and continued to the floor. Natalie picked up her belongings and walked out. Sara burst into tears. Her insides hurt and she was dizzy with confusion. And there was something worse. Like her tormentors, she was beginning to find fault with herself.

Sara saw two courses open to her. She could choose friends from the other outcasts, Coreen Savalas with her harelip and strange voice, or Denise Wilson, a girl with tapeworm who gratefully lapped up everyone's leftovers, which were considerable in that diet-conscious group. She could also wait out the persecution until they tired of it. Both routes pained her. She was not used to humiliation and several times chose to remain in bed, feigning illness.

After one such day the injustice of it washed over her and she decided to cower no longer. She began to raise her hand in class and answer questions, ignoring the groans of disbelief. "Did you hear *it?''* *"It* wanted to answer.'' *"It* raised its hand.'' Nausea plagued her, but she kept her eyes fixed on a silly picture of Jesus coming through clouds until she calmed herself.

Then, in what possibly was the most humiliating moment of her life, Rita Ford ran screaming from her side insisting she had seen an animal crawling from ''its kinky hair.'' The picture of Jesus was of no help. She threw up all over her essay about the California Gold Rush titled, ''A Pilgrim at the Mill—the Diary of a Rusher.''

They shaved her head and rubbed kerosene through her scalp. She was secluded in the infirmary and had her meals brought in on a tray by Sister Joseph. Two days passed, strangely peaceful days which she spent reading old copies of *The Saturday Evening Post*. In a section for younger readers she read a story of a boy who nursed a lame pony and saved him from being shot. She thought the story was badly written and began one of her own about three close friends who promise undying loyalty until one is accused of stealing and the other two desert her.

So lost was she in her story that she didn't hear her dinner tray brought in and was startled to see not the perspiring, red face of Sister Joseph, but Natalie, fresh and composed.

''You don't have to stay long,'' said Sara brightly. ''I know the kerosene smell's terrible.''

''I don't mind,'' said Natalie. ''You're going to get a partner after dinner. Sally Watkin's crawling with them. They decided she's the carrier. Her head's got enough unhatched eggs to stock a lice farm. You only had one.'' Sara remained silent. Natalie's comments, while impersonal, seemed in her favor, but she was no longer curious about the sudden good will. ''Mother Di Blaise says Rita's to write you a note of apology for her outburst, not that that's anything.''

''Oh, I'd like to see it,'' said Sara, mentally composing a long note of abject remorse as if Rita had come to her for editorial help.

''We could play tennis when you get out.'' Natalie's voice as usual was cool and disinterested.

''I don't know how to play.''

''We don't have to really play. Just volley back and forth.''

''Maybe.''

''What about Thursday after my music lesson?''

''Okay.'' She had no interest in prolonging Natalie's stay and began to pick at her food until Natalie gave a small sigh and walked out.

When Sara left the infirmary, Natalie gave her a beautiful silk scarf to wear on her head until her hair grew out. She also spent time with Sara every day, and while Sara was sometimes glad for the company, she was also content to be alone polishing her story, which had grown to twenty pages.

After she mailed the story to Philadelphia, she had her final thought on the subject of her recent ostracism. Maybe she wasn't her old self anymore but a new one who didn't need to talk so much or be liked all the time.

Once the manuscript was in the mail, she followed it mentally each night, picturing it in the post office, in a mail pouch, delivered, placed on a desk, opened, and read. Then she pictured the man who read it being overwhelmed by admiration.

It was a woman, not a man, who finally read it. The reply came exactly three weeks later, a letter addressed to Miss Sara Hopkins Rafferty and typed neatly. She tore into the envelope (it had already been slit open) and her heart nearly burst.

Dear Miss Rafferty:

We have read your story with interest. You write with a facility and depth of feeling which held our attention and, we feel, will hold the attention of our readers.

Therefore, we are pleased to advise that we will be publishing your story, "Fair Weather Friends," in our For Younger Readers section, January issue. Enclosed is payment of $200.

Should you wish to contribute again, please be in touch with me directly.

Cordially,

Roberta Johnson
Juvenile Fiction Editor

For five minutes she sat holding the letter and the check so tightly the imprint of her fingers was clearly visible on both and she wondered if the check would still be good.

When they put the small girl in the car, she decided to start screaming and would not stop. The driver, a terrifyingly fat man with a shaved head, stared ahead as if making up his mind whether to drive or not. Twice in the first half hour he pulled off the road and crossed himself. He stared back at them, his pale, watery eyes questioning.

"How long she going to keep thet up?"

"It won't be long," said Miss Lacey, a prim and proper lady from Catholic Charities. "She doesn't want to leave her mother." She patted Miranda's back clumsily. "There, there. When your mother's better, you can go back. She'll be all right soon."

"*No es seguro,*" said Miranda under her breath, stubbornly speaking in Spanish. That's where she and Miss Lacey parted company. Her mother was not ill, and she wouldn't be getting better. Her mother drank too much and spent a lot of time lighting candles to painted statues of the Virgin Mother and Jesus.

When Miranda did not stop crying, Miss Lacey's tone turned sullen. "This is a very expensive school, and they're taking you in for nothing," she said. "Think about that, young lady."

Miranda thought about it, but not with the gratitude Miss Lacey had in mind. She was furious.

She stared out the window and found herself looking at a cow. The ride was long and smooth and fast, which she liked. She had been in a car one other time. Her aunt Margarita had bought a secondhand Ford convertible, miraculously learned to drive it, and insisted on taking them for a ride. They hadn't been on the road more than twenty minutes when her mother sat upright and unlocked the door.

"Let us out at the next corner, please," she said to her sister, and Margarita did so without a word.

When they were left standing on a strange sidewalk, her mother said that Margarita was trying to kill them because her son's wife couldn't have children. "She thinks I put a curse on her daughter-in-law, just like she did to you." She looked at Miranda, who began to shift her weight from foot to foot wondering how they would get home.

Her mother and aunt believed things that nobody else seemed to know about—magic to protect them from harm. For herself she was certain that nothing would ever harm her.

When they had been driving about two hours, the sun began to fade and the driver pulled into a wide, pebbled driveway. Miss Lacey took her hand, and they were led into a long, cool room. Miranda sat on a stiff sofa staring at the strangely shiny oxfords Miss Lacey had put on her that afternoon. She had never worn tie-up shoes before and hadn't the faintest idea how to lace and tie them. Her heart began to beat faster, and a feeling of anger and despair rose from her stomach. She screamed as loud as she could, kicking and flailing until she was surrounded by the voluminous skirts of at least four nuns, one of whom lifted her as if she were no heavier than a feather and took her away.

The cries from the front parlor could be heard clearly in the library. The voice, young and foreign, was defying Mother Di Blaise *and* Sister Francisca. What's more, Sister Joseph scurried through from the kitchen. Sister Joseph was athletic and could pick up a good-sized child under each arm and take them to wherever she wanted them to go without any huffing or puffing.

"They're going to subdue her by force," whispered Sara to Natalie. She suspected Sister Joseph had been recruited to tame the source of the screams. It heightened the interest in what already was a highly interesting development.

"Who?"

"Whoever it is they're bringing in who obviously doesn't wish to be brought in. You've heard of the expression 'she was dragged in kicking and screaming'? I think we're about to see a demonstration."

They didn't see a demonstration. Sister Francisca shooed them out so the prisoner could be conducted privately to her cell. It was rumored that the new girl had been locked in the infirmary.

Miranda had never liked churches. There was only so much you could do in a church. You could pray, but she did not pray. Today she moved her mouth to make it look as if she were answering the prayers, but she was really saying *mierda, mierda, mierda. Shit.* Everyone was looking at her, which limited her activity. She had to be still.

". . . Hail Mary full of grace . . . ." None of it made sense. It only made her sleepy. She stifled a yawn and wiped the after tears out of her eyes with her fists.

All day they had whispered about her and now they stared. She looked straight ahead. The trick was not to look at the candles. She was terrified that she might fall asleep, which would be humiliating or worse. She closed her eyes to get the image of the tiny flames out of her mind. When she closed her eyes, she felt wonderful; warm and peaceful and far away from here. She would keep them closed one second more.

She slumped against the pew. Dreaming. The sudden wetness between her legs brought her to, and she went rigid with horror. She had peed in her sleep. She had peed—was still peeing—in chapel! It was the most terrible moment of her life and she wished herself dead a thousand times. How she hated this school. Her heart was pounding for all to hear. But what did it matter; soon they would see what else had happened.

Sara, next to her, saw it first. From the start she had tried not to stare at the girl even though she was the strangest looking thing any of them had ever seen. Then she heard this hissing noise—everyone heard it, you could see them all cocking their heads, but it seemed closest to Sara. She looked down to see a thin rivulet of yellow across the polished oak floor. Still unbelieving, she watched the leather padding on the kneeler turn dark. She nudged Natalie, who looked in the direction of her pointing finger and caught on. They stared briefly at each other and then at the girl. They hadn't realized how small she was. She looked terrified.

Sara fished out a ballpoint pen from her pocket and wrote on her palm, "S.F. will crucify her." Natalie nodded without taking her eyes off the altar even though there was nothing happening there. Sister Francisca could patrol a room twice this size and zoom in on every pocket of mischief. Girls were often yanked out for hiccoughing or for giggling and sometimes for yawning. If she came by now, the poor creature was doomed. Natalie furrowed her brow. Then she smiled and began to hoist up her skirt with her fingers while keeping her torso erect. She wiggled out of her cotton slip and passed it to Sara who tossed it in the direction of the wetness and with some fancy footwork mopped up the evidence.

"Stick it in your pants," she whispered to the girl, who was staring in disbelief.

"Como?"

Como. "Stick the slip in your pants till we get out."

"No comprendo," came back the hoarse whisper.

Oh, God. They had risked everything and she didn't even speak English. "In there," she hissed, lifting up the hem of her skirt and pointing up.

Miranda picked up the damp slip and stuffed it somewhere up her skirt. Part of it dragged below her uniform, but she was so small, no one noticed. When they left, they put the kneeler up. It was a miracle that no one caught on.

Miranda could not believe what had happened to her. She could not believe that these two beautiful angels had appeared out of nowhere to change her life. Within hours her confusion and anger turned to joy and expectancy. She stuck to her saviors like glue.

Miranda had a different status than the rest of the girls. She was poor. However, she had her own idea of who she was, and she considered the girls of St. Mildred's pale and weak and completely incapable of managing their lives. Their whining and aspirations annoyed and mystified her. She quickly accepted the fact that Sara and Natalie doted on her. People had doted on her all her life. The women at the pocketbook factory next to her tenement had always brought her presents and fought with each other to comb her thick, black braids. They tried to cuddle her and fed her fruit from the carts. She knew they wished she belonged to them, but she was glad she did not. If perfect strangers wanted to watch over her and give her things that was all right, but she didn't belong to anyone.

Natalie, she decided, was not like the others. She was beautiful, and Miranda made a ritual of kissing her good night even though she knew that Natalie didn't like it. Oddly, the girl Miranda was most at ease with was Nellie, an overweight, lumbering girl who looked middle-aged. Nellie was recruited to look after Miranda and help her with her English (Natalie's idea, accustomed as she was to retinues and servants). Nellie's naturally slow pace was suited to Miranda's halting English. Nellie introduced Miranda to four-letter words, and the two cursed cheerfully throughout long, slow conversations.

One warm afternoon Sara and Natalie left Nellie to wait with Miranda while they snuck out to Marcy's, a tiny grocery/candy store that was out-of-bounds but close enough for them to run there and back without being missed. Nellie and Miranda were instructed to stay put on the far side of the rise next to the ball field. The older girls vowed they would break their record for the trip, but Marcy's was crowded with a group of matrons stocking up for an afternoon of bridge, and it was a good half hour before they returned.

At first they could only see one big lumpish mound in the distance and assumed Miranda had tired of waiting and gone off. They then realized that the large bulk was Nellie bending over Miranda who was lying flat on the ground. "What in the world is she doing?" Sara was puzzled. "Do you think she's wet her pants again?"

The scene didn't look right. There was something wrong in the awkward way Nellie was sitting. When they could see more clearly, they stopped, unable to go closer. Nellie, in a frenzy of ardor, was furiously massaging Miranda's plump mound between her legs. Suddenly her entire head was lost between Miranda and her own huge arm thrust into the folds of her skirt.

Natalie and Sara could not move. Unfamiliar currents went through their bodies. They were fascinated and frightened by what was happening. Nellie continued to rub herself faster and faster. Her normally heavy-lidded eyes were wide open and magnified through her thick lenses. It occurred to them that Nellie was having some sort of fit. When Nellie relaxed, they yanked a bewildered Miranda from under her and straightened her clothes. They decided Nellie was not right in the head, and she could no longer be trusted alone with Miranda.

Sara and Natalie did not speak of the incident. Something had happened. They were no longer little girls.

As spring settled in and the girls returned from their vacations, a calmness permeated the school. No one was being actively persecuted. Those who were friendless had adjusted to loneliness. The good weather gave them plenty of time to be outdoors and get properly tired. In the evenings, kneeling together for night prayers before a statue of Mary, crowded and touching, there were moments of affection among them all. They couldn't help feeling that they had shared an important part of their lives that was now coming to a close. They would—dare they say it?—miss each other.

Unexpectedly Natalie was the one most intoxicated by the idea of lifelong friendship and repeatedly asked for details from Sara and

Miranda on how their lives might proceed when they left. Natalie decided that Harbor's End, her father's estate, would absorb the three of them most comfortably for a summer reunion. The others quickly agreed.

When Sara contemplated Harbor's End, she saw a huge expanse of rolling hills and sentries posted every few yards wearing hats like English bobbies. She wanted to be absorbed by Natalie's wealth, but could not rid herself of the notion that it might all change in the morning. Natalie could once again become indifferent. This made her sad to the point of tears. Her only defense was to be watchful and, most important, to keep her mind on something else.

It seemed to work. Natalie appeared devoted, and one night she tiptoed to Sara's narrow bunk after the nuns had stopped stirring and nudged her awake.

"Are you asleep?"

"Not now."

"Promise me we'll always be friends."

"We'll always be friends."

"What about Miranda?"

"Of course Miranda."

"I'm going to provide for her when my trust comes due," said Natalie soberly. "We'll always keep in touch."

"Of course." The role of devoted correspondent greatly appealed to Sara. She was ready to write every day.

"No matter what happens?" Natalie seemed really worried, which surprised Sara.

What could happen? "Yes, I promise."

"Best friends," said Natalie in a hoarse, formal voice, and Sara did not comment, feeling too frightened to prolong the conversation. Surely a nun would flash her light on them any second. "In the morning we'll tell Miranda."

"Okay."

She felt two long, cool arms encircling her neck and realized that for the first time since they had known each other, Natalie was touching her. That was the last real conversation they were to have for almost eighteen years.

The twenty-fourth of April was an extraordinary day, cool and dry but with teasing gusts of tropical air that made the girls yearn for summer. Sara, Natalie, and Miranda, flushed from an eventful softball game, were stretched out under a large, perfectly shaped maple. One by one they rolled into the sun.

"Oh, my God, what a game," said Sara, blinking at the brightness. "My blood feels like thunder. Nat, you're red as a beet."

"I stole that base. Did you see it?" Miranda was beside herself with triumph.

"We saw it, we saw it," said Natalie rolling her eyes to heaven. Then she rolled toward Miranda and patted her head. "You were terrific. Chubby little legs going chug, chug, chug."

They couldn't stop smiling at each other.

Then they noticed Sister Francisca hurrying across the uneven ground, holding her beads and long skirts against her. She was scanning the grounds looking for someone. She stopped abruptly and stared at the three of them, then headed straight for Sara.

"There's a call for you, Sara," she said primly. "Prepare yourself . . . and remember, God has his reasons."

Sara watched her lips disappear under an expression of moral rectitude. A chill went through her. Sister Francisca had to push her into the tiny vestibule where the phone for the girls was stationed. Her legs felt numb and unwilling to take her there. Left alone, she stared at the receiver lying on its side. Words drifted in from the visitors parlor just a few steps away. ". . . hung himself with a bedsheet. He strung it up on a pipe in the linen closet . . . died in mortal sin . . . took the life God gave him . . . ." What a strange conversation. A moment before she had been perspiring, but now she felt cold. Warily she picked up the phone. It was Aunt Gloria.

"My dear," came the soft, dreamy voice, "your father has seen fit to end it all."

"End what all?" Sara did not understand. All she could think of was that her father had written "the end" somewhere. She could see him holding up a gigantic sign with just those words to explain his feelings about life.

"We're arranging for a limousine to drive you home—can you pack your things?"

"My things?"

"Yes. All your things."

"I don't think so," said Sara. She couldn't move.

"Try, dear. The sisters will help you. I'm so sorry, but your mother needs you now."

For a moment Sara was convinced her aunt had gone off the track. She had just seen her mother. Her father had been home for Easter, too. He had read Dickens out loud to show them he could concentrate. It was a good sign, he told them. A sign of increasing mental responsibility, according to his doctors. Then he had smiled the long-suffering smile of a man at the mercy of fools. Sara had understood. She had wanted to hug her father, but he wasn't ready for that. He was in his handshaking stage. He shook everyone's hand including her mother's, which was the craziest thing Sara had ever seen him do.

"I was just home two weeks ago," she said into the phone. "Mom's okay."

"Oh, dear," said her aunt. "You're not really listening to me." Sara could hear panic in her voice, and she knew her lack of understanding had put it there. She tried to concentrate, and almost instantly her mind made the awful connection. She put the receiver down on the table. It was her father they were talking about. It was her father hanging dead from a pipe in the linen closet. She could see him swinging. She saw his feet at odd angles like Jesus on the cross. Had they cut him down or untied him? She hoped they hadn't just let him drop. Then she looked down at her own thin, helpless arms.

"My father has died and I'm going home," she explained simply to Natalie when they met.

"How ghastly for you," said Natalie. "Ghastly" was a word they had discovered recently. Everything was ghastly, but Sara was surprised that Natalie could use it under the circumstances.

At the very end when Sara's suitcases were side by side out on the gravel driveway waiting for the limousine to arrive, the three friends cried helplessly.

"Crocodile tears," Sister Francisca called them, but she was wrong.

The day they parted, Natalie could not sort out her feelings toward her friend. She was shocked and angry at her own sense of dismay. Sara seemed to be taking both their lives with her and leaving Natalie with nothing.

After Sara left, Natalie wouldn't look or talk to Miranda. She told herself she hadn't meant to become such bosom buddies. Now Miranda expected it, while she really didn't need anyone at all.

Miranda, however, was too disconsolate to be put off.

"You're my friend," she stated simply.

It annoyed Natalie to admit it, but she knew Miranda would not be easy to get rid of. Besides, she looked pathetic with her socks around her ankles. "I'm your friend," she agreed wearily.

"To the end?"

"The end?" Natalie was exasperated. "What end? Honestly, Miranda."

"To the end," said Miranda obstinately. "Friends to the end." Her eyes were wide and steady. Baby beads of perspiration hung above her upper lip.

"All right, all right," Natalie said and quite unexpectedly began to cry. She took Miranda's honey-beige, sweaty hand and held it in her own cool, white one. "To the end."

Chapter 1

IT WAS THAT POIGNANT PART OF SPRING, THE
time of year when you needed a philosophy,
some meaning because another winter had dropped you back, like a
wave, on shore.

The building on Madison Avenue had two banks of elevators, and
Sara realized too late she was on the wrong one. Before starting up
again, she leaned against the cool marble in the lobby and patted her
hair. It was shocking how everything had changed in the few years
she had been out of touch with the city. Three girls walked by in
various stages of nudity. The boys delivering coffee were fashion
plates in high heeled shoes and polo shirts in shades of mauve . . .
mauve!

She was wearing freshly pressed black gabardine slacks and a silky
sweater with twenty-four tiny buttons, each snug in a crocheted but-
tonhole. The effect was modest but appropriate for a job interview.
After the third barely covered pair of thighs passed her, however, she
reached up and unbuttoned the four top buttons of her sweater before
starting toward the elevators. No need to look repressed.

"How do I look?" she had asked Reynold that morning.

"Fine," he answered innocently.

"I mean really. How do I look? Do I look young? Do I look like the mother of two?"

"Yes."

"Yes, what? Young? Or the mother of two?"

"Young."

"How young? Twenty? Thirty?"

"Ummmmmmm," his eyes narrowed. "Twennnnty-six."

"But I'm only twenty-nine."

"So. You look three years younger."

"Ooooooh . . ." she frowned.

"You look like a sullen Irish schoolboy. That's what I think sometimes when I see you coming toward me."

"Oh," her face brightened. "That's not bad. A sullen Irish schoolboy isn't bad at all." She went to confirm this in the bathroom mirror.

Her large eyes were far apart, and stubbornly she emphasized the spacing with eyeliner. *Things could be worse,* she considered. A rosy early tan softened her strong jawline and wide, generous mouth. Her figure was still boyishly slim, a status look in a community where the latest baby could leave you with a spreading behind and Smithfield hams for legs. Blessed Charlie, kind from the start, had exited her womb leaving fuller, nicer breasts. The jitters over meeting the editor had all but vanished. Why should she be less acceptable in the city than right here amid the guarded friendliness of Horse Hollow Estates?

Jane Seymour, articles editor for *Haute,* did not look up when Sara entered. She was making notes on the margin of a manuscript and from time to time took a deep breath and shook her head. Sara considered clearing her throat. Maybe the woman had forgotten she was there.

"I know you're there," said Jane, making Sara jump. "Just hold your horses. This article is a bitch and we're late on it."

Sara settled into her seat and wondered if she had made a mistake. She was already missing the children *and* her tennis game which would now be half over. She was also worried about the sitter who was new and whose pupils appeared strangely dilated.

Twenty minutes went by and Sara grew restless. Was this the time to assert herself? Was she being manipulated? The woman before her was not out to inspire confidence. She had on the ugliest and most dangerous looking pair of shoes Sara had ever seen and was wearing them *with* blue jeans, a western style shirt, and an almost military haircut.

The editor left the room and returned ten minutes later without the manuscript. "All right," said Jane, crossing her legs and lighting a cigarette, "why do you want the job?"

"I'm not sure I do." She wished she hadn't said that. How stupid. She had cracked right off. It was all probably a test to see if she had the temperament, and she had cracked immediately.

Jane searched for an ashtray amid the sea of papers. "I hear a huff," she said, bending over to pull out a sticky drawer to hold her legs. "Are you going to leave in a huff because I kept you waiting? Huh?" She straightened up and looked straight at Sara. "Huff, huff, huff. You're thinking what a big mistake this is. Why shouldn't you be in your pleasant split ranch watering petunias, right?"

"I don't live in a split ranch." Sara was annoyed by her tone and annoyed with herself for not wanting her to think she lived in a split ranch.

"Oh . . . ? Colonial?"

"No."

"Cape Cod?"

"You're cold. It's contemporary. But you're half right. I am on the fence about something."

"What was that?"

"Your shoes." Sara fixed her gaze on Jane's skyscraper-heeled sandals. "Aren't you afraid those straps will stop the circulation?"

Jane grinned. "These were left over from the shoe business issue. Nobody wanted them, so I took them home." She regarded Sara with a glint of friendliness. "Okay, let's begin. Do you know what's expected?"

"I think so. You want me to write captions and connecting copy where it's needed."

"Precisely. A thankless job and it pays badly, but as they say in the classifieds, you'll make the right contacts. 'Good ladder job to the heights' is the way they phrase it." Sara smiled. "Now look, sweetheart," Jane pulled a sheet from a manila envelope, "you've got to write to count, especially under the photographs. The layouts show you how many letters will fit, and the fact sheets will give you information about the merchandise. If it's an article about someone or something with photos, you're on your own. If you can't make it out, ask the writer. Their home numbers are usually scribbled on the layout.''

Sara thanked her and began to gather up the sheets feeling mildly euphoric.

"Uh," Jane rose awkwardly and walked around her desk. "There's just one thing. Our editor would like to meet you. It's just a formality but . . . you know . . . I can't give you the green light until you poke your head in her office.''

"Sure," said Sara. "Now?"

"No. Not now."

"She's not in?"

"She's in."

"Is she in a meeting? I could wait."

"She's not in a meeting. She's perfectly capable of seeing you now, but she doesn't want to.''

"Why not?" Sara was sure she was missing an important point.

"Well, if she saw you now, you would go home sane and relaxed and do the work I've given you more competently than we have any right to expect, and that would spoil all of Tania's fun. She would prefer that you go home crazy with doubt and seething with humiliation.''

"You're kidding, I hope."

"Of course," said Jane and sat back in her chair. "Can you come back at three?''

"I suppose."

"Good. We'll see you then."

It was not a happy three hours. Her passion for the job was growing proportionately with the chance that she might not get it. The silly job had effectively dimmed the life she had been perfectly satisfied with just yesterday.

She decided to do some window shopping, but within minutes was drenched in sweat, done in by her wool slacks, and took refuge in a small, shaded park. Her stomach felt empty but not hungry which she attributed to nerves. It seemed weeks since she had left the house that morning. An hour passed. She thought of the children, and as often happened when she was away from them, she imagined all the terrible things that could happen to children. She saw Charlie with missing teeth, missing limbs, crumpled somewhere on a road. Strangely, she never imagined Rachel hurt. Rachel seemed so much stronger. She realized, not for the first time, that she was the tiniest bit afraid of Rachel. Rachel was six.

She left the park and whiled away another hour trying on bathing suits in a boutique on Third Avenue. The saleslady brought in half a dozen bikinis and encouraged her to try them on. Sara chose a white one, smiling at the size of it. The bottom was held together by two gold links.

"Just as I thought," said the woman when she had it on, "you're the type who looks better naked." She stood back for an appraising look. "Stunning."

Sara liked that, but it also made her apprehensive. She had never worn a bikini. What would Reynold say? What would Rachel say? In the end she bought the suit and stuffed it into her handbag then hurried back for her appointment.

It was five minutes to three, and she rushed to make an elevator just as the doors were closing. A tiny cry of terror and relief escaped her as the doors grazed her arm and she almost collided with the one other person inside. He pulled her in firmly, and for an instant she lay against his chest. She blushed violently. He, on the other hand, seemed unperturbed.

The door opened again and closed slowly and deliberately. They were still alone. The man asked if she was all right, and she nodded and took a good look at him. He was a type she didn't often see, tan and unapproachable in an expensive suit made of the real, old-fashioned linen that looked like hell the minute you sat down. But it didn't look like hell on him. It looked perfect. *He* looked perfect. At least as much of him as she could see—the back of his neck and the slant of his shoulders. He must have someone who took excellent care of him. Perhaps he had several someones. She patted her hand-bag and wondered if he would approve of her bikini as much as she approved of his suit.

"Floor?" he asked pleasantly, turning to look at her.

"Pardon?" She blushed again.

"I want to push your floor so you don't go down again." He said it protectively, as if he assumed she was headed for a lifetime of close calls.

She didn't like that. "Fourteen," she answered primly.

"Do you work for the magazine?" The idea seemed to surprise him.

"I might. I want to, but"—she threw up her hands defensively—". . . who knows." It was stupid to tell him everything. She was surprised he was talking to her at all.

When the elevator stopped and she got out, he got out, too, which confused her. "You work here?"

"In a way," he answered lightly. Then he smiled. "I own the place."

She hurried to the ladies' room to press cold water to her temples and her wrists and the inside of her arms. He may have been kidding but probably wasn't. He certainly looked like he owned the place.

There were so many things to notice about Tania Rivers, one wondered where to begin. She sat poised at a spotless desk, her small hands folded in front of her as if in prayer. The overall picture was one of inordinate neatness. Her hair, clothes, even her complexion, were spotless and controlled. She could have been a painting.

Tania Rivers looked long and hard at Sara's sweater, at her slacks, at her shoes, and at her haircut. She appeared to be boring holes into each spot she focused on, and Sara began to feel as if she were covered in green slime. It's all in my mind, she told herself. The woman is probably wondering what to have for dinner.

"Why does a woman go back to work?" she asked suddenly, as if the idea were a philosophical dilemma.

Sara was taken aback. She had gone back to work because her friend Sally Becker had told her there was a job available when they had lunch last Tuesday. "Because she's capable," she said finally, knowing it was not the right answer. There could be no right answers for the madonna before her.

"Capable of what?"

"Of taking responsibility. In my case of putting words together." She hadn't put words together for years. What the hell was she talking about?

"According to your résumé it's been a while since you held a writing job. We would have to suffer through your creaky preliminary efforts."

"You don't have to be Joseph Heller to write captions that count."

"True," said Tania and stood up. She was smaller than Sara had expected, but packed no less a wallop than if she'd been six feet tall. Her eyes were unblinking and unfriendly. The interview was over.

Sara, confused, stuck out her hand, and Tania, having little choice, shook it weakly with cold, indifferent fingers.

"Yeah? How'd it go?" asked Jane when Sara appeared at her doorway.

"It doesn't look good, but thanks for your vote of confidence." She waited, but Jane said nothing.

"I suppose it's useless to ask for an answer now."

Jane shrugged. "Take the stuff home anyway and call me. I'll let you know."

The ride home on the bouncy Long Island Rail Road was not pleasant. She kept thinking of all the possibilities that were lost to her, and it seemed so unfair. From time to time she thought of the man in the elevator. She had a feeling he would have given her the job. Then in the next instant she was not sure of anything. He probably wouldn't even remember who she was. In some vague way thinking about the man also made her feel disloyal to Reynold.

They met at Columbia in their senior year. Sara had seen him around, could hardly avoid it, visible as he was. His slot in her brain said, good looking, as in Paul Newman, especially the all-out grin. Looks like he just got off the slopes or out of the pool. Oh, yeah . . . he's a brain. I keep forgetting that. Math whiz. Never alone. Seems to need crowd therapy. Always surrounded by people. Ugh. Also he's not available to me. Even if I'd want him. Which I don't.

Once she found herself sharing a table with him in the cafeteria, and his perfection had annoyed her. He was wearing tinted aviator glasses which made him look like a . . . a . . . well, they made him look like a goddam aviator which he could well have been given his proclivity for physics and math. It all annoyed the hell out of her.

"Isn't that you behind those Foster Grants?" she asked sarcastically.

"Pardon?" He put down his egg salad on rye and stared at her out of innocent blue eyes.

"Well . . . see, there's this ad for sunglasses and all those gorgeous people . . . oh, forget it."

"No, please. Go on."

No, please. Go on. He's civilized, she thought. "What they're trying to say, I guess, is that their sunglasses make everybody look famous.''

He nodded and continued to eat his sandwich. She felt foolish and hurriedly finished her own tuna, some of which oozed onto her hand. When she was through, she slunk away.

Each time she saw him, he nodded and she became less annoyed than the time before, until one day she realized that she was always half hoping to meet him. If she saw him with a girl, she was grouchy for the rest of the day.

About that time Sara realized that none of her relationships with men ever lasted more than two dates. The men she wanted to love forever had only wanted to love her for a few hours. The men who wanted to love *her* forever were mostly bearded radicals or graduate students who had married too young. Unwillingly, she too looked radical. Her hair was curly, her figure boyishly slim, and while everyone else was miniskirted, her hems were still at the knee.

Periodically she tried to make herself look better. She learned to draw tiny triangles at the corner of her eyes and valiantly glued on false eyelashes. She even had her hair straightened, but it came out looking sparse and singed, robbed of its healthy shine.

She bought a long, black wig made of real Polynesian hair according to the tag. It was astonishing how it changed her. She no longer looked like Sara, but like some nubile island maiden fathered by a blue-eyed tourist. She wore the wig on a blind date, and her escort was so attentive and interested that she began to behave like the Polynesian whose hair she wore. Instead of talking, she listened. Instead of wisecracks, she offered tantalizing smiles. Her date was enchanted. He called daily, but she wouldn't see him again, certain he'd be horrified by the deception. Suppose he looked in vain for the other Sara while she stood patiently at the door. It was too humiliating.

She didn't wear the wig again except to concerts at The New School, well on the other side of town. Each time she wore it, however, someone tried to pick her up. Hair could make or break you. It was frightening. She resolved to find happiness in her writing. Soon she would begin in earnest.

The next time she spoke to Reynold was one of the coldest days of winter. Subfreezing temperatures had lasted for days, and patches of ice were impossible to see in the general refrozen slush and gray light. He was coming toward her on a path narrowed by mounds of shoveled snow. It was clear one of them would have to step aside, and she decided it would not be her. She wasn't thinking of the icy walk and was soon sprawled on her lower spine feeling as if broken in two.

He rushed to help her which made her feel worse. If only he'd let her get up by herself, she could make light of it, but he was holding her elbow as if she were old or clumsy. She jerked free of him and lay back down on the ground.

"Can't you get up?"

"I can get up."

"Let me help you."

"I don't want you to help me. Just give me a minute and I'll get up."

"Okay. I'll give you a minute." He didn't move.

He was wearing a mountainous coat with a fur-trimmed hood that came out several inches beyond his face. She imagined it was the type worn by explorers who walked frozen tundras and looked ridiculous in upper Manhattan. Also it made her assume he was rich and trendy. "Aren't you going to go on your way?" she asked.

"No. I'm going to wait for you to get up. Aren't you going to get up?"

"I'll get up as soon as you go away."

"Why?"

"Why?" she repeated.

"Yes, why?"

"I don't know why." She knew why, but it was complicated. She wanted him to be more to her than a Good Samaritan. "For some reason," she said evenly, "it makes me mad that you saw me fall."

"In that case I'll help you up and forget I ever saw you." He smiled. She let him help her up, but he didn't go away. "Do you want me to take you to the health office?"

"No. Absolutely not."

"You're not hurt?"

"I may be hurt, but I stand a chance of being made worse by the health office."

"Where can I take you?" Despite his promise he was reluctant to leave her.

"Who says you have to take me anywhere?"

"I could take you to my apartment," he said innocently.

"Your apartment!" She looked at him as if he'd said, "I could stab you." "Those are my choices? The infirmary or your apartment? I'm beginning to feel better already."

"Okay," he thrust his hands in his pockets, "see you around." He walked away and didn't look back.

She stood looking after him, wondering why she felt more lonely than before he had arrived. She began to cry. She cried partly because her hip hurt but mostly because she would have liked to visit his apartment, though not in the way he had in mind. She wanted to be important to him and had no idea of how to make such a thing come about. Working hard at getting someone to like you was the best way to get them to hate you. Natalie had taught her that. It was strange that Natalie had taught her the most indelible lesson of her life and then vanished right out of it.

Several times during the next few weeks he came into the library when she was already there, and he always moved closer when a seat became empty as if they were old friends. On one occasion he moved right next to her and smiled and her heart gave a small leap of happiness. She smiled back radiantly which confused him. She had never smiled at him before.

"Do you come here every day?" he asked.

"I'm not compulsive about it if that's what you mean." She couldn't help staring at him. His workman's blue shirt was rolled up to show lovely, strong arms with golden fuzz and a classy watch. He was beautiful.

"You're a good looking man," she confided bravely.

"You like me?"

"I think so. Yes." She looked away from him.

"That seems to disappoint you."

"I always thought the man in my life would be much older than I. Someone who knew all the classics and would make reading lists for me and interpret *Ulysses* and remind me to eat." As she finished speaking, she realized with a shiver that she had perfectly described her father during his good periods. Her face turned sober.

"If you like me so much," he reasoned, "why are you always so grouchy?"

"Because I'm afraid of you." She hadn't meant to say it, but it was true. She was afraid of him.

"I won't hurt you," he said earnestly.

"Hah!" she snorted and walked out, but her heart was pounding wildly and that night, lying on her narrow bed, she ached with the need to have his arms around her. The stakes were so high. She could end up with him, a stunning addition to her life. Or she could end up with nothing. Either way it was more than she could handle.

She began to think seriously about herself. What was so great about her life and feelings that she guarded them so zealously against invasion? There was pain in her life already. The pain of loneliness. She could just be trading in one kind of pain for another. Maybe it wouldn't even be painful. Maybe she'd have the good sense not to get involved but just take it as it came.

The following week she went to Lord & Taylor's and tried on a slinky but simple jersey dress. "My God," said the saleslady with conviction, "if you don't buy that, you're crazy."

She bought the dress along with a course at Elizabeth Arden's called "How to Create the Face You Want." She didn't know what face she wanted, but Pablo, the master, assured her they would find it together.

Armed with her improvements, she sought out Reynold and asked him to the movies. He accepted but insisted on paying even though she mumbled something about having invited him. She was relieved that he paid, but the rest of the evening did not go well. She talked too much. He'd never call again. Oh, wicked mouth. Wicked tongue. She was so sure he wouldn't call that when he did, she said, "Who is this?" And when he told her, she asked, "Who? Who?" impatiently before it dawned on her that it was he.

He began to take her out about twice a week; to the movies, to Chinatown, for long walks through Greenwich Village. Each time he took her home, he kissed her. Some of those kisses she would never forget—the first one, for instance, which was hands down the most physically exciting thing that had ever happened to her.

He wasn't sneaky or shy about doing whatever he wanted to do. When he wanted to feel her breasts, he took them into his beautiful hands and hugged and rubbed them. Then he unhooked her bra and pulled up her blouse and hugged and rubbed them some more. While she did nothing to help him, she didn't stop him either.

Three weeks after their first date he made love to her. "Are you a woman of easy virtue, Sara?" he asked softly, his head against her breasts.

"Sure looks like it, doesn't it." She was frightened by how far they had come but tried to keep it light.

"You know what I like about you?" He was speaking very softly. In another moment he would be inside her.

"No." She swallowed hard and waited. If he said the wrong thing, it would stay with her forever.

"You don't protect yourself. You're right out front. Right out front."

She breathed out. Whatever that meant, she could live with it. It sounded all right.

They saw each other every day for a month, which brought them well into spring. There were no commitments, but there was a lot of touching which surprised Sara. She hadn't known she needed all that touching. She had assumed she was a cerebral type with a low sex drive, yet his lovemaking made her supremely happy and she walked around in a haze of contentment, refusing to think where it all would end.

He began slipping away from her sometime in April. She could feel trouble coming in the same way one sometimes feels the onset of autumn. There was the absence of that special warmth and closeness. He stopped making love to her. He still kissed her, but they were short, hasty kisses and his heart wasn't in them. She could feel them for hours afterward, cold and distant on her lips. She too became quiet. She would exit with dignity.

One day as they lazed on the grass of Riverside Park, he leaned up on one elbow, and she could tell from the look on his face he was about to say something important.

"I have something to tell you," he said. To his credit his eyes looked no happier than her own. There was none of the sheepishness of someone fallen out of love.

"I would rather not hear it."

"Please, let me explain."

"Unless they make you feel good, explanations are a waste of time." It took all of her courage to look into his eyes. "I have a feeling this one is going to make me feel crummy."

He lowered his eyes and that was her answer.

For the next two weeks she didn't hear from him. Not a word. Nothing. She went to all the places he might be, but he wasn't there.

It was the worst two weeks of her life. Everything hurt her. Her teeth, her joints. Christ, she thought, he gave me arthritis. I didn't know you could get arthritis from screwing.

Worse than the pain was the terrible cliché that kept running through her mind. Why should a man buy a cow when he can get free milk any time he wants it? It also upset her that she couldn't think of a more imaginative way to torture herself. Just about that time, too, she came upon a picture of Natalie in the society pages. Natalie at a benefit for the Actor's Workshop wearing a black, strapless sheath that made her look like a painting. It was a full face view, and she seemed to be looking right at Sara. Why did you screw it up, said the beautiful mouth.

She crumpled up the page and threw it away, trying to remember some good reason for living.

Before Reynold she had thought of her life as a separate thing which she had to propel forward to justify the huge sums spent on her education. Writing was her first love, but the idea that she might live in her head, concoct things, make stories out of nothing, frightened her mother to death. That's what her father had done and look where it got him! In the end she majored in Business Administration because it was solid and reeked of a balanced mind, but her heart was in her minor which was English. She always kept a diary, not of the things that happened to her which were minimal, but of the things that *might* happen to her and to others. She had filled sixteen fat, lined notebooks when Reynold came into her life, and now the notebooks lay dusty and neglected.

Three weeks later she finally saw him, but not in the way she had imagined. There was a girl with him with long, red hair. It was fluffy and languid and full of promise, reminding her of Brenda Starr.

The two of them stood for a moment, poised and smiling, like people in ads to sell luxury cars. The girl swayed toward him and pressed herself against him as if she had done so many times. Finally they drove off in a red convertible, the girl at the wheel.

She saw the car again, parked alone, and noticed it had Maryland license plates. Of course. How could she have been so stupid? He came from Annapolis and this was his hometown girl. The one he would marry when he graduated which would be in three weeks. Men like Reynold did not marry girls like herself. They married the admiral's daughter or the judge's daughter or the doctor's daughter. She was the madman's daughter. Whereas before there had been melancholy, now her heart raged.

Four days later he showed up at her door looking terrible.

"You look awful," she said, trying to make her voice stop trembling. "What have you done to your nice eyes? They're all bloodshot."

"I could tell you I've been busy with finals," he said. His voice was none too steady either, but she attributed that to his general lousy condition.

"Yeah. So why don't you tell me that." She was frowning. He was going to tell her something worse—that he didn't want to see her anymore. She wanted to help him. He was so decent coming in person to dump her. She wanted to tell him not to worry; instead she shut her eyes and tried to imagine a hot, sunny shore. She felt unreasonably cold.

"Sara . . ." he stumbled in and grabbed for her. "Sara . . ." his voice was hoarse but distinct. She heard it clearly. "I love you."

"Don't ever go away like that again," she said hoarsely. "You scared the shit out of me."

Much later he told her briefly about Brenda Starr, also known as Cindy Watson, who had been his girl since they were fourteen.

"And . . . ?" she asked, unexpectedly strong and ready for an answer.

"And . . ." he groped for the right words, ". . . and I found you."

The first three years were bliss. They lived in a tiny apartment on East Eighteenth Street, and Sara bought her vegetables at the outdoor markets on First Avenue. She was feeding his beautiful body beautiful things and felt virtuous. He was feeding her soul and nourishing her spirit. He had taught her to love her body which she now did.

It startled her how quickly she had abandoned her smartness and self-reliance when Reynold surfaced. He was so sure of what he wanted that she was happy to abdicate. After all, she had *him*, a heady experience for a girl who could remember the humiliation of dateless years. Now in an amazing reversal she would be a couple after all. Not just any couple, but a dream couple that made heads turn.

While he did graduate work, she did editorial work for a dental journal. She edited articles about gum disease, improper cleaning, plaque, new methods of root canal. They had a baby girl and named her Rachel. When Sara was pregnant with their second child, Reynold's father died and left him forty thousand dollars which drastically changed their lives. They left their silly cramped apartment and their simple, joyful life and moved to a fancy neighborhood on Long Island. It was a neighborhood for corporate men who did not wear jewelry or cologne. It was a neighborhood where the maids drove Ford Granadas.

He still excited her. He still made her laugh, and she made him laugh, too, but it was different. Now he worked in a large laboratory complex, and his work was so far removed from anything she could understand that they never tried to discuss it seriously.

"Annapolis," she would say, although she seldom called him that anymore, "just what do you do all day?"

"I work with things I can't see, that aren't going anywhere. Do nothing. Ask nothing. Have no hope of personal gain."

"They sound like saints. You work with subatomic saints. Are there any lady scientists out there?"

"Just one. Her name is Mary-Hope and she has long, skinny arms which she regularly wraps around my neck. Why do you ask?"

"Because," her voice would get serious, "I don't want you to stray." He made hearts go thump all up and down the North Shore, but he always tumbled into bed with her, looking boyish and innocent in his Brooks Brothers pajamas. The children looked like him. Poster children who seemingly had nothing to do with Sara. So much for dominant genes, she thought, looking at the two miniature strangers. Blond. Blue-eyed. Straight-haired.

"If I hadn't been there, I'd swear you had these children by some other woman. I want my money back." But she knew she was kidding. She adored the children. She had carried them on her back, papoose style, as soon as they could keep their infant necks from wobbling wildly.

"I won't stray."

"Promise?"

"Yes. . . . And Sara."

"What?"

"You get a maid to help you with the kids."

"Why? I don't want a maid. If I get a maid, I'll have to clean up every time she comes."

"Get one anyway."

"Why?"

"Because lately every time I want to make love to you, you're already asleep."

It was true and she knew it was true, but she wasn't ready to admit it yet. "Oh, my God, do you think we're over the hill, Reynold?"

"Of course not. Just get a maid."

The next day she called her closest friend in the community, Penny Sawyer. Penny didn't understand her jokes, but she genuinely liked Sara. Her children and Sara's were roughly the same age, and they traded off once a week so they could spend one day completely alone. "Penny, do you think your day worker"—she hated the idea of calling someone a maid—"could give me a day?"

"I don't see why not," said Penny. "I know she's looking to fill out her week."

Mrs. Ramirez, as it turned out, was neither a maid nor a day worker. She was a tyrant and a master at the particular torture known as passive resistance. She spoke little, smiled generously, and did exactly as she pleased. She never actually did much housework. She brightened faucets, straightened silverware drawers, and had endless cups of tea. "All in good time," stated in a weary philosophical tone, was her answer to all requests.

"Can't we get rid of her?" Sara asked Reynold.

"You won't like yourself for giving up so easily," he responded.

She nodded and changed the subject. She could not totally explain her feelings about Mrs. Ramirez because along with frustration there was at times a sense of comfort. The comfort came when she heard her speaking to the children from another room. Those inflections and pauses and charming mistakes brought back Miranda so clearly that images from the past kept breaking through. She was surprised at how much she remembered.

The subject of the editorial job had come up over lunch with a girlfriend from the old days at the dental magazine—a girl whose life had escalated to bigger editorial jobs and whose weekends were spent on press junkets and cabin cruisers. Hardly a soul mate for a mother of two. Still, Reynold had insisted she keep the date. "It'll do you good to spend a day in the city,'' he said solicitously, as if she were a patient.

"They ask me every day if they're still on the planet,'' she was trying to sound good-humored yet cynical for her friend who appeared bored. "That's the thing with children, you've got to tell them every speck of information. You wouldn't believe what they don't know.'' She stopped. I'm supposed to be forgetting the kids, she thought, and I've talked of nothing else since I sat down.

Her friend traced little grids on the tablecloth and looked thoughtful. Finally she asked Sara if she'd be interested in writing captions for a magazine. They needed someone and she'd thought of Sara. "You don't have to know much,'' she said, not meaning to be unkind. "Just write some little thing. It's just high shit. Write a little high shit about a dress or event or someone's ultra, ultra living room.''

Sara was having difficulty listening to what the girl was saying. Her writing had been everything to her before Reynold. It came to her in a flash of anger and disappointment how motherhood and marriage had completely blotted out all former dreams as if they had no value except to keep one's spirits up until the real thing came along. Her cheeks burned with indignation. She had left the old Sara, dream in hand, standing on some other shore. And now in front of this girl she hardly knew, she had an intense desire to row back quickly and get her.

That evening when Sara returned home from her day in the city and her interview with Tania Rivers, she was overly cheerful and the children kept giving her sly questioning looks.

After the children were asleep, she and Reynold laughed long and hard because his shirt hung loose and it was called The Hugger. They laughed because her shoes were called Captivators and as Sara pointed out, they had captivated no one. They laughed because Joyce Brothers said on the Johnny Carson show that couples talked the most to each other the year before they separated. That was ridiculous. They talked all the time.

They rolled on the floor laughing and finally rolled toward each other, but the tears coming out of Sara's eyes weren't all from laughing, and when he kissed her, she began to cry in earnest.

"What's wrong?"

"I couldn't get the crummy job."

"But you didn't even want it, did you?"

"When I couldn't get it, I wanted it plenty."

"Why don't you find something else?"

"No, that isn't it. I must look like a hick. My God, I was so stupid. I didn't know how to answer or how to dress or anything. Reynold, I've been living in a different country. I have no idea what it's like out there."

"Do you want to have an idea?"

"No. It's terrible. A bunch of barracudas. This woman . . . you wouldn't believe what she looked like. She barely let me shake her hand. Ugh." She gave a long, slow shudder.

"That bad, huh?"

"I wouldn't take that job if it was the last one on earth and I was destitute and alone."

The next morning at precisely ten thirty the phone rang. It was Jane Seymour. "The job is yours," she said briskly into the telephone.

"Really?" Sara began to hop on one foot and wrapped the telephone cord around herself. "You mean she said yes? But how? She looked like it was no."

"She always looks like it's no. But sometimes it's yes," said Jane pleasantly. "So you can get on that stuff and have it back by Tuesday."

"Yes, yes," she said more loudly than was necessary. And before she hung up, a final "Yes!"

The editorial offices of *Haute* were undistinguished looking. The entrance was a black metal door that led to a small foyer at the end of a long, blank corridor. Inside was a maze of little cubicles separated by glass partitions. The outer rim consisted of tiny offices with removable nameplates at the entrance to identify the current occupant.

Dutifully each month the editors tried to satisfy their average reader's insatiable appetite for two themes—weight and spiritual replenishment (the latter now including heightened sexual awareness and victory over personal tragedy).

There was a miracle diet in most issues (sometimes the same one under a new name) as well as what Tania Rivers called God-pulled-me-through articles—"My faith in God saved my troubled marriage," says Lu Anne Timmins from Two Forks, Iowa. "I just said, God, I'm giving this marriage to you."

The fiction, however, two short stories per month, was of the highest quality and often went on to be anthologized in award collections.

Sara kept her eyes open and said little. She had never been around such smart, confident women. They joked together all the time and cheerfully revealed their weaknesses. Some had terrible lovers who cheated on them and borrowed money. Others had overbearing mothers who sneaked around checking up on their lives. Sinister men followed them home. They all claimed to have upstairs neighbors with bare floors and dogs who scurried around all night with tin plates tied to their legs. Everyone exaggerated and then laughed. They were loose and free. Anything could happen to them. Sara was enchanted but still grateful for the refuge of tight-lipped, sensible Horse Hollow Estates.

Within two months she was writing regularly for *Haute*. Nothing bigger than a paragraph for their "What's New What's Now" section, but it was getting easier and Jane no longer edited her copy. She resisted the impulse to glamorize the job, even to tell anyone about it except Reynold.

Three times each week she came in, wrote up spec sheets, and did most of the work at home after the children were in school. Even so life was not the same as before. There was a definite shift in her awareness of herself. Often, as if it were a physical fact, she felt small random segments of herself opening up to possibility.

When she was at the office, the time sped by and she hardly ever thought about the children. Still, when she noticed their empty tiny sneakers lying in the hall, a lump rose in her throat.

One day Jane asked her to attend an editorial meeting. Whether it was out of kindness or real need, Sara did not know. She sat at the farthest end of the conference table, anxious not to be highly visible.

The table was headed by a man whose importance was unmistakable. She recognized him instantly as the man she had seen in the elevator and wondered if he would feel obliged to say something to her. She hoped not. She was nervous enough.

All eyes were on him and she, too, tried to look him over without catching his eye. He was not much more than forty, lightly tanned, dark brown hair trimmed precisely to an inch above his collar. The suit he was wearing, a soft wool challis, shaped itself around his body which while not muscular, appeared trim and held no tension. He looked crisp and polished, as if someone followed him around and pressed the clothes right on him.

It was more the look on his face than the actual features that was so appealing. It was the look of a man who needed nothing from anyone, and for the first time she understood why power was such an aphrodisiac. When he sat forward, she noted two tiny initials over his heart. She could picture such a heart. She could picture little signs around it that said, "Abandon all hope ye who enter that you can have me forever."

Finally, Tania Rivers, reed thin in a cashmere sweater dress that revealed every available ounce of flesh on her body, said something close to his ear and the meeting began.

Sara was wearing a T-shirt with Calvin Klein's initials emblazoned between her breasts much like half a dozen other women around the table. The only difference was that while theirs curved snugly about their breasts and arms imparting a look both innocent and sexy, hers just sort of hung there, not really touching her anywhere. She was disappointed in herself as if she were only now grasping some obvious deficiency. Tonight she would wash it in the hot cycle and shrink it up.

She was not proud of the fact that she often took off her underwear only after her nightgown was well over her body.

Reynold had been amused at first. "That's a neat trick, Sara, but I've seen it already. Now can you get undressed like a normal person?"

"Sister Francisca said we were never to expose our bodies," she would answer, trying to sound lighthearted.

"Funny"—he would look around and under the bed—"but I haven't seen Sister Francisca in weeks. Why don't you go cold turkey and walk around naked?"

"I can't."

He was wise enough not to insist. "Actually it's more exciting this way. Every time I get a glimpse of a breast or a thigh, I feel like a peeping Tom."

"The first problem today," began Tania, turning to the man whose name, Jane had whispered, was Bill Waring, "is whether to go with the rape story for the Personal Triumph series. We've never done rape before.''

"No?" he was surprised.

"A lot of our readers still feel that any rape victim had to have led the guy on.''

"Well, then we should educate them.''

"This was a particularly nasty rape,'' said Jane Seymour. "There were two men involved and they scarred her breasts.''

"Bill,'' Tania spoke again. "I'm against it. The strongest thing we've had so far in that area is how a young wife copes with passes.''

"A football story?'' His eyes were merry. He was trying to lighten the atmosphere which had been made tense by his presence.

"The passes were made in the kitchen,'' said Tania, not amused, "by the husband's best friend.''

Tania did not like to defer to him in front of her staff. She had tried several times to interest him in subjects that had nothing to do with the magazine, and he had rebuffed her. "You're too strong a woman for me,'' he had told her lightly. "And too sophisticated. You'd make me work too hard.'' Tania knew this was not true. With all the sleeping around that went on in this business, Bill Waring had a reputation for being, if not outright puritanical, fairly conservative. Eighty percent of the girls employed by Waring Communications would have fallen into his bed at the nod of his head. But he never gave the nod. If he was making it, he was doing so privately, far away from the office. She knew there had been a wife, a stiff debutante whose starch had run out one day. Once in a while he would show up at cocktail parties with a model, but more often he came alone.

"Does anyone have a different opinion?'' He looked around the table and Sara felt his eyes rest on her. Oh, God, she pleaded silently, don't let him ask me anything. You don't want to talk to me. No, no, I pass. If I speak, every eye in the room would stare at me. Who was this? Why am I here? And what right have I to an opinion?

"Would *you* put the story in?''

She began to blush right through her Estée Lauder cheek tint. He was waiting for an answer. She had always been a devotee of the Personal Triumph series. She cleared her throat and tried for a low register. "Remembering my own circumstances throughout my life, I've always empathized with the young women in the series who underwent stillbirths, young widowhood, financial disaster, even violent husbands, and came through it all stronger and happier. I felt we were all, myself included, survivors of sorts because understanding on someone's part had taken the shame away. If the terrible shame of rape could be alleviated by simple exposure, then certainly it should be given as much publicity as possible."

"Have you had many trying circumstances in your life?" He was encouraging her to be at ease. To tell him everything.

Why was he focusing on *that*? Hadn't he heard the rest of her answer? "No, no. I mean, well . . . no more than anyone. I meant to say that when you can identify with another soul who's been through something shameful, it must make you feel less alone. I . . . I'm sorry."

"No need to be sorry," he said. "We're all relieved to hear that your life has been no less sunny than it should be."

Everyone tittered which surprised him. He hadn't meant to be funny at her expense. He had been perfectly serious. "Tania," he said, turning to the editor, "I don't like to do this because ninety-nine percent of the time you're dead on target about this magazine. Just this once, however, would you let me have my way?" He was kind and solicitous and Sara admired him for that. He would not embarrass his editor in front of her subordinates. "If you get a lot of hate mail, I'll treat you to a trip to Bermuda."

"Just the two of us?" Tania asked coyly.

"No need to bargain over that," he answered smoothly.

"All right." Tania was all business. "We'll go with the rape."

The meeting continued for twenty more minutes with the senior editors vying to get approval for their sections. One by one they filed out, and Sara slipped out with them. She collected fact sheets for work to take home, and then realized she had left her pocketbook in the conference room.

She saw the bag draped over a chair and darted in to retrieve it feeling like a fraud. Very slim threads connected her to the business world. She should either be really writing or stop pretending that she was doing something. She stood still a moment, mesmerized by the view and the ideas swirling in her head.

"Hello."

She jumped and turned to face Bill Waring.

"Hi." She had crashed in on him deep in thought. "I forgot my pocketbook."

"I was wondering when you would retrieve it." He was in no hurry to let her go. "I see you got the job. Are you a writer?"

"Technically, yes." She was pleased that he remembered her. "I describe things. Captions."

"What keeps you from being a regular writer?"

"Insufficient talent."

"Don't say that, not even in jest."

"I'm not jesting, but it doesn't make me unhappy either. Leading the sort of life I do, it's very nice to slip into the working world to describe the Valentino sari or how Lee Radziwill feels about her living room—what she loves about it and what she doesn't." She didn't like the brittleness in her voice. She had no reason to be brittle. "I'm talking as if I feel above it which is not true. Just now, gazing at the view, I was quite unhappy about what I've been doing."

"What's your name?"

It was not a come-on. He had a clear, unhurried interest in her. "Sara."

"What do you like, Sara? Tell me what you like."

"I love to walk." He made her feel unsure. "You mean something like that? I used to walk a lot, but now I take cabs because I have to curb my natural stinginess. I tend to be a little stingy with myself." Why was she blurting out this nonsense? Why was she purposely acting so stupid?

"What have you got there in your hand?"

She looked down at the information sheets. "Well, this is all about Natalie Wood and her new dressing room. How she feels about it and how it feels about her. Also how Bob Wagner feels about Natalie."

"And how does he feel?"

"Expansive. Very expansive. They've been married twice—once when they were children, by their own admission, and once when they were grown up." His eyes were smiling. He had trapped her three times.

"Yes . . . and yourself?" He glanced at her simple gold wedding band. "Were you married when you were a child?"

"Sure. A very sober child, but a child nevertheless."

"But it has worked out." It was a statement.

"I'm not going to tell you anymore." She realized too late that by saying that she had already told him plenty.

"So you like to walk?"

"Oh, yes!" Again she reminded herself to calm down.

"Well then," he said rising, "let's walk, Sara. Would you like to take a walk with me?"

She was confused yet exhilarated. He was just a few inches taller than herself. She came to his mouth which was not a bad place to come to. It was a simple, straightforward mouth. Relaxed, wide. The lower lip was a little fuller than the top one. "Sure. Why not?"

"We're on our way," he said and held the door for her.

She took his silence in the elevator for discretion. It was crowded with people from the magazine. In the lobby, however, he took her elbow and nudged her purposefully through the crowds until they reached Park Avenue and began a leisurely uptown stroll.

"My car's parked in the garage under the Metropolitan Museum, we could walk there."

"Fine."

He said little for ten blocks, then he pointed out a man who had brushed past him. "That man owes me money," he said tonelessly. "He used to be my friend, but now he avoids me because he owes me money. Never help anyone, Sara. They never forgive you for it." He was silent for the rest of the walk, and there were moments when she felt that he had changed his mind about her. Still, she was determined not to chatter. He appeared deep in thought.

When they reached Seventy-ninth Street, she stopped and faced him. "Thank you."

"My pleasure." He smiled broadly, touched her arm lightly, and strode off. Half a block away he hailed a taxi.

Bill Waring settled back in the cab and gave the address of Lutèce. His guest would be confused at being kept waiting for half an hour. The man was important, a vice president of a large corporation that wished to acquire Waring Communications.

While he did not wish to be acquired, Bill Waring felt he had to play the game. It was the old you-appear-to-be-raking-it-in-so-I-want-to-swallow-you-up game. He had played it himself in younger, more innocent days. Before *Haute* he had acquired two radio stations and his hometown paper in Newton, Massachusetts, home of the original Fig Newton cookie which had been swallowed up by Nabisco.

If he told the man waiting for him that he could have everything except *Haute* and the Newton newspaper, the man would be suspicious and want to include both even though he could show him that the one lost money and the other barely broke even. People always wanted what they couldn't have or what they suspected was making you happy in the hopes that it would make them happy too.

Being late today would give him an edge. The man would assume he didn't care. He cared in a general sense but not in the specific, and he knew that was probably why all his business deals were successful and why his personal deals were disastrous. There were all sorts of women who wanted to belong to him; the problem was they wanted to belong to him forever, a commitment he had made once with dismal results. When they found this out, the women became cool and sometimes cruel. It saddened him to always make love to women hiding grievances.

Perhaps that's why that girl had gotten to him. She wasn't that special . . . nice eyes, slim and athletic. Probably played tennis badly but looked good in shorts. She wouldn't know how to be cool or cruel. If he stood her up, she'd be mystified and hurt. She'd cry long, sniffling cries and confide every quirk of her pain. To his complete chagrin she made him want to use his arms for strength again. To hold and protect her. Why this was so he didn't know, but it made him smile at himself and at the unpredictability of life.

He saw himself as invincible, powerful, manipulative. He knew how to get people to do what he wanted. Yet here was this girl who could without knowing it wrap him around her little finger.

That evening as Sara prepared dinner, she hummed a complicated Beatles song until Rachel came into the kitchen and stopped her.

"Don't sing anymore," she said.

"Why not?"

"You can't sing and think about me at the same time."

She smiled. "Of course I can. I can sing and think about you and cook these hamburgers."

"No, you can't. Only God can do everything at the same time."

"God and mothers," she said with conviction.

"Huh," said Rachel, "mothers are not like God at all. You can't pray to mothers for what you want. It's mostly the opposite."

"You *know* how to pray?"

"No," she answered reproachfully. "How could I?"

She was a tiny bit glad that Rachel didn't know how to pray because if she did, she would probably pray for her mother to stop working and, of course, to stop meeting men like Bill Waring.

Later that night as they settled into their respective sleep positions, Sara said to Reynold, "We haven't done anything about religion. The children don't know how to pray."

"Um." He was half asleep.

"Reynold," she raised herself on her elbow, "do you ever pray?"

"No. I don't think so." He was silent and she assumed he was asleep. "Now that you mention it," he said as if the memory had roused him, "I did pray recently."

"You did? What about?" She was alarmed. As if, perhaps, he had been praying about her.

"At Charlie's party. When you had a flat and didn't show up on time."

"I remember."

"The kids started crying right away. They didn't like being outside. They said all the other parties were inside. There was a little wind blowing, and they were afraid of the wind because it made their napkins flutter. They were scared to death of this tiny wind. Well, after a while I went inside and I stood at the kitchen sink and prayed."

"You did? What did you say?"

"I said, 'Please, God, make these little jerks stop being afraid. Invade their little hearts and make them strong. Take their little grubby palms and calm them.' "

"And . . . ?"

"And I was sure He'd do *something*."

"Did He?" She was overcome.

"Of course not. How could God answer someone who only shows up every ten years." He reached for her breast and began to knead it slowly between his fingers. "Now that you got me to admit all that," he said, pulling up her nightgown, "I think you owe me something."

She smiled in the dark, but her mind wasn't totally on what he was doing to her. She was glad that he knew how to pray and she liked the way he spoke to God, and somewhere way back in some dark corner of her mind she had the idea that he might have need of it again.

Chapter 2

SHE AWOKE TO THE SMELL OF PAINT, AND
her head swirled wildly when she tried to
raise it from the pillow. If she got up now, she would be sick. It occurred to her that with little calculation she could be sick all over Mr.
Simmons, watching her dourly from the foot of the bed, and force
him into some act of intimacy. He would have to lead her to the
bathroom or to bed, perhaps wipe her face with a damp cloth.

No. She would remain still and let Simmons keep his distance.

He stood tall and erect in his blue serge, one of three suits which
he rotated methodically, counting out ten wearings between dry
cleanings. She had heard Dolly and Lucinda discussing it, not in the
snide way they chewed over her habits, but with begrudging respect.
They considered Mr. Simmons a rare bird. She didn't know what
they considered her.

"Madame." He waited to have her full attention. "They're preparing this room for painting today, and you'll be spending the next
few days in the city. Lucinda needs to pack your bag and Mrs. Sandford is coming at eleven." He consulted several bits of paper as if

hers was just one of many lives he had to sort out. "Had you forgotten?"

"No, Mr. Simmons, I haven't forgotten." She opened her eyes and closed them again trying to itemize what she had eaten for dinner. "I can't leave at eleven."

"It's been arranged," he said matter-of-factly. "It's nine thirty now and . . ."

"Mr. Simmons," she interrupted him, "I have to say good-bye to Jeremy. His bus doesn't get in until twelve."

"A call from the city perhaps . . . before bedtime?"

"I want to say good-bye in person." She opened her eye experimentally to see if the room had stopped twirling, then closed it. "He's going to miss me. And of course, I'll miss him." That was the sort of logic that distressed Simmons the most—people missing each other. "Mr. Simmons?"

"Yes, madame." He was correct at all cost.

"Where is Mr. Van Druten?"

"Why he's already gone."

Simmons's face brightened instantly. *He* not *she* had been there to receive the day's instructions from Alden Van Druten, and now she would have to depend on him for information. It would be twenty minutes before she got it all out of him, if in fact she did. He might play cagey and forgetful, leaving her to cope with Alden's icy disapproval if things went awry.

She opened her eyes again, and this time the room was still. Simmons was not going to budge until he saw her on her feet. This was an opportunity for him to have the advantage, and Jake Simmons lived for such opportunities. Sometimes he reached for them boldly and often won. For instance, three days after her wedding Simmons had an appendicitis attack, and her husband had jumped his honeymoon cruise on the Mediterranean and flown to his butler's side, booking a room at the hospital until he was out of danger. Natalie had pictured an aging, devoted retainer, but Simmons in the flesh had startled her. He was tall and distinguished and appeared to be all one color, a cool yet sparkling gray. His eyes were calm and steady and slightly red at the edges as if he showered too often.

At the time, however, she had blessed the unknown Simmons, relieved to be left alone, and spent the remaining days of the trip happily vomiting into the high round toilet in her stateroom and trying to swallow the broth brought hourly by the confused steward. The seas were calm that early fall and Natalie was not ignorant of the cause of her nausea.

On the ninth day she appeared on deck and found the crew standing at attention, ready to dock. They were back in Portofino where they had started out, and Alden was waiting for her with a limousine.

"Did you manage to enjoy yourself?" he asked, not the least chastened for leaving his bride of three days.

"It was lovely," she answered. "We anchored often and I swam and sunned myself." Neither claimed to have missed the other, although they seemed content to be together again. They had known each other five weeks. For his part he never questioned the fact that she was as pale as he had left her.

By the time they left Europe and headed across the Atlantic to Alden's Long Island estate, they had known each other eight weeks, and she decided it was safe to confide that she was pregnant. She broke the news when they were well under way.

He looked at her turquoise eyes, calm and unbeseeching. Then he turned and stared out the window as if the cotton-soft clouds could help alleviate his disappointment. During the last two months they had had intercourse six or seven times. At most she might have been fertile twice, but he had a chronic history of low sperm count and had only been able to impregnate his second wife after years of trying. It was highly improbable that Natalie was pregnant with his child.

She had been clever to wait for this moment to tell him. What was he to do trapped thirty thousand feet above the ground? Show outrage and threaten her with annulment? He knew there would come a moment when he would be furious with her and deeply resentful, but now he was only puzzled. What did she want from him? Legitimacy for the child? Hardly. She was not after his money, either. She had her own trust fund and had readily agreed when he suggested a marriage contract that curtailed her access to his fortune.

With a sigh of resignation he turned to her and searched out her hand, which he noted was surprisingly large and capable. His reasons for marrying her were still valid. She was energetic, cheerful, beautiful, well-bred, and would demand little in the way of affection. Firm in his decision to accept the child, he gave her hand a small squeeze. "I would be a fool not to want to reproduce someone as beautiful as you." His voice was free of sentiment but kind and certain. Satisfied that the worst was over, she fell asleep instantly with her head on his shoulder. He continued to hold her hand, but his happiness was blemished. How could he hope to trust her again?

Seven months to the day after her wedding Jeremy was born weighing a whopping nine pounds. Everyone counted the months and came up with nothing but admiration for Natalie. She had managed to snag one of the richest men in America with the oldest trick.

Alden never questioned the short pregnancy, choosing to play the love-blinded husband. When she began to grow large, he left on an extended business trip to Europe and did not return until the infant was three weeks old, at which time he presented Natalie with an enormous emerald-cut diamond ring and securities in her name valued at a million. It was not gratitude. The practice had been in his family for generations. The women were paid handsomely for sons and Alden was very much tied to the past. It was the core of his sanity.

"This is my first son," he said, looking down at the small stranger. The child did not resemble either of them. His hair was black and his eyes dark. "I hadn't counted on having one, and now you've managed it perfectly without any fuss."

It was true. The baby had emerged easily from his mother and began immediately to flail his tiny arms and legs with more strength than one expected from a newborn. His foreign good looks were a shock to everyone. They looked quizzically from father to mother to baby, but said nothing. At least not in front of the parents.

Natalie felt deeply grateful to Alden for the adjustment she knew he had made. She resolved to devote herself to his happiness. And she stuck by her resolve even when he turned distant and stopped communicating shortly thereafter.

There were many requests for photographs of mother and child. An heir of such magnitude was news and a beautiful bride was news. Tricking one's husband with someone else's child was news also, but not the printable kind; nor was Natalie a person about whom one publicly speculated.

When Jeremy was three months old and his features emerged in more recognizable shape, Natalie invited all the fashion and news magazines to photograph mother and child in her city apartment. Alden refused to have it done at Pheasant Hill for fear of kidnaping, which was ever on his mind. He was strongly against exposing his wife and child to the media, but when he saw how much it meant to Natalie, he gave in.

Natalie appeared in *Vogue* in a full page photograph boldly pointing Jeremy's three-month-old face into Avedon's camera so that each feature could be scrutinized down to the cleft which had begun to deepen in his tiny chin. She left his chest bare so that nothing could detract from his face.

The wire services picked up the photographs from *Time* and *Newsweek*, and within a month Jeremy's face had appeared in most newspapers and magazines in America and in every major magazine in Europe.

All that effort so that one person would see the photograph and realize that she had borne him a son.

Natalie had first laid eyes on Sam Johnson on a dreary day after a week of late spring rain. She had finished Wellesley and was living in New York and attending the Drama Workshop, a prestigious acting ensemble to which she had wangled an acceptance.

"Why should I let you participate?" the director asked when she came for an interview.

"Because my father contributed fifty thousand dollars toward the purchase of this building," she answered calmly. Her tone was respectful but logical. It was a simple business deal. "But that doesn't mean I won't work hard," she added.

The director burst into laughter. "That's wonderful," he said. "Direct and wonderful." He laughed again. "I'll take you, but that doesn't mean I'm soft. If you're no good, out you go."

"I know you're not soft," she said. "And if I'm no good, you won't have to ask me to leave."

They shook hands, and she was pleased to note that he never again singled her out in any way.

At first she had decided on acting to please her father who was passionate about the theatre. But the more she thought about it, the more she warmed to the idea that it was a perfect career for someone who seemed devoid of emotions of her own. After all she had to do something with her time. She had no intention of marrying.

The workshop routine was grueling and the encouragement slight, but Natalie stuck it out and thrived on it as the first purposeful activity in her life. She liked the director, Joshua Epstein, a dedicated genius of few words. If you were good, he said nothing. If you were good and had a bad day, he sent you home with a quick half pat on the shoulder. If you were bad and weren't going to get better, he referred you to someone less scrupulous than he and gave you your money back. "This is a laboratory," he liked to tell them. "We are experimenting. We must be as precise as possible."

On that day in May several workshop students, Natalie among them, had been invited to do a cold reading of a play under consideration at the Murray Hill Theatre Club, a warren of small stages in what once had been a mansion.

The reading was held on an intimate triangular stage situated on the main floor with the audience, consisting of management and friends of the author, just a few feet from the actors.

There was a general buzz in the room, and she soon realized it was caused by a man sitting apart from them all, drinking coffee from a Styrofoam cup and munching absently on a piece of a sandwich. He was wearing clean jeans, a white dress shirt, and expensive running shoes. He also looked vaguely familiar. She decided he was important because he made no move to join the nervous circle of actors and appeared content to wait by himself. Also he had the lead.

When the play began, a complicated story of a monk in the seventeenth century, the man in jeans continued to stay away from the rest, moving to center stage only as long as he had lines to speak which he did so softly the audience leaned forward to hear him. When he finished, he stepped back casually and munched his sandwich. Despite the strain to hear him and the natural resistance to his arrogance, he was easily the best actor there, and when he occupied the stage, a noticeable hush came over the audience and all eyes were on him.

"Who is that?" she asked another actress when the reading was half over and they stretched and crowded around the coffee urn.

"That's Sam Johnson," she said, admiration in her voice and her eyes.

Of course. Now she recognized him. He had won a Tony for the previous year and several Academy Award nominations for supporting roles. She remembered one role in particular where he had played a rich young scion who befriends a handsome but impecunious man trying to break into society. He had maneuvered the man into the right parties and introduced him to the loveliest debs, but privately he was scornful and in the end betrayed him callously. He had been so convincing in the role, she expected him to be callous and arrogant in real life and became somewhat annoyed when she noticed him staring at her boldly with what she took to be an appraising eye.

"You have a nice voice," he said, and she noticed that close up his face was very strong, especially at the jawline, with beautiful teeth and the most determined stare coming out of luminous, brown eyes. A light cleft punctuated his chin.

"I couldn't help thinking of the character you played in *The Striver*," she said. "You betrayed that man with such relish." To her surprise she sounded petulant. As if he had already made her unhappy.

"You prefer goody-goodies?" His eyes were smiling.

"No." She was annoyed that she had taken his bait. "Sometimes it takes more courage to be cruel than to be kind."

"I take it you've had some experience along those lines." He was not smiling anymore.

"Some." She walked away before he could say anything more.

The next day there were two messages from Sam Johnson on her answering service. One said: "I have free tickets to see *Borstal Boy*. Meet me at the box office at eight. Would pick you up, but I've got to see a guy about a job. Also—I don't know where you live. It was tough enough finding out your name."

The second message said: "Plans have changed. I can take you to dinner, too. Call 555-2470."

She didn't meet him or return his calls which came all week. Each time he left long, civil messages without any mention of the fact that she had not shown up for any of the other proposals. She was used to messages and she was used to men. So she did nothing.

In the beginning of the second week he left a message which read: "If you want to see *Bonnie and Clyde* without waiting in line, meet me at Cinema I at eight twenty. The manager will sneak us in through the side door. The feature starts at eight twenty-five so don't be late."

She began to suspect he had no intention of keeping any of the dates, so she showed up at the theatre, and to her surprise he was standing out in front of the marquee peering anxiously up and down the sidewalk.

"Come on," he said without missing a beat, "you're two minutes late and we'll miss the beginning."

When they were seated, he took her hand and held it with decorum. He was dressed in a navy pinstripe suit with a blue shirt and a patterned tie. He was clean and freshly shaved and might have been a banker except for the vitality which radiated out from him. He was too lit up for banking.

"Did you dress up for me?" she asked him in the dark.

"Yes. You and the Merv Griffin show. I taped it this afternoon."

"Did you keep all those dates you made on my answering service?"

"Yes."

"I don't believe you."

"I did."

"Weren't you angry because I didn't show up?"

"No. Women who show up are a dime a dozen. I didn't want you to show up."

"You didn't?"

"No. I wanted you to play hard to get."

"You're crazy." She couldn't tell if he was teasing or not.

"Quite the contrary." After a pause he added, "Maybe you're right. Maybe I'm getting crazy over you."

"You don't know me." He wouldn't get crazy over anyone.

He gave her hand a firm squeeze. "I know you. Now shut up and watch the movie."

She turned her eyes to the screen but couldn't completely forget he was sitting beside her. She couldn't resist one last question. "Did you really have tickets to *Borstal Boy?*"

"Yup."

"Damn."

"Don't worry." He patted her hand without taking his eyes off the screen. "We'll go again."

The following week she checked with her answering service twice each day, certain there would be a message from him. There wasn't.

Against her will she kept remembering how his hands had felt, his thumbs rubbing her cheeks roughly, his lips unexpectedly soft, not lingering long enough to satisfy her curiosity. Damn. Why didn't he call? Why didn't he do something predictable so she could forget about him?

Twelve days later the phone rang at eleven at night. She was just getting out of a hot bath.

"It's me," he said. "I'm at the airport. Don't go to sleep. Meet me at P.J.'s."

Her first instinct was to ask where he'd been, but instead she held the phone until her knuckles turned white and counted silently to ten. "Couldn't it wait until tomorrow?"

"No."

"Why does it have to be tonight?"

"Are you kidding?"

"No." She wanted to hear something that would ease her resentment.

"I haven't seen you for twelve days. Jeez." He paused. "P.J.'s in an hour?"

"Sure. An hour." He knew to the day how long it had been. That was something. The moment she hung up, however, she was disappointed with herself. Why would he want to see her in the middle of the night if not to sleep with her? Well, he could go to hell! She wouldn't sleep with him. Where the hell had he been for twelve days?

"I'm not going to sleep with you," she said as soon as the waiter had brought them their vodka gimlets. He was attacking her hand as if it were a life raft and he had fallen overboard.

"All right, all right." He paused and looked down at his drink. "That's not what I had in mind when I called you. I was scared."

"Scared?" What was he pulling now?

His eyes were serious, and he began rubbing the back of her hand again in an agitated way. "Hollywood scares the shit out of me and I wanted to tell somebody. Don't ever let me go out there again."

Don't ever let him go out there again. He was implying she had some power in his life. Normally she would have felt uncomfortable with such a statement, but not with Sam. "You were in Hollywood?"

"Didn't you know? I left a message on your service. Didn't you get it?"

"No."

He held her chin so she would be forced to look at him. "Hey . . . you must have been madder than hell."

She was ready to lie and shrug it off, but his eyes stopped her. "I wanted to punch you." Against her will she added, "I wanted to punch you because I kept remembering how you had kissed me and then you weren't there to kiss me again." Her small admission hit the jackpot. His face crumpled.

Later that night as they sat in her car outside his apartment building, he kissed her again for a long time.

"Why were you so scared in Hollywood?" she asked when he let her go. She wasn't sorry that he had been scared. "Was it the job?"

"Nothing's real out there. I've never felt so lonely in my life."

The idea that he could be lonely made her happy. If he was vulnerable, she could manage him. She knew she would see him again, but no way would she sleep with him. Not for ages. Months. Weeks.

He took her to plays and movies. She took him to openings of art galleries and museums. They made an extraordinary couple and people stared. At their third gallery preview of abstract expressionist paintings, he looked at three of the canvasses and then tapped her on the shoulder.

"I'm leaving."

"Why?"

"I feel uncomfortable and I don't know what to say about any of it."

"You don't have to say anything. Just look at it."

"I don't want to look at it."

"What do you expect me to do? What do you *want* to do?"

"Eat. Walk. Read. Anything but stand here and look at these globs and make believe I'm feeling something." He paused. "Are you coming with me?"

She didn't want to leave. The gallery owner who had greeted them not five minutes earlier was a friend of her father's and would look for her later. But if she didn't go and he left her there, it would create a break that might not be repaired.

"I'll come with you," she said, knowing she had crossed a line and could not go back.

He made it a practice never to ask her out on weekends, and she continued going home to her father's estate outside of the city even though Celine was there and she found it difficult being with Celine. One rainy weekend she stayed in town and phoned his apartment early Saturday morning. A woman answered. A woman with a lovely voice. Natalie was so undone she dropped the phone. Her heart pounded wildly and her ears felt as if they were hollow.

She went to the mirror and stared at herself for a long time. All her life she had been told she was beautiful. Sam had told her so himself on several occasions. If she was so beautiful why was he sleeping with someone else? She felt humiliated and childish. She was the child and the disembodied voice on the other end of the phone was a . . . a woman.

The throaty "hello" echoed in her head for days, but when he called, she agreed to meet him as if nothing had happened. He had not promised her anything.

Late in July, about two months after she met him, he got a part in a Broadway show and he asked her to come to rehearsals as his script coach. She went with him every day. He was too serious about his work to make such an arrangement without good reason, and she knew that it placed her in a different position than she had been in before. He valued her. He valued her judgment and she helped him learn his lines. They were together constantly, but mostly in the rehearsal hall. Still not alone.

One night as they sat over coffee after a late supper, he put his hand on her thigh and she was so anxious for him to leave it there that it frightened her. "Why don't you want to make love to me?" she asked, her voice trembling.

He thought a long time. "I'm afraid it will change us. It isn't everything, you know."

"What is everything? Is anything everything to you?"

"Yes." He waited a long time before continuing, and she knew it was a dumb question. The answer would not comfort her. He had taken away her confidence and made her ask for reassurance in sneaky ways. She wanted to hate him for doing that, but instead she loved him all the more. He wasn't doing it on purpose.

"For six years I wanted to be an actor more than anything else in the world." He spoke carefully, as if to clear things up for her once and for all. "I thought about it night and day. Went to the movies so often my head ached constantly. When I wasn't out hustling for parts, I was in front of the mirror saying the same line ten different ways. Eyebrows up. Eyebrows down. Tongue-in-cheek. Tongue sticking out. In New York I studied with Stella Adler, and she recommended me to directors and told me when there were closed auditions and readings. Always, though, when I was being considered, the deal fell through and I'd wake up with this hollow fear that I'd never get a part." He paused and took her hands into his, but his eyes, she noticed, were far away. "The fear always passed.

"One day I tried out for a part in *The Last Dance*. I didn't read particularly well that day. I had a cold and my throat hurt. There were two other guys auditioning and I stayed to listen. One guy was really terrific. When I finally got to my apartment, I was so feverish, working was the last thing on my mind. My only regret was not having had at least one job." He took his hands away as if the old regret once again overwhelmed him. His eyes were so bright, she could see herself in them, but they were not bright for her. They were bright for his work and his ambitions.

"The next morning about ten the phone rang. I was surprised because my phone never rang and certainly it never rang at ten o'clock in the morning. I considered not answering, figuring it was somebody trying to sell me a retirement home. But it was Joseph Simpson, the director for *The Last Dance*. 'Mr. Johnson,' he said. 'Is this Mr. Johnson?'

" 'Yes,' I answered.

" 'Mr. Johnson,' he said again very formally—he was a very formal guy—'we've decided that you should play the part of Nicholas Land. If you could come in sometime today, we can talk terms. I am assuming you don't have an agent—at least it doesn't indicate that you do on the information sheet you filled out for us.'

" 'That's correct.' I was in a daze. 'What time shall I come in?'

" 'About two thirty will be fine.'

" 'I'll be there,' I said and hung up the phone.

"After that I danced all around the room until the lady below me tapped on her ceiling. It was easily the happiest moment of my life. Acting is everything to me."

She said nothing. What was there to say.

"Still," he changed his expression and his eyes were all on her. "I find myself pretty excited when I'm going to see you. When I look at your face, it knocks me to pieces."

He didn't look like he was knocked to pieces. Natalie reached out to touch his face. She had never loved him more and tears of happiness came to her eyes. She was free to give everything or not as she chose. It was her decision and he couldn't take it away from her. Despite her fears she would not hold anything back from Sam Johnson. He was everything to her.

"Listen," he said, suddenly tired. "Why don't you take me for a ride in your nice car? I feel like going for a long ride."

"Okay."

They left the restaurant and walked to her car in silence. She slid into the driver's seat, and they were heading toward the midtown tunnel. "Put your arm around me," he said.

She put her arm around his neck except when she needed it to maneuver the car, then she would slide it around him again as one would with a child. When they were out on the expressway, he leaned into her and after a few minutes fell asleep.

Suddenly she had the urge to take him home. She wanted to show him to her father and see how they reacted to each other. It was time he knew who she was.

When she turned off the expressway, he looked up groggily and asked where they were.

"I'm taking you home for the weekend," she said. "Did you have any big plans?"

"No." He looked around at the unfamiliar streets of the small Long Island town. "Where's home?"

"A castle by the sea. We'll be able to swim in the morning and play tennis." She thought of the woman who had answered his phone . and wondered what she would do when he didn't show up.

"Sounds good to me." He snuggled back against her shoulder.

When she reached Harbor's End, her father's estate, she stopped at the foot of the long driveway and waited for him to come fully awake. "We're here."

He squinted out the window, trying to make out his surroundings as she drove to the top. The grounds were lit and the mansion glowed from within.

He gave a long, low whistle when she stopped the car again. "You weren't kidding when you said castle."

"No."

She turned on the interior light of the car to watch his face. His eyes got wider. "Oh . . . Jesus . . . *that* Davidson. Well, whatta you know. Okay," he said straightening his tie, "I'm ready. Take me to the slaughter."

They rang the bell long and hard before anyone answered.

"Good evening, missy." The butler was Japanese. Celine had decided the Japanese cowered her less than the English and had changed all the help to Orientals.

"Good evening, Oni. Is my father still up?"

"No, missy. Father sleeping, but lady still awake. Watch television."

Natalie smiled. Celine had them calling her lady. A pretender to the throne? "Oni, could you put my friend, Mr. Johnson, in one of the guest bedrooms. I think we'll both go to bed right away." She look at Sam.

"Uh, yes, long day," he said. When Oni disappeared up the stairway, Sam shook his head. "I haven't been to sleep this early since I wore Dr. Dentons. I'll go stir crazy. Are you serious?"

"It's either going to sleep or making conversation with Celine."

"Is she the Wicked Witch of the West or what?"

"No. It's just that I wanted you to meet father first."

"Fahtha," he spoke in a nasal voice and pulled Natalie to him, "has retired. You tricked me, you snotty bitch." He smiled and kissed her.

"I didn't trick you. You never asked any questions."

She realized it was the first time she had felt his chest which was hard and warm and enveloping. She remembered his hand on her thigh earlier in the evening, and the warmth spread throughout her body and she felt a tremor between her legs.

"Natalie? Is that you? Why didn't you tell me you were coming, dear?" Celine suprised them in the hall.

"Just came on impulse," she backed away from Sam. "Celine, this is Sam Johnson . . . a friend from the city. We thought we'd stay a couple of days."

"Of course." She studied him curiously and stuck out her hand which Sam shook zealously.

Celine was deeply tan and without makeup looked surprisingly young. She wore thin, cotton batiste pants and a shirt to match which clung snugly to her body. Long, brown hair fell carelessly around her shoulders. She hardly looked like anybody's stepmother.

"You might have called, Natalie. We would have arranged some fun things for you and . . . Sam." Celine stood straighter and licked her lips. "Where is Oni putting your friend?"

"I don't know. One of the rooms on the second floor. He'll need some clothes," she gestured helplessly toward Sam. "We didn't bring anything with us."

Sam walked away from them inspecting the paintings on the walls and whistling softly.

"I'll ring one of the girls," said Celine. "I'm sure someone's up."

She walked toward the servants' wing and Sam looked at Natalie. "The plot thickens."

"I know what you're thinking. She's beautiful. Is she your type?"

"What I was thinking is that she's too young to be your mother unless she had you when she was ten."

"She's my stepmother."

She led him into the den. The television was turned to Johnny Carson. Sam and Natalie sat together on a couch, and when she returned, Celine faced them. During the next half hour she was up and down half a dozen times, and each time she passed Sam, she paused. Natalie had never seen Celine so animated and Sam appeared appreciative. Was he more than appreciative? It was hard to tell, but one thing was sure. He wasn't indifferent.

"I'm going to sleep," she rose abruptly. "The pool's to the right of the house down a little hill. We can swim before breakfast," said Natalie. Sam raised his eyebrows as if asking what was expected of him, but then, sensing that the tension between the women was of long standing, he nodded and said good night.

"Where did you put Mr. Johnson?" she asked Oni who was coming down the stairs.

"I put him on third floor, missy. I tell him now."

"Why not on the second floor?" The only other bedroom besides hers on the third floor was the one that had belonged to her nanny.

The Oriental looked innocent. "Mioshi tell me she see ghosts on third floor. Might frighten you in night. Better have someone nearby on same floor."

"Oni," she said. "I don't believe in ghosts and neither do you."

"Oh, yes, missy. I believe in ghosts. In Japan ghosts are part of life. We have respect, not like in America. Oni believe in everything."

When she entered her old room and sat down on her bed, the feelings of childhood began to crowd in on her. Nothing had changed since her mother had decorated it fifteen years ago. The paper was pink and white with a woven design of blue ribbon through organdy eyelet. Little bouquets of lily of the valley and stephanotis floated amid square trellises of blue ribbon on a background of dusty rose. The curtains and bedspread were white organdy with deep ruffles.

The environment was not appropriate for a woman of twenty-three, even one who had only made love four times in her life. There had been Larry Epstein from Dartmouth who came to Wellesley each weekend and put his hands all over her in a frenzy of passion that lasted all of twenty minutes before he exploded all over her Hadley cashmere and Evan Picone skirt.

She stripped off her clothes and looked at herself critically in the mirror, wondering idly if Sam was Jewish. She was too thin. Her breasts, while not insignificant, were far from voluptuous. Nothing like Celine's which were large and pink and always in need of more space than Celine ever gave them.

Finally she put on her terry robe and sat primly on her narrow, ruffled bed. When she heard his steps in the hall, something totally unexpected occurred to her. She was going to follow him into his room and sleep with him.

As she padded down the hall in the dark, something else occurred to her. Some of her eagerness to get into Sam's bed was a need to short-circuit Celine. Sensuous, bovine Celine, neither cunning nor smart, had always provoked her into taking drastic steps without even knowing she had done so.

To his credit he welcomed her into his bed and showed no surprise; nor did he bring up past ultimatums. He kissed her face and shoulders and embraced her wholeheartedly. When he began to go down her body with his lips, she struggled to raise herself.

"Relax," he said gently, parting her legs. She waited, holding her breath and feeling shy and awkward at what he was about to do. She tried to hold her legs together, but the pleasure produced by his mouth and tongue overpowered her, and she raised her knees and let him in.

Through a haze of memory she remembered she hadn't touched him yet and reached for his penis. He groaned and rolled over on his back beside her. "Not too much," he whispered. "I'm so excited now, it wouldn't take much."

"What do you want me to do?"

"Sit on me. Just straddle my hips until I calm down."

She did what he asked but found she couldn't keep still and began to slide across him rubbing herself against him.

"Oh, no," he murmured. "That won't do. I want to go in."

He raised her high enough to enter, and she leaned forward on her hands and raised and lowered herself on him, keeping well forward. She wanted to ask him if that was all right, but the words wouldn't come out.

"Yes," he said suddenly and let out a low moan. Her hair was floating around her face, and he pushed it back and smoothed it against her head over and over. "I wanted to make love to you since the first time I saw you."

Did he expect an answer in kind? At that moment she couldn't have spoken if her life depended on it. The friction was becoming so pleasurable, she couldn't keep from making her own noises, and each time she did, he moved inside her. Finally when she was on an upward slide, he turned her over and wound himself all around her, thrusting deeply and pulling her legs around his waist as if their closeness meant his life. She felt her own burst of release just seconds before his body shuddered against her and the last long moan exploded in her ear.

"Well, we survived it," he said into the darkness. "All that worry for nothing." He was half joking.

She wasn't so sure. She had been lying there trying to build fantasies of their future happiness, but the images wouldn't come into focus. He was already slipping away from her.

The next day dawned brilliantly sunny, and they swam and played tennis as she had promised him. While he had been still asleep, she went into the village and bought him swimming trunks and tennis shorts. She didn't want him to wear any of the clothes at the house, which technically belonged to Celine. She wanted to take care of Sam herself.

When her father appeared at the pool, she was shocked at how old he looked. His once vigorous body looked fragile and slightly bent, and she blamed Celine who appeared indifferent to his comings and goings. Celine's eyes that morning were all on Sam. Her father, too, seemed pleased with her young man, and they quickly found a common ground on which to get to know each other. They were both insane for theatrical trivia, and Sam was astonished to find that Jack Davidson could match him in dredging up endless facts.

They began to play a game of obscure play titles wherein Sam gave the name of the play and her father had to come up with the stars or the author or both.

"Yes, My Darling Daughter," said Sam, looking up into the cloudless sky with a grin.

Jack Davidson answered from under his tennis hat without shifting position. "Peggy Conklin and Charles Bryant. Marlo Reed wrote it."

Sam lay silent a moment, not quite so buoyant as before. *"Boy Meets Girl,"* he said after a long pause.

"That was the Spewacks play. I invested in it and made a lot of money. It ran a long time. Allyn Joslyn was in it."

"Here's an easy one, but you have to give me the stars and the date it was first produced." Sam was sitting up now and regarding Jack Davidson with open admiration. *"The Women."*

"Clare Booth. She wasn't married to Henry yet. The year was 1936. I went to their wedding, you know. What's more, I dated the star who was Ilka Chase."

"I give up," said Sam, rising from his chair. "Oh, wait. One more. *He Who Gets Slapped.*"

Jack Davidson shook his head. He thought and thought beneath the tilted hat. Finally he opened one eye. "You got me."

Sam came and stood by the older man. "I didn't want to get you," he said. "You know as much about the theatre as anyone who's in it. I don't know two things about horse racing or skeet shooting or any of the things you excel at. So there you are."

Natalie could see her father was touched by his speech. It was generous and full of feeling and just right for a young man to an older man who had begun to feel his years. Sam Johnson knew just how to handle her father who was the best person in the whole world. She would marry him.

The idea that he might not wish to marry her never entered her mind.

Celine left the trio at the pool and went indoors to get some relief from the heat. She would go over the dinner menu and perhaps make a centerpiece for the table. I'm the mistress of the house, she told herself. Being the mistress of Harbor's End was usually like being the mistress of a mausoleum, deadeningly dull. The house in Captiva, Florida, was no better nor was the farm in Vermont. More infuriating than the dullness was the stiffness of the people in her husband's life. "You all have a stick up your backside that goes up to your neck," she had said to Jack on one of the rare times she had voiced her frustrations.

"Perhaps we do, my dear," he had answered calmly, "but we've had it there for a very long time and it's quite comfortable. We won't change." It was an explanation and a warning not to expect anything different in the future. Celine could not even get angry because he continued to be civilized and for the most part ignored her sexual activities.

The first time she knew that he was aware of her infidelity was in Italy when they were vacationing on the Amalfi coast. "My dear," he said one evening as he got into bed for a nap before dinner, "if you're going to hump the bellboy, at least let him use his influence to have the sheets changed afterward. You must push your advantage wherever you can." His tone was professorial, instructing her in the ways of commerce. "But be sure he arranges it before the act. Afterward you've lost your bargaining power."

Had Celine been more sensitive, she would have been wounded by his civility. As it was, she was merely confused, wondering how he would punish her. Would he throw her out? Change his will? Would he send her back to Macon City, Virginia, the hometown she had left twelve long years ago in a blaze of glory?

Celine Davidson, née Tobias, had not been the prettiest girl in Macon City. Her mother encouraged her to *do* something to make herself stand out.

"Celine Marie," she said, "you're a pretty girl, but if you don't do a little something, you'll never get in the public eye. You want to end up with a bunch of kids and urinary complications?"

Celine took up baton twirling and became quite good at it. The fact that she was pretty and also had a skill made that skill all the more remarkable. A representative of the Rheingold Beer Company who had been sponsoring a local bowling league caught her baton act and took her picture as a likely candidate for Miss Rheingold, a title she won the following year.

As often happens to near celebrities, men hesitated to ask her out lest they be refused. Celine was lonely in New York and bored.

At a Rotary Club luncheon ceremony where she was seated between the mayor (middle-aged and balding) and the commissioner of baseball (even older), her boredom became acute, and to distract herself she took off her shoe and tried to touch the man opposite her with her toe planning to make believe it was accidental. To her embarrassment she contacted the most sensitive part of a man on the first try. Blushing violently, she retrieved her errant foot. The man, however, was enchanted and asked her out for the evening. When she realized who the man was and the extent of his fortune, Celine thanked her resourceful guardian angel.

Celine's ardor had cooled almost immediately, and now she would have difficulty remembering why on earth she had considered herself lucky to have become Mrs. John Halsey Davidson, the second.

She went to her bedroom and took off the tight bikini that was beginning to make her breasts feel uncomfortable and put on a thin, silk robe. Thinking she heard Oni in the hall, she came out to ask him to serve cocktails in the den. It was not Oni she saw but Sam going up to change for dinner.

She hesitated only a moment before following him silently, the thick carpeting absorbing all noise. Her husband always swam at least half an hour before dinner. She would have enough time. Seconds after he entered his room she was inside with him and had opened her robe and let it fall to the floor. When he saw her, his eyes became narrow and distant, and he reached down to retrieve the robe and place it around her shoulders.

At that moment Natalie for the first and last time in her life opened a door without knocking.

Her only thought was to get as far away from him as possible, and she booked a seat on the next plane to London which left at noon the following day. At the airport she called her father.

"Was it Celine?" he asked when she told him her plans.

"No, Dad." She couldn't hurt him. "I don't think women are his first choice."

"Oh." He seemed deeply disappointed. "Well, in that case it's better this way. Look up the Raymond Craigmyles, my darling. They'll show you a good time. I'll phone ahead and tell them you're coming."

"Not right away. Give me a few days to sort things out."

There was nothing else to say. "Good-bye. Take care of yourself."

"Good-bye, darling." He sounded forlorn and it occurred to her that he, too, was alone. But there was nothing she could do for him right now. She was too forlorn herself.

Two weeks later she woke up in her London hotel room and knew she was pregnant. To begin with she felt warm all the time, as if her thermostat had been turned up. Then there was the giddiness that overtook her at certain times of the day.

She found out from the desk clerk that all the gynecologists in London that she would find suitable had their offices on Harley Street, so she chose a name at random and sat there the following morning with seven other women in various stages of pregnancy. The doctor, whose name was Colin Botswith, confirmed the news, and she cried for two hours in his shabby but comfortable office. She had not cried since she was twelve years old and now it seemed as if she would never stop. Not only that, but she was happy to be crying in full view of a little plump nurse and a grandfatherly doctor with hair growing out of his ears who were going about their business and only stopped to pat her shoulder in between patients.

"Gulping oxygen she is, each time she sucks in," said the nurse to the other patients as if she were recommending such crying to all of them. "So beneficial to the wee one."

Natalie couldn't remember when she had felt more sincerely comforted and remained there until four when they closed up. She blew her nose, paid them, and left. After a bath and a nap and cold compresses on her swollen eyes, she called the Raymond Craigmyles and they insisted on moving her to their Belgravia flat.

That night she accompanied them and their daughter Ismelda to a dinner dance given by a duke and duchess in a huge stone house in Mayfair. She didn't want to go but was so relieved to hand over her life to someone else, she would have followed them to the Mojave if they had so designated.

The evening was a fog of handshakes and Ismelda's friendly, high-pitched voice trying to amuse her with comic gossip about the guests. Then suddenly the fog lifted. Natalie noticed a deeply tanned, tall and distinguished man staring at her.

"Who is that man?" she asked Ismelda.

"Don't you recognize him?"

"No. But he's been staring in the general vicinity of my bosom for the last five minutes." Her breasts were swollen and had outgrown her bras.

"I should be so fortunate," said Ismelda tugging at her bodice to reveal more of her childish breasts. "That's Alden Van Druten. America's answer to royalty."

"I thought he was an old man?"

"You're thinking of the *père,* who's quite dead. This is Alden, the two, no more than forty and in between wives. Shall I ask father to introduce you?"

"No." Natalie was confused. She kept remembering anew that she was pregnant. "I . . . I . . . . He looks too arrogant."

"That's not arrogance. That's what's known as the natural assumptions of the very, very privileged. Oh, God, Natalie," her voice got higher, "he's coming over."

Those were the last words Ismelda spoke to Natalie that night. From that moment Alden Van Druten did not leave her side. As it happened, he didn't much leave her side for the next several days except to deliver her home each night. But soon that, too, became unnecessary, because on the nineteenth of October, five weeks after they met and nearly eight weeks after she had conceived Sam Johnson's baby, Alden made her his third wife in a brief ceremony in the historic Caxton Hall.

Chapter 3

HE DROVE HIS GREEN LINCOLN CONTINEN-
tal smoothly down the winding roads of
Ryder's Goose Neck to the cinder track at the local high school. It
was 5:10 A.M. on a warm for March morning, and with any luck an
hour would pass before anyone else appeared on the track to run
alongside him. Alden was not used to being alone with people who
were not aware of who he was. Occasionally fellow runners greeted
him. He was forced to make small talk.

There was a man who spoke to him regularly and dribbled information in a way that made Alden uncomfortable. Still, he could not
afford to turn him away.

"Mind if I run with you?" the familiar voice would say. The
stranger was short and stocky with a lopsided grin that never sobered.

"I don't want to run as fast as you do." Alden, jogging on the inside track, knew the man would have to run a little faster on the
curve.

"Naw, naw," said the man. "I'm doing seven-and-a-half-minute
miles." Alden would remain silent. "You play tennis?" asked the
man.

"Why?"

"I notice the shoes. They're no good for running. Once a year *Runners' World* does a shoe review. These are the best." He pointed to brand new running shoes.

Again Alden kept silent, but his mind now settled on his hurting ankles. As if tuning in, the man continued. "Your kind of feet . . . maybe the Puma last is better. I don't know. Geez . . ." He was suddenly exasperated. "You shouldn't run in tennis shoes. What do you wanna do that for?"

Today he walked to the cyclone fence surrounding the track and pulled himself forward with legs far apart to stretch his muscles. He pulled his knees to his chest, a dozen times for each leg, then sat on the ground and bent over from the waist until he felt sufficiently loose to begin a slow, easy run.

Everything was going well. There would be enough time to hit his stride, settle into a rhythmic run, and wait for his mind to empty itself. Then? Well, then he would just wait for it to happen. He would wait for his reverie.

A more pretentious man would have called what Alden did with his mind at the Ryder's Goose Neck High School track a mystical trance, but such a description would have been abhorrent to Alden, who had only contempt for the faddish. Having all his life had an excess of money and social advantage, he had never had to make more of anything than what it was.

This approach served him well until the day his stepdaughter by the first marriage asked him to speak to her class at Farleigh about his profession as some of the other fathers were going to do. He didn't much like the little girl, who in no way filled the great void in his life and heart that his own child would have, but he agreed dutifully to participate.

Joselyn White's father spoke to them about financial planning—which sounded unintelligible but important. Patricia Derby's father spoke about being a lawyer, and Allyson Sinclair's father, by far the most interesting, told them how it was to manufacture bathroom fittings. Mr. Sinclair bought brass and plated it with chrome and cast it into the little spouts they were used to. He even showed them a fancy gold-plated lion's head spout and told them it was purchased by people with more money than brains. He said it was no better (in fact less efficient) than the plain unplated spigot he had used as a child in The Bronx. The girls missed the object lesson, enchanted with the idea of water spouting out of the lion's mouth.

When it was Alden's turn to speak, he told the children simply that he had no job, which shocked his stepdaughter. At times, he went on to say, he did sit in on meetings for various organizations because he was a member of the board. The children heard it as "bored" and began to giggle, making his stepdaughter burst into tears. She ran from the room and refused to return.

The incident brought home to Alden the dismal track record of men like himself. So many had committed suicide or died under curious circumstances which might as well have been suicide. There was Marshall Field II and Trenton Baker and poor Mr. Woodward who had been shot by his wife, who thought him a burglar. He was well aware of how easily his life could disintegrate.

It didn't seem to matter what one did as long as it was *something*. George Reems, an English duke, once his best friend, had bought an exterminating company in Algiers and couldn't have been prouder had it been a bank. "I said to myself," he told them, "where would a rat catcher be busier than in Algiers? The Casbah must be riddled with rodents. We have a band of thirty men whom I visit twice a year to deliver pep talks and bonuses. Their gratitude is touching. Now we've engaged Pierre Cardin to do some nice green and white uniforms."

Alden could not convince himself that renting office space and pretending to manage things would have made him feel any more useful, and he continued as before.

Running had become for him a means of personal exploration. While he had never had to work by the sweat of his brow, now he had an obsessive need for hard physical toil. The idea of pushing his body to the point of sweat, to continue beyond endurance, greatly appealed to him. Time seemed to slip by without awareness. He eased into those moments of forgetfulness as pleasantly and easily as he slipped into the warm bath that Simmons had waiting for him on his return. Only recently had he discovered that these periods of non-awareness were preludes to something more important. His mind emptied itself of normal thought and spontaneously unreeled stored scenes from the past in a manner so vivid that Alden would often emerge moved to tears and afterward experience incalculable comfort.

When the reveries were over, Alden turned his attention to his stride, which had taken weeks to perfect. Run from the hips and thighs he said to himself. Strike with the heel, hold yourself erect, shoulders relaxed, hands in loose fists. He was satisfying something internal; perhaps it was simply a long standing need to play—to take pleasure. Such an idea made him smile.

Chapter 4

ALL THE PAPERS COVERED THE FUNERAL. The young man in the car crash was to be married within weeks, and his fiancée, bravely dry-eyed, absently drumming on the casket with nervous fingers, was unusually beautiful. It was a story to touch every heart. Bob Paxton had died while returning home intoxicated from a farewell-cum-bachelor's party celebrated early because he was leaving for a new job as well as a new life.

Miranda felt the flashbulbs illuminating her face and sat straighter, placing both hands in her lap. She didn't want to be described as bowed in grief. Everyone assumed she was too shocked to react to Bob's death and urged her to let herself go. The truth was, there wasn't much to let go. She hadn't ever planned to marry Bob and expected to tell him so on the day he died. While she was very, very sorry that he *had* died, her sorrow was of the detached variety—what she might feel for war victims or orphaned children.

Miranda's photograph easily dominated the second section of the *Times* the following day and stopped almost everyone who saw it.

The couple, said the paper, was to have settled in Sunnydale Acres, a small community in central Long Island.

Sanche Ray scrutinized the photograph from his French Provincial bed in the Navarro Hotel on Central Park South for a full minute before turning the page. Then when he finished the section, he returned to it and tore out the story, placing it next to the telephone.

Sanche Ray had waited for fame to transform him, but it had not. He still had his compulsions. His mother still ridiculed him. She still threatened seizures, hemorrhages, ulcers because he, Seymour (as she still insisted on calling him), fell short of her expectations (as she intended). She was a first-rate blackmailer. But more troublesome to Sanche was the fact that winning the Academy Award for his original screenplay had not created a tidal wave that carried him off to more dazzling shores. Important voices came over his telephone. Important letters came in his mail. But life was dismally similar to what it had been before.

Sometimes at night he awoke fearful and confused, as if fame had just been one more of his mother Sophie's tricks. He was determined to prove that things were different, and on those days he was especially cruel to anyone he could be cruel to—his agent's secretary, the underlings in the publicity office of the distributor of his picture, the waiters at "21."

The morning Sanche saw Miranda's picture he had spent a particularly troublesome night. To obliterate his own problems he lost himself in the poignancy of the situation. An unusually beautiful girl loses her fiancée in a horrific car crash just as they are about to marry.

Instead of settling in Sunnydale Acres, middle-class but pleasantly predictable, she will end up elsewhere. Perhaps on Park Avenue with vastly altered dreams. Or maybe she, too, ends tragically. A modern Romeo and Juliet.

The dramatic possibilities made his head swim with creative excitement. Writers made novels of news stories all the time. Why couldn't he make a movie out of this girl's life?

He would locate the girl in the photograph, pluck her out of obscurity and tragedy, and make her life shine again. That was power, wasn't it? Seymour Rubinstein, now known as Sanche Ray, had the power to change someone's life.

*   *   *

Miranda herself stared at her image in the paper with relief and detachment. The affair with Bob had ended as it began—with a photograph.

When Miranda was eighteen, a man approached her in Bloomingdale's where she had a Christmas job while attending Hunter College and asked to photograph her. He was doing an essay on typical New York faces and wanted her face for typical young woman. She had laughed. Typical was blue-eyed and freckled, or at least blond with bangs. Not her.

"You don't see what I see," said the photographer, a serious, thin-faced young man. "Once we get all the gook off your face, the camera will do the rest."

He was expensively dressed and had a camera over his shoulder, so the next day she was at his studio on Twenty-third Street, a grimy loft filled with overflowing ashtrays and dirty hairbrushes left by other subjects.

The photographer, whose name was Theodore Perry, scrubbed her face until it hurt and her eyes smarted. He parted her long hair in the middle and pushed it carelessly behind her ears, rubbed a creamy brown stick under her cheekbones, and put mascara on her lashes.

Two huge rolls of paper hung from a ceiling track, one black and one white. He stood her against the black paper and took one hundred and fifty photographs of her face, after which he tried to make love to her on a paisley-covered daybed that sent up puffs of dust when they sat on it.

Although she had no desire for this thin, priestly man, Miranda felt overly burdened by her virginity and considered letting him rid her of it. It had to happen some time, why not him? They'd never see each other again.

"What's the matter?" he asked when she hesitated.

"Nothing. It's just . . . I've never gone all the way." It sounded stupid, as if she were on a bus and someone had asked where the end of the line was. But how else could she say it? She didn't want to say 'fucked' or 'screwed' which would make her sound more experienced than she was.

"Jesus." He rose, tucked his shirt into his trousers, and offered her his hand. "Come on, kid, I didn't mean anything. Come on, I'll take you home."

More than a year later, a few days after her twentieth birthday, a business card came by mail. "Go to the Union Carbide Building," it said on the back. "Through the main entrance and to the right you will see Typical Young New York Woman. I think you'll like her. Good luck!" It was signed TP. The front of the card said, "Theodore Perry Photographs You."

Indirectly Theodore Perry was responsible for her losing her virginity after all, because Bob Paxton, a boy she had known in high school, saw the photograph and called to ask her out.

Miranda had been the last of the three to leave St. Mildred's. Except for summers she lived at the school until she was fourteen, after which her scholarship stopped and she entered a city high school. For the first time in her life she was around boys and it wasn't easy. Her directness was not endearing to the opposite sex. They considered it pushy, preferring girls who were coy or shy or snobbish. They didn't know how to deal with someone who told the blunt truth and behaved as their equal.

For herself Miranda considered the boys childish and stupid. Except for Bob Paxton. From the beginning he treated her differently. He had a secretive smile which he bestowed on her whenever their eyes met in class. When she smiled back, he let his tongue slip out between his teeth which made her tremble and heat up inside.

They had never dated in school, although once while handing her a test paper in chemistry class, he had held it over his crotch and when she reached for it, he pressed her hand down hard and she felt a lump. He regularly brushed against her in the halls but continued to date a blond, accomplished ballerina who was always on the program at school assemblies.

"Miranda, you look terrific," he said when he saw her. "Different. In school you always looked . . . well . . . I don't know but . . . you looked foreign."

Bob Paxton appeared mature to Miranda. She liked the way his clothes fit and the way he smiled. She forgot that he hadn't thought much of her in high school. He had a good job as a junior accountant in an advertising agency and seemed sophisticated. Definitely sophisticated.

On their first date he took her to see *The Graduate* at an art theatre on Third Avenue, and she realized as they stood in line along with haughty braless girls and their attentive men that she and Bob made an attractive couple. They were noticed and stared at with just a little bit of envy.

After the movie they went to a coffee house in Greenwich Village and watched old Charlie Chaplin films and drank cappuccino coffee in tall, slender cups. Bob was ecstatic in his praise of Chaplin. "Look at that, hon," he kept saying. "Isn't that great, hon?" Miranda thought Chaplin was all right, but Bob's calling her "hon" was somehow disappointing. Still, there were other good things.

On their third date he took her to a Japanese restaurant and made a big show of ordering without a menu. He seemed to have a special relationship with the waiter and commented that only tourists ordered from the menu. She thought the food was terrible. She couldn't identify anything on her plate which made her timid about eating, but the good news was that he was touching her thigh between courses, and she liked that very much.

After dinner he took her to visit his friend Hal and his live-in girl friend, Judy, who served them strong drinks made with rye and ginger ale and put on a record of Ella Fitzgerald singing Cole Porter songs. Ella began to sing "Love for Sale," and Hal and Judy, who had been dancing, now kissed openly and stood very close. Bob took the opportunity to fondle her breast, and then he squeezed his hand under her seat.

Viewed from above all was proper, and the idea that they might be discovered at any moment excited Miranda tremendously. The combination of having her thighs tightly around his fingers and the angle of his hand from beneath touched certain parts of her that had never been touched before. The feeling was remarkable.

She looked up to see what Hal and Judy thought of all this, but there was no one there, only the voice of Ella singing ". . . if you want to try my wares, follow me and climb the stairs . . ." which she incorporated into her fantasy of what was about to happen.

He took her hand and put it on his bulge. She squeezed it tentatively.

"Open it, honey," he said.

She tried to straighten the zipper so it would not catch him, but it was impossible. He stood up impatiently and opened it, and she saw a round, nubby end peeking out of the opening in his shorts. Next he removed his jacket and in one stealthy motion removed a condom from his wallet and placed a towel, left nearby by a thoughtful Hal, under her hips. He lowered himself alongside her carefully so that his hips traversed the towel and began to put his tongue in her ear. Miranda was mystified. It felt cold and uncomfortable. Then he began to alternately pull at her nipples and rub his palm over them as they turned hard. This she found mildly exciting, but nothing compared to his finger in her crotch from below. She wished she could get him to do that again.

Finally he pulled up her skirt, pulled down her panties as far as her garter belt would allow, and climbed on top of her, rubbing his penis against her general pubic area. She was surprised at the force it had. It could jab and squirm all on its own. It was jabbing and squirming all over her, sometimes on her garter belt. She decided to guide it toward the center, and perhaps it would find its way.

The moment she touched it Bob began to pant wildly and grope frantically to find the opening.

"Tell me you want me to fuck you," he said in a hoarse whisper.

"What?"

"Say you want to be fucked. It makes it more exciting." He seemed annoyed that he had to explain all this.

"I want to be fucked," she whispered, feeling silly.

Bob began to move furiously against her. "Resist me, honey," he croaked.

What did that mean? "I don't know what you mean." She had lost all sense of her body. When she closed her eyes, it felt as if her head was alone in a room with a disembodied voice.

"Tell me I can't put it in."

"You can't put it in," she said mechanically, eyes closed. "I won't allow it," she adlibbed.

"Not like that," his voice was petulant. "Say, 'You can't put it in until you suck me.' "

The words wouldn't come out. "I can't."

"Come on, honey. It makes me hotter when you say things. That's the whole fun."

"What shall I say?"

"Tell me to suck you."

"Suck me." She could not imagine where he was supposed to suck her.

"I will if you let me put it in a little."

"All right. But just a little. Not all the way." She was pleased with her improvisation and its effect on him.

"That's it, honey. Oh, that's good." He was now trying very hard to enter her and was pushing her legs wider and wider apart. "Put it in, honey," he said. "Put it in, yourself."

She felt timid about doing that, but he was so insistent she began to try. It would not go inside because of the way she was lying. She tilted her hips and jabbed at herself several times until it began to go inside her, though by no means easily. He immediately began to hump up and down, straining and pushing, and she felt several sharp stabs of pain as he groaned and heaved and made a loud grunt before collapsing on top of her.

"Oh, shit, I didn't pull out," he said, but she was too engrossed in her own predicament to pay much attention. Liquid was coming out of her, and she knew without looking that some of it was red and would probably stain the couch.

"Bob," she said, "I think I'd better get up and go to the bathroom. I'm probably bleeding."

"Bleeding?" He was confused and alarmed.

"Don't you bleed the first time?"

"Jesus, this was the first time for you?" He was unbelieving and somewhat peeved.

"Wait. Let's see." She eased herself up to a sitting position and pulled down her skirt. There was a big, red spot on the towel and he moaned.

"Oh, no. Hal will be mad as hell." Miraculously the stain had not gone through, or if it had, the nubby tweed of the couch did not show it.

She wasn't bothered by Bob's reaction, being too relieved to care. The couch was not stained and she was no longer a virgin.

In the days that followed, attending her classes at Hunter and demonstrating Charles of the Ritz cosmetics at Bloomingdale's, Miranda would suddenly find herself thinking about Bob's lovemaking and her underpants would get damp. Her complete awareness was centered on the space between her legs. Sometimes it alarmed her how much she enjoyed sex and how often she craved it. It made no difference that Bob's lovemaking was predictable, an exact duplicate of the first night with some variation in the dialogue he requested. Miranda was too interested in her discovery to care much about technique. Besides, she had no one else to compare him with. Her desire was so strong and frequent, she would sometimes go to the bathroom an hour after making love and rub herself to a quick orgasm so she could face Bob without attacking him.

That fall Miranda turned twenty-one and her mother died after a lingering illness. It wasn't the drinking that ultimately killed her but pneumonia. Miranda cleared the apartment of all the statues of Jesus and Mary and cartons of votive candles which her mother had used to buy divine protection right to the end. She didn't want to remain in the sunless railroad flat. When Bob suggested they get an apartment together, it seemed the solution to everything.

Incredibly, three years passed. She finished Hunter, but all she had to show for it was a secretarial job with a public relations firm. And Bob. From the beginning Bob seemed intent on thrusting her at Judy, implying that the association would be beneficial to Miranda. Judy knew the ropes and might teach them to her.

Bob wanted to mould her in a certain image which did not include talking to the men she waited on at Bloomingdale's, a part-time job she clung to as a source of glamor. He said their crude remarks cheapened her. Miranda, however, looked forward to being noticed by the well-dressed men who flocked to her counter. They wore expensive shoes and crisp poplin raincoats left carelessly unbelted. She would have liked to leave at the end of the day with one of those men. They did not wear strong cologne the way Bob did, and their hair was long and stylish which Bob considered silly and unAmerican.

Miranda felt more alienated than ever from Hal and Judy and Bob. When she and Judy met for lunch, she was bored with talk of Corningware and silver patterns and the virtues of the IUD over the Pill. She got tired of looking into Judy's maple hope chest and having her drag out the patterned sheets and the Waring blender and the Detecto scale all in matching avocado. Most of all she didn't want to see the lingerie which Judy brought out with giggles and blushes. There were panties in there that had printed on them: "F. Y. E. O." For your eyes only!

Mostly she wanted to tell Judy that she had no intention of making Bob the last person to see any part of her.

She had just about decided to move out when Bob was offered a better job in a small suburban ad agency, and he announced that they would now have to search for a house and make it legal. She said nothing, deciding to break the news at the right time.

On a windy Sunday in early March they borrowed his mother's car and drove to Long Island to house hunt. Bob's eye had been stirred by an ad in the real estate section that asked: "Now that you're making over thirty thousand a year, isn't it time you became a success?" It certainly was, he agreed, and asked to see the model home. It didn't matter that one-third of that thirty thousand dollars was Miranda's salary.

The Beechmont was an overly decorated split ranch with oversized flowers as the main decorating motif. The master bedroom was papered with cabbage roses. The guest bath was papered in cut velvet poinsettias. The dining room sported large daisies with all the petals separated from the center as if someone had been playing "He loves me, he loves me not."

She could tell Bob liked the house because he was opening every closet and measuring things. He stood back and visualized his possessions already in there. Miranda said nothing and took a modest interest in the kitchen.

"Well, honey, what do you think?" he asked when the salesman left them discreetly alone.

"Lovely."

"I know my mother would give us the down payment as a wedding present. It wouldn't be that much each month. You could get a job out here."

"Right." She had her head in the wall oven and was glad he couldn't see her eyes.

"Next weekend," he continued, "we'll test drive some cars." He came around from behind her and kissed her cheek. She realized that in his convoluted way he had just proposed.

Ten days later he was dead.

The day after the funeral Miranda had a call from a man named Sanche Ray who claimed he was a screenwriter greatly touched by her story. He got her number from Bob's mother whom he had tracked down from details in the newspaper.

"It's a rotten shame what happened," he said.

"What . . . ?" She couldn't connect Bob's death with what the man was saying.

"About your boyfriend."

"Oh, yes . . . a shame."

"Look, I know this sounds a bit irregular, but I'm very interested in your story for . . . for its dramatic possibilities. Please don't misunderstand. I don't mean to be crass." There was a moment of silence. "Hello. Are you still there?"

"Yes. It's all right." Miranda didn't quite know what he was talking about, but she was interested.

"You can check me out of course. Actually . . . well, actually, I'm well known."

"I believe you," she said soberly. "It doesn't sound irregular." She wanted to add that what was irregular and strange to her were the last few years of her life.

He gave her his address, and she went to see him late in the evening. It was a very posh hotel on Central Park South. She had never been on Central Park South.

His suite had a large bedroom with the beds well away from a small sitting area consisting of two very formal chairs separated by a round table on which sat a tall lamp. It was difficult for them to see each other around the lamp, but, indifferent to the obstacle, they talked for several minutes.

Finally he got to the point. "Would you be interested in telling me your story?"

"Yes."

He liked the fact that she wasn't fawning all over him. She was better than the photograph, he decided. Much better. He went to a small desk and picked up a tape recorder and several cassettes. "I want you to talk into these. Put in everything you can remember about your relationship from the very first day you met your fiancé. What your hopes and dreams were. It must have been a terrible adjustment when you realized it was all over." She nodded and looked away. "Don't be afraid to put in small details. The more details, the better."

"I understand," she said.

"When you fill these," he handed her the cassettes and a piece of letterhead with his name and address, "send them to me."

He watched her stuff the cassettes into her handbag. Her nails were badly bitten, and he was reminded of a child stuffing crayons into a too small box and felt tender and protective.

"We'll have a contract of course. I can have one drawn up and your lawyer could look it over."

"Why do we need a contract?"

"To protect your rights. You would be getting a percentage of the film or a lump sum for the rights to your story."

She shook her head. "Let's see what we get on these tapes before we talk about contracts."

He nodded. "As you like."

She started for the door and then turned back. "What kind of films do you do?"

"Regular ones . . . feature films."

"Would I have seen any of them?"

"Yes. You probably have . . . especially this year."

"Why this year?"

"Because this year I won the Academy Award."

"Oh." She had no answer for that kind of information. "That's very nice. Really." She didn't even ask him which film.

Miranda talked into the cassettes several hours each day, but the story that emerged was not about love at all. The only poignancy was in the way Bob had found her—through the photograph in the Union Carbide building. After that, ennui, deceit, and cowardice had held them together. She had never mustered up the emotional energy to leave him. Was this art? She worried that Sanche would be disappointed but remained faithful to her story.

Much later Sanche would reassure her that it was better than he had hoped. Love stories were a dime a dozen, but this mindless, loveless coupling finally interrupted by fate fascinated him much more. It was a parable of modern life. He liked the idea that she had always planned to leave Bob. It meant she was free to love him.

She spoke it all out with unselfconscious simplicity and mailed it to California. Each day she expected to hear from Sanche, but the call never came. Two weeks passed. One night just as she was preparing for bed, there was a call from Italy. She assumed it was a mistake. Who would be calling from Italy?

"Miranda?" boomed a strange voice, "this is Sanche Ray." It took her a few seconds to understand. "I've listened to all the tapes.'' There was a lot of static, but she heard the word wonderful and something about could she come there. Then, miraculously, the line became perfectly clear. "I'm finishing up a project here, but it needn't take up all my time. We could work on the script together." She couldn't remember that voice at all. He could have been a stranger. "Can you make it?"

"Yes."

"Good. Now listen carefully. I want you to get in touch with my agent . . . his name is Jack Martell at the Martell Agency. That's M-a-r-t-e-l-l. He'll give you a ticket and all the details. Do you have a passport?"

"Yes," she lied.

"Good. Then I'll see you soon."

"Don't worry," she heard herself saying. "I'll be there." She wasn't surprised by the call or the turn of events in her life. This was what she had expected all along. It had just taken some time.

Chapter 5

TWO WEEKS AFTER HER WALK WITH BILL Waring Sara was asked to lunch by Jane Seymour, which wouldn't have been unusual except that Jane called her at home and made a lunch date on a day she was not due in at the office.

"We want you to do a story on home births," said Jane when they were seated at Le Madrigal. It was an expensive restaurant, a courting place where editors took name authors. She was happy but suspicious. They had never given her an assignment before and certainly never asked her to lunch.

She was so buoyed by the prospect of writing a full piece that she spent the rest of the afternoon in the city shopping for presents for the kids and Reynold. She would be supermom and superwife in payment for this terrific windfall. After dinner she wrote a letter to Reynold's mother, something she usually only did at Christmas.

"I'm writing to your mother," she said as Reynold flipped through the evening paper.

"Unexpected presents, unscheduled letters to my mother—you must be having a terrific affair," he answered jokingly.

She blushed and thought of Bill Waring, startled that he came so instantly to mind with the word affair. "I got an assignment today to do a real piece, and I'm trying to pay back the gods."

"I understand perfectly," he said, taking a pointed look skyward.

She began immediately to prepare for her article. She contacted a clinic run by nurse-midwives in lower Manhattan and asked if she might observe their classes on natural childbirth and participate in a midwife attended home birth. They agreed and she was at the clinic at ten on Monday morning.

Sara watched a woman give birth, her husband there with her. She remembered her attempts at interesting Reynold in participating in natural childbirth for Rachel. He had done the exercises with her and gone to one preparatory meeting, but his heart wasn't in it, and in the end she had done it with the help of a young nurse who hired out for labors. She was called a monitrice and accompanied Sara to the hospital. Rachel's birth had been a triumph, the most dramatic moment of her life.

She finished the article by the end of the week and mailed it to Jane Seymour with a sense of accomplishment followed by great anxiety. Suppose they thought it was terrible?

Jane called excitedly two days later. "My God, you wrote a masterpiece the first time out—a goddam Greek drama. It's really good and I want to make it a cover story with the whole bedroom scene at the moment of birth as the cover photograph. I'll show it to Tania this afternoon."

Her spirits were high all day, and she took the children to the playground after school and swung with them on her lap, went down the slide and bought them awful turquoise and fuschia ice pops from the vendor. She felt light and happy. The children, startled to see their mother so giddy, hung back, a little shy.

When she returned home, the telephone was ringing. It was Jane. She was apologetic and sober. "I'm sorry, Sara. Tania killed the story. She says it belongs in the *Soho News,* not *Haute.* I don't agree—natural childbirth and all kinds of even more radical stuff is all the rage among the debs in Europe ever since that duchess's daughter wrote a book about silence and darkness in the delivery room. I told that to Tania, but she's adamant. I got the feeling she was prepared to reject it before she even read it. Have there been any bad feelings between you two?"

"I guess there have," said Sara glumly and hung up. Tania had seen her with Bill Waring in the lobby the day he had asked her to go for a walk.

The next few days were lost in a blur of self-chastisement. To make matters worse, Jane called again and told her they were hiring someone permanently to do the captions and would not be using her as often. She began to feel jinxed.

Now that she didn't have the outside work, the household chores seemed too much for her. Mrs. Ramirez thought she was staying home deliberately to check up on her and appeared more sullen and inefficient than ever. Nothing got done, and Sara spent the days halfheartedly picking up things in one room only to put them down in another.

One day Charlie brought home a circular from school advertising a house tour of the area.

"You gotta buy a ticket," he said seriously. "We need the money to get a new rug for the library."

She was chagrined that Charlie was so easily convinced that every cause was sincere; still, it was better than sitting around feeling sorry for herself.

The circular listed the houses on the tour, and she noted that one of them would be Pheasant Hill, a nearby estate that had always intrigued Sara. Outside of the modest enclave of Horse Hollow Estates with its one-acre zoning, the acreage in the area was given over to large estates whose mansions were rarely visible. The only sign of life was the occasional delivery truck that quickly disappeared behind the tall screens of rhododendrons or overgrown boxwood.

Pheasant Hill, so identified by a discreet, weather-beaten sign at the end of a long, winding driveway, was situated high on a hill. Several huge, gray stone chimneys were all that was visible from the road. Sara was sure only a winter-feebled sun ever reached inside.

Once she and Reynold had walked far enough up the driveway to actually see the mansion before they turned back.

"It's made of Manhattan schist," said Reynold matter-of-factly, and Sara had laughed.

"That would stop the dinner party cold."

"That's schist," he poked her. "The stone they dug up to make room for the subways. Not particularly attractive. It's all one color, but very heavy. Solid."

"Who do you think lives there?"

"Probably a respectable investor who clips coupons in Palm Beach in the winter and Bar Harbor during the summer. This is residence number three, good for a month in the spring and a month in the fall."

"Oh, no," Sara said quickly. She was surprised at how much information was in her head about the house and how strongly she felt about it. "Somebody lives there all the time. I see service vans going there. United Parcel delivers almost every day, and during the summer there was a pool maintenance truck."

"Come on," Reynold said, taking her arm. "Technically we're trespassing. They could send the dogs out after us."

Two weeks later she found herself driving up that familiar winding road. The driveway wrapped around three quarters of the hill before the mansion was in full view. It was more imposing than anything Sara could have imagined, but not in the least attractive. The facade was classic Georgian, and the front door with its peaked trim looked much too small for the triple-storied stone structure around it.

The leader of the tour was small, thin, and effeminate. "Here we have basic, boring Georgian with some rather horrendous deviations," he said snidely. "It's always been a mystery to me why the very rich in America always choose the Georgian style when its original popularity was among the middle class to separate themselves from the bourgeoisie. Notice how symmetrical everything is—that was Palladio's joke—he related everything in the house to the human frame."

Sara remembered reading that the whole Georgian style had been a rebellion against the brutality and disorder of the seventeenth century. The symmetry was reassuring. It made everyone feel dignified. It certainly was that. She looked around the grounds. To the left was a large L-shaped greenhouse attached to a modest cottage. Two other medium-sized cottages were situated behind the greenhouse bordering what looked to be a stunningly neat vegetable garden. Directly in front of the house, about two hundred yards away, was a screened swimming pool and tennis court. She was surprised to see a child's swing set and sandbox. The idea of children in such a formal house seemed absurd.

"This is Mr. Simmons who will show us around," said Mr.

Watts, the tour leader. "He has been with the Van Drutens since Mr. Van Druten was a little boy." The name sounded vaguely familiar to Sara.

A man in a navy suit with black tie opened the door wide and bowed slightly to the women. "We will tour the lower floor and top floor only," said Mr. Simmons. "The middle floor contains the family bedrooms. However, on the third floor the present Mrs. Van Druten has a less formal apartment and a studio for painting where she spends much of her time. She thought the ladies would enjoy seeing it."

Sara couldn't concentrate on what was said, so busy was she assimilating the bare bone facts of Pheasant Hill. There *was* someone living here and a young someone, too, if the age of the child was any indication.

The front hall where they were all assembled was covered in red damask and lighted by exquisite, tulip-shaped, etched wall lamps. Everything was museum perfect with extraordinary paintings and furnishings that could well have been on exhibit. A dark oak dado wall extended into all the rooms except the main salon which was painted yellow but looked as if no one ever set foot in it. To the left of the main hall was the dining room, large and formal with four corner cupboards sporting a gold leaf eagle on top and displaying ornately painted dishes.

Sara trudged with the group to the top floor expecting more of the same and was pleased to find a bright, cheerful room. The entire floor was one big area divided for activities. It was sparsely furnished with canvas pillows on built-in banquettes. Japanese parchment lamps hung at intervals and track lights spotlighted several large abstract paintings. The last third of the room was dominated by a twenty-foot, slanted skylight festooned with plants. An easel with a half finished painting stood under it.

Sara hung back staring moodily at the painting when the others followed Mr. Simmons to the greenhouse.

"I don't know if it can stand such close scrutiny." Sara jumped, not expecting to be found and feeling like a snoop. She did not turn around immediately. As a child she had played a private game of voice divination, predicting the outcome of events, good or bad, by the quality of a person's initial utterance. If her mother said, "Come, Sara, change your clothes. We're going shopping," she would know whether it would be a pleasant expedition or one steeped in arguments and ill will by the special nuance in the voice. From time to time she practiced it as a private voodoo. She had not played the game for some time, but now her mind was flashing out its old signals that something incredibly good was at hand.

She turned to face clear, turquoise eyes that were instantly familiar. And then, it was as if all the unwanted partings of childhood gathered strength and thrust themselves into her consciousness. It was Natalie . . . all grown up.

Chapter 6

SANCHE RAY TRIED FOR THE FOURTH TIME TO get the overseas operator, but the local operator just kept saying "pronto" in her slow, lazy voice, and he knew it would take several more minutes of intensive effort on his part to get the call through. Their slowness infuriated him as did the bitter coffee they brought him every morning and the wads of currency that he had to stuff into his pockets. On top of that he was annoyed over what was happening to his script and because he had no one to complain to. He sat glumly, both hands holding his head. The phone rang. His agent, Jack Martell, was on the other end.

"How the hell are you?" boomed the confident voice from California.

"It took me twenty tries to get this call through. That's how I am."

"Pardon me for saying so, but it wasn't my idea for you to go over there." His voice turned serious. "Sanche, I've got fifteen offers on my desk. *Fifteen!* No dogs in the bunch. Why the hell don't you come home? We'll give them their money back. Tell 'em to shove it."

"I didn't spend an hour trying to get you to listen to that, Jack.

Everything's the same. I'm learning a hell of a lot and Ferlinghetti is still the master." Two years ago he couldn't get Jack Martell to answer his telephone calls. It gave him satisfaction to refuse him now.

"Jesus, I thought you'd have gotten some sense by now. From what I hear from the PR man, the rushes are ridiculous. It's going to bomb, Sanche. Come home."

"Lay off, will you. You have no taste. Besides, you're too young to remember Ferlinghetti's best stuff. What's the sense of being on top if I can't do what I want."

"All right, all right, I don't want to argue with you. Give it another few weeks." There was a significant pause and a sigh that could be heard over the Atlantic. "Yeah . . . so why did you call?"

"I want you to find a house for me in Malibu. It should be right on the ocean. And hire a couple for me—you know, cook, housekeeper, handyman kind of thing."

"I'll do what I can . . . jeez, I don't know, on the beach . . . That's not going to be easy, but I'll see what I can do, Sanche." He took a deep breath. "Think about what I said. Fifteen offers and the phone keeps ringing. You can clean up now. I can play them one against the other. Think about it."

"Okay, okay, I'll talk to you soon."

He went to the closet and chose a pearl-gray shirt, a dark gray suit, and a black tie. From an ornate bombe chest he chose clean white underwear and black socks. Four times each day he took off his clothes and replaced them with exact duplicates. Also he bit his nails way below the fingers' edge. Whether it was unloving Sophie or more complicated demons, Sanche was a man hounded to prove himself which he did admirably. But at a price. He regularly turned out television plays that won Emmys, and his first screenplay had won an Oscar. His current price was stellar, and when he refused a job, it was taken to mean the money wasn't right and the offer usually doubled. It was exactly this sequence that accounted for his being in Europe doing a patch-up job on a mediocre adaptation of a silly English play.

The money enticed him, but the opportunity to work with the director, Enrico Ferlinghetti, whom Sanche idolized, cinched the deal. The movie would probably be shelved to save everyone embarrassment, but Sanche would still be half a million dollars richer, and his fame and fortune unblemished.

The transatlantic circuits were busy day and night with offers and invitations. Scattered on his bureau along with the gold cuff links and change were stacks of cables—Robert Evans, Alan Ladd, Jr.— disquieting accomplishments for a boy from The Bronx whose hair grew in unmanageable clumps and whose head had the unfortunate habit of skulking forward giving him a menacing look from the time he was seven or eight.

The knock on the door startled him. He opened it and was puzzled to see the girl from New York. He had forgotten she was coming today and he had forgotten how attractive she was. His spirits began to rise.

"Hello," she smiled. "I'm here." A shy pause. "A man is bringing the luggage . . . well, the bag. One bag."

"Welcome to Rome . . ." He was about to say her name, but he had forgotten that too.

"The man at the desk asked me about the skiing at St. Moritz," she said as soon as she put down her handbag and sat down on a damask-covered love seat. "He said, 'Bon giorno, mademoiselle. How was the skiing at St. Moritz?' Why do you suppose he said that to me?"

"That's easy. You're quite tan for the season, and he assumed you got tan while skiing St. Moritz which is in Switzerland. It's a very ritzy place to ski. What did you answer him?"

"I said it was pleasant. Very pleasant." They smiled at each other, and she noticed he looked taller and thinner than he had in New York.

"Where *did* you get your tan?" he asked.

"I'm not tan—I'm foreign."

Feature for feature Sanche was a pleasant-looking man with a broad forehead, rounded jawline, and an acceptable nose and mouth. His eyes were the least attractive feature because he was wary of people and never opened them completely. Despite this his more or less average face caused many women to telephone him daily, slip him notes at parties, and send him pornographic books delineating the adventures he might enjoy with them. If he had stayed in bed all day, he could not have availed himself of the amount of pussy offered him.

But it was Miranda he made love to from the first night she arrived, and only Miranda. Why this was so, no one could tell, nor

why he had even imported the girl. Sanche himself was not quite sure
except that he had enjoyed the adventure of tracking her down.

Then, too, lying in the darkened room as he had done, listening to
her sweet, high voice on the tapes had made him aware of her vulner-
ability. Certain passages still haunted him. ". . . I had never done it
before and I was already in my twenties. In the beginning that's all I
could think of . . . touching myself or having him touch me. But
then I got to hate it. Now I think he didn't do it right and I began to
wonder how other men would do it. Especially the sleek, young executives who came into Bloomingdale's where I worked part-time.
Some of them were beautiful, and I knew they thought I was beautiful in a different way than Bob did. I think Bob was secretly ashamed
of my looks. I looked too foreign for him, but those other men considered it an asset. . . ."

Sanche considered it an asset too. Her simple declaration of lust
was stunning and made him feel more like fucking than any come-on
from the Hollywood glamour girls.

Each night a wordless scenario was played out without variation.
He waited until she was stretched out between the crisp linen sheets
changed daily at his request. Then, stealthily, without a word and
with a prearranged understanding that there would be no word from
her, he proceeded to busy himself with her body until Miranda cried
out with passion and satisfaction. Only after she had reached orgasm
and could be counted on not to contort or twist to achieve sensation,
did he hoist himself up on strong, hairless arms and push himself into
her. He wanted her hips relaxed and the opening moist. Then he was
free to move her body to suit himself. This he did with an amazing
agility not evident in his upright movements.

Miranda had never known such sensual excitement as took place
the first night he opened her like a bursting peach and used his tongue
so artfully on her. Astonished and grateful, she was certain that she
had joined a small select group of life's fortunates.

If he had intended that her sexual favors were payment for the job
and its lavish fringe benefits, then so be it. But there was no such
confusion in her mind. From the first day she had arrived in Rome in
response to his call and through their travels to Hamburg and Berlin
and back to Italy, she reveled in the sensual feast before her—stately
European hotels with gleaming wood paneling, polished brass, heated
towel racks, sleigh beds, chocolates on her oversized eiderdown pil-

lows, and gorgeous ceramic buttons to summon starched maids and waiters. She heard French and Italian and German spoken with ease, like beautiful background music. Superb meals were served with flourish and deference by impresarios who might have confused her not long ago. She had been transported into a magical world just as she had always intended.

Sanche, on the other hand, was not transformed by Europe's stately charms. His demons were faithfully by his side. Sometimes to relieve his frustrations he was mean to Miranda. He ridiculed her manners and girlish enthusiasm, but she would shrug it off as a busy man's impatience which infuriated him. It made him mad that he couldn't blackmail her with his moods.

He tried.

At times he showed his streak of sadism to the German waiters who refused to speak English.

When they had to go to Hamburg on location, he insisted the busboys translate the entire menu into English three times a day.

Each time the busboy approached their table, Miranda would get a sinking feeling knowing what was to come.

"Could you translate?" Sanche would ask coolly.

"Where?" the busboy would respond innocently.

"Everything."

"*Everything?*"

"Yes." There followed a long silence before the hapless boy began.

"Ochsenschwanzsuppe . . . oxtail soup. Suppe mit Einlage . . . uh, how you say . . . boullion with all kinds of floats. Terrine Nudelsuppe mit Rindfleisch . . . uh tureen of noodle soup with beef." The boy stood silent a moment, his cheeks red with effort.

"And the entrees?" Sanche would prompt him.

"All of them, sir?"

"All of them."

"Rehruecken mit Spaetzle und Preisselbeerin . . . saddle of venison with noodles and lingenberries. Rinderschmorbraten mit Krautsalat . . . beef potroast with cabbage salad . . ."

During the recitation Sanche stared straight ahead as if fixing each selection in his mind. If the boy hesitated, he would urge him to continue. Not once did he allow them to stop.

Miranda refused to be cowered by these lapses or allow them to dim the rosy light in which she viewed her new life. She was aware, but uncaring, that Sanche had done no work on "her" story. To keep herself busy she offered to transcribe the tapes against the day he could begin writing the script.

The only thing that made her spirits plummet was Sanche's obsequious idolatry of Ferlinghetti. Sanche simply did not see the foolish old man who was there. He saw a pioneer in cinema verité who had given every other filmmaker a blueprint for making real movies, a man who could film some foolishness between ordinary people on a street corner and make film history. Twenty years had passed since he had done that, but Ferlinghetti was still trading on it.

Ferlinghetti was definitely an irritation in Miranda's otherwise sunny life, but soon he, too, ceased to perturb her. Something had happened to obliterate anything that disturbed her feeling of perfect happiness.

One day she awoke in her sleigh bed amid the puffy quilts and oversized pillows and knew there was something different about herself. At first it was a special smell, not unpleasant, that exuded from her body. That body was also sending signals it had never sent before. She felt warm most of the time, almost feverish. Now and again a faint nausea converged on her and she felt dazed and drowsy. Certain aromas—chicken, coffee, an overripe pear—were magnified beyond anything she had smelled before. It was as if her metabolism had speeded up. There were many ways to explain it—foreign climate, foreign foods, the water, the constant excitement. Six weeks passed before she realized she had not had a period. There were slight, constant cramps, but no period.

In the middle of the night the idea finally formed itself completely. She was pregnant. She was carrying Sanche's child. She would be indelibly bound to this man who offered her this exciting life.

During their lovemaking the following night, when he was about to rise over her, she broke the news. "I think I'm pregnant." He continued as if he had not heard her.

"That's the oldest trick," he said when he had finished. It sounded like a line of dialogue he had written for himself.

"It's not a trick," she answered logically. "You've made love to me every night for two months—how could it be a trick?" It was one of Miranda's most lucid statements.

"I'm certifiably sterile," he said triumphantly and for the first time she caught a glimpse of a little boy in his heavy-lidded eyes. He was trying to get her to refute what she had said. As if his not accepting it would make her take it back.

"Well, consider yourself cured." She was sure that in time he would get used to the idea and be as excited and happy as she was. He never did.

One night he called her from the studio where he was looking at the day's rushes and asked her to meet him at Santanini's, a restaurant where all the actors ate. It overlooked a beautiful spot on the shoreline named Bagño Celeste.

The restaurant, as always, was swept clean and fresh flowers were everywhere. Two tables had been put together with a "reservado" sign across them. She saw Ferlinghetti approaching her, hands outstretched.

"Ah . . . Cara . . . beautiful." He squeezed her hand, and she tried to smile but found herself cringing from his self-assured grin.

There were two women seated at the table, the present Mrs. Ferlinghetti and the recent ex. Usually they spelled each other during filming, each staying a few weeks, tactfully leaving when the other appeared. The last few days, however, they both stayed and came together to the set every day, watching the scenes, approving, smiling at Ferlinghetti and at each other.

The tables began filling up with cameramen and the actors, but Sanche did not appear until they were almost finished. He hardly spoke at all, but practically bowed to Ferlinghetti.

"Excuse me," Miranda got up. "Sanche, I have to go back now."

"No." His forehead creased. "You can't go now, sit down."

She was about to protest, but Ferlinghetti interceded. "Das all right. She wanna go, we go." He touched his two wives, who rose immediately, as did Sanche although he hadn't yet eaten.

"We go to my room for one leetle drink," said Ferlinghetti.

The suite was exquisite. The management of the hotel obviously idolized him and furnished his rooms with great care. The furniture was the best of Italian modern, yet it looked perfectly at home in the period room with its huge fireplace and French windows. The wives headed for the couch. The present wife was pale and blond, the other dark-haired. Neither was especially pretty, but both were perfectly groomed and expensively dressed. The present wife was named Nadia and the ex was Norma.

When Miranda reentered the room after visiting the bathroom, Norma was unbuttoning Nadia's blouse and scooped out a breast. She took a large bosom in her hands as if she were handling a newborn puppy. She turned it this way and that, then took the nipple between her fingers and began to rotate it slowly. Nadia stared meaningfully at Ferlinghetti who was now standing very close to the women.

Miranda looked down at his pants and saw what was happening.

"Slowly," he cautioned them.

"So long as your having such a time with mine," said Nadia with some effort, "I want a chance at yours."

"If you can find them," Norma teased.

"Perhaps this will make them come out." She put her hand under Norma's skirt and dug her fingers between her legs.

"Please . . . Enrico." Norma thrust her hand at Ferlinghetti's crotch, but he pushed her away.

Nadia continued to stroke Norma while they sat face-to-face without moving or making a sound. Ferlinghetti stretched out on the couch looking up at the ceiling. After five minutes Nadia looked at her husband with a mixture of pride and longing. "She's ready."

There was no misunderstanding what had happened. Wife number two had prepared wife number one so the great man wouldn't have to work at all. Ferlinghetti did not get up. "Not now, Nadia. You finish her for me."

Norma went to kneel next to him and touched his lips. "No, Rico. I want you."

"Not tonight, darling, I want to try something else."

"Her?" Norma glanced at Miranda. "You want us to do something to her?"

"We have to ask her," said Ferlinghetti.

"Ask me what?" Miranda turned to Sanche for the first time.

"Ferlinghetti specifically asked for you." He said it as if she should be proud.

"Asked for me?" Miranda moved closer to him wanting to shake a better answer out of him. "You mean to take part in this . . . this scene?" She was shocked, but not that shocked. She wasn't completely insulted either. Group sex was as casual as eating in the movie business.

"I haven't felt well all day," she said simply, looking only at Sanche. "I'm going back to the room."

"She say no?" Ferlinghetti was looking accusingly at Sanche, a disappointed child.

"She say no," repeated Sanche. It sounded forlorn and silly and Miranda began to laugh. She left the room laughing and holding on to her stomach, certain she'd never feel so lonely again.

When he joined her in their room, Sanche was quiet. He never was one to show great movement, but now he seemed to be doing everything in slow motion. He took off all his clothes and folded them neatly on a chair. He brushed his teeth and showered and put on fresh pajamas.

Just before he slid into bed, he said, "You have to go back to New York. You're an embarrassment to me here."

"That isn't true," she answered without raising her head from the pillow. "Ferlinghetti is an embarrassment to himself. He's a spoiled brat, and everyone indulges him because of some crap he did twenty years ago. Why? He's not following your script. The picture is stupid." She got up and went to sit on his side of the bed. "Why don't we both go back to New York?"

"You don't know what you're talking about. I want you the hell out of here tomorrow."

"That isn't going to happen. I'm pregnant, remember? Not that I'm appealing to you on that score, but I'm not going to give up on you yet."

"Give up on me?" He snorted. "Oh, God . . . crazy bitch." He turned over and went to sleep, and she knew she had won a small point.

Chapter 7

SOMETIMES WHEN FRIENDS MEET AFTER LONG absence, they despise each other and the conversation becomes grim, filled with black silences. The silence that fell on Sara and Natalie was from a different source. Sara was stunned by the possibility that they might just as easily have missed meeting.

She had sneered at the opulence of Pheasant Hill during the tour, but now that it was Natalie's ormolu, her Dutch Masters, her trompe l'oeil, and Ming, it made her sober and shy. She began to whisper even when they were alone sipping the sherry brought grudgingly (it appeared to Sara) by the butler. Natalie had a butler and countless other people who behaved as if they disliked her. While it made Sara nervous, it didn't bother Natalie at all.

The only time she showed the least anxiety was when Alden Van Druten crashed in on them flushed from running. Then she rose instantly, and Sara took it as a sign to leave.

Sara had assumed Natalie would call the next day and felt let down that she did not. When the rest of the week went by without word, she began to feel that perhaps seeing Natalie again would be of no benefit at all. She played back their conversation for proof of Natalie's sincerity. That hateful first day at St. Mildred's came back with painful clarity. Ultimately she was disgusted with herself for over-reacting. Maybe Natalie was away. Or busy. Or sick.

At the time Sara and Natalie met, their lives had taken vastly different turns, and though Natalie believed she lived simply, her wealth created both a physical and psychological barrier. She didn't answer her own telephone or her door. No one ever just dropped in. Wary of being snubbed, people waited for her to call which she rarely did. Outside of Pheasant Hill she wielded great power, partly because of her status but also because she was an aggressive political fund raiser, an activity Alden encouraged, feeling it to be their responsibility to keep liberals out of public office. Two days a week she worked in a small dingy storefront on Madison Avenue for Bill Haas, a reformed playboy who had served four years as a city councilman and was making a serious bid for a congressional seat.

The Tuesday following the house tour, Charlie was invited to invade the mansion after school and play with Jeremy. Mrs. Remington, the governess, transported him both ways. All attempts to get Jeremy to the Reynolds' house were politely refused.

When it was Sara's turn to visit Pheasant Hill, it was for a luncheon presided over by a woman in crisp uniform whose presence made normal conversation impossible. Getting beyond the preliminaries exhausted Sara. There was nothing to talk about. Natalie didn't cook, clean, or visit a supermarket. Sara's voice became overly cheerful. The word money kept popping out. There were painful silences. True friends, she had read in a small-circulation religious magazine Mrs. Ramirez was always leaving, are comfortable in long silence. If this were true, it put Natalie out of reach. Sara didn't feel comfortable at all. She wished fervently for a second and third visit to prove that her reappearance really mattered to Natalie.

As they were parting, Natalie mentioned casually that she was probably pregnant. "I haven't told anyone yet," she whispered, though no one was around. Sara looked down at her waistline. She didn't know whether to say "congratulations" or "too bad."

"Good luck," she said finally and kissed Natalie on the cheek.

"Can you believe I blurted out 'How's your money' instead of 'How's your father,' " she told Reynold that night.

"That's funny. Did she laugh?"

"No. She didn't know what the hell I was talking about. During dessert I was so still, one foot went to sleep and I almost fell when we left the table."

"And the rest . . . was it all so tense?"

"I think she found it screamingly boring," said Sara wistfully.

"What about you?"

"I don't remember much of it. My hands were cold, so I suppose I was nervous."

"You don't have to prove yourself to her," he said with real concern.

Their second meeting went slightly better. At least it began better. They met at the cafeteria of the Metropolitan Museum, planning to view an exotic exhibition of Russian artifacts and jewels. During lunch Natalie asked detailed questions about Reynold and Sara's life together. It was as if she had regretted not asking all these questions before. Sara answered happily. She felt comforted by Natalie's interest. She even felt comforted by Natalie's wealth, remote as it was, sensing it as a huge warm blanket that would protect them.

"Any big loves before Alden?" she asked when it was her turn to play inquisitor. For a moment it seemed that Natalie was going to answer, but instead she rose abruptly saying she had to make a telephone call.

After a few minutes a small, impeccably dressed man with a trim goatee hurried to their table and introduced himself. "I'm Harold Kruger. Regrettably, Mr. Hoving is lunching out today. If only you'd given us a few hours' notice . . ." His voice trailed off, and he gestured helplessly with his hands. "I'd be pleased to escort you through the exhibit if you like."

"That would be lovely." Natalie gave him a dazzling smile and introduced Sara.

It was impossible to keep abreast of the little man who scurried through the rooms like Peter Rabbit looking for a way out of Mr. McGregor's garden. Sara, bewildered by what had taken place, brought up the rear. The running commentary was lost on her. Natalie had made a deliberate show of clout. She had behaved badly and it made Sara extremely uncomfortable.

She wished now that she had made Natalie reveal more of herself or else had not been so free with her own information. One gave confidences in order to be confided in.

*   *   *

When she got home there was a note from Mrs. Ramirez that Jane had called. She dialed *Haute*'s number unenthusiastically.

"Seeing as we treated you so decently," said Jane wryly, "could you do me a tiny favor?"

"You personally?"

"Not exactly. I need someone to check out Bill Haas—he's running for congress. We don't want to commit ourselves to a story until we see if he's for real. Can he talk, does he make good copy, etc. The editor who was going to do it is out with appendicitis. It's either you or someone off the street. I'm swamped."

Sara waited, torn between her affection for Jane and feeling like the world's biggest chump. "Let me get this straight. I'm out of a job, but I'm supposed to help you out just to remind me how nice it is to work so that I can feel really rotten about not having my job?"

"When you put it that way, I feel like a snake. I'm sorry. Forget it." Jane's voice was barely audible.

"I'm not directing this at you. You know that."

"Of course." She was quiet for a full ten seconds. "I could tell you that I'd use your generosity as a wedge to melt Tania's heart, but I can't promise anything."

Sara sighed. Jane was manipulating her just the tiniest bit. It was masterful. First show remorse, then hold out hope. She didn't doubt that Jane really liked her, but she was also doing her job the best way she knew how. She was a survivor which was exactly what Sara wanted to be. Now put that all together and what have you got? A woman who feels foolish. "Jane, I feel like a dope. Why is the injured party always the one that ends up feeling like a dope?"

"Beats me. Life is full of conundrums. Will you do it?"

"Okay. It'll look good on my résumé."

The park was misty in April. There was just a hint of dampness that made breathing a pleasure. Alden stretched his legs pushing against a giant oak. He concentrated on his stride until he got it perfect and then put it out of his mind. Slowly the jumpiness drained out of him, and he felt more comfortable. His breathing became regular and soft, hazy images began to appear and retreat playfully.

He began to concentrate on his mother. She had been trim and blond and often wore diaphanous gowns. Silk georgette. He could hear her saying to someone on the telephone, ''I think I'll wear my silk georgette.'' The name had stuck in his mind. The few times he saw her at breakfast, she was in a silky dressing robe with a matching gown beneath. The sleeves and proportions were always voluminous, yet there was no doubt of the voluptuousness beneath. If anything, the folds accented the hidden treasures.

But those treasures were denied him. Only once had she pressed him to her bosom. He had fallen off a pony and lay on the ground. She rushed to him—''Oh, my god, Alden!''—picked him up, and held him to her, rocking his head back and forth. How old could he have been? Five? Six? He could remember the smell and feel of her more vividly than his own wife.

Thinking about his wife now made him lose his rhythm, and he stumbled in the near dark. She was pregnant. He was certain, and the knowledge made him so uncomfortable that the gains he had made in controlling his restlessness were eroding. His needs had increased. Often now he went out in the middle of the night.

At times, when he left his sleeping wife to steal off the grounds of Pheasant Hill, he could see that the servants' lights were still lit at that late hour, even though they were expected on duty by eight. Were they drinking? He felt a grave responsibility for them all, especially the women whom he had taken into his house when they were barely in their teens. Dolly and Lucinda were not fit to go out in the world. Lucinda because of her drinking and Dolly because of her mental deficiencies. They were devoted to him and knew him better than his wives did.

His valet was closer to him that anyone in his life had ever been. They had grown up together, and while there had always been that invisible but unalterable line that prevented a true friendship, the closeness was there.

Was it any wonder he valued Jake Simmons? They shared the same English tailor, and their shoes were made by the same Italian firm; the only difference being that while Alden chose from many styles and fabrics, Simmons had remained with the same blue serge suit and the same black seamless shoes since his early twenties.

Once late at night Alden, with a splitting headache and no idea of where to find aspirin, buzzed the servants, and Simmons had appeared in a plaid bathrobe and slippers. Alden couldn't have been more startled had he appeared naked. Simmons in a red plaid bathrobe was not a comfort. He was a threat. My God, the man's neck was thick, a fact gone unnoticed beneath the constant white shirt and tie. His complexion, ruddy from sleep, his light, gray-brown hair falling rakishly over one eye, were not the embodiment of loyalty, companionship, and servitude.

"Never mind." Alden had waved him away, unable to articulate his disappointment and discomfort.

"Is something wrong, sir?"

"No. It's just . . . I'm not used to seeing you without your blue suit. It's somewhat of a shock."

"Yes, sir," Simmons whispered, wounded by the rejection. It seemed a failure on his part. He would not make such a mistake again.

The incident had been unnerving, but not for the reasons Simmons supposed. Only now during his reverie did Alden realize that he had wanted to touch Simmons, to rub his fingers along that strong neck and smooth the hair back from his forehead. He wanted a different sort of comfort from Simmons than he had ever sought before. It was a turning point for Alden. Simmons, the one unshakeable constant in his life, was no longer available to him. The circle of those from whom he had to distance himself was growing. There was Natalie and the child inside her. And now Simmons.

Sara met Bill Haas three mornings later at a coffee shop in a hotel near Penn Station. He was of medium build and gave the feeling of being well-coordinated. His clothes fit perfectly. The overall impression was of paleness—his hair, eyes, and summer suit were all in the same family of nondescript light tan. Overriding this were the bearing and slight indifference of someone who had never scrambled for funds.

There were two other men at the table. One, Robert Redding, was an Ivy Leaguer of the same pale, classy ilk as the candidate. The other, introduced as Rudy Sorbentino, Haas's campaign manager, was pudgy, ill-dressed, with hairy hands impudently defining more than his share of the table. He appeared supremely confident, obviously the brains behind the campaign, and barely able to stifle his disinterest in her arrival. She noted that some butter clung to his lower lip, and her first impulse was to daub at his chin with a napkin as she might do to Charlie or Rachel.

Sara explained what would be involved, purposely directing herself to Bill Haas. She had taken an immediate dislike to Sorbentino.

"This is an exploratory meeting," she said, wondering if they knew what she was talking about.

"You don't want to get our hopes up?" Sorbentino finally looked at her, and she realized how dumb it was to think he would misunderstand anything.

"I don't want to mislead you," she said primly.

"Nor I, you." He pushed back his chair and surveyed Bill Haas with an appraising eye. "As you can see, the candidate is personable. He doesn't stutter or drool. He drinks moderately, sleeps in pajamas, doesn't play with himself in public, doesn't have ulcers or piles. Goes to the Marble Collegiate Church at least twice a month and screws his wife about the same. They don't have children because they're still kids themselves. By the way"—he reached over and pulled up Bill Haas's upper lip, revealing innocent pink gums— "these are his own teeth. No caps. Not even gum disease." He took a deep breath and returned to his breakfast. "He wasn't a star at Harvard, but he didn't cheat." There was a moment of silence. "He's not a fag, either, although he looks like one."

Bill Haas smiled good-naturedly. Sara knew there was no way to best Sorbentino. He could and would say anything to her. She decided to play it dumb.

"That's cute," she said with a revolting giggle. Sorbentino looked puzzled, as if he had miscalculated, and she let out a small sigh.

"What do you think, Rudy?" Bill Haas sipped at a glass of orange juice.

Sorbentino stuck half a piece of toast in his mouth and washed it down with a gulp of coffee. "It won't do us any good if that's what you mean. It wouldn't be out until after election day." He rolled his tongue around his mouth to dislodge bits of food and turned to look for the waitress. "You want a nice glossy spread in a ladies' magazine, go ahead." His eyes shifted. The subject was not worth more discussion and he avoided looking at Sara.

"Belinda might get a kick out of it," said Bill Haas, again looking to Rudy for approval.

"Do it. It don't mean a thing one way or the other." Sorbentino rubbed his palms together impatiently, and Sara noted a gold identification bracelet twinkling coquettishly amid the forest of his body hair. Below that a lavish pinky ring and Cartier tank watch completed his ensemble. Nobody had ever told Rudy Sorbentino that he shouldn't wear all his jewelry at one time.

While she squeezed some consolation from her private joke, she also realized that Rudy Sorbentino was well aware of the image he created and had perfected his crudeness for effect. It was not without appeal, especially when you considered that the man exuded power. That it was not obvious where the power was coming from was all the more stunning. He gave the impression that he could get you anything you wanted if you did exactly what he said. She could see that the men at the table, perhaps wisely, had chosen to follow Rudy Sorbentino wherever he might lead them. She hoped to God she would never need such a man.

Cora Sandford was already downstairs when Natalie finished dressing. She and Cora now had a routine which sometimes suited her and sometimes did not. When Cora had had enough sleep and not too much brandy for breakfast (she claimed to need it to get her heart *really* started each morning), and when she was not agitating over her safety (a man had exposed himself exclusively at her commodious window as her limousine was caught in a traffic jam on Park Avenue), Cora was as much fun to talk with as anyone. She wore well. Now that they were working at Bill Haas's headquarters and did not have to talk to each other nonstop, she wore even better. Each Tuesday they were driven to their Madison Avenue storefront office, stayed two nights in their city apartments, and returned to the country on Thursday afternoon.

The balance suited everyone except Jeremy who missed his mother. Natalie missed him, too, but she liked the respite from Simmons and Dolly and, now, the decorator, Cardon. In the city she did not feel as if secret eyes were watching her every move and secret ears listening for the sounds of her life. The apartment had only a housekeeper who engaged the building staff when she needed extra help. A part-time cook came during the week. It was as close as Natalie came to complete privacy and freedom.

Alden had discovered the reservoir around Central Park as a per-

fect, impersonal place to run, and he got in the habit of taking a cab
to Eighty-sixth Street and doing six or seven miles before walking
home. He always walked home to wind himself down. He liked to
run in the park at dawn and dusk when the sun was not too hot and
the number of runners had thinned to a manageable number. It was a
pleasant routine.

Natalie was relieved they were not going to Europe for any part of
the summer. If she had had to, she would have used the pregnancy as
an excuse, but that hadn't been necessary. It seemed Alden had no
more of a wish to be alone with her than she had to be alone with
him. He was dedicated to his running and more enthusiastic about his
new routine than any thought of azure seas and skies in Italy.

She hadn't told him about the pregnancy because she feared a
crisis between them. Each would have to make a decision, and she
was not prepared to make any decisions. She also suspected he knew
about it in his own way.

"Darling, you look wonderful," Cora greeted Natalie with genuine affection. She had known Alden all his life and befriended both
his previous wives, although she now claimed not to have liked either. "The first was demented, my dear," she confessed to Natalie,
"and the second a tart. I swear it, a tart."

Cora was thirty-two years Natalie's senior and along with Letitia
Reeves the dowager of their set. She was beyond looks or fashion.
There were many branches of the Sandford family, but Cora had
inherited the major portion of the estate. Over a hundred million,
people said. "Who knows?" Cora was quick to speculate along with
everyone in a spirit of fun.

But there was another side to Cora. When she wanted to manipulate, there was no one more tenacious, and few were strong enough
to thwart her. Even Letitia, who had nothing to fear from her, crumpled when Cora stood firm. The trouble was, no one was ever sure
when Cora was standing firm and only realized their entrapment after
the fact.

Natalie placed her hands on Cora's shoulders and pecked the air
near her cheek. "I want to say good-bye to Jeremy," she said
quickly. "Were you planning to leave right away?"

"Suit yourself. I've nothing but that dreadful dinner at the Waldorf
tonight. If I see one more piece of overdone beef on institutional din-

nerware, it will be the end of me. It's revolting. Makes one want to turn vegetarian. Do you realize my New York houseboy doesn't eat one speck of meat and he's beatific looking. Never bad breath or body odor."

Simmons entered, bowed slightly to Cora, and handed Natalie a slip of paper with Alden's schedule for the day. He left without a word.

"You mustn't let Simmons have the upper hand. Janet," said Cora, referring to Alden's second wife, "was virtually reduced to the trembles whenever he spoke to her. After all, servants are meant to be servile." She assumed the air of someone who has just stated a badly forgotten fact. "And why does he dress so somberly? Ugh. Looks like an undertaker. My mother used to tell me that when she was a girl servants dressed so stylishly, it was hard to tell the mistresses from their maids. The liveried footmen were matched for height and weight and wore padded silk stockings in case nature hadn't endowed them with curvaceous legs. Now they have padded everything and think it's so original. They even pad men's underwear, did you know that? They call them Buns. *Buns!* I've seen them advertised in the back of magazines. Suppose you went and touched a man and then it all came off with his underwear. Wouldn't that be a switch?"

"Cora, I've got to go down the hill and wait for Jeremy's bus. He likes to see me waiting for him."

"You're devoted to that child. I admire it and Alden must be enchanted. He never saw his mother more than ten minutes a day when she was in residence, which was seldom. Did he give you her pearls? They were magnificent. Janet must have kept them. She played lady meek, but now we know that was just an act. She's opened a restaurant, you know. And hired a greasy brute to run it for her."

Natalie rose impatiently. Cora could be silly and stubborn and hated to be made to leave before she was ready. Also the conversation was not as aimless as it seemed, and she wondered just what it was that Cora had in mind. "Walk down the road with me," she said.

The older woman rose and put her arm through Natalie's. They walked down the winding driveway to the main road and the bus stop. "Alden's mother was such a gay woman," Cora continued, undaunted by the lapse in the conversation. "It almost killed the old man when his only son and heir, Alden's father, married a middle class Irish girl. She was vicious and destructive without ever knowing it. She always served champagne at dinner parties. 'We have to liven these people up,' she used to say. 'Wine just puts them to sleep.' She was so *lively* the rest of the family didn't know what to do with her." The way Cora used the word lively, Natalie knew she did not mean energetic. "The rest of the family were walking zombies by comparison. Alden's grandmother barely spoke a word after Alden's father was born. Has he ever shown you her diaries, they'd make you weep. She used to sit in her parlor and work on her crewelwork every day. On the day she died, they didn't discover her until teatime when they found her slumped over her sewing frame. I sometimes think Alden takes after her, although heaven knows his mother was just the opposite. Stupid. Destructive."

Cora was silent, surprised that her bitterness toward Jenny Van Druten was still so strong. She had been in love with Alden's father and despondent when he married the flamboyant Jennie. But barely two years later, rebuffed by his pregnant wife, Max Van Druten had become her lover. Coached and encouraged by precocious Cora, somber Max had been transformed into wild, passionate Max, and together they explored every hidden crevice that might possibly bring them pleasure. No one in all New York, they agreed, knew as much as they about sex. For Cora it became a religion, and even now it was ever on her mind.

It had been Alden who ended it. Innocently, he had bungled his way into the cottage where they met. "Father?" he asked wonderingly. He had never seen his father naked. He hadn't recognized Cora at all, so fascinated was he by her round, full breasts. That capricious entry had ended the happiest years of her life. Max, haunted by this tiny son's look of confusion, refused to see her again.

She had despised Alden for many years. Now it was a dull frustration searching for an opportunity to pay him in kind. When he had married Natalie, Cora was ecstatic. Natalie could not live out her life in Alden's bed. A grand passion would one day overwhelm her. Cora would live through each encounter and feel each kiss vicariously. In fact she had made it a personal mission to search for a proper candidate and bring it about.

*   *   *

The bus was approaching, and Jeremy's dark head was easily visible in the window. "Strange," said Cora, peering steadily at the little boy, "neither you nor Alden has black hair. Now who do you suppose he takes after?"

For the first time that day Natalie felt uneasy. Jeremy was five and a half, and no one had ever suggested by word or deed that he wasn't accepted as Alden's son. Cora's sudden interest was no idle musing. If she had decided to bring it up, there was a reason. Was it Alden who had put her up to it? Alden was so secretive lately, it was hard to know what he was thinking.

Once on their way to the city, however, she relaxed, trying to forestall the slight nausea that still plagued her for some part of each day. It soothed her to hear Cora prattling. The people she felt most comfortable with were those who, like Cora and Letitia, she could not intimidate. They took her up with affection and slight bullying, a relationship that suited her.

It was not the main ballroom of the Waldorf, but the smaller one which was the familiar arena where old money did its social work. Natalie had sat there many evenings wishing to be elsewhere, then finally succumbing to the stupor and daydreaming through the speeches.

Her mother had sat away her young matronhood in this very room, and likely as not her own daughter, if she had one, would do the same. She squirmed into the hard banquet chair and wondered if the pain in the small of her back was caused by the poor contours of the chair or. . . . She would think about that later.

Alden, seated like exotic bait at the thousand-dollar-a-plate table, was far away from her. It mystified her that people were willing to pay such money simply to be near him. It mystified her even more that she had been placed at the five-hundred-dollar table with Cora.

"Who do you suppose paid so much to sit with us?" she asked Cora who was seated four chairs away from her at the large, round table.

"I wouldn't doubt the men would pay that and more to sit with you, but I think they got a celebrity to titillate the ladies. Letitia says the table was oversubscribed."

Natalie shrugged and sipped her wine. The table was filling up with familiar couples who made the society columns in the New York papers. Natalie nodded pleasantly, but the women, who knew each other well, fell into private conversation. Her back kept hurting. Ting. Ting. Ting. She thought of the other time, when she had found out she was pregnant with Jeremy in London. It had not concerned her half so much as this pregnancy. She could no longer predict what Alden would say about anything. He slipped in and out of her life like a shadow and said little.

One day she had come into his dressing room and found him sitting in the dim light with one shoe on, one off.

"Is something wrong?" she asked softly.

He passed his hand over his eyes as if clearing the things he was looking at and faced her with an openness that surprised and frightened her. "I must concur with John Jacob Astor," he said thoughtfully, "that money has never brought me anything but a dull anxiety."

She sat down next to him and took his hand in hers. It seemed much lighter than she had imagined, and she got a mental image of his bones being hollow. "Would you like to go away? Shall we spend some time away from here?"

"Oh, no." He pulled his hand away. "I couldn't do that. I'm just getting it under control. The whole thing is coming under control."

"What, Alden? What have you got under control?"

He looked at her, but the veil was back. "My condition . . . my condition with my legs."

"Of course." She sounded bright and hopeful. "I'm so glad to hear it."

Tonight, thinking of the long evening before them, she had been anxious for him. "Are you sure you want to go tonight? Are you up to spending all those hours sitting still?"

"We must go," he had said. "We must help Bill Haas. I knew his uncle. His uncle once saved me from drowning."

She found it hard to imagine that his life had ever been so tractable. That he had been a boy. And had nearly drowned. And had been saved from drowning by Bill Haas's uncle.

One of the men at the table had asked Natalie to dance. Peter Duchin's band was playing *The Way We Were,* and the man was humming in her ear which was irritating. When they returned to the table, there was a new arrival. Rudy Sorbentino was seated directly across from her. He was the opposite of the soft-haired, even-featured men around him and seemed to occupy more space than the others. He caught the look of distaste on her face and smiled knowingly as if he had planned on being disliked and enjoyed it.

Natalie looked away. She didn't see him often because he conducted his business from hotel rooms and restaurants. He liked people to come to him, and they did. Technically he was her boss. She had a title—public relations coordinator—and her name on the letterhead. For this she received a nominal salary which made her an employee. "Take the title *and* the money," Cora had insisted. "One never knows when one will need a résumé and something to put in it. Besides, what is PR but speaking well of people, and you can do that better than anyone."

Whenever they went out for speeches and rallies, Sorbentino always positioned her on the platform to the left of and slightly behind the candidate. "Window dressing," he had muttered sarcastically. He was satisfying the venal tastes of Haas's constituents.

The seat next to her at the table was still empty, so she had nowhere to look but to the small stage and was relieved to see someone approach the microphone and ask for silence. The waiters began to serve, and as Cora had predicted, it was peas, mashed potatoes, and two slices of gray-brown beef. She felt the queasiness return and left the food untouched.

Sorbentino was still staring at her, and she turned steadfastly to the speaker, Senator Fitler, who was discussing the problems of the inner cities. It sounded poetic, "the inner cities." Too poetic for what it really meant—a pocket of deprivation and unrest, alien to the surrounding calm. She had an inner city herself, in the center of her heart where she had locked away all her feelings. Natalie's Inner City, population: 1. Pregnancy made her feel more alive and radiant than ever. All those hormones galloping through. She toyed with her bracelet and tried not to look at Sorbentino. He was all wrong, yet it was not unpleasant to be looked at so longingly by a man. The men she knew were so bloodless. Perhaps she was bloodless, too, except now. Pregnancy had fired her up.

There was a sound of a chair being pulled back, and she realized without looking that her dinner partner had finally arrived. She would have to make small talk and try for pleasantries. After all, he had paid plenty to sit with her. In a few minutes she would speak to him. She was just so tired of doing her duty. She didn't realize he was touching her arm right away. It was so unexpected. Reluctantly she turned and found herself staring at Sam Johnson.

He leaned close to her. "Are you going to eat those peas?"

Chapter 8

MIRANDA ARRIVED AT KENNEDY AIRPORT IN the midst of the worst rainstorm of a cold and dismal June. The plane had circled for two hours only to be rerouted to Boston where she spent a restless night alternately vomiting into the chipped seat of an unusually high-perched toilet and trying to put in a transatlantic call to Sanche.

He was not at his Rome hotel. And if he were? Would he accept her call? They had not parted on the best of terms. Still, the shouts and accusations had been a relief, like a rainstorm after a muggy day. Looking back on it, she felt as if she had spent the emotional equivalent of sixty-five muggy days with Sanche.

At quarter after three, Boston time, the call went through. He seemed relieved to hear from her, as if he had reconsidered her departure and found it not quite what he wanted. His tone reassured her, and she asked if she could use the hotel room his agency kept while she looked for an apartment.

"Call Jack Martell and tell him to arrange it. Someone else might be in it. They give it to whoever's in town. If it's free, use it and . . . ." He had been about to say something else, make some small commitment, but had stopped himself.

"I'm in Boston. We couldn't land at Kennedy. I've been throwing up all night."

"Uh . . . ask Jack for the name of a doctor, too. I've talked to him about it and he can arrange it. They have a doctor for everything—he'll give you the name."

She didn't want to know what he wanted the doctor to do for her. If the suggestion was innocent, she'd find out soon enough. She also knew better than to ask when she would see him again because that would send him into a whirl of excuses, so she just said good-bye. She had a place to stay and he had arranged for a doctor. What more could she want.

It was a typical upper class obstetrician's office. Pale green walls, a pea green carpet smoothed and worn where many edema-filled legs had trodden out their last few months of pregnancy. The room was long and skinny, due no doubt to its having originally been a regular apartment in the luxury building. The furniture was well-bred tacky, maroon and gray upholstery on a mix of fake Regency and Queen Anne.

There was no noise in the room beyond the occasional rustle of a . magazine or an unexpected (impatient) sigh. Three women sat primly, legs crossed at the ankle. All were on their first visit and discreetly slim. This was unusual and the nurse, a homely but compassionate woman who had survived successive and increasing dips in the population curve, decided that perhaps the magazines were right—women were having babies again.

"Do you have to kill something?" Miranda was undressed and waiting when Dean Whitley entered the room. Her hair had come undone and framed her face, loose and innocent.

"I beg your pardon?"

"To tell if I'm pregnant? Can you do it with an examination, or do you have to kill something?"

"We can tell a lot by examining the cervix." He was surprised by her directness. She looked so angelic and young. "It's usually spongy and beginning to soften when there's conception. Depends on how far along you are also. But we're getting ahead of ourselves. Just lie back and relax."

"Don't say that. I don't want to relax." He was younger than she had expected and less threatening, but that didn't mean he had her best interests at heart.

"If you don't want to relax, that's okay with me, but you've got to lie down." Was it nervousness or just defiance? Most women were embarrassed by their curiosity. They asked questions timidly.

"I would like to know what your connection is with the Martell Agency." She settled her legs into the stirrups but kept her head up. Despite his long established, impersonal attitude, he found himself admiring them.

"I have no special connection." He didn't know what she wanted to hear. "Why do you ask?"

"They made this appointment."

"They probably use me because I'm centrally located. Also, I've delivered some of their clients . . . a singer and a television newslady. I'm sure they have nothing more in mind than that I'm a known quantity." He could see this did not satisfy her. She was tense and still half sitting up. "I can't examine you until you lie flat on your back."

She was surprised by his sudden stern voice and did as she was told. He tried to concentrate on what he was looking for.

"Just what do you intend to do about this pregnancy?" She was dressed and facing him across the mahogany desk. There was a picture on it of his ex-wife, and he was startled to see it there. Why had he never thought to remove it?

"Is that what doctors ask now?"

"Excuse me?"

"Do you just routinely say—what do you intend to do about this pregnancy?" She mimicked him slightly. "I thought you were supposed to say, 'Congratulations, little mother.'" She was baiting him. "What happened to, 'Congratulations, little mother?' And what happened to, 'Keep your weight down,' or 'Drink more milk?'"

"I used to say all those things," he was enjoying himself, "but recently I attended an obstetrics convention, and one of the doctors, a very savvy guy, told us not to talk that way anymore. He said it was sentimental and old hat. He said, 'If those girls want to call us John instead of Doctor Smith and if they don't want us to call them our girls, then it's going to be grown up to grown up all the way. We can't assume every woman wants a baby.' " He noticed with relief that she was smiling for the first time. "This is the first time I've ever said it," he grinned at her. "But you're probably the wrong candidate. You must want to keep your baby more than anything in the world."

"Oh, I do. I do!" She surprised herself. She hadn't known how strongly she felt about keeping it until he put it into words. Miranda liked him despite herself. He had thoughtful, calm eyes. And he was handsome too, although she suspected he needed someone who could make him merry. His blond hair was parted at the side and combed neatly across his head. He was definitely of the old school . . . a tie and proper shirt under his white jacket, wing-tip shoes. A Harvard man according to the diplomas. She could see his mother serving tea in some Boston brownstone. She trusted him. "The only reason I came was to make sure. Did it look all right . . . the way it's supposed to?"

"It looked fine. You're about ten weeks along and the cervix is engorged and purplish which is exactly the way it should be. Let's just wait for the test results." He stood up. He was taking a disproportionate interest in this girl and the waiting room was filling up. Ms. Wasserman, his nurse, would be grumpy. He turned professional. "Don't take anything you don't have to, not even aspirin. If you smoke, better try to give it up as well. We know that smoking affects the birth weight and maybe other things as well. Be good to yourself and everything will be fine." This last was said with a different inflection. He was telling her to watch out, but he didn't quite know why.

She nodded, gathered her purse, and expelled a sigh of completion. Her face was as vulnerable as any he'd seen, although pregnancy often did that to women. She shook his hand firmly, a gesture he found endearing, and left. Something about the pregnancy disturbed him. He was not so self-confident as to think he could predict which pregnancies would turn out well and which would not. Still, there was something here that bothered him. Perhaps it was nothing. She looked healthy enough. Clear-eyed, vibrant, at the peak of her womanliness. He was relieved that she had not asked for an abortion. He liked bringing babies into the world.

*   *   *

Until his wife left him and broke his heart, Dean Whitley had succeeded with ease in every endeavor into which he put honest effort. In childhood he was Sonia Whitley's total pleasure, a first and only child who never had to wait for food, nurturing, or divertissement. That pattern would hold until his adult life, and contrary to popular belief it had not made him selfish and self-absorbed but generous and trusting.

He was fair, well-proportioned, with wide-spaced eyes and a freshness that made people eager to be part of his life. He excelled in everything he did—sports, scholastics, and friendships—and upon graduating third in a class of four hundred Harvard, recognizing a life worthy of their special input, readily accepted him.

His star did not shine as conspicuously in the brilliant Harvard sky as it had at Prevolt High. He didn't own a car nor could he fly to the Caribbean on winter weekends to share mumsy and dad's condominium in St. Maarten or St. Croix. Still, he was the boy most often invited to join young scions as a houseguest, an activity at which he also excelled. He played tennis, swam well, and looked terrific in sports clothes.

On one such weekend holiday in the home of a man who manufactured (among other things) a remarkable kitchen appliance that pared and cored vegetables with ease and speed, he met his future wife and his charmed existence came to an end.

Marcia de John was bold from the start. The first night at dinner while her tall, thin mother defended Orval Faubus and gave long and complicated opinions on the debacle at Little Rock, Marcia placed her hand in Dean's lap and searched out his crotch. Expertly she located the most sensitive part of his penis beneath the soft seersucker of his trousers, and as his face grew red and his thighs began to twitch, she flicked the end of it back and forth. Dean was astounded. No one had ever held it with such authority, much less under such titillating circumstances. Up to then his sexual experiences had been furtive, backseat flings with girls who knew less than he did and who, if they touched him at all, did so with an awkwardness used to handle raw eggs.

Only his growing sexuality and healthy appetite brought him to orgasm in those tangled gropings. What this girl was doing to him was remarkable. He had never felt such an instant and complete need to come. When he could contain himself no longer, she returned both hands to the table and daintily broke off a piece of Parker House roll, buttered it carefully, and proceeded to lick the fingers which had just recently caressed him.

He fixed his mind on the gory dissections of his med school classes to keep himself from ejaculating on Mrs. de John's Aubusson carpet.

After the main course while they waited for dessert to be served by a gaunt and morose butler, she took his hand from under the table-cloth and placed it under her voluminous skirt, separating his tallest finger which she guided to a little nub buried in her pubic hair. She was not wearing underpants.

Dean had never felt such a thing. When he touched a girl, it was in that general soft, warm place that got slippery and smooth as it was rubbed. But the thing he was feeling was well-defined and grew under his touch. After she had used his finger to make it grow, she slid his hand down a bit and he felt warm liquid flowing out.

When her mother paused in her conversation and the butler had served the dessert, she removed his hand from her lap and placed both of hers on the table.

Dean was shocked at her aggressive behavior but also felt hornier than he had ever felt in his life and wanted nothing more than to have her show him what else she knew. Insanely, he wanted her to fondle him again under the table, but her hands remained stubbornly on her ornate silver spoon dipping into a quivering soufflé.

Marcia de John continued to orchestrate this game of give-and-take until he married her two and half years later when he graduated from medical school.

Dean Whitley was not a complicated man in the psychological sense, and it was a severe blow to his sunny view of life when Marcia divorced him. She was still baiting him after five years, still taunting him with her excesses, her drinking, her spur-of-the-moment lovers. She was an exciting woman, not beautiful, and when she entered a room, you had to look at her. In all their years together she never allowed him to show tenderness. She had assigned him the role of a cold son-of-a-bitch and he had not disappointed her. Now the only picture that remained with him was of a fresh, young girl wearing a picture hat that dipped to form a shadow across her brow. She was coming to him over miles and miles of green lawn because it was their wedding day.

* * *

It was a Thursday that the stains began to appear. Five or six altogether, although she couldn't be sure. On Friday there were a few more. On Saturday Miranda looked and saw nothing more than an innocent white rectangle. *To be a woman,* she thought with slight relief, *is to always be looking in your underpants for information.*

On Sunday she had run out of food and patience. With no new spillage to unnerve her she found a drugstore around the corner from the hotel and asked an acne-scarred clerk in a lab coat for a Nata-Kit. The blood had scared her. Suppose she wasn't pregnant any longer? But he had said ten weeks along. Ten weeks would bring more than ten spots of blood. She wanted to be sure.

"It's a pregnancy test kit," she said to the clerk when he made no move to get it.

"Yes." He stared at her. "They're very reliable. Within ninety-eight percent."

"So I've heard." Did he stand around reading the literature from all the women's products? The things that went into vaginas and near vaginas?

"I guess it's cheaper than going to a doctor?" He leaned over the counter. "What's the matter, honey? Did your boyfriend knock you up? You let him put it in your pussy?"

She stared at him for several seconds. Then with a bold sweep of her arm cleared the counter of a pyramid display of Colgate toothpaste and St. Joseph's aspirin.

"Hey . . . what are you crazy?" He rushed from behind a hinged partition and started after her, but she was out the door, surprised and grateful for the sudden coolness. For the next three blocks she laughed, remembering his expression.

She found another drugstore and from there stopped to pick up milk, eggs, bread, cottage cheese, and orange juice before hurrying back to the hotel. In the empty elevator she patted her belly reassuringly. She would take good care of whoever was in there.

The instructions were simple. The test required a fasting urine specimen. "Now you can be the first to know," said the pamphlet and she shuddered. She didn't want to be the first to know. She wished for calm, solicitous Dean Whitley to be calling with the happy news which she would quickly relay to the happy father. As it turned out, the father wasn't all that happy. Not even interested.

That's what money and power do to people. Events that are monumental to the poor, just make a rich man shrug.

The Nata strip finally turned a bright, positive orange, and she let out a sigh of relief. The baby was still alive and kicking. Or something.

As dusk became night, however, old fears overtook her. Suppose the test wasn't accurate? Although she didn't totally trust him, Dean Whitley was the only one who could really reassure her. Dare she call him on a Sunday night? Doctors were such shits. They had everyone scared to death to inconvenience them.

She stressed to the answering service that it wasn't an emergency, but he returned her call within ten minutes. What's more, he was not annoyed at being summoned away during the dinner hour. His voice was concerned.

"I told them it wasn't an emergency," she apologized. "Were you having your dinner?"

"Yes. As a matter of fact I was."

"You left the table to return my call?" She felt mildly guilty.

"Not exactly. I was eating a can of tuna fish at my kitchen counter. What's up?"

"I've had some bleeding."

"Oh . . . spotting or continuous?"

"Spotting. Maybe a dozen spots in all."

"Bright red or brown?"

"Bright."

"Has it stopped?"

"It stopped two days ago. Does that mean . . . do you think I'm still pregnant?"

"I would say so. Spotting is not so unusual, but bleeding is something else. Stay off your feet for a few days. Do you have someone to help you?" He was not asking solely for professional reasons.

"Yes," she lied.

"Good." He paused. "And, Ms. Lesley, if you begin to spot again, don't wait three days to call. I'm your doctor, remember? I'm supposed to take care of you."

"Yes, doctor." She lingered over the word "doctor" to make up for her previous snottiness. They loved to be called doctor. He was really a decent man, if a little stuffy. At another time with less in her head and heart she might have encouraged him to be her friend.

She stayed in bed and fell into a fitful sleep and dreamt her old dream. She was in a new apartment. Or a new house. A place to live that was better than the one before. During the dream she was either arranging a lease or inspecting the rooms. When she awoke, she decided it was time to look for a place of her own and perhaps put an end to those dreams.

At nine she was awakened by the telephone. It had to be Sanche. No one else knew she was in New York.

"I'm going to look for a place tomorrow," she said, hoping this would bring an invitation to join him in California. It did not.

"Good idea," he said quickly. "They could ask you to leave any day and then where would you be?"

Out in the street pregnant, she thought dismally. "You've got to come back for your stuff. There are things of yours here." Her voice was matter-of-fact. He held most of the cards, but she knew how to be calm. Now there was a silence on the other end. She couldn't be sure if he was annoyed or only thinking.

"Did the . . . uh . . . doctor confirm it?"

"Yup."

"And what did he . . . advise?"

"Advise? He told me to be good to myself and not take any aspirin." She knew that wasn't what he wanted to hear, but she was not going to help him.

"You're going to keep it? You're going to manage the whole thing yourself?"

"Perhaps."

"Jesus."

"How's the script going? Do you need any more tapes?"

"It's going okay. I haven't really worked on it."

"I could help."

"I'm not at that point yet." There was a long silence. "Hullo . . . you still there?"

"Yes."

"I'll be in New York two weeks from today. Let me know your new address. We'll talk then."

The next day she was up before eight searching the real estate pages of the *Times*. There were three possibilities she could afford, on West Twenty-second Street, East Forty-ninth, and East Eighty-third. After inspecting all three she decided on the efficiency on East

Eighty-third. A small park and playground were only two blocks away. It was a quiet, tree-lined street where you could easily push a carriage, and there was a doorman who could help you get the carriage in and out.

The rent was two hundred eighty-five dollars a month, a figure she could afford if she worked to the end. She had saved all her salary when she was living with Bob. He had told her they would use it for a joint capital expenditure which had made her want to squander it immediately, but she had not. There was two thousand dollars left of it which she put into a sweet, one-story colonial bank two blocks from her new apartment. The next few days she spent on the Lower East Side buying bolts of calico prints to decorate her long, skinny one-room palace.

The room's one good feature was a deep window seat banked on either side by deep bookshelves. She painted the shelves white and stapled a dainty, blue and white flower print to the inside of the alcove and made a dozen pillows to match. She bought a slab of foam rubber for the seat and found to her delight that she could sleep there. It was wide enough and long enough for a bed, but it also gave her a wonderful nook in which to sit and croon to her baby while watching the life on Lexington Avenue go by.

After a week, when she had done as much as she could afford to the apartment, days of total silence took their toll. She had no girl friends. No one to eat with or go to the movies with. It would be best if she got a job, any job that offered simple human contact. And she had better do it before the pregnancy became more obvious.

The next Monday morning found her trudging up the soiled steps of a Third Avenue walk-up. On the second floor the only sign of life came from an orange door, slightly ajar. White lowercase letters read: ONLY WHEN YOU WANT TO . . . TEMPORARY JOBS FOR FREE WOMEN.

Some of the desks were still empty and the lights still out. She sat down to wait. Finally a yawning, frizzy-haired girl in a T-shirt that said "Not Now" opened the top drawer of her metal desk and threw a stack of applications on a little ledge in the waiting alcove.

"Each one fill in a form and drop it in the wicker basket," she said. "And don't lie about the shorthand. We test."

They sent her to a cosmetics firm on Fifth Avenue, a sumptuous modern office that smelled of roses and lilacs. The office manager, whose name was Lee, was not thrilled to see her. "Are you the temporary?"

"Yes. My name is Miranda Lesley."

The woman sighed and straightened some papers on her desk. She did not want to know Miranda's name.

"What's wrong?" asked Miranda. She could not imagine what she had done to cause that expression of distaste.

"Your clothes . . . they're not. . . . These are *the* executive offices of Lancia Cosmetics. We care about how our girls look to people who come here."

Miranda looked down at herself. She had on a lightweight muslin top over matching drawstring pants. The material was meant to look slightly wrinkled. It made her look delicate and slightly mysterious. Or so she had thought. It took her a moment to accept that she was being chastised by this power-hungry tarantula from Queens.

She was placed in a corner with an electric typewriter and hundreds of blank labels on which she was to type names and addresses from a list. For three days she typed and no one spoke to her except to answer when she asked where the ladies' room was and to ask if she wanted a sandwich when they ordered out. No one asked her name. No one asked her to have lunch. No one said good morning or good night. She might as well have been at home or walking the streets except that the money was decent and allowed her to save the nest egg she had accumulated. Also it delayed any dismal thought about Sanche and the outcome of their relationship until the late evening hours when, in her condition, she was too sleepy to think at all.

On the fourth day Lee Wallach strode to her desk with a set chin and disapproving eyes. "What is that?" She pointed to Miranda's dress which was cut like a kimono with a bib effect below the bosom. It perfectly hid her condition.

"It's my best dress," said Miranda, her eyes wide and innocent.

"We don't dress like hippies here."

Miranda stared at her. *Did she say hippies? Did people still say hippies?* "Mrs. Lancia needs you to run an errand," Lee continued coolly. "She'll give you the details. Mrs. Lancia's office is down the corridor, past the advertising department, and then left. It's the last door on the right. She wants some things picked up at Saks."

Miranda was delighted to be taken off the labels and allowed a trip out of doors. It was a beautiful sunny day, perfect for a stroll down Fifth Avenue. "We're going out," she said to her stomach.

On the way to Barbara Lancia's office she inspected all the cubicles along the way. Everywhere she looked were slim, attractive women dressed like models out of *Mademoiselle* or *Vogue*. They sported gold chains or designer scarves artfully arranged around their heads or waists or necks. They had a knack for looking delectable and fresh and fashionable. They probably cooked tricky French dishes for equally delectable men who would never leave them pregnant and alone.

As she approached Barbara Lancia's office, one of these young women caught up to her and they entered together.

"Lee said you wanted me to pick up something from Saks," Miranda answered Barbara's inquiring look over half-glasses. She was a tiny, elegant blonde with chiseled features. Older than she looks, Miranda guessed.

"Yes. Just sit a moment while I go over these." She took the sheets from the girl who had entered with Miranda. They were ads for Lancia's new perfume, More. The headline on one ad said: "More by Lancia . . . For Women Who Don't Want to Make Do With Less." "I don't know what that means," said Barbara Lancia. "A woman puts on perfume because it makes her feel better. There's a touch of the whore in it. How would you react to a headline like that?" She thrust the ad at Miranda.

Miranda looked at the headline. "That's a little vague for me. I wear perfume because . . . well . . . frankly . . . it makes me feel expensive. It sounds like I'm selling myself, but I mean it in the best way. I'm merchandising myself not only for a man but to myself as well. It raises my self-image. It makes me feel . . . *expensive.*" Miranda was so pleased to have a normal conversation, she could hardly stop.

Barbara Lancia looked at her shrewdly and thumped her palm down on her antique Queen Anne desk. "That's it. That's just what I'm talking about." She wrote down some words over the ad on her desk: "More . . . it makes you feel expensive."

"But Barbara," said the girl who had brought in the ads, "that sounds like you're appealing to whores."

Barbara Lancia took off her glasses and settled back in her chair.

"That's exactly who we *are* appealing to . . . the bit of the whore in every woman. My God, if you don't know that, you're in the wrong business."

The girl wearily picked up the bundle of advertisements. "Is that the headline you'd like to go with?"

"I want to see at least ten versions of that thought . . . and I want the word expensive in all of them. Tell that to the agency and have them back to me by Friday."

The girl left and Miranda rose. "You wanted something picked up from Saks?"

"Yes. Ask for Mrs. Raffia in the lingerie department." She took off her glasses and looked at Miranda. "And when you come back, I want to see you again. Why are you running errands?"

"Let's just say I like fresh air."

From that day on Barbara Lancia called Miranda into her office daily. She asked her opinion on ads that were waiting for approval, or new colors for the lipstick line, or any of a hundred other things that needed to be decided. "Come over here," she'd say in a tone that hovered between friendliness and command, "let's see how Cinnamon Pink looks on you. You shouldn't wear that black mascara," she would continue when Miranda was seated in front of her, "your eyes are dark enough. Wear brown mascara and beige eye shadow. Did you ever think of modeling?"

"No. But once I was Miss Typical Young New York Woman."

"That's ridiculous," said Barbara Lancia. "You don't look like a typical anything. But you do have an interesting face, and if you don't get gaudy and paint yourself like a gypsy, you can look beautiful. Why do you always wear those mumu tops, you're not fat? Those things are for fatties or protestors. You're not a fattie, are you a protestor?"

"I appreciate your interest, but I'm hardly a permanent fixture here. I was brought in as a temporary by your office manager, Lucrezia Borgia."

"A temporary what?"

"A temporary anything. I sent by 'Only When You Want To . . . temporary jobs for free women.' "

"Good lord, it sounds like a sexual rights movement." She turned serious. "Why are you wasting your time on that kind of arrangement? You're a smart girl. Would you like a permanent job here? I need an assistant for my personal life as well as my business life. . . . It would involve some travel—I spend a few months of the year in East Hampton and St. Maarten.''

"I think you should know something." Miranda rose, took a deep breath, and sat down again. Then she rose again. "You see . . . well . . . I'm pregnant."

"*What*? Oh, for goodness sake." Barbara Lancia rose from her chair and pulled up the top Miranda was wearing. "Well . . . what . . ." she sputtered as if not comprehending such waste and stupidity. "Now, I see—you're going to play the martyred single mother. I can't believe you'd want to ruin your life that way, not to mention the child's. What are you thinking of? Who is the father?"

"He's important." Miranda's voice sounded high and childish. "A screenwriter . . . very much in demand at the moment and trying to cope with his success and the amount of work it's brought him. He'll come around when the baby's born."

"Huh. It'll be worse then. If he can't get dewy now, don't expect much later. Nothing can compete with success, my dear, to hold a man's passion . . . not beautiful women, not newborn babies." She shook her head. "How people mess up their lives."

"I don't see it that way." Not Barbara Lancia or anyone else was going to take her triumph away. It *was* a triumph. The baby within her was all the fulfillment she needed. A sweet knowing that bathed her in hope and satisfaction. How could anyone know how she felt.

"All right," said Barbara wearily, "suppose you stay as long as you can. Who pays you?"

"The agency. You pay them and they send me a check for two thirds of the amount."

"Well, stop working for them and I'll tell Lee to take you on. As a matter of fact, I'm giving a party, the last party before everyone leaves for the country. I'll need all the help I can get to keep track of the invitations and arrangements. We'll work out of my apartment."

"There'll be days when I can't make it. If he comes to town . . ."

"Are you giving *me* stipulations?"

"That's the way it's got to be." Miranda was adamant, and Barbara while she appeared put off by her stubbornness, secretly admired her spunk.

As for Miranda, she wanted to like Barbara, who was smart and elegant and generous. However, she could also be selfish and cool and sometimes cruel.

Chapter 9

NATALIE LOOKED AROUND THE BALLROOM with a feeling of confusion. It felt as if she'd been there for days. Her voice sounded as if it were coming from a distance. "Excuse me?" She couldn't focus on what Sam Johnson was saying. She felt completely disoriented. He had lived in her mind for so long and now here he was, in person. Was she hallucinating?

"Your peas . . . ." He pointed to them. "Are you going to eat them?"

"No." She glanced at the mound of shriveled vegetables on her plate. She could see right away that nothing had happened to take away any of his strength or any of his certainty, and she had to struggle to fight back tears of disappointment.

"Would you mind?" He motioned for her to transfer them to his plate. "I've had nothing to eat all day . . . just flew in from California."

She was startled. She remembered another time when he had asked her never to let him go to California, and the memory of those days made her chest feel constricted. She picked up the plate and carefully tipped it and transferred the peas and turned her face to the stage again. He didn't remember anything.

A few minutes later she felt the nudge on her arm again. "Are you going to eat your roast beef?"

"No."

"Would you mind?"

"Not at all." She was in control now and stabbed the meat and laid it on his plate. "I don't suppose you want the potatoes too?"

"Well, I . . ." She heaped them on his plate.

"Tell me," she whispered, leaning close and looking into his eyes. "If you were planning to ask for the meat and potatoes all along, why did you only ask for the peas first?"

He grinned. His mouth was full and he waited before answering. "My mother told me never to ask for big things right away. People don't like it. So"—he broke off a piece of the roll he had taken from her plate—"I always ask for something small first."

She turned again to face the stage. Her face was burning. She wanted to hit him. Pummel him. To wipe that senseless, satisfied grin off his face. He could still hurt her. After all these years the wounds were just as raw. Just as painful.

Cora Sandford had not touched a morsel of food on her plate either, but for a different reason than she had offered to Natalie that morning. From the moment Sam Johnson had entered the room, she had been transfixed. He was just the person she had been looking for. She recognized with a flutter of her heart that he was looking at Natalie in a certain way, exuding . . . what? *Energy. Sexual energy.* Exotic visions of the two of them in the most intimate poses swam through her head, and she blushed as if she, too, were involved.

The talent portion of the evening was about to begin and the lights dimmed. Sam Johnson rose. "I'm the emcee," he said almost apologetically. She smiled and tried to look pleasant. Then he leaned close to her and whispered in her ear. "You're still the most beautiful woman I've ever seen. To me you're the most beautiful."

It was the first acknowledgment that there had been anything between them. Her heart lurched and she was no longer calm. She looked around the table to see if anyone could tell what was happening. Sorbentino was still staring.

Out of the corner of her eye she saw his hand resting on the table, his pinky ring picking up the light. Black wisps of hair curled about the stiff, white cuff. The fingers were puffy and looked as if they held tremendous strength. The hand curved inward.

She refused to look at him. She looked everywhere else instead. Respectability was everywhere, and the guests did not seem to be having a good time. Possibly they wondered why they were there or whether because they were rich, they were supposed to behave differently. When it was finally over, Sam Johnson said, "Thank you, everyone, and good night." Everyone began to file out and the band played "Hello, Dolly!" For no reason anyone could understand the vocalist sang the lyrics in French.

Sorbentino continued to stare. She could not make him look away. In a way it was interesting being his victim and not unlike the delicate balance she walked with Simmons and Alden, or Cardon. They all had power. For instance, Dolly, the kitchen helper, had power which she proved often by oversalting the soup or underbaking the potatoes. Everyone assumed Dolly was not quite "there" and could not be held responsible. Natalie suspected Dolly was as there as she chose, matching her degree of sanity to the amount of effort she wished to exert. Her lopsided grin probably became a normal mouth when she returned to the servants' quarters. Actually Sorbentino was more interesting because it would be so easy to take the advantage away from him. She had only to smile and he would be hers.

"I've thought it all out," said Cora, approaching Natalie and Alden who were standing together. "We all deserve a nightcap at the Carlyle." She had Sam in tow, having rushed to the stage the moment the lights went up.

"Thanks," said Sam, looking curiously at Alden, "but I can't. Not tonight. I haven't been home in a week. All I can think of is taking off my clothes and sleeping for two days straight."

Natalie felt a wave of disappointment. He didn't even want to be with her, while she wished nothing more than to take off his shoes and undress him. She wanted to put him to bed and watch over him as he slept.

"George Shearing is there this week," insisted Cora, "and Letitia and I could never go alone. We're not liberated." She took a deep breath. "Alden, you look exhausted . . . all that running. Simmons tells me you're up before dawn every morning. Well, go to bed, my

dear, but please let us borrow Natalie. She'll liven up the old ladies.''

Alden appeared relieved and almost fled without remembering to
peck Natalie's cheek.

"Now, Mr. Johnson," Cora said sternly, "we've all seen your
plays and they're wonderful. You're wonderful. Won't you give us a
treat? Natalie seldom gets a chance to kick up her heels, and she can
hardly do it in the company of Letitia and myself. We're almost a
hundred and fifty put together. Of course, Letitia makes up most of
the hundred.''

Sam looked at Natalie. "All right." It was both a question and an
answer.

They were squeezed together with Cora in the back of a taxi, Letitia riding in front with the driver. Natalie could feel his buttocks and
his arm. She could not keep from touching him, and her heart was
pounding so loudly, it was hard to hear anything that was said. Cora
was not unaware of the currents, and she grinned mischievously to
herself in the dark. She kept eyeing them, more and more certain it
was a perfect match.

The show began almost immediately after they were seated, and
Natalie was grateful not to have to make conversation. Her thoughts
were tumultuous. Shearing sang wonderful, complicated love songs
in a voice so unpretentious and innocent, it could break your heart.

After an hour and a half there was a short intermission, and Cora
began to breathe heavily and agitate in her seat. "I'm sorry," she
said to Natalie and Sam. "I don't know what's wrong with me. I feel
perfectly dreadful, but I don't want to spoil your evening. No, don't
bother to come with me," she said as Sam began to rise, "the doorman will get Letitia and me a cab. You stay with Natalie and enjoy
the rest of the show.''

"Visit us at Haas Headquarters anytime," she called over her
shoulder. "Natalie and I are there three days a week.''

That was it. They were suddenly alone. He said nothing for a long
while and then quietly reached over and took hold of her hand. "My
beautiful, beautiful girl. You can't imagine what it does to me to see
you again.''

"I've thought of you every day," she said and realized that it was
true.

"Come on," he said hoarsely, "let's get out of here.''

They were in a cab kissing and holding each other all the way to his apartment. She was embarrassed to get undressed in front of him. She knew her belly was rounded and she feared he would think it was fat. He looked tan and fit. His hair was longer and it made his head look larger.

She needn't have worried about her shape. He made love to her immediately, roughly and furiously. In the middle he became angry, as if he wanted to hit her. "Why didn't you wait?" he groaned. "Why did you run away from me?"

She was dismayed that he had brought it up. It seemed rude. Like pointing out someone's deformity. What could be done about it now? She said nothing but burrowed into him wherever she could.

When it was over and they were lying quietly holding each other, she said, "You're the only man I've ever wanted," and was immediately sorry. Where was his equally committing statement? Once again he had her at a disadvantage. She realized with horror that it was on her lips to tell him about Jeremy. *You have a little boy. He looks just like you. He is like you.* She would not tell him anything. That was her only advantage against him and the yearning he aroused in her. Somehow she felt that if he knew about Jeremy she could break his heart, and beneath everything that's what she wanted. To break his heart. But not yet.

Later he was asleep in her arms, and she remembered what he had said about not having slept in three days. She eased herself out of the bed and dressed quickly, asked the doorman to get her a cab, and went home. It was three o'clock and she had no idea what she would say to Alden.

Her heart began to pound as she entered the apartment. He would want an explanation. He might even be angry. She took off her shoes and crept into the bedroom. If she didn't turn on any lights, he might remain asleep. She wouldn't even put on a nightgown but just slip into bed. She looked across to see if he was still sleeping. The bed was undisturbed. There was no one there.

She snapped on the bedside light and looked around the empty room. Alden's tuxedo was draped over a chair. Where could he be? She looked in his dressing room where he had sat that afternoon taking off his running clothes. They should be there where they always were, but they were not. The shoes were gone too.

* * *

Alden had not intended to go to the park so late and couldn't even remember getting there. But now all his senses were alert. He knew the park was dangerous. The danger was real.

He forced himself to concentrate on his breathing and soon relaxed. He continued for twenty minutes more and then only dimly became aware that someone was running behind him. The someone was still far away, perhaps thirty or forty feet. The sound of the steps was like a whisper. He slowed and tried to assess the size and weight of the man by the heaviness of his step. The steps were light and the cadence steady. It was a slim man of better than average height. He became exhilarated by the idea of the two of them in the dark, strangers yet trusting that neither would violate the other.

It was then that he tripped. He caught a rock with the side of his right foot, and it turned in and made him go down. Unwillingly he yelped in pain. The footsteps behind him faltered, stopped, and then began again at a slower pace.

"Is someone there?" It was a soft, yet masculine voice.

"I've twisted my ankle." Alden tried to make out the face. He was not afraid.

The man was at his side and moved closer. He knelt and their faces were inches apart. Their eyes met and both concluded they were in safe company. He appeared young.

"Let me help you," said the young man and leaned down to offer Alden his weight until he was up and leaning against the fencing.

They were silent a moment, deciding what to do. Should they be polite but quick or . . . the young man spoke first. "My apartment is not far. I could take you there and wrap it up."

It was obvious to Alden that this was unnecessary. He could take a cab to his own apartment or to the nearest emergency room. He had many options, but there seemed an inevitability about the events that had befallen him that night, and he wanted to see them played out. "That would be kind," he said. "I'll accept."

He leaned on the young man who offered his weight and wrapped his arm around Alden's waist. They hobbled out of the park, emerging on Eighty-sixth Street at Fifth Avenue where the young man sat Alden on a bench while he went in search of a cab.

"I'm David Laver," said the young man as he let them into his apartment, but Alden did not reciprocate. He didn't want to say yet who he was.

The apartment was tastefully decorated and greatly appealed to
Alden. Everything was in a rough muslin and close to the floor.
There was a feeling of tremendous space in what was an otherwise
ordinary layout. Alden sat in one of the muslin-covered sections and
stretched out his injured foot.

David brought out a pan filled with warm water and a box of
Epsom salts. He took off Alden's shoe and sock and as carefully as
possible bathed the swollen foot. He wrapped it snugly in an elastic
bandage and cradled it in a bag of ice.

"Would you like a drink?"

"Whatever you're having will be fine."

"Scotch and soda . . . although I think I'll have mine straight
after all this. You should try a slug of Scotch after a good run. Your
temperature shoots way up and the water begins to pour out of you.
Then into a shower, and after a huge cup of coffee."

As he spoke, Alden stared intently at David. He was beautiful, no
more than thirty-three or -four and expensively dressed in a well-fit-
ting exercise suit. He looked to Alden like a model out of the *Times
Magazine*. Now he realized how much he had liked having him bathe
his foot and touch him. He was sorry that it was over and wished the
young man would sit next to him.

After he handed Alden his drink, the young man did just that. He
sat right next to him. Alden was consumed with interest because he
knew what was about to happen. His body was totally relaxed. His
legs were no longer restless. It was a moment out of time.

When David Laver woke up the next morning (technically it was
only later that morning), the man was gone. He sat up confused. It
was close to ten and he had a client meeting in half an hour. He took
a quick tour of the apartment to see what evidence there was of his
visitor. The bag of ice had melted and lay flat in the pan. It seemed
unreal, yet he felt better this morning than he had felt in a long time.
He felt . . . comforted. He felt as if for the first time in his life he
had someone to turn to. He realized this was foolish, since he had no
idea of who the man was. He could very well be little better than a
bum. Worse, he could be someone dangerous. He had not even found
out his name, but he knew the man would be back.

For the next few days Natalie began to spend more and more time
in the city, zealously went to work earlier than she needed to, and

stayed until they closed at five. She regretted being away from Jeremy, but the idea of seeing Sam again totally obsessed her. As the first days passed and there was no sign of him, she began to hate her need and was disappointed in herself.

He had said he loved her. Was it possible that it was said simply to fill out the moment? He was a sucker for drama. He was also a good actor. Several times she had the distinct feeling that he had used her. It was *she* who had gone to his apartment. *She* had let him make love to her. *She* had cradled his head and soothed him to sleep. Then she had gone home. She had read that he was in a play that was going to try out in Washington. Had he gone without letting her know? She licked envelopes, sent out press releases, and waited every moment for the phone to ring. If he had really been glad to see her, if he loved her as he had said, why hadn't he been in touch with her immediately?

After five days when he still hadn't called, she asked Sara to have lunch with her. She didn't want to confide in Sara, but Sara was her only friend.

It was a small French restaurant in the West Fifties. The food was served all on one plate with a minimum of ceremony, but it was carefully prepared and delicious. Sara had been there twice with Jane Seymour and was happy to introduce it to Natalie.

They ordered a litre of cold, dry white wine and sipped it thoughtfully as if it could help them deal with each other. They would have to work through the shyness.

"Where are you hiding the baby?" asked Sara. It was a dumb question. There were lots of better questions she had in mind, but they were variations on the theme of truculent servants, snotty butlers, unsmiling husbands, etc., etc. She had no right to reach conclusions. One had only to look at Natalie to see that suffering agreed with her.

"I haven't been to the doctor yet. It's not official."

"That explains it," said Sara lightly. "The child won't grow until the doc gives it the go ahead. Such is the power of the AMA." She waited. "Are you happy about it?"

"I haven't given it much thought. The alternative is pretty gruesome."

"I suppose." Sara was eager to tell Natalie about Sorbentino. He was someone they had in common. It wasn't much, but it was a start. "By the way, I met your Mister Haas but not under the best conditions."

"Was his wife with him? She talks a lot."

"No. There were two men with him. A perfectly bred Harvard type and a guy named Sorbentino. King Kong among the choirboys." She thought Natalie might take offense at this. She was the female equivalent of a Harvard type.

"Mr. Sorbentino likes to give the impression that he's ruthless."

"*Impression*. Beneath that ruthless exterior is a ruthless interior."

"I suppose. But he's got to be like that. He gets people elected and that's what counts." She smiled, amused to be defending Rudy Sorbentino and remembering the way he had stared at her.

"I tried to explain that our meeting was no guarantee that *Haute* would actually go through with the profile and he was all over me. God, I felt so naive and . . ." She stopped in mid-sentence and looked straight ahead. Bill Waring was walking toward them. Her first thought was that he would be bowled over by Natalie, and she was sorry to be the one to introduce them.

He saw her immediately, smiled, and walked to their table. He nodded politely to Natalie but did not look at her. He looked at Sara. "I haven't seen you at the office lately."

You've been looking? "I haven't been there." It came out more sarcastically than she intended.

"Oh?" he asked pleasantly. "You don't work for me anymore?"

She hadn't thought of it that way. "I did a piece on home births and"—she took a big breath—"as it happens, it wasn't right. And . . ." she looked away from him to the far side of the room, ". . . since then there just hasn't been much free-lance work. That's all I meant."

"It doesn't sound as if any big doors have closed on either side," he said.

He was implying they were negotiating from equal positions of power, and it annoyed her. It wasn't true and he knew it wasn't true. She wouldn't be patronized. "I wouldn't put it just that way. You have a big, big door that you can close, but I . . . I don't have a door." She gestured with her hands to show there was nothing hidden there. ". . . No door."

He wasn't smiling anymore. In fact he looked annoyed. "I read your piece and it was remarkable. But Tania is right. It wasn't for us." He walked to the back of the restaurant before she could answer, and she felt confused and let down. She had forgotten all about Natalie who had been watching the exchange avidly.

"Is he your lover?"

She jumped. *"My lover!* You heard the man. I work for him. Worked is the word."

"He didn't look at you like a boss." Natalie's tone was conversational but certain, and Sara wanted to ask her in detail how he *had* looked at her. What special emanations had come from Bill Waring that were visible to the naked eye? She studied the menu and wiped her clammy hands on her napkin. The waiter came to take their orders.

"What would you do if someone you loved betrayed you?" Natalie continued in the same intimate voice.

"No one I love has ever betrayed me except my father." Both became silent, surprised at the mention of her father, remembering that wrenching parting. When they looked at each other again, Sara's eyes had misted.

Natalie cleared her throat and spoke very softly. "But if someone did, could you swallow your pride and go on as before? Would you mind giving more than you thought you could ever get?"

Sara relaxed and buttered a piece of roll. "If you're really in love, there's not much of a choice. For myself I would probably let him betray me and keep on wanting him. It's a sad but true rule of life that those who betray are always more interesting than the betrayed. No doubt I'd love him all the more because he wasn't totally mine."

"I couldn't do that."

"Of course, *you* couldn't," said Sara indignantly. The idea of anyone betraying Natalie was ludicrous. "But the rest of us . . . well . . ."

Natalie was not satisfied. "Why should you be able to forgive someone and continue to love them and not demand absolute adoration . . . and I cannot?"

"That's easy," said Sara before she could stop herself. "You've always called the shots." It came out as an accusation, and they were both glad the waiter was standing there with their food. Sara decided to put the subject to rest. She was saying things to Natalie based on their life long ago. How stupid to still be harboring resentment. It was the wine. Wine made you jump to conclusions.

Natalie ate her food and said nothing, and Sara had the unhappy thought that she was gathering her forces to surprise her in some way. She wanted the luncheon to end on a cheerful note. She wanted to be invited to Pheasant Hill and to have Charlie and Jeremy be good friends. A friendship like theirs gave continuity to life. It was precious. As for herself and Natalie it seemed they had a way to go before they could enjoy themselves. "Is there someone else who has perhaps started calling the shots?" she asked timidly. She was certain that Alden was not the man in question and felt immense relief that there was someone else in Natalie's life.

Natalie nodded. "I'm not the most important thing in the world to him." A look of abject pain crossed her face and Sara felt her defenses melt.

"I'm sure you're very high up there," she said reassuringly.

"That's not enough."

"No, of course not." For the first time Sara noticed a deep cleft above Natalie's lips that looked as if someone had chiseled it lovingly and with great thought. When you turned away from such a face, you wanted to look right back. How could she hope to answer questions for Natalie? "Do you love him very much?"

Natalie's face became noncommittal. "As a young girl I was told I didn't know how to let love out. It's one of the many popular myths about blond, attractive women. We're icy, selfish, empty-headed. How could I possibly love anyone?"

"Oh, God," said Sara with mock envy, "to be icy, selfish, and empty-headed. It sounds wonderful." She was ready to go to safer ground. She was ready to talk about recipes and children, but Natalie was not.

"What sort of man is he?"

"Who?"

"Your boss."

"Oh . . ." She yearned to talk about him but at the same time was afraid.

"Yes . . ."

"Well, he doesn't say much which makes everyone feel insecure. Also it makes him appear cold and too controlled, but I don't think he's like that at all. He seems to have his own special view of the world, and it both amuses him and disappoints him. But it doesn't amuse him or disappoint him enough not to play the game. He plays it all right."

"You're in love with him." Natalie buttered a roll slowly.

"I'm not." She didn't like the smugness.

"A woman doesn't defend a cold, calculating man the way you did unless she's in love with him."

Sara tried to make light of it. She was not going to protest too much. "We're all in love with him . . . every woman and child at *Haute*. The men, too, for all I know. It's harmless."

"Perhaps it's harmless for everyone else, but not for you, Sara."

"Why do you say that?" She didn't feel good anymore. The wine was making her slightly sick.

"Because he wants you back."

"That's ridiculous. He never dates anyone from the office."

"If you really think so, you're either blind or dumb, and I know you're not dumb. I saw the way he looked at you." She stopped to chew several mouthfuls of calves' liver slowly and thoughtfully. She seemed pleased with her neat deductions. "There's something else I have to say . . ."

Sara, unwilling to take it further, pushed around her sole meunière until it resembled a hundred bits of chewed white rags.

". . . he's going to get you."

There. She had done it.

Blessedly, they stopped talking above love and what might or might not be in their hearts. They talked about the new longer skirts and relived in detail the birth of their children. Yet each without knowing it had come to a new understanding of herself. One that she could give up nothing for love, and the other that she could give up everything.

One evening as she entered the elevator to her apartment, Miranda saw that she was sharing it with a man she had noticed several times before. He was slight and young with thinning hair and perfect features. He always wore three-piece suits and looked straight ahead giving the impression that he did not want to be consulted about the time, the weather, the state of the halls, the garbage pickup. He wanted to ride in silence, alight on his floor (which was hers as well) and be absorbed into 11J quickly and silently.

Sometimes when she came home late in the evening, he was wearing a stretch suit for running, but even though his face was flushed and it was obvious that he had been doing strenuous exercise, he still appeared perfectly groomed.

Once she had seen him with another man, taller and equally well-dressed. The other man had been older, and she remembered thinking that it had been strange to see two men like that; they seemed too different to be friends. The two of them had stared straight ahead and seemed even less friendly than one alone. She had pegged them as Wall Street or corporate law. Well, she decided, eyeing him now in the otherwise unoccupied elevator, this is cold, callous New York. What do you expect?

Today the young man stared back. He began to stare at her grocery bags which she had placed next to her. And he was also staring, less openly, at her slightly protruding belly, which was now straining through her regular clothes. She was definitely beginning to show.

"Let me help you with those," he said.

"I can manage."

"Of course you can, but I'd like to help you." He was wearing his exercise suit, and his face was flushed and boyish.

She smiled. "Okay." She held the door while he stepped out with her groceries. "I live on this floor, too."

"I know," he said. "I know when you moved in."

"Ah . . . then you will understand why my apartment is still bare. I sleep on the window seat. I'm beginning to like it. Nothing to clutter up my space. Nothing to dust or trip over . . . or to have cleaned or shampooed. Nice bare space."

"Aha," he sighed when she opened the door. He stepped back and viewed the room. "Cluttered house, cluttered mind, I always say."

She smiled again. "Like it?"

"It looks . . . let me see"—he rubbed his chin—"we can call it Monastery Modern. The look is . . . frugal. As if someone is doing penance."

"How do you know all that? Are you a decorator?"

"No. I'm a partner in a small advertising agency and one of our clients manufactures pillow furniture . . . those stuffed, cuddly squares that snap together to make beds or chairs or whatever. He'd have you think that's all you'll ever need."

"Sounds great. Where can I buy some?"

"That's for me to know and for you to find out . . . unless, of course, you'd care to join me for a hamburger and a beer?"

He took her to Friar Peter's, an overly decorated Third Avenue pub. When they were seated across from each other, she stared at him and he didn't flinch or look uncomfortable. She decided he looked like Tony Perkins. He was the first person she had socialized with outside of work in six weeks.

"Now," he said, looking over the huge menu, "let me caution you. The DeLuxe burger is not really deLuxe even though it costs more. It comes with bacon which they must prepare a few weeks in advance. It's tough and chewy. Whereas the humble, down-home burger is delectable and comes with everything except the fancy name *and* the bacon, which you don't want anyway."

"Don't you ever get serious?" She really didn't care if he did or not.

"Of course. I'm going to get serious right now and ask why you're pregnant when there's obviously no delighted daddy waiting in the wings." He waited to see if she was offended. "I'm not trying to be uncouth, but it's a mystery to me why a great-looking woman like yourself would be in such a predicament."

"Why do you want to get involved?"

"Because we live in the same building, the same floor as it happens, and I'll probably bump into you dozens of times. Each time I'll worry about what you're going to do when the baby arrives. Who will take care of you? If you will fill me in now, I'll be able to think about other things when we meet. We can begin with a clean slate, so to speak."

"If I tell you, what's in it for me?" She grinned into his warm brown eyes. She would tell him anything.

"Well . . ." He appeared to be thinking. "It gets pretty lonely at holiday time. Spooky. We might need each other. We could have . . . uh . . . an alliance of convenience. The French have a word for it, but it usually implies marriage which, I can say, is of no interest to us at the moment." His tone grew serious. "Since our hearts are busy elsewhere, we will have an alliance of convenience."

"Okay," she said heartily. "I need a friend." They shook hands over their beers, and he said, "David Laver, here," and she said, "Miranda Lesley, here."

They got into the habit of seeing each other a couple of times a week, usually on the weekends. She cooked for him, mostly omelettes, perhaps a chicken on Sunday. He cooked for her, Chinese food brought in from outside and served on exquisite china which he claimed he had stolen from his mother. He also said that his mother deserved to have it stolen, but that's all he would divulge.

When he did talk about his past, which was almost never, it was with black humor. "My sister Cynthia is so fucked up, she has razor blades in her cunt. And she was the one my mother loved best."

In reality it was a middle class Jewish story with a few original twists and turns. His father had owned a pharmacy in New Hyde Park. His mother filled the textbook profile of the maternal Jew for the first five years of his life. Then, quixotically, she had drifted into fanaticism. She had to have things her way, especially things that concerned her children. His sister had emerged from this domineering tyrant, a thin, nervous woman whose mouth was so taut, it created a tight, white ring when she spoke.

David, on the other hand, was soft and relaxed. From birth he had radiated self-assurance, but only in later life did he admit that the calm was only skin-deep.

Miranda was now working full time in Barbara's apartment which was in the East Sixties and wrapped around Park Avenue. It was a triplex with a grand, sweeping staircase that began in a marble foyer and ended in a turret-like third floor that quickly became Miranda's favorite spot. It was not as sumptuous as the red-silk-covered walls of the first two floors, but the views were breathtaking and the wicker and chintz suited her more than velvet and ormolu.

She found it difficult to believe that anything enclosed by an ordinary building on the streets of New York could be so grand. The kitchen alone could have held her entire apartment. Footsteps made no sound on the thick Oriental carpets. Barbara had doubled her salary with the excuse that she was now doing executive work, and Miranda happily stashed some of it away but also indulged herself with luxuries, feeling there was more where that was coming from.

The work she did seemed more like play. She placed calls to important people by placing cards into a sleek console with a telephone receiver. She was always answered with friendliness and consideration. She kept meticulous records of Barbara's social life—where she went, what was served, how it tasted, and what gift was sent the following morning. She was surprised and chilled by the swiftness with which Barbara discarded bores and climbers. There were certain invitations she never intended to return, and to these she sent elaborate gifts. Miranda knew the more elaborate the ''thank you'' gift, the less likely it was for the recipient ever to be invited in return.

Callous as it seemed, Miranda secretly admired Barbara's single-mindedness in getting her life to work perfectly. She seized opportunity as she had seized Miranda, and she used everything efficiently.

Barbara's friends, all past child-bearing age and coping with children who had either not married or refused to have children, outdid themselves in coddling Miranda. They wanted to have a hand in a baby that had no father to close up the familial triangle. Several had offered safe havens after the baby arrived. At the very least she was the recipient of the most elegant castoffs. Hardly a day passed that Barbara or one of her friends didn't show up with a hardly worn item of clothing that had cost as much as she earned in a month. When she ceased being pregnant, she would be the best-dressed woman in New York.

At twelve thirty precisely each day one of the smiling Orientals on the house staff padded in with her lunch, after which she napped in a wicker chaise, snuggled into a patchwork quilt against the air conditioning. Before she left each evening, she atomized a dozen hanging plants. The pace was mesmerizing.

It was not a perfect life, but it was civilized. She would survive in style until the baby came.

Chapter 10

THE LAST FEW DAYS OF MAY WERE A LES-
son to Sara in the antic quality of life.
Three weeks earlier the bad news was coming in the windows, and
then two events (within days of each other) completely turned her
around again. Her dearest friend was now part of her life and living
down the road, if you could use such a phrase to describe the thirty-
odd-acre Van Druten estate. The day following her luncheon with
Natalie she had received a call from Jane Seymour.

"Could you come in, please? We have some work." Jane's voice
was evasive.

"You said you hired someone permanently." She was delighted to
hear from Jane but not eager to show it.

"Well . . . uh . . . this is something else."

"I won't be a yo-yo for that emaciated loony." There was a
long silence. Jane said nothing. "What kind of work?"

She could hear Jane take a deep breath. "Do you promise not to
breathe a word?"

"Of course, what's wrong?"

"Who said anything was wrong. Bill Waring asked me to get in touch with you."

She felt her stomach collapse. "What does he want?" He had been so snotty in the restaurant. Now that he wanted her, for whatever reason, she wanted to resist.

"How the hell should I know. He just said to get that young woman, Sara, the one that does the captions, on the phone and to tell him when you could come in so he'd be there. When can you come in?"

"Tomorrow," said Sara lamely.

She changed her outfit three times the following morning and was still not satisfied. If she delayed any longer, she'd be late. In desperation she chose a wraparound dress made of thin, clingy material. Her nipples stuck out an inch ahead of her. It occurred to her that he would mistake her intentions. Once in the car and heading for the expressway she was sorry she had worn it. The dress was too obvious, too sexy, too everything. It was a dress that said, "Fuck Me." She was appalled and at the same time oddly expectant.

"I'd like you to do a piece for us," he said when she came in and sat down in the chair next to his desk.

"Suppose it's rejected again? What makes you think she'd like this one any better?" She sounded resentful and hated it.

"You'll receive a three-hundred-dollar kill fee. Is that acceptable?" He refused to be baited and she felt unsure of herself. She felt young and dumb, but mostly she felt inexperienced in the ways that women deal with men.

"Yes. It's acceptable."

"Good. Now this is what I have in mind." He leaned back and put his feet on a corner of his desk. "A lot of women now are faced with the emotional upheaval of having a husband fired or furloughed. It's humiliating no matter what fancy name they give it. But worse than having your husband fired or furloughed or laid off is having your husband defeated politically. How does a political wife cope when her husband loses an election? I'm looking for something from the gut. . . . Did he cry? We all assume she cried, but did he? Did she resent all the adulation and press attention he got and now feels the tiniest bit triumphant—now that he's dumped? After all she sees the guy in his underwear. She hears the idealistic speech a hundred times.'' Sara stared at him, trying to look serious and professional but feeling tense and guarded. Could he see how nervous she was? ''Most men,'' Bill Waring continued, ''lose self-esteem when they're fired because they have no place to go in the morning, but it's worse for the politico. Imagine the press hanging on your every word for weeks and then one morning nobody cares except the woman facing you at the breakfast table. Is she sympathetic? Or does she turn on him, too?'' He paused. ''Well, do you want to do it?''

''Oh, yes. Yes! Do you have someone in mind?''

''The congressman's wife . . . Mrs. Oliver Martin. After twelve years in the Congress he ran for the mayoralty and lost in the primaries. They have a suite at one of the residential hotels on Park Avenue. Jane will know who to call for the address.''

Before she left, Sara got a good look at his face and decided what she liked most about him. It was his eyes.

Mrs. Oliver Martin had a suite at the Park Lane, a posh residential hotel. Sara was surprised that a congressman's wife could afford such opulence, seeing as their salaries were so paltry.

''Do you live here all the time?'' she asked the thin, pallid woman who greeted her in the impersonally furnished parlor of what looked to be a three-room suite.

''We have a regular apartment, but Oliver . . . it's hard to conduct a campaign from your own apartment . . . there are intruders, crank calls . . . people can be vicious.'' She looked frightened, as if someone had been vicious to her that very morning. ''We'll be moving out in a day or two.''

Sara could see traces of what must have been a beautiful face gone pale and harried from too many exhausting days and too many hurried dinners. Then she saw Mrs. Martin's shaking hands and realized it wasn't just the campaign trail that had made her look like that. The lady had tremors. Was it drugs or liquor?

''Was it a blow when Congressman Martin lost the nomination,'' Sara paused before finishing the sentence, hoping to catch a telling reaction, ''. . . or was it a relief?''

Mrs. Martin laughed a hollow laugh which could have meant anything.

''What is the first thing you remember feeling?''

"The first thing was . . . that I could sleep late in the morning and maybe just sit around in my bathrobe . . . not put on any makeup . . . And poor Ollie was so exhausted, I think he didn't have any immediate anguish . . . it's so exhausting, no one can guess . . ." her voice trailed off. ~nd she looked vague and helpless. "Would you like a brandy, my ʳ ʳ?" she asked.

"No, thank you," said Sara. ʳ ʲ it was liquor.

Mrs. Martin went to a decanter and poured herself half a glass of brandy. Sara was not aware of her drinking it, but when she thought to look it was almost empty. The lady had learned to drink when no one was looking.

"What else are you grateful for? I mean after the rest and the regular meals have restored you. What then? How does it affect your relationship at home? Was he angry with himself for not being more effective? Were you angry with him? Had you given him advice he didn't take? What were your feelings?"

She looked at Sara confidentially. "I had to hide my feelings for such a long time, because the aides don't want the little woman interfering. I had ideas, of course, good ones, but a candidate is like a child star in the hands of promoters. There is a brain trust that moves him from place to place and decides what he should or shouldn't say. What he should or shouldn't do." She looked like she was about to cry, and Sara moved closer and wanted to take her hand and soothe her and tell her that no one was going to scare her anymore. But Mrs. Martin was using both of her hands to hold her brandy glass.

"Does he turn to you after it's over? Do you move in and comfort him?"

"It's not easy. You've been apart so much. A strangeness sets in. You don't equate the man you see on the evening news with the man you knew in high school. He gets further and further away from you and . . . and . . . you find other ways of consoling yourself."

"When the aides are gone and he's all alone," Sara persisted, "doesn't he need you then?"

She began to laugh. "You've read all those stories of how Jack Kennedy shared his decisions with Jackie. Ha, ha. In the loneliness of the night they turn to their wives for solace and comfort. Ha, ha. That's the old American apple pie machine at work. They seldom turn to their wives, my dear." She looked suddenly sober. "They often turn to someone else."

"And what about the wife?" Sara whispered.

"The wife . . . finds amusements." Mrs. Martin was staring at her in an odd way. Her eyes were clouded over and her second glass of brandy was empty. She reached over and placed her hand firmly on Sara's breast. "You're so young. You haven't had to find . . . other ways." It was over so quickly, Sara wasn't sure it had happened, but still she wouldn't have done anything to hurt this woman anymore. As a matter of fact, she felt a kinship with her and wanted to tell her of her own dilemma, a dilemma she hadn't known she had until that moment. Suppose you are lovesick for someone who isn't lovesick over you, she wanted to ask?

She gathered her notes. "One last question . . . what do you do to cheer yourself up. When things are looking so gloomy, what cheers you up?"

"Oh, that's easy," said Mrs. Martin with the brightest smile she'd shown all afternoon. "I go roller-skating. I love it more than anything."

Sara thanked her, determined to leave her with some dignity. "Do you have any background material on yourself and the congressman?"

"Sure. There's a stack of press kits over on that table by the door. They'll tell you where we were born, where we want to be buried, and everything in between. Are you going to write all this?" She waved her hand to indicate the sofa where they had been sitting.

"No," said Sara. "I'm going to write about how a congressional wife helps her husband keep his self-esteem when the phone stops ringing. You'll be an inspiration to all the women with men out of work." Sara smiled reassuringly.

"Thank you, my dear." Sara held her thin, pale hand for a moment and left.

It was one of Barbara Lancia's smaller parties. Just twenty people. But the "right" twenty, Barbara had said. She had also said that an invitation to one of her parties was as good as winning the lottery.

"Why?" asked Miranda. "Why are your parties better than anyone else's parties?"

"I run the best salon in New York. On Sunday evenings I have my Sunday evening group which includes a managing editor from the *Times,* an anchorman from CBS, and a top editor from one of the major publishing houses. Naturally every writer or actress or producer, aspiring or otherwise, wants access to these people.''

Miranda knew this to be so. If anything Barbara was being modest. It took more than money to create an attraction in New York. Barbara had something of the bully in her and people responded.

"What's your secret?'' Miranda was fascinated by the certainty with which Barbara planned the smallest details.

"I serve simple but expensive food. I don't let them drink more than one cocktail before dinner or else they ramble and bore each other. After dinner I let them watch television.'' Miranda smiled. "Oh, very important . . . .'' added Barbara, "never invite more than one celebrity in any field. There's nothing worse than having two anchormen or two Broadway actresses waiting stiffly for homage from the rest of us.''

"That's not all,'' said Miranda. "I've heard you say that to be really successful a party has to have a good portion of nobodies. Why do you need nobodies?''

Barbara's sigh came from her feet and implied volumes. "You are so naive, Miranda. For people who have made it there's nothing worse than going to a social event where everyone is on an equal footing. They lose their celebrity status. Nobodies allow the stars to shine.''

The first guests were arranging themselves around the windows and fireplace. They inspected the paintings and picked up porcelains from small tables. Miranda knew they were nervous and self-conscious, wondering if they belonged in this rarefied atmosphere. Beyond that there was the anxiety of wondering if they would be asked again. They had already begun to miss what hadn't yet been experienced. An eager young man in a gray flannel suit and with nervous eyes came purposefully toward her. "Hello, I'm Jeffrey Selwyn, ABC News.''

"I beg your pardon?''

"ABC News. I'm on the nightly news.''

"I'm sorry.'' She didn't want to embarrass him. "I don't watch the news. Are you an anchorman?''

He looked disappointed. "How could I be an anchorman? There's only one anchorman. I'm a street reporter. I'm the guy who asks the bereaved wife if she wants revenge on her husband's killer.''

She had always thought reporters who did that despicable, but she didn't tell him. As part of the hired help it was not her place to insult the guests.

"Excuse me," she said. "I think Barbara wants me to circulate or I won't get my full pay." He looked puzzled and she left, smiling to herself.

Barbara Lancia approached her with a man who looked vaguely familiar. "Miranda, this is the most important man here tonight, but the only person he wants to meet is you. . . . Bradley Gifford . . . Miranda . . ."

"That man," said Miranda, pointing to the news reporter, "works on the evening news. I don't do anything."

"That's a relief," said Bradley Gifford. He was handsome in the way well-cared-for men are handsome. His hair and clothes were well cut, and although overweight he carried himself gracefully. His eyes were the color of an overcast sky and unwavering. He was not the sort of man you would speak to unless he spoke to you first. "Barbara," he said, taking Miranda's hand, "am I seated next to this shiftless woman for dinner?"

"Of course."

"Good. Maybe she'll ask me about *my* career and talk about *my* life plan. All I seem to meet are corporate women who know precisely what their moment-to-moment goals will be for the next ten years. It makes me feel absolutely slovenly. I don't know what I'm going to be doing tomorrow."

Miranda smiled, aware of his look of admiration. Barbara had dressed her carefully, like a favorite doll, in off-white, satin lounging pajamas that clung to her breasts and buttocks and flowed over the rest of her body. She loved the feeling of the material against her skin and decided she was exuberant for the first time since Sanche had left. The rich, if not entirely reliable, certainly knew how to make a person feel good.

"Miranda," said Bradley, pronouncing every syllable, "I want you to stick to me like glue." An overweight television actress was coming toward them. "That woman is going to ask me for a job, and I don't want to give her one."

"Bradley, darling," said the woman, "I hear you're producing again . . . a musical of *Jane Eyre*. A brilliant thought . . . and I want a part in it."

"Only in the talking stages, Sylvia."

"Don't lie to me. Linda Evelyn has a part. She told me so."

"I don't cast, Sylvia. I'm only the money man."

"Oh, God," said the woman, "if only someone in this business told the truth. Nobody tells the truth."

"The truth is often painful," replied Bradley dryly.

"Not as painful as evasion, no one likes to be evaded." Miranda had to agree with her. Evasion, as she had learned from Sanche, was the worst.

"All right, everybody," Barbara swept down on them, "if we don't start eating immediately, we'll miss the Streisand special."

The actress strode away in the direction of the dining room, but Bradley continued to look dismayed. "Barbara promised not to have any tiresome people here," he said. "Now why would she invite a woman like that?"

"What's wrong with her?" asked Miranda, who considered the woman brave and spunky to have told Bradley what she did.

"She's a two-bit actress and Barbara's in a bigger league."

"But I'm not anybody. Why am I here?"

"You're a looker," he said matter-of-factly. When he saw that she was serious, his expression changed. "That's no mystery. Powerful men like to be surrounded by beautiful women."

"You mean I'm part of the amenities . . . like the flowers or the air freshener?"

"I doubt that Barbara has any need of air freshener. And no, you're not an amenity either. Actually, my dear," he said with mock seriousness, "you're more like dessert."

The remark made her uneasy. There was a connection she was not making and it annoyed her. She didn't delude herself that Barbara's interest in her went further than liking an employee who was reliable and attractive to have around. So why was she a guest at this special party? Bradley Gifford, too, was being overly solicitous, considering that *he* was the celebrity.

At everyone's place at the table there was an elaborately wrapped favor. A small packet of Lancia cosmetics for the ladies, including lipstick, perfume, and facial soap, in a simulated leather pouch that resembled a jewelry wrap. For the men there was a similar packet filled with Lancia pour l'homme preparations. Miranda noticed that the familiar pouch which she herself had placed around the table was missing from her place. Instead there was a small, unwrapped box from Tiffany's. She sat down, opened it, and lifted out a pair of fat, gold hoop earrings, simple and shiny. A card underneath said: "You are a find, Miranda."

It was Barbara's way of thanking her for the long hours spent perfecting the party arrangements. She often gave gifts for work well done. In her case, however, the earrings served to remind her that she was spending too much time on Barbara's life and not enough on her own.

"Don't you like your present?" Bradley was nudging her arm.

"No . . . yes . . . I don't know." I feel obligated, she thought.

He took the hoops into his hands. "Would you like to put them on? I'll help you." He placed the hoops on her ears and let his hands linger on her cheeks. Either by design or accident his hand also pressed on her breast on the way up and on the way down. She decided to say nothing. It was not unpleasant. The man was educated, witty, and she liked the way he smelled. She had also had too much wine before dinner.

After dinner, true to her word, Barbara called everyone into a room with a giant television screen and rows of upholstered swivel chairs. In one corner a man in spotless chef's whites was dispensing espresso from a large machine. Another man in a dark suit was ready to serve one of fourteen brandies. When everyone was seated in the semidarkness, Barbara took Miranda aside.

"I want you to take Bradley home. He doesn't handle liquor well, and I want him out before he makes a fool of himself and ruins the evening for everyone. See that he gets safely into his apartment, will you?"

Miranda was glad for the excuse to go home, her back had begun to ache. Bradley didn't appear as intoxicated as Barbara claimed but was quite willing to be taken home.

"Would you like to come home with me now," she said, smiling.

"Yes, mommy," he answered.

The doorman hailed a cab, and within minutes they were at his apartment in River House and he was fitting the key in the door.

The room was breathtakingly simple with carpeted platforms as the only furniture. The walls were lacquered white. Pristine compartments hid the paraphernalia of living. The lamps were made of cold chrome on cold marble bases. It was not a room for a shy person.

"Doesn't it give you a complex?" She sat gingerly on one of the platforms, surprised at how soft and comfortable it was. There was foam rubber under the carpeting. Seeing as the rich had such skinny behinds, it was great foresight to pad the seating platforms.

"There's a platform for everything," he said, ". . . eating, sleeping, sitting . . . whatever . . . except elimination. That I do in a more or less conventional bathroom lined with mirror tiles. Whenever I take a crap, thirty-two Bradley Giffords smile back at me." He led her to a balcony and left her contemplating the twinkling lights of Manhattan. "I'll be right back."

She felt exhausted and wanted nothing more than to lie down in her own slab of foam. Her handbag was on the platform nearest the door. She would leave quietly. Just then he walked back into the room stark naked and turned out all the lights.

"Bradley, the lights . . . what happened?" She felt his hands busy under her tunic.

"I knew you'd have tits," he said hoarsely. "Real tits, Jesus, I'm crazy about tits. Get this stuff off. I want to suck you for an hour. Standing up just like this while they're hanging."

She had been set up from the start. The party, the wining, and dining . . . perhaps the entire job for all she knew, had been geared to . . . *this*. She felt seriously sick to her stomach and thought of the beautiful carpeting.

He had let her go and gone to switch on the lights. His plump belly shook as he walked.

"Get undressed."

"I'm going home."

"You don't know why you came here?"

"To bring you home."

"You're supposed to service me," he said sarcastically. She stared at him in disbelief. "That's right. Service me. You have to take care of my cock." He took the now distended penis into his plump hand. "You have to kiss it or lick it or pump it or sit on it. Whatever it takes."

She had been angry, but now the look on his face frightened her.

Suppose he hit her? Suppose he hit her in the stomach? He looked greedy and petulant.

"Come on, I'll get you hot first." He thrust his hand up her legs and probed with his fingers. Then, impatient, he went inside the elastic of her pants, delving deeper, searching through her underpants for an opening. He found her pubic hair, yanked it harshly, and then began strumming her clitoris. "I'll make you good and hot," he said.

She blinked back tears. She was as angry as she had been in her life. Barbara's parties were famous . . . each guest got everything his heart desired, including a willing partner to take home.

She pushed him away with all her strength. He was panting and groping for her breasts, now loose from the thin, shapeless brassiere. He pushed up her tunic and began to suck noisily. Then he stepped back and looked at her in amazement.

"There's something in it! It's dripping liquid. Jesus, there's milk in them!"

"That's because I'm pregnant, you shithead," she shouted in contempt, but he wasn't listening.

"I've never had that before." He was incredulous, and the look of greed on his face turned to frenzy. She took the moment to straighten her clothes and walk away from him. "Didn't she tell you I was pregnant?"

"What are you so asstight about? You're having a good time. Your pussy's wet as can be." It was true and it made her all the more furious. She felt betrayed by her own body.

"I decide who makes love to me. Not anybody else."

"Who would you prefer to fuck you if not me? You got someone else in mind? Tell me about it. What does he do to you? There are dozens of women who would give anything to fuck me."

"To get something from you," she shouted. "They only fuck you to get something."

"Not necessarily." His calmness was infuriating. "But is that it? You want something? Money?" He grabbed her breast again. "Name your price, baby, just let me suck the milk." He went down on his knees and pressed his face against her thighs. "Breast feed me, mama. Please."

Her hands felt cold and there was a metallic taste in her mouth. He was not going to let go. She could see little pads of fat hanging over his buttocks. Looking down on him, a bald spot was visible with hair artfully styled to cover it. She struggled against him, but he pulled her down with little effort. There was no resisting.

"No . . . no." She struggled harder, but he was suffocating her, pressing too hard against her stomach. He was pressing her with his head much too hard. "No . . . please, the baby . . . don't."

"Get them out." His voice was cold and distorted. She stopped resisting and let him do what he wanted. Through the jumble of thoughts she remembered a time before St. Mildred's, before she was quite seven. Two little boys had walked her home from school. Rain or shine, they taunted her with the same verse each day. They considered themselves very clever for saying it and were always in a frenzy of excitement after the first or second line. It played itself over and over in her head.

> Two, four, six, eight.
> Who do we appreciate?
> Miranda! Miranda!
> Why? Why?
> She's starting to die.
> When? When?
> Tonight at ten.
> Where? Where?
> In the electric chair.
> Pull down her underpants and
> See what's there.

She often wondered why in their innocence the boys had coupled death with sex and their curiosity about what was in her underpants. Were they two sides of the same coin? Sex certainly had not been a joyful experience in her life. Bob Paxton had been clinical, like a mortician preparing a body. Sanche was self-engrossed, never speaking, twisting and turning her to suit himself, then turning away when he was finished. And now . . .

She couldn't remember how long it went on, only that at some point he said, "Jesus, they're bleeding." After that he straddled her, putting his full weight on her stomach, and placed his penis between her breasts. He pushed them together until they smothered his engorged organ. Then, unable to achieve the friction he wanted, he began to jab them with strong random thrusts. *He's trying to fuck my breasts,* she thought dimly, feeling a great distance from her body, but he won't be able to. Afraid of what would happen next, she tried to take his penis into her hands, away from her wounded nipples. It would be a relief if he just placed it in her vagina. He struggled. "Oh, no," he said, "I don't want your pussy. I want these."

Again he straddled her and squeezed her breasts against himself until she could stand the pain no longer. She remembered being sick all over the rug and feeling very, very cold. After a long while she got up and he was nowhere in sight. Her nipples were bloody. When she rolled the tunic over them, the pain was excruciating. Blood began to seep through the soft satin, and she thought of Barbara Lancia and how carefully she had dressed her that evening. She collected her handbag and found the bathroom. She washed her face and turned to the wall of mirrors. Thirty-two pairs of vacant, unbelieving eyes stared back at her accusingly. In some terrible way she could never understand, it was her fault.

When she reached her apartment, she was dumbly happy to see David Laver's lights streaming under his door and rapped lightly.

"What the hell happened . . . oh, my God, what happened to you?" He all but carried her to a couch and she began to cry. He cradled her in his arms and soothed her, but she couldn't stop crying.

When she could talk again, she said, "David, I want the baby's father to marry me." She hiccoughed between words. "I want him to want this baby as much as I do. I want to live happily ever after."

He got up and began to pace the room. "Oh, shit, piss, fuck, Miranda, the guy's not going to marry you. Grow up, for God's sake."

She sat up pale and startled. "Why not? What's wrong with me? Aren't I attractive?" David's outburst frightened her.

"Of course you're attractive, but the guy's not buying it. He's buying something else right now. Forget him." He stuck his hands in his pockets and stared out the window. "I want you to come and work for us, Miranda. Come and work for us until the baby comes. We'll figure out something to do." He turned to face her. "What can you do?"

"At the last job," she said sarcastically, "they made me breast feed a fifty-five-year-old man. He offered me any amount of money if I'd just let him suck the milk out."

"You're kidding . . . there's milk in them?"

"Not real milk"—the horror of the night was beginning to recede—"something sticky."

"How does it taste?"

"How the hell should I know?" She began to laugh and cry at the same time. "This guy loved it."

"I hope you charged him enough to live comfortably for several months."

"He did it for nothing." She was sober again.

"Why for nothing?"

"Because," she said, lowering her eyes, "I was afraid he would kill us. The baby and me. . . . David"—she looked more innocent than he had ever seen her—"if he just violated my breasts, is it still rape?"

He shook his head mystified. This was a stray cat. He happened to like cats. He wanted very much to help her. He decided when she was feeling better, he'd make sure she accepted his offer. She would need a new job, that was for sure. He looked over at Miranda. She was asleep, curled up against him. He put her down, straightened her fancy pajamas, and covered her with a quilt. A stray cat, he thought. A beautiful stray cat. What would happen if he weren't around to take care of her? Suppose she were all alone? He shuddered at the thought.

Chapter 11

"IT TOOK YOU LONG ENOUGH," SAID CORA when Sam finally strolled into Haas headquarters. She twitched her nose as if something didn't sit quite right with her.

Natalie was so glad to see him, she forgot her frustrations of the last few days.

"Can I take you both to lunch?" he asked.

"You may take Natalie to lunch," said Cora. "I'm only allowed Perrier and cottage cheese, and the chauffeur brings it precisely at one. Then I'm going to see the new show at the Whitney, so don't take off the whole afternoon. You may go and play until two and then I expect Natalie back. And . . ." she looked sternly at Sam, ". . . I expect her back in a good mood."

Sam smiled and rolled his eyes to heaven. When they were outside he asked, "Do you suppose Cora wants us to sleep together?"

"Looks that way, doesn't it?"

"Isn't she your husband's friend?"

"I suppose. But Cora gets bored. At her age she must have reached some conclusions about life. It must be complicated to sort things out and decide what's really moral and what isn't. She seems to enjoy playing matchmaker. Perhaps she hasn't thought it out beyond that.''

"And you . . . have you thought it out beyond that?''

"I wanted to hear from you. I wanted you to be as . . . shaken as I.'' Even though she tried, it still came out an accusation.

"Were you shaken?''

She stopped dead on the street and a man behind her cursed. She pulled him to the edge of the sidewalk. "I went home with you.''

"That seems to be a big point with you, but in love . . . in love . . . sex isn't everything.''

"What is everything in love?''

"A sense of trust. Commitment to each other.''

She began to walk again. She didn't trust him, and she certainly didn't feel that he had a sense of commitment to her. If he was so crazy about her, how could he wait a week to call?

The conversation had turned solemn and she didn't want that. She didn't want to pout. "Does that mean we can't go to your place and make love?'' she asked cheerfully.

"Is that what you want?''

"Yes.''

"Don't you want to have lunch first?''

"You don't want to go.'' Her smile wilted.

"Of course I want to go. Let's go.'' They were walking past St. Patrick's Cathedral, and he pulled her up a few steps and kissed her. His eyes held hers. "I want to do something to you right now. Right here in front of St. Patrick's.''

"Sister Francisca would turn over in her grave,'' said Natalie, but she, too, didn't want to wait.

Once inside the apartment, however, they stood in the middle of the room feeling awkward and looking around. It was a pleasant room, sparsely furnished and filled with colorful pillows. Sun streamed in through a large window and Natalie blinked and wondered what to do. Sam sat primly on the sofa, his legs crossed, his fingers drumming nervously on a pillow. He was not at ease, and she sat next to him and burrowed her face into his neck.

"I wish I had known you in grade school,'' he said huskily, "and pulled your pigtails. By the time we were fourteen, I'd have asked you for a date, and by now we'd know everything about each other.

We'd be dynamite wherever we went . . . even in the middle of the day." He stood up. "This place is too goddam sunny. It's too stiff . . . not a good place to go into a clinch." He ran his hands through his hair and looked out the window. "There were many days . . . all I thought about was making love to you." She came and stood next to him, and he tilted her chin and kissed her tenderly on the lips. Then he led her into the bedroom. "Now, tell me," he said as they sat shyly on his sleek modern bed, an upholstered box with a mattress in the middle, "who was Sister Francisca?"

"She was a nun at the school where I went as a child. She never liked me after I won the St. Mildred's day prize."

"Why didn't she like you?"

"There were three of us. She had no use for the other two girls, and I was *non grata* by association."

"What was the prize?"

"Ah . . . it was promises. St. Mildred would see us through our womanly struggles and whatever we touched would be a success."

He smiled at her seriousness. "Yeah . . . and did she keep the bargain? What happened to the other two girls?"

"I just saw one of them recently." She smiled broadly, only now realizing how glad she was that Sara was back in her life. "It seemed as if she hit the jackpot . . . loving husband, beautiful children . . . even a career."

"And . . . ?"

"We were having lunch and a man came into the restaurant. He was an exciting man, the kind that knows how to get exactly what he wants out of people."

"And he wanted to get something out of your friend?"

She looked up at him, surprised that he understood so well. "He wants to get everything out of my friend."

"What about the husband and the kids?"

"I don't know." Natalie was thoughtful. "I really don't know."

"And the other girl? Did you ever hear what happened to her?"

"No. We never did. We do talk about looking her up when we're in the city, but we always forget. Miranda"—she tried to reconstruct Miranda's face—"Miranda was . . . unusual, to say the least. Beautiful in her own way . . . and so fearless. Absolutely fearless. Of all of us Miranda really needed St. Mildred's promises."

"Why don't you look her number up right now?"

"Right now?" She saw that he was more relaxed and showed none of the strain he had felt before.

"Sure." He took the directory from under a small table and began flipping the pages. "What's her last name?"

"Lesley. Miranda Lesley."

He found it right away. "It just says M. Lesley, but it's the only M. Lesley. Why don't you give her a call?"

"Not now. It might be awkward."

"Please. I'm fascinated by the girls of St. Mildred's."

"Oh, you're not. You're teasing."

"Maybe. Maybe not. Give fearless Miranda a call."

She dialed the number, making faces between digits to show she didn't think it was a good idea. The phone rang five times, but there was no answer and she hung up.

"Cora wants us back in half an hour."

"I know." He was studying her face as if to memorize it and moving slowly.

She liked the room which seemed to enclose them. She liked the fact that they were chatting idly as if they had all the time in the world. As if they were friends and shared a life. She knew, too, that it would make parting all the more painful.

He had to go to Boston with his play for a week, and even though she knew she wouldn't see him, she was at Haas headquarters at nine every morning. Her nights were restless, filled with dream images that left her confused and eager to get out into the clean, early summer sunshine. I'm out all day, she thought wryly, and my husband is out all night. But this thought also filled her with fear. Was Alden's going out at night her fault?

"Does Mr. Van Druten appear pale to you, Mr. Simmons?" she had asked the valet. He knew that she meant more than that and his eyes flickered. While he considered women in general lazy and needlessly secretive, he was not totally against her, especially since her pregnancy had become obvious.

"Possibly he loses a lot of his body salts when he runs." His eyes were noncommittal. He wasn't ready to confide in her.

There were many times when she found Alden sitting alone in his dressing room wearing his athletic shorts and shoes. She spoke to him, but he didn't answer. If his friends or anyone else noticed his extreme aloofness, his secrecy, they chose to remain silent. The servants would never mention it. They seemed determined to punish her, as if she had done something unforgivable to them. She badly needed someone to confide in, but there was no one.

Her father had had a stroke and no longer spoke. She often sat with him for hours, shooing the nurse away. Celine was never there. Sometimes she thought of her body, firm and supple as if it had been kept on ice all these years. There was no mark on her body even now with the baby growing inside it. It was such a waste. Alden had stopped seeing. He had stopped seeing everything. She lived now just to see Sam.

At the end of the week, unexpectedly, Sam came through the door of Haas headquarters grinning wildly.

"You're supposed to be in Boston," she said and then quickly looked at Cora.

"I've got a day off and I came home to pick up my mail and . . . well . . ." he looked from Natalie to Cora ". . . has anybody had lunch?"

Cora was staring at him as if he were an apparition. He was freshly shaved, crisp and pressed, and it gave her physical pleasure to look at him. "What makes you think you can just get us at the last minute?" she asked haughtily.

"Oh. You have plans?"

"Certainly. With my hairdresser. He's a little too graceful, but at my age you can't be choosey." She looked from Natalie to Sam.

"And you?" Sam turned to Natalie.

"I can go at one," she answered, trying to appear calm.

"Why don't you get a head start, dear," said Cora. "We can leave the place locked up for half an hour and hope Mr. Sorbentino doesn't drop by." She giggled. "It wouldn't surprise me if he slapped us around and called us names." She giggled again. "I'm scared to death of him." She got up and forced Natalie out of her chair. "Well . . . go ahead. Shoo."

They walked out into the sunshine of Madison Avenue to Fifty-third Street. He was tall and striking and everyone who passed stared at him. He put his arm under hers in a gesture of protection that touched her and seemed to come naturally to him. He liked women. She could see his mother explaining how he must always behave well toward women and protect them. "Now Sam, you hold a woman's arm when you take her through the streets. No telling what could happen to her."

When they were seated in the restaurant, he ran his fingers through his hair. "I have a lot to tell you, and I've got to talk fast because there's only an hour before I'm due at CBS. I've had a job offer to host a series of documentaries." He waited for her to speak, but she just stared at him. "If I take it, it will mean twenty-six weeks of steady work, plus the play which is sure to come into New York. The money's great. And, see . . . well, it's the first time I've had another job before finishing the job I was on."

"The job at the network sounds wonderful." It was clear he wasn't going to say anymore until she spoke. She felt disappointed that his plans were so personal. They had nothing to do with her. The luncheon was just to share his good news. He had really come down from Boston to meet with CBS.

He was suddenly agitated and grabbed her hand and held it tightly. "Don't you understand why I'm telling you all this?" She shook her head. "I've been thinking of a way to be with you. Part of this move has to do with us. With us . . . Natalie, don't you understand?"

She was so relieved, tears began to slide down her cheeks. She nodded dumbly and waited while a waiter took their order. She realized with some difficulty that he was happy because he could tell her he had a more reliable source of income. Now he felt entitled to make plans for them. She was astounded. Money had held him back. He wanted to be able to support her.

Then it occurred to her that he knew nothing about the baby. He was making all these plans without knowing she was carrying Alden's baby. And what was he thinking? Was he expecting her to leave Alden? For the first time she realized how difficult it would be to leave her husband. What would happen to him? He needed someone to look after him . . . someone who knew how unhappy he was . . . someone who cared about him.

But this was not the time to bring that up. She wouldn't take away his triumph. Then, too, perhaps just telling him about the baby would scare him away. Again she thought about Jeremy; his name was on her lips to pass on to his father, but she knew it wasn't the time to bring that up either.

They ate quickly, mostly in silence, adjusting to their discoveries.

When they finished, he paid the bill and walked her part way back to her office.

"I've got to leave you now," he said and held her hands together next to his chest. "I would like to be alone with you for five minutes," he added wistfully. He looked at her with such longing, her chest felt as if it could burst. No one had ever looked at her like that or spoken with so much emotion.

When he was halfway up the block, she realized she hadn't wished him luck or told him about the baby. "Hey . . . hey," she shouted after him, "good luck."

He looked back. "What?"

"Good luck . . . Oh! . . ." She ran to where he stood. "I think you should know . . . well, I'm pregnant. I'm pregnant."

"Don't look at me, lady. I didn't do it." He was smiling at her. "I know you're pregnant."

"How could you know?"

"My dear, growing up in the city streets, a boy learns many things. There's a certain look on a woman's face when she's pregnant."

"What look? You could tell by my face?" She was impressed. "That's incredible."

"Your face and . . . uh . . . one other thing."

"What's that?"

"Well . . . uh . . . I don't want to be indelicate, but you . . . show."

"In the front?" She looked down at herself.

"Yes. And . . . uh . . . in the back . . . a little. You see I know exactly how you used to look."

She put her head next to his chest. "And . . . you don't care?"

"Certainly, I care. I want you to be healthy and have a lovely baby."

"Oh, Sam." She was eager to say his name and placed her arms around him. It was easily the happiest moment of her life.

She returned to the office and was relieved that Cora had not returned to prod her with questions. She wanted to take her happiness and stash it away to be parceled out carefully as she needed it. She could see now how grotesque her life had been these past few years.

In the late afternoon she called Jeremy and was pleased to learn that Charlie was visiting.

"Please come home early tomorrow," he pleaded.

"All right," she said impulsively. "I will. I'll be there in time to have a swim with you if the sun's out."

"What about Dad? Is he coming too?"

"I think so." She realized with a start that she hadn't spoken to Alden for two days.

They said their good-byes, and she stuffed a hundred envelopes and wrote two releases which she hoped would get Haas press coverage for what she called his Subway Raps—he stood by the entrance to the subway during morning rush hour and answered questions. She was cleaning the carbon smudges off her hands when the phone rang.

"Hello," said a husky voice, "this is Sorbentino." She had known it was he. "I'm having a load of books delivered there for Bill to pass out at the subway tomorrow. You gonna be there awhile, or should I come down?"

"I'll stay," she said slowly. "I thought he was going to pass out shopping bags. We have thousands of shopping bags."

"Shopping bags are okay, but this is better. It's a booklet on how to keep from being mugged with a little commercial for our boy between the lines."

She saw right away that the booklet giveaway was an inspired idea, but she wished he wouldn't call Bill Haas "our boy." It made it sound as if she and he were in cahoots.

"You going to the country tonight?" he asked casually. She was surprised that he knew that much about her.

"No."

"Bill and I are at the Plaza having drinks. . . . You're free to join us . . . *after* the books arrive, of course." He said it jokingly, but there was an undercurrent of one-upmanship that annoyed her.

"I don't drink," she said curtly.

"That's a shame," he clucked sympathetically.

For the first time in her life she had a drink when she got home. She gulped down a brandy and asked Eva to run a bath. She would soak herself into a stupor and sleep all her fears away. The call from Sorbentino had changed her mood. She knew there was nothing to be afraid of, but she was afraid anyway, not so much of real events, but of some terrible overall current in her life. Even the idea of happiness with Sam frightened her, and she thought again of the matter with Celine. If he could betray her once, would he do so again?

The next day she didn't return to the office but left immediately for Pheasant Hill and Jeremy, determined to shake her gloom.

She was aware that Sam's play had opened on Thursday, and she drove all over the Island on Friday trying to get a Boston paper to see the reviews. She realized he didn't even know her number in the country, even if he had wanted to call her. She relaxed and enjoyed two beautiful summer days, swimming, walking, and patiently volleying tennis balls with Jeremy. Alden was jovial and also paid special attention to Jeremy, which pleased her. At one point on Sunday they were all three together splashing in the pool, and it struck her that they had never done that before.

It was Tuesday before she saw the reviews which were good for the play and superb for Sam. He called her during the day and said he would probably be home on Thursday. When Thursday came, she washed her hair and wore a new beige-silk pants suit that looked especially nice with her tan. She stayed in the office until six waiting for his call, but it did not come. Finally, disappointed, she left for the country where she spent a restless night. She had a need to see Jeremy and be with him. It was almost as if he made up for his father's less than total commitment to her.

Twice during the night she got up and had a brandy, but it did not help. A little after midnight she went into Jeremy's room and watched him sleep. She traced his features lightly with her fingers. He was a miniature of Sam except that he had never disappointed her. He was more than she had ever expected.

The following morning Dolly knocked at her door with a breakfast tray. *The New York Times* was neatly folded on her tray, and she looked through it casually until she got to the Style and Family pages where there was a set of photographs taken at a party at Sybil's the previous night. It was a birthday party for the female lead of Sam's play. One of the pictures showed him dancing with her. He was holding her very close, his face in her hair. The article said they were inseparable, but she knew how those things went. Reporters often presented as fact, things that were mere conjecture, sometimes outright lies. Yet something inside her believed that Sam was involved with the woman in his arms. Her insides felt brittle, as if they would break at a touch. There was a metallic taste in her mouth.

She had waited for him all day, dressed up like a fool, and he had chosen to go dancing with someone else. The idea that he could hurt her so casually left her trembling.

She thought briefly of the baby who had begun to kick inside her just several days ago. How bad all this must be for him. Surely anything living inside her must feel the terrible hopelessness—and the anger.

The cast of Sam's play took the three o'clock shuttle out of Logan Airport which was due in New York at four. A few minutes into the flight a man in first class began to moan and gasp for air in the throes of a heart attack. The plane circled and the pilot requested permission to land again. It was an hour before they were able to get back in the line of departing planes, and they didn't reach LaGuardia in New York until ten minutes past six.

The phone at Haas headquarters went unanswered. Sam could picture it ringing shrilly in the empty office and cursed softly. How could he reach Natalie? Information was adamant in refusing to give out the Van Drutens' unlisted number. He pleaded, cajoled, and demanded, but the supervisor insisted that only a life or death situation would warrant revealing a nonlisted number and that that decision would have to be made by someone higher up than herself.

Having done all he could, Sam hung up and resigned himself to the situation. Natalie could not help but understand. She must know that he loved her and wanted to be with her, which was all that mattered. Given his business, their life would always be fraught with last minute change of plans and small disappointments. Maybe it was even for the best.

As it happened, it was not for the best. Natalie had made a decision. She opted for the well-being of her unborn child. She was no longer available to Sam, and his repeated efforts to speak to her went unheeded.

Sara's story about Margaret Martin was a masterpiece of invention. It was a touching story and clearly there were no villains.

Jane Seymour liked it and told her to sit tight. She would ask to run it in the November issue. Sara was disappointed that Bill Waring didn't comment on it personally, but then maybe he didn't want to stick his neck out.

A week after completing the story, when she had despaired of ever hearing about it again, Jane called her at home. "Waring loves the piece." This meant absolutely nothing. It was a stock phrase in the magazine business that meant anything from "it stinks but we have nothing else to replace it, so we'll use it" to "it's a decent piece of work." The only other qualitative expression used to describe what a person felt was "it's a piece of shit." Sara was mildly pleased. "Waring loves the piece" was preferable to "it's a piece of shit."

"Oh, yeah," she answered Jane. "If he loved it so much, he certainly kept it to himself."

"He's been away. He just got back to the office today and wants to see you."

Jesus, why didn't you say so! "I can't come in today. Charlie has a doctor's appointment."

"He doesn't want you to come in today. He wants to see you tomorrow."

"Well, I can't . . ."

"For lunch. He never asked me to lunch. Just go, please, and see what he wants. We're all dying to know."

"All right."

She didn't know what to wear. I won't send any hot signals this time, she decided. If I dress carefully, he'll think I care what he thinks. But if I don't dress carefully, he'll think I look awful. Oh, shit. Why do I care what he thinks? I'm a married woman with two children. Why do I want him to think I'm beautiful?

When she wasn't thinking about what to wear, she was rehearsing her reaction when he told her why they couldn't use the piece. Then, cautiously, she rehearsed her reaction when he told her how good it was and why didn't she work for him all the time.

They were to meet at Guillermo's on Forty-ninth Street at one P.M. She wore a linen shirtwaist dress that wrinkled when you looked at it but did not reveal her anatomy in a provocative way. That'll confuse him, she thought. Then she realized he might not give a damn if her anatomy were revealed or not.

The maitre d' became overly solicitous when she mentioned Waring's name and fussed over her until she was seated in a corner banquette at the back of the first section of the long, skinny room.

"A glass of wine?" he asked.

"No. Yes. All right." A glass of wine wouldn't derail her. It might even relax her a little.

She was sipping the wine and munching a carrot stick when he appeared. Her first thought was of how neat he looked and how wrinkled her dress was getting to be. He slid in beside her and motioned to the maitre d' to bring him what she was drinking. A vote of confidence. She felt a little better.

"The piece was good," he said evenly. "It wasn't great, but it was good."

"But . . . ?"

"No buts. We're going to use it."

Relief flooded her face. "Why wasn't it great?"

"You ought to be glad it wasn't great. If it was great, we'd have to scrap it. Magazine articles should be good, not great. Great is for the stage or a book . . . which, by the way, you might also consider. You have a natural style." He paused to take a sip of his wine. "It's wonderful."

She didn't know whether he meant the wine was wonderful or her style. "You mean the wine?"

"Your style is wonderful. The wine is okay."

Wonderful. She had almost missed that.

"What was wrong with the piece?" she asked finally, assuming he had saved the criticism for last.

"Nothing. It was charming."

"I made it all up."

"You made what up?"

"I made it up. Her husband sleeps around and she never has a chance to go near him." Sara looked at his clear eyes focused totally on her. "She made a pass at me. That's where she's at. She calls it her way of entertaining herself."

"Why did you make up any story at all? Why didn't you just tell me?" He took her hand in his.

"I wanted to do it for her. She's pathetic. She drinks a lot, and maybe the story will help her keep her head up among her friends."

"When she made a pass at you . . . did she . . . uh . . . touch you?"

"Yes." She felt herself getting warm and something was happening to him, too. She could feel it in the air between them. She was aware that he was still holding her hand, but she wasn't sure he was aware of it. She knew right then that she would let him do anything he wanted to her, no questions asked.

The waiter came toward them with enormous menus, and he let go of her hand. She was glad to bury her face and not have to talk. She wanted to touch him. She wanted to touch his hand, his cuff, his thigh, anything. She had to hang on to the menu.

"I'll have the sole," he said, and she nodded to indicate the same. What did it matter what she ordered? She wasn't going to taste anything anyway. He appeared to be deep in thought and she didn't want to intrude. When their food came, he ate in silence, smiling at her from time to time. When he was finished, he pushed his plate slightly away and folded his napkin neatly.

"Sara," he said simply but with some emotion, "I want to see more of you. I want us to be together. I'm sure this is not so surprising, is it?"

She looked startled, as if he had told her she should undress before the collected diners. "No," she whispered. Then she worried that he thought it meant she was agreeing to everything, but she could not speak.

"I'm not going to ask you what your situation is at home because that is of no concern to me, although I'm sure it is of concern to you. Suffice to say that I want to be with you as much as possible. I sense that you might feel the same or at least wish to make a try. Don't answer now." He called for the check, touched her cheek lightly with his hand, and rose to leave. She sat there for twenty minutes more, unable to move. She was shaken. A feeling of dread and incomprehensible joy made her lungs feel strained.

She refused to think about what had been said, as if thinking about it would immediately make it so. When she got home, the children were cranky and wanted her to spend some time with them. They wanted to play a card game and she acquiesced, her mind a million miles away. Mrs. Ramirez kept giving her sly, suspicious glances, as if she knew precisely what she was up to. All of a sudden Sara noticed Rachel's chin quivering.

"What's wrong?"

"You're not playing right."

"Yes, I am."

"No, you're not." Her eyes filled with tears. "You're supposed to leave the cards in the middle, not take them to the side."

"You're wrong." She was suddenly exasperated and not up to a confrontation. "This is the way I play it—if you want to play, play it my way."

Rachel gulped, peeled a card from her pile, and thrust it in the center of the table. Then Sara put a card down. Then Rachel, through her tears, gave a little cry of delight and slapped her chubby hand over the card. "Oh, mommy. I saw it first. I did slap Jack."

Sara felt tears well up in her own eyes. She had not been playing slap jack. She had been playing war. Of course you weren't supposed to take the cards until you slapped the jack. She took Rachel in her lap and rocked her back and forth. She had not even done anything yet and she was already going crazy.

Chapter 12

Her second break with Sam brought Natalie new grief and desolation with each passing day. She moped in bed unwashed and refusing food. She could not bear to put him out of her mind. If she put him out of her mind, there would be nothing left for her. But there *was already* nothing left for her because she couldn't forgive him. This reasoning took hold of her head for hours at a time.

On the third day Cora arrived grim and determined.

"Are you sick?" she demanded, arms crossed in front of her.

"No."

"Well, then come along. I've got the car waiting."

"Cora, I'm not going."

"Of course you are. I can't possibly manage the office by myself. We're very busy and getting busier. A shower will do wonders and a strong cup of tea will do the rest." Cora could smell a lovers' quarrel a mile away. Yet she had not been prepared to see Natalie so wasted by it and so bereft. Natalie needed to get back to her routine and put Mr. Johnson in proper perspective. Out of the corner of her eye she noted that Natalie had swung her legs over the side of the bed. "I'll be waiting downstairs," she said softly and left.

Going back to the office did effect a change in Natalie, but not in the way Cora imagined. The possibility that Sam might call or walk in at any moment brought a new emotion. She never knew when he might call. The few times he had, she had been quick enough to avoid speaking to him. There was always a way. She was overcome with anger. She hated him with all her heart and yearned for revenge.

A few days later she found a way to get it.

"Where the fuck is Haas?" said Rudy Sorbentino into the telephone late one afternoon.

"I haven't seen him. He hasn't been here."

"Yeah . . . well you tell him where the hell was he when the guy from *Time* came to interview him! I had to double-talk my ass off."

She knew it was useless to be offended. In Rudy's mind they were all of a kind with himself on the other side, tolerant but stern. He considered Bill Haas naive and childish, but as he often said, not any more childish than those asses who were already on Capitol Hill. What he could not stand was sloppiness, and that included not keeping appointments which he had painstakingly set up. He was right to be angry, not that she would tell him. She knew, too, that Bill Haas was probably playing racquet ball at the Athletic Club, thinking the man from *Time* would wait for him.

There was a long silence and she thought he'd hung up. "You there alone?" His voice had softened.

"No."

"Too bad." Before she could ask him why, he hung up.

After Cora left, Natalie locked the outside door and sat in the empty office. That this grimy storefront, once used to sell cheap lingerie, should hold memories of Sam depressed her. She felt the baby straining feebly against her. Poor baby. Alden never mentioned it. There had been a brief acknowledgment when she told him, but now she wasn't sure he remembered. Why did her babies never have a proper father? She felt unbearably alone.

The ringing telephone startled her.

It was Rudy Sorbentino. "I'm at the Plaza," he said. "Room 1538. You don't have to call from the lobby. Just come up." The line went dead.

She continued to stare at the dirty window almost obscured by posters of a smiling Bill Haas in shirtsleeves and jeans. Her mind was still. Quite clearly she could see that what Sorbentino was suggesting would effectively dissolve her anger toward Sam. It would defile what they had shared. Make it cheap and insignificant and perhaps take some of the hurt away. After several minutes she rose casually, let herself out of the office, relocked the door, and hurried to the Plaza.

Given the early traumas of his childhood, Rudy Sorbentino had a remarkably balanced view of himself. He had been the shortest and frailest of three brothers, the middle child of Jacob and Sophia Sorbentino. His father, a gardener who rotated his services among several large estates on the Connecticut side of the Sound, was known for his violent temper. He would chase a man who cut in front of him on the road fifty miles to "show the son-of-a-bitch he can't cut off Jacob Sorbentino."

From early adolescence Rudy suspected his father's fits weren't all due to temper. Certain things made him believe his father had moments of true and dangerous insanity, but it would have been heresy to say so. Rudy was not liked, and his observations had no weight in the family. He was bookish and dreamy, qualities that made his brothers scornful and his parents suspicious. If he were a homosexual, as they suspected, they would find it impossible to live with him, and this possibility made them extremely uncomfortable. It would be best all around if he could get out of the house as soon as possible.

One night, awakened by sounds from the cellar, he found his father cursing and holding his fingers in the flame of a candle stub. Rudy was transfixed. His father was muttering wildly, "Goddam clumsy shit fingers. I'll burn you off."

Rudy saw a spray gun filled with yellow paint oozing on the floor next to a chest of drawers that was half painted. Apparently the gun had slipped out of his father's hands.

Jacob Sorbentino alternately pulled wildly at his fingers and held them to the candle as if they belonged to someone else. Rudy jumped down the stairs and grabbed the candle, which earned him a stunning blow across the side of his head. Blood began to trickle down his neck, but he was too frightened to search out where it was coming from. He ran up the stairs, locking the door behind him, and telephoned the police who arrived within minutes.

Seeing the blood trickling down his cheek, they assumed Rudy was the emergency and began leading him to the squad car. He pulled away and led them to his father who was heaving himself against the cellar door with maniacal grunts of rage.

Rudy pointed to his father's hand, grotesquely swollen. The tips of his fingers were charred and oozing. The police thought that the pain had made him crazy and took him to the hospital.

After they attended to his father's burns, they found his wrist was dislocated and were astonished that a man could dislocate his own wrist from the frenzy of pain. Rudy knew differently but didn't say so. He wasn't feeling too well himself and passed out in the emergency room. Blood was trickling out of his left ear, and the side of his head was badly swollen. He heard the cops tell the young intern he had fallen down the cellar steps.

After that incident Rudy spent all of his energies plotting his departure. He was convinced that his father would soon kill himself in a rage, and he didn't want to witness such a thing. He knew also that he was a disappointment to his parents who valued qualities that he did not possess. His mother had wanted a girl, and his father hated him for his height and frailty and God knows what else. Sometimes he even blamed himself for his father's mental problems. It would be best all around if he left.

Because of his dark complexion and early stubble he appeared older than sixteen and got himself a job as a messenger delivering packages from Connecticut to Manhattan.

He liked the job because he was his own boss and didn't see the same people every day, but more important he had entry into all the grand offices where he made deliveries.

The receptionists were some of the best-looking girls he had ever seen. Gorgeous, leggy brunettes and blondes and redheads. They all had long, polished fingernails and fancy rings with a single large pearl and beautiful teeth which they showed generously when anyone approached their desks.

Some were snotty and only perked up when a well-dressed man came into the reception room. They didn't even turn from their typewriters for Rudy but simply motioned indifferently that he should leave the package, even though they knew he couldn't leave without getting a signature. They would roll their eyes to heaven and sign his soiled slip of paper as if he personified the aspects of their jobs that demanded superhuman patience.

Rudy loved the snotty girls best. He liked to fantasize about how he was going to kill them with surprise when he made it big. He had no doubt that he would eventually make it very big.

Whenever he had to wait for a pickup, Rudy sat in his truck and read biographies of famous men and any book he could find that detailed the lives of the rich. He was relieved to find that most men who made a great deal of money had usually suffered great deprivation in childhood. The picture that came to mind was of a lonely child, grubby fist in tear-filled eyes, accepting the loss of parental love and facing a dangerous future. He was happy to have already fulfilled this prerequisite.

A loving, stable household, he was convinced, was a booby trap to keep you happy and content. And poor and lazy. Happiness only led to a predictable, middle-class, humdrum road with just enough money to keep you alive. In his circumstances he didn't have to worry about breaking his mother's heart or letting his father down. He could go out in the world and take chances. He was quick to note that taking chances was the other noticeable thread that ran through rich men's lives.

The third thing he had in common with men who made it was that wealth and success were ever on his mind, and his particular hero in this department was a Mr. William Appleton, a new England merchant who wrote in his diary, ''I am quite eaten up with business. While in church, though I try to pray, my mind flies from city to city, ship to ship.'' That was Rudy. He was eaten up with business.

Rudy's break came quickly. When he had some money saved, he bought himself a chauffeur's uniform and hired himself out as a driver to a limousine firm. Before long a favorite customer, a partner in a Wall Street firm, hired him as a permanent chauffeur for the company. By keeping his ears open he picked up enough good tips to make himself several hundred thousand dollars in five years. At one point he was worth a quarter of a million dollars and continued to work as a chauffeur.

The rest had been easy. He bought out a public relations firm and learned everything he could about getting people to do what he wanted. At the same time he developed a style that capitalized on his weaknesses. Instead of trying to hide what he was, he emphasized it.

The one constant that followed Rudy into his new life was his penchant for snotty girls. The only conquest that ever intrigued him was the woman who appeared completely out of his reach.

Sorbentino opened the door before Natalie knocked, and she suspected he had been listening for her in the hall. He was completely naked and she couldn't help but be fascinated by his body. She had not seen many male bodies and certainly none like his. It was . . . the word "Mediterranean" came into her mind.

The smell of cologne was strong and made her stiffen up. "Take a shower," she said, "and don't wear cologne when you're going to see me."

Those were the last words she spoke, although he said many things. He seemed to be sulking about the cologne remark, and when he came out of the shower, his eyes were no longer neutral.

"Take your clothes off and sit in the chair with your legs over the arms." His voice was surly. He was paying her back.

She did as she was told. She put one leg up and then took her time before raising the other. She noticed as she raised the second one and her lower body split open that his eyes narrowed and his penis began to enlarge. She noticed, too, that her own body began to tremble, but she fought not to show any sign of involvement.

He knelt before her. "Put your fingers down on your pussy and open up. I want to see everything. I want to see what a blond, icy bitch pussy looks like up close. I might want to suck it."

Liquids began to form and exude from her, and she wished she could keep it a secret from him. She didn't want him to know anything about her.

He knelt down in front of her and kissed between her legs. She could feel his loose chain bracelet grazing her inner thigh. He held a cigar in one hand, away from her, as if he were taking a sip of his drink before another puff. His smallest finger was in the air. She was fascinated. In between small kisses and nips which he took as she held herself open, he puffed deeply and watched carefully for a reaction. She didn't move or make a sound. He smiled and bent down again as if experimenting with a recipe and patiently measuring out ingredients.

After several minutes the perspiration was pouring down her

cheeks. Her hair was wet. Both the hair on her temples and the hair below. He smiled broadly and told her to get up. Then he sat down and told her to sit on top of him and guide his penis into her. The idea of touching him came as a surprise. She hadn't counted on that, but now the desire to do it was strong. She wanted to grab him, and it took all her control to ease herself carefully, one leg at a time, through the armholes of the chair and onto his lap. She couldn't lean forward because of her belly, and he could see she didn't much like being that close to him. He laughed. "Don't touch the wop, huh? Just use the cock and leave the rest." He seemed to think that was very funny. As if he had planned it.

She was impressed with how accurately he had read her mind, but he was wrong about the rest of him. It helped to see his plump body with its unexpected patches of hair. She now brought her legs out and bent them behind her so that she was sitting like the girl on the White Rock ads. That was what she thought of. This way she could squeeze herself against him. It seemed to have an effect on him, too, because his cheeks puffed out and he began to concentrate saying, "Oh, Jesus," as if something unexpected and uncontrollable was taking place inside him. This excited her more than anything.

Finally he pulled her down from the waist harshly and thrust himself into her leaving the chair for a moment and supporting her totally on his buttocks. She fought to keep the contact for the instant more it took to find her own release. When it came, she was stunned by its intensity and immediately afterward devastated by what had taken place.

She pulled on her clothes as he watched. As she struggled into a ridiculously thin summer jacket and ran a comb through her hair, he crossed from the chair to the bed and stretched out lazily. "I'll call again when I have an hour to spare."

She left without answering.

All sorts of things have been said about men and how they take illness, that they get childish and morose and that the strongest of them gets petulant and demanding because they really feel they're going to die. When Reynold got appendicitis that summer, he was sober and quiet, but when all danger was past, he turned anxious and talked about dying.

"When I thought I might die," he said in the hospital late one night when Sara had ignored the last call to route visitors out, ''I had one big regret.''

''My God,'' she stiffened. ''What?''

''You know those cards we get every Christmas that say a donation has been made in our name to the Heart Fund. Who used to send us those cards? I can't think of their name and it's driving me crazy.''

''Friends of your mother,'' she answered smugly. ''Remember? They moved to New York and had us to dinner once a month, piling up the food as if it were going to be our one good meal till the next time they asked us.''

''Oh God, yes. Now I remember. Mr. and Mrs. Roland Smith.'' He grimaced. ''What did the card say exactly? Do you remember?'' He shifted painfully to face her.

''Of course.'' She turned mockingly serious. ''It said, 'Seasons' Greetings. A donation has been made in your name to the Heart Fund. Mr. and Mrs. Roland H.A. Smith.' ''

''That was it!'' His eyes glistened. ''That used to make me so mad. A donation has been made in your name—which is to say, don't think this crummy card is all we can afford. Instead of showy, showy, we will do something worthwhile. We will let the heart fund keep the money and send you this cheap card instead. We made a donation for *you*. Get it, dummy? Until you get on your feet.'' He lay back on the pillow and looked serious. ''I don't want to die before telling those people not to send us cards like that anymore. Remind me at Christmas how angry I was. And don't just throw it away before I see it.''

''Okay.'' How superior one felt when visiting a hospital. She felt a responsibility to take care of all his grudges. There were so few.

''Sara?''

''Yes.''

''Remember the first time we met, you thought I was so dumb?''

''I didn't.''

''Yes, you did. You thought I was dumb because I was good-looking. You didn't think anyone who was good-looking could be smart too.''

''You're exaggerating,'' she lied. She *had* thought that.

''No, I'm not. Think about it.''

''Well . . . maybe.'' She smoothed his forehead and then retrieved her hand as if she'd done something wrong. ''It's hot in

here,'' she said. Her voice seemed too vigorous for the room, her
hands too strong. But that wasn't true. What made her strong was
righteousness. She was still a pure wife. She had chosen fidelity. But
for how long?

"After I'm out, let's go away for a week together. We haven't
done that in a long time."

She nodded weakly without answering. That was not what she
wanted right now. She had work to do. She really wanted to wheedle
more work out of *Haute* and . . . and . . . stay close to home. How
could she go away with him when her every waking thought was of
Bill Waring and what he wanted to do to her?

Since her luncheon with him she had begun taking languorous
baths during which she considered her limbs anew. His interest made
her body more valuable, and she began to handle it like new merchandise, bathing often and creaming herself lovingly. He *wanted* to
touch these thighs, these arms, these breasts. She felt her skin as it
might feel to him and imagined his hands everywhere. Sometimes
when she was answering Reynold or one of the children or the touchy
nurse at the pediatrician, she was also at the same moment dealing
with one of Bill Waring's hands on some part of her. It was frightening.

Fortunately the nurse came in with a juice and sandwich cart and
spared her the need to answer him about going away.

"Can I get you something?" she asked.

"Yes, please. Grapefruit juice."

Sara held it as he sipped. He could have held it himself, but he
seemed to want her close to him. She was tired and wanted to start
home and unconsciously began to drum her fingers on the Formica
tray table.

"Sara," he smiled wryly, "you are becoming the sort of woman
who taps impatiently with her fingernails."

"What?"

"You know . . . tap, tap, tap, as if you're itching to be in more
important places doing better things. You tap on the kitchen counter,
you tap on the stove while you're waiting for the eggs to cook. What
the hell are we supposed to think?"

He seldom said "hell" and it surprised her. Also he had a point.
She *had* become the sort of woman who had a working wardrobe and
went regularly to the dry cleaners, and yes, she did tap nervously on
counters, but only when she was thinking of how hectic her life had

become. She even liked to say it to strangers in line at the super-market when the line was slow. "My life is hectic now," she would say but her smile contradicted the remark.

"At least when you're home," Reynold was saying, "when we're all together, it's not unreasonable for the children and I to want to be your 'better thing.' "

"I like the work," she said seriously. "I like it more than I thought I would. Is that wrong?"

"No." He was relaxed again. "But the last time I tried to make love to you, you tapped your fingernails on my chest."

"I did not." She threw the pillow at him and almost spilled his juice.

"Please," he laughed. "I'm a sick man." He put his fingers on her knee and let them travel up her skirt.

"What are you doing?" She held her skirt stubbornly in place.

"I wanted to see what my lungs and heart felt like when I really needed them."

"And . . . ?"

"I didn't get far enough. You want to touch me under the covers and I'll do the same to you?" He had never been coy about lovemak-ing, and she had always found his straightforward requests exciting. "I figure if something happens and I can't make it, they'll have all the rescue equipment right here. What do you say?"

She didn't know what to say. "You've got to be kidding."

"Yes. If you say so." He let his hands drop to the outside of the covers in a gesture of defeat. "You'd better go. You've got a big day tomorrow."

"No, I don't. Why do you say that?"

"All your days are big now."

"Reynold"—she was suddenly annoyed—"I don't say things like that to you. I don't ridicule your work."

"True enough." He was contrite and reached for her hand. "That was second-rate. It's just that . . . you look so pretty and I'm so horny."

"Now you're talking," she punched his arm. "Really . . . I look pretty? How pretty?"

"Very pretty. No kidding. Now you really better go. The night nurse is mean and she weighs three hundred pounds."

She kissed his forehead and left.

* * *

The next few days were spent in a mental fog, either weeding compulsively in the unevenly sown vegetable garden or wandering aimlessly around Lord & Taylor and Altman's picking things up and putting them down. One day she bought a pair of boots in Bloomingdale's that cost one hundred dollars. They were suede and breathing on them created spots. She would probably never wear them. And what's more it was August. Why should she buy suede boots that went to the knee in August? Falling in love, she noted wryly, created an immediate clothes crisis which the boots would in no way alleviate.

When she wasn't shopping or weeding, she was jumpy and prowled the house. On the worst of her jumpy days she fired Mrs. Ramirez and was so relieved, she drank a bottle of beer on an empty stomach and felt sick the rest of the day.

The phone rang and she let it ring. If it were he, he would call again. She didn't want to answer. She wondered if he would give her another assignment. Having Bill Waring waiting for her decision while she went about her life gave her a momentary sense of power.

She finally answered the phone toward the end of the week. It was Jane.

"Tania's given your piece on Congressman Martin's wife a small kudo."

"Oh? What did she say?"

"You want a direct quote?"

"Yes."

"Well," Jane cleared her throat. "She said it wasn't your usual piece of shit."

"Nice. Lovely."

"Tania wants to go ahead with the profile on Haas, and seeing as you do so well on political matters, she wants you to do it. Are you listening?"

"Sure."

"Well, the piece is obvious, a Choate-Harvard boy with straight blond hair and thin, white feet, who is the spitting image of Nick Nolte running for Congress. You'd have to follow him around for a week and find out what makes him tick . . . within the bounds of good taste of course."

"What's so special about him anyway, and as for his campaign manager . . . Rudy something or other . . . well, I don't want to get mixed up with that guy. Can't you get somebody else?''

''Tania thinks Haas will win and she wants to get on the bandwagon. Besides, his family's loaded, just the sort of heartthrob *Haute* readers go for . . . pale and unattainable.''

''Who's idea was this assignment?''

''Tania's.''

She was confused. She wanted it to be Waring's idea. ''You're sure about that?''

''Yeah.''

''Why didn't Tania call me herself?''

''Well . . . uh, no offense, but Tania would rather not deal directly with the hired help.''

''Yeah . . . right.'' She stared out her picture window at Charlie riding his new two-wheeler. With Rachel at day camp he was lonely. ''Jane, I'll think about it. I can think about it, can't I? The kids are out of school—maybe I should be spending time with them.''

''Sure, sure. Take all the time you need, only let me know by nine o'clock tomorrow morning when the cashmere tarantula will expect an answer. Lucky for you she's left for the shrink or I could only give you five minutes to make up your mind.''

''Jane?''

''Yeah.''

''I love you.''

''Don't get any weird ideas. This GI haircut doesn't mean a thing, and say, speaking of all that stuff, what happened when Waring took you to lunch?''

Sara was glad not to be facing honest Jane. ''Nothing much. He liked the piece and wanted to tell me he would use it.''

''Funny. He never takes writers to lunch unless it's Michener or someone like that. Are you holding out on me? He's not after you, is he?''

Sara was uneasy. ''Does he . . . does he often go out with women from the office?''

''Oh, God,'' Jane sighed with mock grief and regrets, ''would that he did. There's a waiting line and I'm first. Seniority and all that. I've been waiting ten years for him to break down. I have the scenario all written. Picture this: The two of us are working late in our separate offices. Finally with a giant yawn I head for the elevator and

voila! at that precise moment he, too, arrives. Those lovely mausoleum doors seal us in. Alone. Then the elevator stops between floors
and goes dead.

"When every hope of quick rescue is gone, he turns to me without
skipping a beat. 'Jane,' he says in that fastidious voice, 'remove your
blouse, I want a good look at you.' You know how he is, don't you
think that's just what he'd say? 'Jane, remove your undergarments, I
want a good look at your . . .' "

"All right, all right. I get the picture."

"Tell me, is that him?"

"It's him," Sara said weakly, thinking of her own fantasies. She
had a recurring dream. It was always a business situation. Bill Waring was either on a plane surrounded by executives or in a boardroom
or at his desk reading mail. When she appeared, he looked up,
smiled, and said, "Oh, yes. I've been expecting you." He rose, took
her in his arms in front of everybody, and kissed her. She looked
around to see what the people thought of that, but they had disappeared.

"I'll call you in the morning," she said into the phone.

"You sound funny," said Jane thoughtfully, "but I gotta go."

It was shaping up into a muggy, airless day and she called Natalie
to wangle an invitation for a swim at Pheasant Hill for herself and
Charlie. Natalie was pleasant and agreeable over the telephone. She
seemed genuinely eager to see Sara, but when she arrived, Sara was
appalled and disbelieving. Natalie was tense and guarded. She had
deep circles around her eyes, and her normally shiny, bouncy hair
was listless and looked in need of a good washing.

Was it the pregnancy? Were the servants getting to her? Or was it
the man with whom she had not yet become number one? It troubled
her deeply that she could not simply ask her friend what was wrong.
There was still some distance between them.

On the plus side Sara was too preoccupied with her own life to be
intimidated any longer by Pheasant Hill or the staff. She and Natalie
left the boys outside and went to see the master bedroom, newly
redone in shades of beige. They passed Mr. Simmons on the stairs,
and Sara successfully stared him down. He, too, seemed to have
withered over the summer.

The room they entered did nothing to change her opinion that
Pheasant Hill and its people were in a general decline. Shirred beige

drapery had been used as a backdrop for the bed which rested on a huge beige platform. It looked to Sara like a gigantic, open coffin.

"I take it you like beige," she said, looking for a likely place to sit.

"I had nothing to do with it. Alden hired this man from Paris and he's doing it all himself." Natalie threw herself across the bed which seemed a sacrilege.

Sara stared uncomfortably at her surroundings, finally focusing on Natalie's shoes, now highly visible. They were flat and stiff-looking with a small edging of gold in the shape of a horseshoe. Had it some equestrian meaning like the hood ornaments on the cars parked around the village? An emptily gilded shoe seemed too frivolous for Natalie.

"Don't you want to have a say?"

"Not especially. I detest the little man and he detests me. If I started to take issue with anything he did, we'd have a dialogue and that's just what I want to avoid."

"Why?"

"Because that's precisely what the little man wants. He wants us to be pals and talk all the time." She said this wearily, as if she had been plagued all her life by people who wanted to talk all the time.

Sara lifted her eyebrows and whistled. She now had a firm image of a vicious little gnome angrily trying to break down Natalie's defenses. "And what about Alden?"

"He wanted everything uncluttered and simple, and"—she waved her hand to take in the room—"that's what he sees, I suppose. I haven't discussed it with him." It was a dull statement of fact.

Sara rose and went to sit on a beige, velvet window seat and stared out at the sculpted hedges and graceful shade trees. How could you not discuss the décor of your own home with your husband? What did they discuss? Their bank balances? Their holdings? Their wine cellar? In the silence Sara was distracted by a high, squeaking noise that sounded like some small hurt animal. She remembered that Natalie had nervous little dogs.

"Do you hear that?" asked Natalie.

"Yes. Is it the dogs?"

"It's he. He's sucking on antacids. He sucks on antacids all day, except when he's eating. Now he hardly eats because cook won't get what he wants."

"Who is *he?*" she whispered. "Who is sucking on antacids?"

"The decorator. Cardon." Natalie smiled which seemed totally inappropriate. "He seems to have a delicate stomach."

The sucking noises came closer and then slightly foreign sounding male voices clearly audible. "If madame has no interest on where she will place her fine ass, it isn't our job to reprimand her. Mr. Van Druten hired us and it is he we must please. Or rather ourselves," he reconsidered. "We must please ourselves."

Sara colored and felt immediate outrage for Natalie.

"Don't be upset." Natalie rose to lead the way out of the house. "I have a way of dealing with that sort of thing." When Sara did not change her expression, she added, "It's not as unusual as you might think . . . or important."

Yes, it is, thought Sara. It's both unusual and important. But only to me. It occurred to her, not for the first time, that she had no real understanding of what motivated the privileged class. They seemed to shrug at human failings, their own as well as those of others.

"What about yourself, Sara? What are you up to?" Natalie asked.

It seemed as good a time as any to discuss the assignment. "I've been asked to do the piece on Bill Haas. What can you tell me about him?"

"Personally or professionally?"

She knew Natalie would now be on her guard. "As you like."

"Alden knows the family. Bill's older brother has a drinking problem and less than the total use of one leg. The father insists someone has to be in government. I can't explain this to you, because they're hardly idealists, but they really believe they can do a better job than someone who is motivated by making a living."

Sara admired the shrewd use of details to present the candidate. It was PR, but intelligent PR. "Suppose he makes it?"

"*Suppose?*" Natalie was annoyed and Sara regretted her flippancy. "He's supposed to make it. Don't write him off just because he's rich. Poverty doesn't insure high-mindedness and foresight in public office."

They walked toward the pool. The weather had cleared, and the temperature had dropped by several degrees. Natalie called to the boys to join them. The pool area appeared newly planted and bare of any signs of casual living. There were no glasses with melting ice leaving rings on smooth, sectioned concrete. No chair out of place.

Once in the water all tension slipped away. Sara and Natalie played shyly with their sons, smiling over their heads from time to time.

A light, cool wind began to blow, and Charlie climbed out and shivered at the edge of the pool. "I'm cold, mommy."

Sara got out and covered him with a towel and pulled him next to her on a chaise. "We're going home soon." She saw a flicker of disappointment cross Natalie's face but cautioned herself that she might be imagining things. While rubbing Charlie's puckered fingertips she wondered why life was so complicated. What could be simpler than two women being friends. Yet it wasn't simple. Sara was thinking things, and Natalie was thinking things, and they couldn't always tell each other what they were thinking.

"Everything's perfect except for the puddle I made." Charlie was looking down at an irregular wet spot on the otherwise spotless paving. Sara nodded and looked around again. There was not a leaf out of place, and the ground under the bushes was raked in perfect concentric circles. Her own chaise, pushed sideways to catch the last rays of sun, was the only jarring note. "What are you thinking?" Natalie hoisted herself out of the pool.

"How neat everything is."

"Yes," Natalie agreed as if concurring that the sky was blue. "It's important to Alden."

There seemed to be nothing further to say and both were silent.

Jeremy was the first to be aware that Alden had come and called out. "Over here, sir. Watch me dive."

Sara turned to see him sitting at the corner of the pool. He was dressed in swimming trunks and a terry jacket. He had running shoes and socks on his feet. He nodded slightly and fixed his eyes on the boy who executed a clumsy dive into the deep end of the pool. Sara was relieved to see him bob up again, certain from the plaintive quality of Jeremy's voice that he would have risked his life to impress his father.

"Isn't that much better than before?" Jeremy had hoisted himself up again and stood dripping and wet.

"Yes," said Alden. "I think it is."

With his black ringlets plastered against his head, Sara was struck by Jeremy's face. It was unique, not at all childlike, and there was little in it from his parents. His eyes were dark and intense, deeply set, and his small chin was dominated by an indention. It was not a cleft, it was a dent. She looked back to Alden searching for some small similarity and was startled to find him staring intently at a spot just below her legs. Then she realized that he was staring at her chaise as if he saw something structurally wrong with it. As if it might collapse at any moment. But that wasn't it. She looked down and saw it was as perfect and sturdy as those around it.

An idea formed in her mind, as if he had transferred it there. He was dismayed because her chaise was not in line with the others. No, that couldn't be it. But yes, yes it was. That was what was making him stare in that troubled way.

It was time to leave. She rose quickly, turned the chaise, giving it a final nudge with her toe, and said good-bye.

When she reached home, it was a relief to return to the old dilemma, and she rushed to call Jane Seymour before the switchboard closed. She had the beginnings of a fine career which she should be nurturing with care. Also she should allow herself to feel some happiness over all the good things that had happened to her.

That night she and Reynold drank a bottle of champagne that had lain in the refrigerator for at least six months. She took it to the hospital for his last night.

"They liked my piece," she said in explanation. "The editor said it wasn't the usual piece of shit."

"That's nice to hear," he said, raising his glass to toast her.

Their festivities turned out to be a farewell celebration. Reynold was going to live in one of the cottages at the lab that they kept for visiting scientists. He wasn't allowed to drive a car or climb stairs for a month. It would be better that way. He would come home on weekends.

Chapter 13

THE STATEMENT FROM THE BANK WAS broken down into several columns against a background of blue on blue. Miranda had read somewhere that they chose the color scheme because it was hopeful but not frivolous which was exactly the way they wanted people to feel about money in general and the bank's money in particular. She had been both frivolous and careless, perhaps because she hadn't bothered to open the statements which lay in a neat stack on a shelf near her bed.

She was not only broke, she had dipped into the bank's cash reserve, money they had assured her was hers for the asking, providing (it now turned out) she gave it right back. She had assumed her generous salary would keep her afloat.

What would happen when the baby arrived and she could no longer work?

Barbara Lancia, furious over the way she had handled Bradley Gifford, had stiffed her out of a whole month's pay. She had done so not out of stinginess, but simply to teach Miranda a lesson.

She remembered a sampler that hung over Barbara's Queen Anne desk: Learn to function in disaster and to finish up in style. Miranda had not finished up in style, and Barbara wanted her to reap the rewards of her foolishness just as she wanted women who were too lazy to remove their makeup each night to be punished with large, coarse pores.

"You are foolish, foolish, foolish," she had screamed into the telephone, and Miranda, prepared to hear apologies in the elegant voice she had come to admire, was dumbfounded. Who was this harridan and where was her well-bred mentor? "If I were a pregnant girl without hope of support," Barbara had continued with contempt, "and a gentleman of taste and means took an interest in me, I would seize the opportunity." Barbara's exasperation was compelling, and for a moment Miranda was sure she had behaved stupidly. "You could have had the best of what New York has to offer."

"Not with him." She stood her ground.

"Dozens of girls would have been delighted to take your place."

"That's what he said," answered Miranda dully.

"It's true."

"He was a bully and a . . . a . . . pervert." She knew that sounded childish and it was not what she had intended to say, but her mind was not working.

"My God! It's a little late to play Mary Poppins."

Miranda, too muddled to answer and too embarrassed to describe what had happened, hung up, but afterward hated herself for handling the call so poorly. The illogic of it all made her angry and confused. She wished she could believe Barbara. The best of what New York had to offer was exactly what she wanted. It made her think of Judy Garland in the movie *Easter Parade* which she had seen on television. When she thought of anyone really making it in New York, she thought of Judy Garland, dressed to kill, walking down Fifth Avenue on the arm of Fred Astaire while a band played something cheerful.

That night she called California hoping to hear something cheerful herself from Sanche. She did not want to be, as Barbara put it, "without hope of support."

"Is it . . . coming along?" he asked immediately. He was referring to the baby. Sanche was used to dealing with projects, and projects were either coming along or stalled. "Yes. I can feel it sometimes. I can feel his ankle."

"What do you mean? How can you feel his ankle . . . you poke in there?" he asked nervously.

"Not poke. Sometimes he kicks me and I grab this knobby little thing."

"You shouldn't do that, Miranda," he said gravely. "I've never heard of anyone doing that. Promise me you won't do that anymore."

"Okay. I won't do that anymore," she lied. She was going to do that every chance she could. Feeling for the little foot made her feel better on certain nights when she didn't see David Laver or anyone else. She was pleased, however, to find he had opinions about the baby and instantly felt better.

As a bonus he told her she could come to California for a visit and that he would call her about it in a few days. With that hazy promise she crept into bed and tried not to think of the things Bradley Gifford had said. His cold, flat voice had not left her, and the things she still heard in her head were riveting and sinister. Sometimes she accused herself of being excited by them, an idea that made her so uncomfortable, her uterus stiffened and her back began to ache.

When this happened, she massaged herself until she felt relaxed and tried to trace the baby's outline with her fingers. She wondered if they would end up in one of those overcrowded city hospitals where you could bleed to death because it took so long to get admitted.

Bolstered by the real offer from David and the halfhearted offer from Sanche, Miranda stayed away from Barbara Lancia's apartment for two days. On the third day she went in to say she was quitting. Barbara said little, although her mouth twitched and the look on her face was a mixture of pity and contempt.

For two weeks after quitting she moped in bed, hardly leaving the apartment. David had given her a small television which she kept on even when she slept which was much of the day. Sanche had not called as he said, and her dream of being whisked to California now seemed improbable. She gained weight and the baby seemed to grow larger overnight. She felt swollen and clumsy. Parts of her, the ankles and hands, were visibly swollen, and when she poked a finger into them, a dent remained.

Quite often she ate nothing all day but a box of saltines which made her mouth dry and sore and her lips crack. The salt, she knew, was making her retain fluids. She had read in *How to Help Your Unborn Child* that salt was enemy number one of a safe and uneventful pregnancy, and she tried to picture all the unsafe, eventful things that would befall her. Mostly she saw her organs and the baby floating amid great gushes of water.

She had gotten to know David's step in the hall, but he didn't always stop to see her. Once he asked when she was planning to start at the agency, and she told him she wasn't really ready. The truth was the idea of starting over again and, worse, that a probable fag was her only friend made her want to burst into tears. Thinking how disloyal this was to David also made her want to burst into tears.

On August third, three days after the rent was due, she decided to try and return the earrings Barbara had given her. Tiffany's in August was subdued and unfriendly, and the nasally disdainful clerk was suspicious. To begin with, Miranda in a too tight, gauzy top and thin drawstring pants did not look like their typical customer. What was the reason for the return? She didn't need them. Didn't *need* them! Nobody *needed* earrings. The explanation exasperated him.

She stationed herself firmly by the customer service counter, feeling warmer and more swollen than ever. She was dimly aware that her back hurt, too, and looked glumly down at her feet swelling around the thin, cutting straps of her sandals. The shoes in her closet—high heeled, skimpy, possibly dangerous—were firm testimony to her recklessness.

When the man put the money into her hand, she went straight to the bank and added it to her dwindling account leaving out ten dollars for groceries. The ten dollars had to last a long time. Even if she didn't feel like eating, she had to start thinking about the baby. She bought cottage cheese, eggs, and a small box of powdered milk because it was cheaper than fresh milk. She added up everything in her head except the milk which was unmarked. The bill came to over four dollars and her heart sank. She hadn't expected to spend so much.

On the way home someone in front of her yelled, "Hi." It was Judy of Hal and Judy, flailing her arms to flag her down. Judy seemed to have grown shorter. How could that be? She hadn't remembered her being so . . . so squat. Judy had gained weight and most of it was in her hips. She looked like one of those unappetizing brown pears that were supposed to be sweeter than the green ones.

"Miranda, it's me. Gee, how are you?"

"I'm okay," said Miranda. She couldn't get over how Judy had changed. Judy had been pert and bouncy with long, shiny, dirty-blond hair, and while Miranda had never liked pert and bouncy, it was better than this. In place of her long, simple hairdo, were three distinct tiers of unevenly cut, straw blond hair. In place of her normal hips were two intimidating mounds.

"It was really too bad about Bob," Judy lowered her head.

"Yeah. It's been over six months," answered Miranda trying to account for her lack of grief. "But what about you? Want to have a cup of coffee somewhere?" She thought of her five dollars and eighty-one cents and realized she couldn't afford a cup of coffee, but Judy looked so beaten she felt sorry for her.

"Oh, I couldn't do that. The sitter goes home at four and I have to get my train."

"Sitter? You have a baby?" That explained the hips.

"A little girl. We live in Hewlett. Hal's in electronics."

"Hewlett?" Jesus, Hewlett. Electronics. It occurred to Miranda that while she might feel sorry for Judy, Judy in no way was feeling sorry for herself. She was a little smug in fact.

Judy looked pointedly at Miranda's abdomen. "I see you've found someone too."

For a moment Miranda didn't know what she was getting at. "You must have married right away," Judy continued. "Anyone we knew?"

"No. I . . . well . . . I didn't get married."

"Oh, geez . . . geez, I'm sorry. I just assumed . . ."

"That's all right. Don't worry about it."

"Me and my big mouth. Miranda, I didn't mean . . ."

"I know you didn't. It's okay. I mean it."

Judy was not convinced and continued to look sorrowful. "Judy, it's *all right*. It's more than all right. The man . . . the father's rich. And . . . and famous. We're supposed to join him in California next week. Everything's super, really. In fact you've probably heard of him . . . Sanche Ray?" Judy looked nonplussed. "He wrote that movie that won the Academy Award . . . You know the one . . . *Wall to Wall*."

"We haven't been to the movies lately. The baby's so little." They were both silent.

"Call me when you're in town again," said Miranda because there was nothing else to say.

"Will do," said Judy, but when she was a half block away, she yelled back, "Hey, you forgot. How can I call you when you'll be in California?"

That was the trouble with Judy, thought Miranda, trudging the last few blocks home, she didn't know when to shut up. Bob had wanted her to be just like Judy and have Judy's hopes and dreams. By now she'd also have her ass. She thought of Judy's hope chest. The dainty bikini underpants with the coy message—For Your Eyes Only. She hoped Hal was still looking at them.

When she got home, she looked in the mirror and knew why Judy had looked at her so pityingly. Her eyes were swollen to slits. Her skin looked mottled and her hair, once so lustrous and silky, was a tangled mess. While she had been feeling sorry for Judy, Judy was busy as hell feeling sorry for her. For the third time that day she felt tears welling up in her eyes.

The next day she was due for her monthly visit with Dean Whitley, but when she stumbled to the bathroom and looked at herself in the mirror, she couldn't make herself go out. The effort of untangling her long hair and bathing was too much. She dialed his office to cancel the appointment expecting the service, but instead it was his voice on the line.

"I'd like to cancel my appointment for today." She tried to sound cool and businesslike.

"Who is this please?" He knew who it was.

"Miranda Lesley."

"What's the reason for cancelling?"

"Well . . . I . . . well, I just look too awful and I'm too tired to do anything about it."

"You're canceling your appointment because you don't like the way you look?" He tried to sound stern and outraged, but he was pleased that she cared how she looked to him.

"If you saw how I looked, you wouldn't think it was ridiculous." She relaxed, feeling reassured by his voice.

"I can't force you to come in, but I strongly urge you to do so. Are you retaining water, is that it?"

"Among other things."

"Well, that's serious. If you don't want to make the effort for yourself, think of your baby." He knew that would get her there.

"All right. But it won't be this morning. Can I come around three?"

"I'll make room for you at three." He hung up before she changed her mind.

When he saw Miranda, his concern was real. He tried not to show his surprise at how much she had changed. He examined her carefully and said nothing. He did the internal, draping her chastely and trying not to focus on her firm, round buttocks. He palpated each breast. Finally he took each of her legs into his hands and pressed gently around the badly swollen calves and ankles.

"You've gained ten pounds since your last visit," he said soberly. "You're almost crippled by edema. I can tell by your nails and hair that you're not eating right or getting fresh air and exercise." He stepped back and pushed some stray hairs back from her forehead. "Why are you doing this to yourself?"

His genuine concern undid her and tears began to roll down her cheeks. As quickly as they began, however, they stopped, and she struggled to sit up and rubbed angrily at her eyes. "Just dumb, I guess."

"Has . . . did something happen to make you unhappy? Are you worried?"

"No, no." She sniffled one last time into the Kleenex. "I'll be fine."

He helped her down from the table, and for an instant she had an intense desire to put her head on his white coat and tell him everything that had happened to her. But she didn't. He would just feel sorry for her and, God knows, she didn't need that. "I'll do better next time, don't worry."

For the next week she drank two quarts of water a day, added no salt to her food, and urinated constantly. Sometimes it would take her a full minute to finish, and she could almost feel her body deflating. Her face took on its normal contours and her eyes looked clear for the first time in weeks. Most important her clothes fit again, and she decided it was time to accept David's offer. Who else was going to hire an increasingly pregnant woman?

"I'll make you a junior account executive on the Sinclair Fabrics account,'' David said, looking out his office window with a visionary stare.

"It sounds like you just made that up." Miranda was softened by a wave of affection for him. Sudler, Laver, and Ross was much larger than she had imagined, and he looked impressive and capable behind a large, modern rosewood desk. There was no Sudler and no Ross, she found out. David had bought them out when the agency was young and poor. A few shares had gone to his creative director, Donald King, and the research man, Nelson Ackerman, in lieu of big, taxable salaries. "David, I'll learn that space buying," she said earnestly. "Read me a lot of numbers . . . go ahead. I have a photographic memory . . . really!"

"Miranda, will you just sit down and shut up . . . and *please!* stop putting me in the role of furry, lovable daddy. My motives are as ulterior as anyone's."

"You want my body?" She shot him a sultry look and then crossed her eyes, but the look of pain on his face was sudden and acute and she was sorry to have said it. This was a part of his life he had not shared with her other than the initial, tantalizing revelation—his heart was elsewhere. She knew where it was, too, and didn't like it. It was with the tall man she saw regularly in the hall. The one who stared straight ahead and wore serious, heavy shoes. He certainly didn't look like someone to trust with your heart.

David wheeled his chair to face the window again and his voice was thoughtful. "I've decided you should be very visible. . . . Chauvinistic or not, it would be a waste to hide you in some back office."

"But there is some *real* work you have in mind?" She sank into a chair beside his desk and looked suspicious.

"Very hard work. You have to be a liaison between the agency and the client. Show them campaigns, sit in on their strategy meetings, and occasionally take your opposite number over there to lunch at a fancy restaurant. On this end you'll coordinate work that comes out of here. Hound the copy people, the art department, and make sure we're on schedule. Also there's the space buyer, the market research people . . . it's a big job."

"I don't know anything about coordinating and . . . and suppose they ask me something?"

"It's all common sense. If they want your opinion, give it. Be-

sides, by the time an ad comes out, it's hard to trace the blame." He
rose and stood beside her. "Uh . . . there is one thing."

"What?"

"Try to wear stuff made with their fabric. It makes them feel
you're on their side. And . . . you don't have to actually announce
that you're an unwed mother. Okay?"

"Okay." She smiled grudgingly. "I'm grateful. I just don't know
how to behave grateful."

"It's okay. Grateful is boring."

Somewhere between the second and third weeks at Sudler, Laver,
and Ross Miranda began to notice that she was positively eager to
dress herself in the morning and reach her ten- by twelve-foot cubicle
overlooking the minuscule gardens of well-tended, private brownstones. Each morning and evening she walked the twenty-odd blocks
to work and back in sturdy new lace-up shoes she had purchased in a
fit of concern over her safety.

She liked checking the progress of her work orders and opening
her interoffice mail and straightening the increasing wad of papers on
her desk. While David had not discussed salary, on the fifteenth of
the month she received a pay envelope along with everyone else, and
her interest turned to zeal. She had taken charge of her life. Her favorite part of the day was spent sitting in on creative bull sessions
and watching campaigns take shape.

Before long she arrived at a puzzling realization. It amazed her, for
instance, that no one at the agency could think simply about a problem. It took layers and layers of trade lingo and endless meetings to
come up with what to her seemed obvious solutions. When she
timidly offered her fresh ideas, everyone stared as if she were newly
arrived from Mars.

"Were you just sitting on that?" Donald King would ask, annoyed
that she had kept such a good idea to herself while they floundered.

"Well," she would stammer with relief that she hadn't made a
fool of herself, "I know the words aren't right."

"No, listen. The idea is terrific. Right on target."

"That's very kind of you, Donald." It wasn't kind of Donald at
all, but she had decided to make her way carefully. Donald, a near
alcoholic who was always dissolving into long-winded defenses on
why he didn't get out of the business and settle down to *real* creative

work, would have cheerfully stabbed her if he thought her a threat. But in his eyes she had strike upon strike against her. She was a woman, and a pregnant one at that. Also he was just enough of a lecher to want to keep the pathway clear for a possible liaison between them.

She soon found that people in the advertising business behaved even more childishly than those in the movie business. Jeans were practically a uniform, and the more prestige and salary one had earned, the more eccentric was their behavior and the décor of their offices. One art director always sat on the floor when he presented anything and spoke so softly that everyone had to bend over to hear him. Another had an office that looked like a morgue for cast-off medical furniture. He sat in a dental chair, his drawing board was mounted on a specimen cart, and an old apothecary shop cabinet with millions of tiny drawers held God knows what. He dressed only in leather and wore elaborate, gem-studded cowboy boots which, he claimed, had to be insured.

Donald, she noted, called everyone on his creative staff "kid." If he were trying to humor them, he said it in an amazed way: "How could anyone under a thousand create something so clever?" They were prodigies to be molded by Papa Donald. When he was nervous, he used the word "kid" like a threat: "Hey, kids, you haven't come up with any dazzling answers lately. We don't need any green kids around here."

Miranda's immediate mentor was Lola McKay, a buxom, motherly blonde with a British accent that made Miranda's name sound like a sinfully expensive perfume. She taught Miranda everything with cheerful generosity, the ins and outs of scheduling, campaign presentations, and persuading the copy department to deliver things on time.

Then one morning Lola did not show up at the office. At noon she called to tell them she would not be in that day or any day in the near future.

"My back's out, darling. You'll have to do my running for me for a few weeks. There's a meeting at Sinclair. Talk to SueEllen if you can make sense out of her. She knows what you need to take. If not, call me back."

"SueEllen . . . is that right?" Miranda approached her timidly.

SueEllen Greenberg was redheaded, plump, and supremely bored with earning a living. She wore alarmingly short skirts and had great interest in her breasts on which she lavished cologne and isometric exercises. She was not impressed by her regular boss and even less so by the temporary replacement.

Miranda stood by her desk. "Is that one name?"

"Yeah. My mother loved *Gone With the Wind,* but she couldn't name me Scarlett. So . . . she named me SueEllen after Scarlett's younger sister." Miranda listened transfixed. SueEllen spoke in one run-on sentence that defied interruption. "I wish she had named me Ashley. I love Ashley. I would spell it Ash and l-e-i-g-h."

"SueEllen," Miranda tried to divert her. "What happens at a client meeting?"

"Ashleigh Greenberg . . . God! I love it." SueEllen treated herself to a long, rubbery stretch. "Nobody had any imagination in those days. They were scared to fart. A girl was named Susan, Pat, or Mary, you know what I mean?" Miranda did. "Anyway you've got a client meeting at three at Sinclair. Their secretary called to confirm.

"You're supposed to take copy ideas and rough layouts for Sintrell," she paused for emphasis, ". . . as in Sinfully Luxurious. It's a piece of crap. It pills and stretches when you sit on it for ten minutes. Oh, well . . ." She walked to a small mirror mounted on a file cabinet and applied bloodred lipstick.

Miranda followed her. "SueEllen, could you brief me?"

"What do you mean?"

"What happens at a client meeting?"

"Nothing. You sit around a long table and talk."

"Who talks? Do I talk first or do they?"

"You sit opposite each other, and you can only talk to the person at Sinclair who corresponds with your salary and position. If you want to pee you can only ask your opposite number where the can is. If the office boy were the only one who knew where the can was, you couldn't ask him and he couldn't tell you."

"That's ridiculous."

"That's the way they do it." SueEllen was delighted to be the bearer of such disturbing news.

"Why for God's sake?" Miranda followed SueEllen who began to regard her as if she were a dull and tiresome child.

"They're scared someone will take their job, of course. Everybody's scared except for the steno pool and the office boys. You'll see. Don't speak to anyone over there but the ad manager's assistant—that's all I can tell you.''

The boardroom of Sinclair Fabrics was on the fourteenth floor of the Sinclair Building, an architecturally boring skyscraper on the Avenue of the Americas behind the little sign for Honduras, Guatemala, and Costa Rica, which was incongruous since Sinclair was a British-owned firm. Around the highly polished, burled wood table were seated the advertising manager, the stylist, the account man for Sintrell, two secretaries, and the assistant to the advertising manager. The air conditioning was much too high, and everyone was huddled into themselves against the blast of cold air. Normally the advertising manager would have headed the table, but today he had been displaced by the president of Sinclair, Warren Stokes, and with him was Albert Sotheby, the head of the parent company in England, who had surprised everyone by showing up on an unscheduled trip.

The agency side of the table was dismally empty except for Miranda and a marketing man, Rock Newell.

''Suppose we were to look at everything from a fresh point of view.'' Albert Sotheby was addressing Warren Stokes who was trying to look attentive while everyone else doodled on their pads. Miranda heard the account man for Sintrell whisper, ''Oh, God, this is going to be one of those fresh-point-of-view meetings.''

Albert Sotheby's voice clipped along innocently. ''What would make a woman choose an easy care fabric over a natural one? What is the true emotion behind such a purchase?''

As if on cue everyone shifted in their chairs and looked blankly into the air in front of them. After sixty seconds of stunning silence the advertising manager sat up straight.

''Sir,'' he said, ''the agency has a campaign for us to consider this morning. They've been working on it for weeks.'' He looked meaningfully at Miranda and she handed him the portfolio of rough ads. ''Would you like to see it?''

''Frankly. no. I'm sure it's quite clever,'' said Albert Sotheby, looking around the table, ''but I was more interested in getting everyone to contribute some ideas . . . extemporaneously . . . let our imaginations run riot.''

"Oh, God," whispered the account man under his breath, "it's going to be one of those let-our-imaginations-run-riot meetings."

Miranda thought of SueEllen and waited for her opposite number across the table to invite her ideas, but the woman was crouched in the fetal position, either from cold or fear.

"Who'll be brave enough to start the ball rolling. Don't wait to be brilliant. It's just an informal exchange." The account man snorted audibly and then realizing he had been heard, sunk lower in his chair.

Albert Sotheby sounded kind and encouraging, and Miranda found herself wanting to please him.

"I would go to TV spots," she said quickly. "No big fashion extravaganzas, just ten-second spots showing a woman in real life situations."

Albert Sotheby focused his entire consciousness on her. "Could you describe some of those real life situations?"

"If she's in a supermarket," Miranda continued, "she really is squeezing the tomatoes—but more importantly, she's saying things that women really say. She might ask the vegetable man, 'How do I know when this melon is ripe? The last one was hard for a month and then it just died.' Or she might be in a market where they package all the vegetables in huge quantities and she only wants one lemon. She begins to have a fit about it. 'Why can't I buy just one lemon, aaagh.' That sort of thing." Miranda stopped. There was dead silence around her.

"Go on," said Albert Sotheby in his gentle English voice.

"Another vignette might be in group therapy." She didn't know where she was pulling these ideas from, but if she just went with the forward motion, she'd be okay. "The woman is saying—it could always be the same woman for quick identity—'My mother never listened to me. She always knew what I was going to say. In fact that's just what she would say to me: "Cynthia, I know just what you're going to say." ' The vignettes can be moving. They don't have to be comic like everything else. If the woman's at the dinner table with her children, there may be an argument in progress. 'Jeffrey, did you wash your hands? Doesn't anyone like the green beans amandine? Amandine means with almonds, Jeffrey. With almonds.' Just little bits of real life. People would look for them because they'd be provocative—the woman would represent their own frustrations—they

wouldn't be like commercials at all. At the end would be a tag line
. . . something like—'Sintrell . . . easy care fabric for real people.
One less thing to worry about.' ''

She took a deep breath and looked around. She could see the advertising people weren't going to react until Albert Sotheby reacted,
and he was staring at her calmly, one eyebrow higher than the other.

"Does anyone else have something to say?'' he asked.

No one did. Warren Stokes suggested that perhaps they should all
think about it and jot down some things that occurred to them and
they would have another meeting, but Albert Sotheby said that wasn't
what he had in mind at all. He had not wanted them to think about it
because that was inhibiting. Warren cleared his throat and the advertising manager cleared his throat, and Albert Sotheby finally said,
"It's near lunchtime,'' as if he were giving up. Then he glanced at
Miranda. "Perhaps you could join us for lunch and continue your
very interesting presentation.''

"Of course.'' Warren Stokes stood and looked questioningly at the
advertising manager. He had no clues as to who she was.

Miranda, seeing his confusion, seized the situation. "I'm Miranda
Lesley, how do you do.'' She stuck out her hand to Albert Sotheby
who had no choice but to pump it, which he did heartily.

"Well, SueEllen,'' said Miranda when she returned to the office,
"I didn't exactly follow your advice, but it went okay.''

"We heard,'' said SueEllen disdainfully. "You made a grandstand.''

"What's a grandstand?''

"When you show off. You know . . . say something really wacko
hoping to have one of those movie endings . . . whiz kid saves the
day—unknown rockets to stardom.'' SueEllen puffed furiously on
her wet nails.

"That's just what I did, SueEllen. That describes it perfectly. I
made a grandstand.'' She was sorry she had ever said anything to
SueEllen, and she would not let her have the last snotty word. "And
when you finish puffing on those Fu Man Chu nails, come in and take
a memo.''

"What you did wasn't smart,'' SueEllen said calmly.

"Why? Mr. Stokes didn't seem to mind.''

"You talked with and addressed Mr. Stokes? Warren Stokes? The
president?'' SueEllen's voice was a shriek of disdain.

"Yes."

"It may have worked out today, but you'll be sorry in the end."

"I really don't care."

"That's up to you."

Miranda couldn't help but be impressed by the way SueEllen held her ground, but she tried not to show it. She went into her office and slammed the door.

The next morning David stopped her in the hall as she was leaving for lunch. "I just had a call from Warren Stokes. They want to go national with a ten-second spot campaign on TV and radio. Network. That means half a million dollars in additional billing, fifteen percent of that a direct gain for the agency. Jesus, what did you say to them?"

"There was a man from England, Mr. Sotheby . . . . Sir Albert actually. He asked if we had any ideas and nobody did. It was embarrassingly quiet, so I gave him my ideas." She was confused. They had been very polite at lunch and asked her a lot of questions, but nothing was said about actually using any of it. "David," she said earnestly, "I'm no longer deadwood." David was quick to agree that she was not. He felt like telling her all the other things that she was not and some things that she was, but he decided to keep it simple and just treat her to lunch.

"Did you know you had diplomatic abilities?" he asked over their veal piccata. "In the Roman days you would have been the trusted diplomatic courier. Just think, you've been sitting on this terrific talent and it took me to get it out of you."

She realized that was precisely what had happened. "Can I still work for you after the baby comes?" She didn't need Sanche, she didn't need anyone. She had made a place for herself.

Albert Sotheby's interest in Miranda did not end with their luncheon. He began to call her every few days. "I wanted to speak to you, my dear," he would say frankly and innocently. It was not sex. He had found out that she was an unwed mother and the thought of protecting her quite overtook him. Miranda could visualize his mother, Lady Something or Other, speaking in her high English voice, "Albert, we must always behave decently. If we fail in our responsibility to the race, we are nothing." Miranda had grave doubts as to whether Sir Albert would be as solicitous if he knew the circumstances of her pregnancy. As of now he saw her as a duped innocent who had the courage to refuse abortion, something he abhorred.

At times she fantasized shattering his view of her by protesting that she had wanted to get pregnant and would do so again. When they were talking calmly over tea at the Palm Court of the Plaza and listening to the string quartet, she had the urge to whisper in his ear, "Sir Albert, let's screw," thinking the shock might scare him and send him flying off his seat. The idea that she could scare the hell out of Sir Albert who had a company on the New York Stock Exchange was irresistible, except that she would not do anything to queer David's business. She knew, too, that he might make believe he didn't hear her. He was too smart to let her shatter his serenity. Once he had asked where she lived and wrote down her address in a small pad that fit neatly into a slim billfold. The next day the doorman handed her a basket from Charles & Company filled with jams, oranges, nuts, and exotic soups—cream of quail and vichyssoise. Tucked in the center was a round thing imprisoned in a thick black, plastic crust which proved impossible to penetrate.

She brought the basket to David's apartment, and together they mauled the black thing with their fingernails and teeth. Finally with a tiny saw from his Swiss army knife David succeeded in making a jagged tear and looked inside. It was a wonderful, sharp and smoky cheddar which they ate in huge chunks. While they laughed and ate, David hugged and kissed her and Miranda began to cry.

"Don't worry," she said tearfully. "I cry all the time now. It must be the hormones. Jesus, it's weird, the invasion of the body snatchers."

Her relationship with Sir Albert accelerated. He took every opportunity to see her. He wanted her to go over the commercials with him and the print campaigns and study the potentials of each one. He wanted, quite simply, to be involved in her life.

For herself Miranda felt she was a fraud, although her sins were sins of omission. With his high, broad forehead and narrow face he reminded her of someone who had renounced the world and spoke only to God. He would be a natural in some abbey off the coast of Scotland, except that he was a cultured Englishman with a company that made millions. Still, he didn't behave like any businessman she knew. She was sure he had never lied for profit or done any other ungentlemanly thing. She knew he was completely taken with the idea of being her protector, and she never said anything that would alter his idealistic view of her. Often he would stop in at Bonwit's or Saks and pick out a scarf or a shawl which he thought perfectly complemented her coloring.

Only once did he mention the baby's father. A stitch in her side made her cry out in pain. He waited until she was composed and then inquired, "Uh . . . the father . . . do you know his whereabouts?"

"Oh, certainly. He's very well-known. In the movie business."

"I see." His nose twitched. "There's no financial worry then . . . ?"

"Well, he hasn't given me any money if that's what you mean."

"Why not for heaven's sake?"

"I haven't asked for any, I suppose." She wondered if Sanche would give her money for the baby. Perhaps he wouldn't. Perhaps that's why she hadn't asked.

"It sounds to me as if you could use some legal counsel. Would you like me to recommend a lawyer?"

"No, Sir Albert." She loved calling him Sir Albert. She liked the sound of it and it kept their friendship formal. He continued to take her to plays and often for tea around four in the afternoon, a practice she came to adore.

As if in response to Sir Albert's indignation Sanche called twice that week. He seemed to be leaving out what he really wanted to say and the conversation was uneven. He asked if she felt all right and also mentioned that the weather in California had been especially good and smog free and the climate in Palm Springs where he went on weekends was even better. He was leading up to an invitation. Or so it appeared.

"Can you travel . . . it isn't bad for the baby or anything, is it?"

"No."

"How would it be if you came here for a few days?"

"A few days?" She couldn't imagine going all the way across the country for a few days.

"Yeah." There was a silence on her end. "I'm not sure how long I'll be free to be with you, so I can only make it definite for a few days."

"Which days would those be?" She felt detached and powerful.

"Well . . . I don't know. How about the next few days?"

"You mean tomorrow?"

He became impatient. "Yeah . . . tomorrow . . . until the week-end."

"I can't come tomorrow and probably not for the rest of the week." She wasn't going to go at all but wanted to see how far she could take him. Would he protect himself at all costs?

"When can you come?"

"For a few days?"

"Yes, yes. For a few days."

"I have a job."

"A job?" He was surprised. "How can you have a job?" There was a pause. "Don't you show?"

"It isn't a sin, Sanche. Anyway, I feel fine and I'm working for a friend." She said it in a way that sounded as if the friend were more than a friend.

When he responded with a knowing, "Oh, I see," she let it go.

Miranda did go to California, spurred by a tiny item in the paper stating that Sanche Ray had purchased an original property which he would call *The End of Love.* Purchased? *She* was the original property and no money had come to her. It made her furious to think he might stiff her. Was that why he had been so skittish over the telephone? Promising David to be gone no longer than five business days, she set off for Beverly Hills.

She hadn't told Sanche she was coming and expecting the worst, was gratified to be greeted warmly over the telephone and met at the airport. His first shocked glimpse of her, however, evaporated all of his good humor and most of his composure. Her size, the enormous belly that trembled as she sat erect on one of his armless sectionals, confused him. She had tricked him in some terrible way.

"I never believed you would really keep it," he said. "Why'd you do it?"

"Why not?" She held herself protectively.

"How are you going to take care of it?"

With the joyous father's help, of course. "I've done all right. There's enough money to last for a while and then . . . I have a job." She smiled wryly. "It turns out I have all these hidden talents. I'm not your usual party girl."

He appeared relieved and became more animated. "I'm glad you showed up," he said. "I want you to make some more tapes for me. We've found a producer for your movie, John Summertime. It's not going to be schlock, Miranda. It will be a metaphor about the ruinous state of love. Like *Marty*. Or *Woman Under the Influence*."

"Will I get paid?" She knew he was only calling it *her* film to flatter her. Did he think it would flatter her into giving it away?

"You'll get five thousand up front, and the contract spells out the percentage deal once the movie comes out. You can look it over while you're here."

Seeing that her trip was going to pay off, she relaxed. "And what *is* the ruinous state of love?"

"When people talk about love today," he said, his eyes wide and serious, "they're really only talking about fear. Fear of being alone. Love is dead."

She thought about that. Did that mean nobody loved anybody? That nobody had ever loved anybody? That wasn't true. She searched around for people she had loved and who had loved her. She and Natalie and Sara had loved each other. She loved David. She had loved Sanche when they were in Europe, although that really did fit his description. It had been a fear of being alone. She could see that clearly now. She sighed and wondered why she had come and if she should stay.

That night he made love to her carefully. His methods were posturally good for her condition and she experienced an extraordinary orgasm which made her hopes flicker once again. Soon after, however, the sight of her naked profile made him brood again.

He paced across the room, far away from her. "What bothers me is that you had it on purpose and now expect me to feel something. I don't like that. I don't want to feel anything. Girls get abortions right and left. Where do you get off keeping it when I never promised you anything?"

"If that's what you think, forget it. I'll be all right."

Her calmness infuriated him. "*All right?* How can you be all right?"

For the first time she realized he hadn't set out to desert her or "do her dirt" as SueEllen was fond of saying. It was worse. He simply hadn't thought of her at all, and now that he had to, it annoyed him. He wanted to think about his work. His connections. His screenplay. His Oscar possibilities. His grosses and his nets.

He had no connection with the squirmy, knobby-heeled being inside her. How could he think about it? He had never felt it move or kick or hiccough. She felt desolate, yet relieved that there would be no more false hopes and dreams. Through the misery and fear of what was to come there was a renewed determination to have the baby.

In the morning he was all business and handed her a list of questions about Bob Paxton which he wanted her to answer on the tapes. He wanted to know what Bob Paxton slept in. Did he brush his teeth before he went to bed? Did he bite his nails? Did he insist she wash before making love? Did he cry out during lovemaking? What was his favorite food? What kind of underwear did he wear? Did he like seafood? Who was his favorite author? Did he ever kiss her back? Her neck? The inside of her hand?

"No, no, no," she whispered into the microphone, eager to be done and head back to New York. "He kissed my mouth, my forehead, my shoulder. He slept in pajamas and wore Jockey shorts. He liked to read Louis L'Amour novels and Ian Fleming. He liked shrimp, hated lamb, hated rice, hated pork. He played handball with his friend, Hal. As a child he played the trumpet. He was allergic to many things—wool, tomatoes, certain synthetics. He had to wear all-cotton shirts which were hard to find."

"What did he love about you?"

"I don't know. I think he had just made a decision about it and he . . . he just stuck by his decision. His friend, Hal, was getting married."

The second day in the afternoon the producer, John Summertime, came to the house dressed in an open-necked shirt and wearing a heavy gold chain around his neck. His hair was frizzed out around him.

"This is John Summertime, my producer," Sanche said in an unnatural voice. She could see he was nervous, afraid she'd say something unsuitable that would queer it for him with John Summertime.

"Hello." She stuck out a limp hand without rising. It was hot and the air conditioning was not functioning.

John Summertime straddled a chair and turned it so he could look directly at her. "You're a good-looking girl." It sounded as if he were mad at her for being good-looking.

One guy didn't think she was good enough to meet his friend, and the friend was annoyed because she was good-looking. She slumped inside and wished for her window seat, Sir Albert, and David.

After his second drink Summertime began to tell her what a socko story they had. "It won't be crap," he said seriously. "It'll be human. Boy meets girl. Boy does girl a favor. Boy fucks girl. Boy feels superior to girl. Meanwhile girl sees the light. Sees boy isn't going anywhere. Sees boy is shit. Girl hankers for more, but she's afraid. Then, whamo! Plucky fate steps in." He took a deep breath. "It's not your usual boy meets girl story."

She wanted to tell him it perfectly described the sequence of her feelings for Sanche, but she didn't think it was worth five thousand dollars for one smart-ass remark.

Two days later she was back in New York, exhausted but pleased with herself. Five thousand dollars would buy her several months with her baby.

After a week of brilliantly dry weather the beginning of September was muggy and sunless and seemingly without one clear whiff of air. Miranda began to have daily headaches and what was worse, a crushing fatigue. Sometimes when she left the agency and went home, she could do no more than drag herself to the window seat and lie there watching the dusk disappear into night. Overwhelmed by the need to sleep, she could not rouse herself and the street noises became part of her dreams. In the middle of the night she would be prodded awake by the urge to urinate.

Then she'd splash cold water on her face and pad down the hall to David's, knocking gently. They had an unspoken agreement. If he didn't answer right away, she was to go away. If he did answer, they would talk and drink beer and later fix each other scrambled eggs, after which she would go back to her own apartment feeling less alone.

When her knock on David's door went unanswered, she knew the tall thin man was there. She now recognized his step in the hall. She never questioned David. There were some things she could live without knowing.

Chapter 14

FOR TWO DAYS SHE FOLLOWED BILL HAAS around Manhattan as he visited two public schools, attended an electrical workers' union meeting, and in a complete about-face petitioned the city council to clean up the massage parlors that were cropping up alongside boutiques and dog grooming palaces.

She came away with the notion that Bill Haas was the darling of the teenyboppers, climbers, and women over forty. He was poetic-looking, rich, and boyishly charming in front of a camera. He rode his bike on Sundays in Central Park, nodding and smiling to everyone who cared. His suits were Savile Row and his accent pure Harvard, but he knew when to pump a hand with earnestness.

His opponent, on the other hand, was short, balding, and suffered a chronic postnasal drip which had him frequently making impolite noises. Unless Bill Haas turned out to be a child molestor, he was a shoo-in.

On the third day, for variety, Sara decided to follow Mrs. Haas on one of her typical days. Belinda Haas was one of those slack-mouthed debutantes who (one imagined) had been so indulged as children, they showed no inclination to work at anything, including keeping a firm hold on their lips. Her full, red mouth was always slightly parted. One expected drool to begin seeping down, but it didn't, and her generally outdoorsy glow was appealing.

She had an almost lanky figure that wore everything well. Her thick brown hair was loose and full, surrounding a round, innocent face in two loose triangles ending in a blunt cut that would have been described in *Vogue* as a "good blunt cut."

Belinda hadn't toned down any part of her personality for her husband's campaign. Bootsie, as she called him, would not win or lose because of anything she did or said. Bootsie would win or lose depending on how much money his father sank into his campaign and on the quality of the photographs they took of him and how he appeared on television. Bootsie's image was impeccable. He was the sort of man people wanted to trust with their lives and money. He was great at sports, came from an old Boston family. If she behaved badly, it would only have the effect of making the public gallop to his support.

Sara trailed Belinda in and out of Saks and Bendel's and watched her put in a perfunctory ten minutes at St. Anthony's orphanage to dedicate a new playground donated by her father-in-law. After a quick stand-up lunch at Nedick's Belinda retired to Bloomingdale's where in the space of thirty-five minutes she purchased a raccoon coat, a pair of Dior jeans, and an even dozen of Calvin Klein's silk shirts that came in twelve dazzling colors.

While Belinda was in the dressing room struggling into skintight leather pants, Sara timidly slipped into a short fur jacket. It was long-haired in shades of beige and fit her perfectly.

Belinda came out of the dressing room and surveyed the effect. "Amazing."

"What's amazing?"

"With a little fixing up you could be a knockout."

"Hardly." Sara put the jacket back on the hanger. "Cute maybe but not a knockout."

"For myself I hate cute." With a flounce of her leatherbound derrière Belinda rummaged through a rack of leather vests.

"This is my best middle-of-the-week outfit, you don't like it?"

Sara wasn't about to get into a hassle with Belinda Haas, but she could not pretend the remark hadn't stung.

"Want to take some advice from a spoiled brat?"

Sarah looked uncomfortable. "I'm not here to pass judgment."

"No, but I know what you're thinking. You think I'm a rich, mindless bitch who never did a day's work in her life. As a matter of fact"—Belinda looked thoughtful—"I work very hard, but convincing anyone of that is of no interest to me."

"Okay, okay, the thought has crossed my mind . . . and I'm sorry. It's none of my business. It's probably sour grapes. I suppose if I were asked to trade, I wouldn't exactly turn it down. So it must be sour grapes."

"Don't feel rotten. At least you're honest." Belinda's face lit up. "Now that everything's out in the open, would you take a little friendly fashion advice?"

"Like what?"

"Let me choose a whole outfit for you . . . everything. It won't be a present, it'll be a . . . a hand-me-down from me to you. I have an appointment upstairs for a cut and makeup, and we'll make them squeeze you in, too. We're going to the theatre tonight and you're tagging along, right?"

"Yes."

"Okay. You'll look gorgeous."

Under Belinda's direction they attacked Sara like the beauticians of Oz had attacked Dorothy. Her hair was cut short, disciplined to one side, and sculpted around her face. Her eyes, already wide apart, were further emphasized by plucking a wide path between her eyebrows. A facial brought a glow to her skin and contouring foundation made her cheekbones stand out like the "damn Rocky mountains," according to Belinda.

"See," said Belinda, who jumped from her seat every five minutes to look at her, "I knew you had good bones, and you've been just letting them go to waste."

As a last touch they inserted extra lashes among her real ones with the assurance that she could count on the extra fringe for a couple of months. She looked both sultry and childlike. When Sara saw the finished product, she smiled shyly, shocked at the change.

*　*　*

In the cab on the way to the theatre Belinda and Bill Haas spoke to each other in sullen voices that were almost identical in accent and timbre.

"Your mother called. She wants us out there this weekend," said Belinda, looking at the back of the driver's neck.

"Oh for Chrissakes, didn't you tell her that's impossible?"

"No, darling, I'll leave that to you. She might think I was trying to keep you away from her."

"Jesus"—he pronounced it *cheesus* and Sara couldn't help but be impressed—"don't you ever let up?"

"No," Belinda replied good-naturedly, arranging the folds of her skirt with infinite care.

Sara made herself as small as possible while trying to keep her clothes uncreased. Each time she hunched over the slightest bit, she caught sight of her breasts—the dress Belinda had chosen plunged to the waist—and suspected Bill Haas caught sight of them, too, but remained more interested in belittling Belinda.

The fact that she could feel so totally different about herself in the clothes and hairdo Belinda had chosen for her was unsettling. Where the hell was the real Sara she had been banking on and shoving up the ladder of life all these years? She had been shown that without much fuss she could be a totally different person. It wasn't a small point.

That she was having such an epiphany while these spoiled strangers were throwing poison darts at each other didn't amuse her. Life was often bizarre and the closer you got to the apex of money, success, and power, the more bizarre it became. Still, she wished Bill Waring could see her tonight.

The theatre was jammed outside and there was not much breathing space, much less walking space in the tiny lobby, but money soon talked. Out of nowhere a man appeared and ushered them to the manager's office. Political candidates, Sara found, don't sit down until everyone else is seated and the lights dim. Their seats are always on the aisle and they are "discovered" like buried treasure at intermission, after which they are allowed to escape by any exit that suits them. She wasn't complaining. It was fun to be with the favored group, even in the retinue. People stared at her and wondered out loud who she was.

Within minutes she forgot about herself and the Haases. The actor who played the lead, Sam Johnson, had completely captured his audience and in addition seemed very familiar to her. She had seen that face before, and it wasn't on a movie screen or on the stage. She had seen it recently and close up.

At intermission she called home and the baby-sitter assured her the children were safely asleep; Mr. Reynolds had called to speak to them before bedtime.

"Will you come with us to supper at Shepheard's?" asked Belinda when they returned to their seats.

"Only for an hour or so. The last train is at twelve fifty-five."

"Sam Johnson's going to join us."

"You mean him?"

"Uh huh. He's an old friend of Bootsie's from the Athletic Club."

"Why do you want me along?"

"Because you look gorgeous . . . and . . . it will be better if there are four of us." There was mild sarcasm and mischief in Belinda's voice which left Sara mystified.

Once inside Shepheard's and facing a drink she did not want, Sara had some regrets. The crushing decibels made conversation impossible. It also made her stomach hurt. Because there was little else to do, she stared at Sam Johnson openly. He invited close attention and had perfected a short-range stare that focused on absorbing action taking place a few inches above everyone's head. He appeared perfectly at ease saying nothing. He didn't look lonely or left out. As a matter of fact he made everyone else look lonely and left out.

Belinda was inspecting a plate of food that had been set before her. "What is this," she asked, stabbing at a dark object, "a turd?" No one answered. "And this . . . what would you guess this is?" She turned to her husband who was looking around absently.

"Belinda, shut up. Why do you order food in these places?"

"Because I'm hungry, Bootsie. I'm starving." She turned appreciative eyes toward Sam. "Sam's performance took everything out of me." It sounded as if she'd had an orgasm.

Belinda left her food untouched and stared pointedly at the dance floor. It was impossible not to focus on the frenzy of movement before them. Sam, it now appeared, had not read any of Sara's cues—signaling that she wished to remain invisible until she could leave. He expressed an interest in dancing the hustle. But not with Belinda. With her.

Sara froze. What did she know of the hustle? If he were just being polite, it would kill her.

He held her firmly and she found herself moving correctly in a strange new body. Did it come with the hairdo, this new twitchy body? It felt as if she were looking down on herself from some high place, like the grackles and mourning doves that perched on the wires near her house. *I am in it, but not of it,* she said to herself and thought of Sister Francisca's disapproving mouth because she had paraphrased Jesus. Never mind. She would console herself with private jokes. These were not people to confide in.

Sam Johnson's arm tightened on her back. "Let's get out of here."

"What! Are you kidding?" She was appalled at her own lack of finesse, but he had surprised her. "Was this a setup?" What was her will against this giant of the stage and screen?

"I need your help." His manner was totally winning. "Belinda is placing her hand farther and farther up my thigh. She's an excitable girl and I'm fond of Bill."

"You're fond of Bootsie?" She couldn't keep the sarcasm out of her voice.

"Bootsie can keep his cool. He isn't aggressive and has a remarkable knowledge of art and literature. He can't help it if he's rich. Also," he paused significantly, "he wears well which is more than I can say for most people."

Was he putting her in her place? She was having an increasingly difficult time knowing where her place was and felt suddenly very tired. She didn't want to keep her shoulders up another minute.

"I'm exhausted," she said, not caring about anyone. "This dress is like a booby trap. If I don't stand straight as a rod, my breasts fall out. Besides, I've got to catch a train."

"I'll drop you off at Penn Station, but to simplify matters don't mention that at the table. As far as they're concerned, I'm wildly interested in you. Do you mind?"

"Mind? Why should I mind? You're terrific." They smiled at each other for the first time. "Be as wildly interested in me as you like. I'll bite the bullet."

He smiled again and it struck her anew how familiar he looked.

She knew someone with just those intense dark eyes, just that set to his head. The chin. The dent.

She was relieved to be alone again even though her outfit was woefully out of place on the dingy train. Her day of beauty was over.

She crawled into bed without removing her make-up and was startled to find Reynold asleep in the bed.

"One of the men was passing this way and gave me a lift," he said in the morning. "I thought I'd take tomorrow off." He was clearly surprised by her appearance. "By the way what kind of a hairdo is that?"

"It's my *African Queen* haircut," she answered lightly. "If I were deserted on a lonely island without a comb, I'd still look okay when the rescue team arrived."

As she began to set the table for breakfast, he tapped her on the shoulder. "Could I see you inside a minute?"

The children were drinking their juice, and she followed him into the bedroom where he promptly locked the door. "I want to make love to you and your new haircut," he said. "Come on." He began to unbutton her nightgown.

"You're crazy. Aren't you supposed to lay off this stuff? Pardon the pun."

"No, I'm not crazy. The deadline is next Tuesday. I won't be home."

"The kids are waiting for their breakfast."

"They can wait."

There was some scuffling at the door. "Why is this door locked?" asked Rachel imperiously.

"Mom and Dad are having a serious discussion," said Reynold as he dropped his pajama bottoms.

"About us?" asked Rachel sternly. "Is it about us?"

"Of course," said Sara weakly. "Who else would we discuss?"

"That's good." She was mollified. "Shall I give Charlie his cereal?"

"That would be wonderful," said Sara, and then it was blessedly quiet.

On Sunday night she drove Reynold back to the compound for two additional weeks of recuperating. The following day she had lunch in the city with Jane and turned in a rough draft of the Haas piece which had come quickly and easily. What Sam Johnson said about Bill Haas made sense. He kept his cool, was intelligent, and wore well. He was also, as she had observed when she had seen him with Rudy Sorbentino, a pragmatist. She saw nothing wrong with that. It was an intelligently upbeat piece.

As she walked out of the elevator, she saw Bill Waring striding toward her, and her body reacted so violently she was certain it was obvious to anyone who could see her.

"Excuse me, can I get back to you later today?" he said to his companion, a man from the sales department. "You look wonderful." He rested his hand lightly on her shoulder. She struggled to remember what she looked like and what she was wearing. "I hear you're doing a piece on Bill Haas and I'm anxious to see it. Come with me."

He took her arm and led her gently through the maze of desks to his office. She was aware of people staring, but he took his time and nodded pleasantly from time to time. Once inside he motioned her to a couch and sat next to her. She was aware that his thigh was inches from her hand, and she drew away, lacing her fingers close to her chest as if in prayer. This seemed to amuse him and he smiled.

"Have you given some thought to what I asked you?" he said gently.

She let out a tortured grunt and rose as if the couch had become too hot. *"Some thought!* I've given it every thought." She looked ready to cry. "I think about you all day."

"And when you think these thoughts, what is it that you think, Sara?"

"Mostly . . ."—she tried to look into his eyes but couldn't—". . . mostly, I think about you touching me." She was amazed to admit such a thing in broad daylight to a man she hardly knew. She might as well have asked him to fuck her which also crossed her mind.

He pulled her down beside him and took her hands in his. She looked so woebegone, he seemed genuinely sorry to have caused her trouble, but touching her made it worse. It made her instantly damp and she blushed, retreated, and gripped her small leather pocketbook.

"You're not the only one affected," he said wryly. Her eyes traveled to his crotch. The soft linen was distended and he made no attempt to hide it. She could see the tiny basketweave zigzagging wildly and she yearned to touch it. She looked away and to her horror began to laugh helplessly. She crossed to the window and looked out trying to control herself.

"You find my erection amusing?"

"Oh, no. It's not that kind of laugh. It's just . . . I'm just too keyed up. Please don't think that."

He didn't think that. He knew precisely why she was laughing. She was nervous, but not nearly as nervous as he. That he could be crouched in a corner of his office fighting down an erection caused by holding someone's hand was not quite believable. She wasn't even beautiful, although her eyes were. She was merely vulnerable. She telegraphed her every emotion. She knew absolutely nothing about holding her cards close to her chest. Added up, it touched him beyond reason. Blinded by her body, she would have done almost anything he asked and been forever sorry. For the first time in his life Bill Waring thought twice before taking something he wanted. He had to think it out again.

"I have a meeting," he said with a sigh, "we'll speak again." He started to rise and then sank down again. "You'll understand if I don't see you out," he said dryly as she let herself out.

Strapped safely into her hunter's green hatchback and speeding home to Horse Hollow Estates, Sara felt neither guilt nor remorse. Her attention was centered on a throbbing ping, ping, ping all over her body.

Up to that day her timid fantasies of Bill Waring had not gone beyond a tight embrace, the hasty placement of her mouth on his, heads burrowed into necks, probably her head burrowed into his neck. Their hands remained chastely above the waist. There was a general amorphous hardness in the vicinity of her hips, but she had never, *never* visualized Bill Waring's cock as it had appeared straining against the expensive fabric of his pants.

Now the images were chaotic. There was no kissing or nuzzling. There was only a montage of filled orifices. His cock in her mouth, her breasts in his mouth, her cunt in his mouth, and finally, blissfully, triumphantly—his cock in her cunt.

She had never thought in those terms before. She had never thought of a man's penis as a cock or referred to her own vagina, the place where her children had emerged, as a cunt. Yet there was no other word for it. It felt swollen to twice its normal size. She felt bold and reckless and free, as if she had shed her skin. Her mind was clear and generous.

As she turned off the expressway, a small child in the car in front waved out his back window. She wanted to ignore him, knowing he would continue to wave for miles, but something about the child was naggingly familiar. He had a mass of black, curly hair and fleetingly she assumed it was Jeremy Van Druten. At that moment she remembered who it was that Sam Johnson looked like. He was the spitting image of Natalie's son, Jeremy.

On the Thursday after Labor Day, visiting the ladies' room, Miranda found blood stains on her underpants and afterward sat in her office with the door closed and her feet on the desk.

A few minutes later David walked into her office with an enormous grin on his face. He placed a check on her desk for fifteen hundred dollars. It was made out to her.

"What's that for?"

"Did your friend Sotheby mention anything about sponsoring a Sinclair Hour of Song as a television special?"

"No."

"Freda Heller just got the okay to buy the time. An hour of prime time on ABC for two consecutive weeks. Do you know what that means in cold bucks?"

She tried to look interested, but her fervent wish was to be transported home by some magic means and placed in bed. "A million?"

"A million to ABC and one hundred fifty thousand for us. Want to go out and celebrate? Have dinner at a fancy place, huh? Hey"—he moved her face so he could see it clearly—"don't you feel well?"

"I feel as if someone slipped me something. Could you just get me a cab and put me in it. I don't think I have the energy to raise my arm and flag one down."

"I'll do better than that. I'll go with you." He stuffed the check into her handbag. "Don't forget this is in here."

He got in the cab with her and she promptly fell asleep against his shoulder. The bleeding seemed to have stopped. During the ride he could see her belly moving and at one point felt a distinct jab against his arm which made him jump and startled Miranda.

"I think the kid kicked me."

"What kid?"

"Your kid. He just kicked me in the arm. You think he's trying to tell me something?"

She smiled and said nothing.

"There's something really in there."

"Mmmmm."

When he got her in bed and removed her shoes, he looked around at the bare, empty room. "Where were you planning to put the baby? You don't even have a proper bed for yourself. Suppose he's premature? He could be born tomorrow and he wouldn't have a place to sleep. No wonder he's kicking me. He's worried."

"David, they're tiny when they're born. They can sleep in a drawer. A box. Anything."

"A drawer? You'd put him in a drawer?" He looked at her as if she'd lost her senses. "A box? Miranda, are you sure you've thought this out?"

"I'll buy something next week. I promise."

"What about Saturday? We'll go to Bloomingdale's on Saturday. Everyone's still going to their weekend houses. We'll have the store to ourselves."

She started to point out to him that it was not his baby or his worry, but he looked so pleased by the idea, she didn't have the heart. "All right, David. Now go back to work. I'll be all right. Really."

She stayed in bed most of the weekend except for the brief trip to Bloomingdale's where David purchased something called a Port-A-Crib which could be used as a crib or a playpen and folded flat for travel. She liked the idea that she could travel with it, although David argued for a much sturdier model—a Danish sleep box featuring mobiles and red and yellow graphics. But Miranda shook her head. In the end he gave in and insisted on paying for it, adding a stuffed koala bear at the last minute which made Miranda cry.

"Jesus," she said, blowing her nose. "I cry all the time."

The spotting had not returned, but she was glad her monthly appointment with Dean Whitley was scheduled for Monday. Now that she had a crib and a koala bear, she also wanted to get some answers from him.

After her examination, when he motioned for her to come into his office, she bypassed what she liked to call the poor-dumb-son-of-a-bitch chair across from him and perched instead on the edge of his desk. It was a massive desk, solid mahogany, dark and self-righteous. The desk went with the precise part in his hair and the nice rep tie under his white coat. It was probably his school tie.

The bleeding had frightened her, but the idea of telling him and having him confirm some dread complication frightened her even more. In the end she convinced herself she'd be better off knowing the truth.

"Dr. Whitley," she leaned forward, swinging one bare, tan leg in front of him, "why do I bleed? You must have some idea."

"One can never be su . . ."

"I'm not asking you to be sure," she leaned closer. "Why don't we discuss what it might be . . . Jeez," she turned her face away, ". . . you doctors are so touchy."

He was touchier than she supposed. He wanted to take her perfect tan calf and rub his cheek against it. He thought of stern Nurse Wasserman innocently trying to manage a roomful of patients before they became cranky. Nurse Wasserman would not approve of Ms. Lesley who besides taking up more than her share of his time, was unwed and probably unprincipled as well. She was also full of life which is what attracted him. That and her looks, of course, which were dazzling. He answered her with measured primness.

"Placenta praevia."

"What?" She stood up amazed. "I have it?"

"You might. It happens to be my specialty, so you're in luck."

"Well? What is it? Is it a disease? Is it terrible? No, it wouldn't be terrible or you wouldn't tell me. You guys don't want any scenes."

"You seem to have hardened your heart against the medical profession," he said with mock civility.

"Personally I think they should list your medical school grades along with your telephone number."

"That, Ms. Lesley, might wipe out half the country's doctors and create a serious health hazard . . . or a health bonanza, depending on one's views. . . . Now," he straightened the edges of her records, "about placenta praevia . . . it doesn't have to be terrible. We have ways of dealing with it, and if we know it's a possibility, we take precautions."

"But *what* is it? Just a simple description will do," she added sarcastically.

He showed her a replica of the placenta from a plastic see-through model he kept on his desk of all the paraphernalia women needed to procreate. The placenta was broad and busy-looking with angry colors, red and blue and purple. The cord at its center looked angry too.

"I like to call placenta praevia the 'Catch-22' of the birth process," he began, gratified to see her eyes alert and neutral. "The placenta, usually attached at the fundus or top of the womb, has grown too low and covers the opening, the cervix, partially or completely. As the cervix begins to dilate in the last few weeks of pregnancy, the placenta begins to tear and ceases to be a lifeline. If the placenta remains intact, there's no opening for the baby to come out." He paused. The complication intrigued him. The placenta did such a miraculous job for the nine months, a marvel of genetic ingenuity, the pièce de résistance of God's perfect creation. "Usually," he continued, "the placenta does the job quietly and when it's over, after birth, the cells and appearance resemble those of an eighty-year-old human being. Spent. Unsung hero."

"My God," she sighed. "You make it sound so . . . so . . . . personal."

He smiled and tried to sound tough. "I'm going first this time, baby. When you go first, nobody thinks of me. From now on it's gonna be different." She was grinning and he wanted to kiss her. "It would make a good film, don't you think? *Placenta praevia,* starring Jimmy Cagney as the placenta."

She laughed out loud but then turned serious. "Suppose it begins to tear away? What can you do to save the baby?"

"In the extreme case there's always Caesarean, if the woman is at term anyway. Sometimes bed rest helps. It might repair itself. So you see," he paused significantly, "we have options."

He stood up to see her out and she walked and stood in front of him. He was not like any other doctor she had ever met. She meant simply to kiss his cheek in gratitude, but when they were inches apart, something other than friendliness passed between them. Instead of his cheek her lips sought and found his proper Boston mouth. His response was unmistakable—hungry and probing. She backed away in confusion, gathered her things, and left. It was the best and worst thing she could have done to him.

After her talk with Dean Whitley Miranda began to feel stronger and resumed her normal routine. One evening Albert Sotheby called her as she was leaving work and asked if she was free for dinner. She didn't want to go. She still tired easily, but he seemed determined and she couldn't refuse him.

"I'll meet you in the lobby," she said. It wouldn't do for David's best client to see her bare apartment.

She showered and dressed carefully in the white tunic and pants that Barbara had given her. It was still the best outfit she had, and while it no longer hid her belly, it covered it elegantly.

He arrived shortly after seven thirty in a chauffeur-driven car and got out to look for her. The doorman, who had many times been crude in the way he looked and spoke to her, was impressed.

"Sir Albert," she crowed pointedly, "how nice to see you." She was hoping to elicit two or three very British sentences out of him to further dazzle the doorman.

"My dear," he took a long look, "you look absolutely beautiful. But what have you done with the baby?" He blushed at his own daring. He had never mentioned the word baby, referring to it only as her "condition."

"Oh, he's in there." She grabbed his hand impulsively. "Want to feel a kick?" Albert Sotheby looked flustered and uncertain. He clearly considered her belly much too intimate a part to touch, with or without a baby. Even if he had secretly wished to devour Miranda, a thought he had never given quarter to, the doorway of a building was not the place to make such an advance. He cringed noticeably. "My dear, you *are* exuberant tonight."

The reprimand was not lost on her. She felt a twinge in her lower back and fatigue began to seep into her bones. Sir Albert could be a jerk. She had to keep in mind how stiff he was, and the thought tired her even more. Why had she agreed to go out with him? She certainly wasn't hungry and not in the mood to sit and make inane conversation no matter how elegant the restaurant. She wished she were at home watching something dumb on television with David. Anything would be better than this.

"I want you to meet someone," he said when they were seated in the back of the limousine.

"Someone else is coming?" Shit, shit, shit. Would this evening ever end.

"Yes. A wonderful chap. Amusing. Knowledgeable. Absolutely first-rate in his field. I feel most fortunate to have him working on our behalf."

"An American?"

"Ummm. The producer of our television special."

She was only mildly interested. She looked past him out the window to the chic stores along Second Avenue. They were going downtown toward the Fifties. The sun was fading and she caught him looking intently at her face.

"You look so innocent, my dear . . . and so beautiful. Are you sure you're going to be all right? I could help, you know."

When some people said they could help, what they really meant was that they wanted to own you. They wanted to drop in on your life and take over. She wanted to say, *Sir Albert, I would let you help, but the fact remains that you would drop dead just looking at my apartment before we even got to the rest of the details. You would not survive the shock.* "You're very kind," she said in her poor-but-resourceful voice.

When they entered the restaurant, an expensive French one, she knew immediately something was wrong. Peering straight ahead, waving a breadstick at a waiter and then suddenly altering his appearance when he noticed Sir Albert, was none other than Bradley Gifford.

"Sir Albert," he rose and turned to Miranda. "Well, we meet again. How have you been?"

She was sure he remembered the outfit and was looking menacingly in the direction of her breasts. She would burn this hateful tunic in the bathroom tonight.

The men quickly settled into intense conversation, Bradley not quite as intense as Sir Albert. The conversation slipped in and out of her head, and she was not able to hold on to one word. She was aware that intermittently Sir Albert asked her opinion and she gave it. They were loosely hammering out the details of the special for Sinclair. Her ribs began to hurt from sitting so long in an uncomfortable position. The banquette gave her back little support, and her ribs were being displaced by her rising uterus. She yearned to lie down. She was holding herself stiffly, too, which didn't help. At one point she was certain Bradley's hand had lingered menacingly close to hers.

Bradley had lost weight and appeared tan and dapper in a light-weight, beige linen suit. She thought of his beige apartment and the platforms and mirrors. Did he get lost when he sat there in the suit? She thought of Sanche and his sober outfits. The two of them had a lot in common, but Sanche would feel naked in such a suit. Transparent.

When Sir Albert finally delivered her to her apartment, he kissed her impulsively on each cheek and smoothed her hair. "You look awfully tired, Miranda. Isn't it time you stopped working?"

"I'd be too lonely. What would I do at home all day?"

"Don't you have a family?"

"No." He looked so dismal, she would have gladly produced a perfect Norman Rockwell family to get the frown off his face. "Don't worry about me. I'll be fine. I love going to work. I don't think a baby ever suffered from his mother working while she was pregnant."

"Probably not." He patted her hand and left.

The phone was ringing before she opened the door. She knew who it was but was afraid not to answer. He would continue to call. She picked up the receiver and held it to her ear.

"God, I got so horny just looking at you." He didn't waste time with hellos. "Can I come over?"

She stared at the calico print covering some pillow and at the tiny, innocent flowers covering the recess above her bed. Each little design was distinct, but overall it seemed just a jumble and made her dizzy. She could not say anything. Not even no.

"Are you there?"

"Yes."

"Let me come over. Please. It won't be like before."

She thought of Sir Albert and of David. Could Bradley do something terrible to her through them? Could he do something terrible to them through her? Oddly, the terror she felt was not personal. It would affect everybody. "Please, don't call me again."

She put the receiver down, but it rang almost immediately. "We'll just sit and talk. I've got to see you."

She considered how powerless she really was. Who could she turn to to make him stay away? Only another equally powerful man. But what man? Her life was complicated by the fact that she cared about

David and would do nothing to hurt him or his business. He had given her a job and looked after her. The way not to hurt David was to keep Sir Albert happy. Sir Albert was leaving for England by the first of November, just two short months away. When he left, she could do as she pleased. Well, not exactly. By December her baby would be on the outside.

"I can't speak to you right now, I'm very tired."

"I'll call you tomorrow."

"I won't be here. I work. Let me call you."

"That won't be necessary, Miranda," he said as if refusing a second cup of tea. "I know where you work and I'll be waiting there for you."

The next day she didn't go to work and called SueEllen to tell her if anything important came up to ring her twice and then hang up. She was entitled to stay home after last night's stint with Sir Albert.

"Trying to shaft some guy, huh?" replied SueEllen with her customary directness.

"Of course not. I just don't want to talk to anyone unless it's business."

"Okay. Two rings it is," said SueEllen with a yawn and hung up.

It was only a delaying tactic. Bradley Gifford had not become what he was by being respectful of the rights of others. Still, she didn't know what to expect or how far he would go or if he were in control or out of control—all that vagueness frightened her.

Thinking about this, she stayed in bed most of the day, rising only now and then to drink a cup of tea or a glass of juice while she stared out the window. Her throat felt dry. She couldn't get enough to drink.

At six thirty there was a light tap on her door. She assumed it was David and exhaled with relief, then realized the footsteps had not been David's. She knew his sound.

"I know you're in there," said Bradley. "Come on, let me in."

The doorman had let him up, probably for money.

"Come on," he said when she finally opened the door. "After all I'm not asking to fuck you."

"What are you asking?" she said in a tremulous voice.

"Not much." He was coming toward her. He was smiling and small beads of perspiration had formed on his upper lip. "Very little, actually.'' As he got closer and actually touched her, his voice became less casual. "Don't turn me down. Don't turn me down.''

When he said that, she became very uneasy. He was not the sort of man who pleaded for anything. When he discovered he was pleading in vain, he would be angry and vengeful.

She brought her knee up clumsily to where she thought it might cause the most trouble and he doubled over. Then she heard another light knock and knew this time it was David.

"What's going on here? Miranda, are you all right?'' David looked around perplexed. She saw that he and Bradley knew each other. "Bradley . . .'' He looked at Miranda. "You know him?''

"Yes,'' she said dully and reminded him of the night she had dragged into his apartment weeping and distraught.

"But why didn't you tell me?''

"I didn't want to be the cause of anything going wrong with the Sinclair account.''

Bradley was straightening out and looked at David with contempt. "Why should you care? Her cunt can't be of any interest to you.''

David's eyes went wide with surprise, and he punched into Bradley first in the stomach and then in the mouth. Bradley recovered, composed except for the wild look in his eyes and the fact that when he tried to speak, he was out of breath. "You'll both be sorry,'' he said, and they didn't doubt it.

Bradley's power was more decisive and swift than either had imagined. Even though it had been his idea to befriend Miranda, Albert Sotheby now was convinced he had been set up and Miranda had been used to manipulate him. He was determined to repay the cunning seducers in kind. He took his account and its millions in billings from David's agency.

The money they had counted on from the Sinclair commissions had already been used to finance pilot projects in market research. It couldn't have come at a worst time. The blow was almost lethal to the agency. David showed none of this and he told Miranda over and over not to blame herself, but she saw what it did to him. He retreated into himself. He became secretive and not as well-groomed as before. The tall, thin man came more frequently and many times she heard loud quarrels.

She tried to think of what she might do for David but had to confront the fact that her life wasn't exactly pointed toward a rosy future. She was again alone and without hope of support. Only this time her time was running out.

Chapter 15

THE SECOND TIME NATALIE MET RUDY Sorbentino it was at the Summit Hotel and he apologized for the room. There was a convention of orthodontists in town and this was the best he could do. She suspected he was lying, that he had chosen it because the location was convenient for him, but she didn't mind. The room was gaudy and impersonal, and it made being there less dramatic than the first time in the high-ceilinged Plaza suite.

She also felt less tense knowing what to expect, but he surprised her by sitting in a straight-backed chair, totally clothed with his legs slightly apart so she could see the activity in his trousers. He held her hand as if they were courting in some Victorian parlor and massaged it.

"Whenever you feel like it," he said calmly, as if reasoning with a balky child, "just reach over and pull down the zipper."

She wondered if she were strong enough to outlast him, but then the picture of Sam and his actress came to mind and she couldn't act fast enough. In the end she did everything he wanted, wondering through a haze of excitement if these were true and tested scenarios that Rudy had perfected over the years.

The third time they saw each other, two days after the second, he offered her cocaine which stunned her. She had rationalized that their meetings were outside of her life, and that made them bearable. To take drugs and get "high" with Sorbentino was insane. After that he offered her a drink of Scotch which she gratefully accepted and drank straight down. He pointed out that it was Chivas Regal and that made her smile. She knew also that he would not be embarrassed to find that she considered him socially clumsy. He would laugh, too, and agree with her, and this meant that there was no easy way for her to hurt him.

"What are you trying to show me, you need to get drunk to make it with me? That's silly, baby. Think about how silly it is," he said amiably when she finished her Scotch.

He was right. If she didn't want to make it with him, why would she be there.

After the second time he stopped trying to make her talk. He talked for both of them and didn't expect her to answer, in fact seemed to enjoy calculating her answers. He was always slow and deliberate but never failed to begin with the slightly contemptuous appraisal of her cool exterior and her hot interior. He didn't want to let her forget it.

When she asked herself why she kept seeing him, several ideas occurred to her, the most compelling one being that pregnancy had made her highly excitable and that it would pass. Also she imagined Sam watched them.

"How many guys have you screwed?" he asked one afternoon as if he already suspected the score was poor.

She looked away.

"Don't tell me it's only *him*." He turned her face back. "How many others . . . one?" She lowered her eyes and refused to look at him. "Only *one* other guy?" It wasn't true, but it might as well have been. "Boy . . . he had to have been some guy. Huh . . . ?" He kept going. ". . . Was he some guy? Some good-looking guy who didn't go for you, was that it?"

She continued to look down shivering a little. "No, of course he went for you, babe." He reassured her as if her feelings were hurt. "What guy in his right mind wouldn't go for you?" She jumped as if he'd hit her, which in a sense he had. How had he known?

He took a long, lazy puff on his cigar. "Ah . . . I thought that would get you. How does old dumb Rudy know the guy didn't go for you? Well . . . your face just sort of crumpled when I talked about him, and I know you're still hot for him. You gave it away, sweetheart. The minute I mentioned his name, your little titties got hard." He waited for this to sink in. "But you know something? Even though you loved that undeserving bastard, you didn't love him enough. Rudy knows. If you had loved him enough, no man in his right mind would have left you." This unexpected conclusion touched her and two fat tears began to roll down her cheeks.

"What happened to Mr. Wonderful? You've seen him since?" He tried to figure it out, searching her face for clues. She had wiped away the tears. "Don't tell me. He fucked you a couple of times and then he split. Son-of-a-bitch. Insensitive shitheel. How could he do that to you?" For a moment he seemed genuinely concerned. "But what are you doing wrong, babe? There's something you're not ready to give the guy, or he wouldn't have split. Listen to Rudy . . . a broad like you could have anyone." He sought out the place below her belly and settled his head there. He played with her and kept burrowing his head back and forth just above her pubis. He seemed to think by rubbing back and forth against her skin, he might hit upon some other way to get inside her. She finally pushed him down between her legs, and he willingly complied until she again made her wishes known and he entered her. They rocked back and forth, entangled like two halves of a hobbyhorse, until they climaxed facing each other, their necks and arms strained, veins showing, fingers hanging on for dear life.

The next two times he called she didn't go. She wasn't sure what he did when she didn't show up because from the beginning she never said on the phone whether she would or wouldn't come and he never asked. The third time he called she was caught off guard. "I'll be there," she said and immediately regretted it.

"What are you going to do when I'm gone?" he asked when it was over and she was dressing to leave.

It made her angry, but then she understood that he wasn't being sarcastic, but trying to figure it out. "Your old man's not going to get any better," he added seriously. "If he knew about you . . . about us . . . he's nutty enough to kill you."

Alden was not unaware of the changes taking place in Natalie. As a matter of fact, his predilection for meditation made him particularly observant, and he noticed that she dressed more gaudily and that a certain energy exuded from her that had not been apparent before. She was restless. All those quiet hours spent at Pheasant Hill were incompatible with the twitchy woman she had become.

One day as he bent to kiss her, the strong odor of cigar smoke rose from her hair. She caught his look and muttered something about people smoking in the tiny office she shared with Cora. There were other smells which he caught from time to time.

"My wife is sleeping with another man," he said one day to David, "and I don't know what to do about it."

David shrugged. "Does it bother you?"

"That isn't the point."

"Isn't it? I would think you'd be glad not to have the responsibility for . . . for . . . her sexual needs." He was about to say, "screwing her," but he knew Alden hated coarse talk and seemed exceptionally touchy. He had had enough glimpses of his violent temper not to want to arouse it unnecessarily.

"It's the deception," he said. "She's willfully . . . no . . . it's careless. Carelessly deceiving me."

"Oh, come on. What do you want her to do, ask your permission?"

"You don't understand," said Alden, and his voice was weary. "It isn't the sex . . . it's the pregnancies. Why should she do that again? It's high contempt, wouldn't you say?"

David was bored with the discussion. "I've heard of *haute couture* and *haute cuisine*," he said lightly, "but never *haute contempt*."

Alden was not amused and sat grimly, two fingers holding his forehead.

"If it bothers you so much, why don't you divorce her?" asked David.

"A divorce? What good would that do? That would just relieve her of all responsibility. No," he grimaced, "not a divorce. It has to be something that will cause her continuing anguish . . . as she has caused me."

David didn't like the trend of the conversation or the emphasis on the word "anguish." Also, he was trying to get up the courage to ask Alden for a loan, and this talk about his wife's affairs made him anxious. They had not been getting along so well lately, and he was afraid Alden would end the relationship before he asked for the loan. Now he was afraid there wouldn't be enough time to bring it up gracefully. He didn't want to be crude about it. He wanted to give Alden the background of his financial difficulties so as not to appear irresponsible. He prided himself on having good business acumen, and it distressed him that it appeared he had lost clients through carelessness or stupidity.

Finally one night he broached the subject.

"Alden," he said quietly, "my business is in serious trouble. It has nothing to do with my abilities or bad business practices—it was just . . . well . . . one piece of bad luck. If I can get a temporary loan of three hundred thousand dollars, it would pull me through."

He could see that Alden was surprised. Alden had not expected anything like that.

"Requests for money have a bad effect on me," he said. "Sometimes I feel as if I have never had a true response from anyone in my life, even as a child. As if every encounter had been carefully calculated to get something from me." He gulped his drink. "Don't misunderstand. I'm more afraid of the supplicants than they could possibly be of me. After all, they know what they want which gives them a certain advantage. For myself my attitude about money seesaws wildly between a desire to flee with a modest annuity and a desperate need to involve myself in every decision even down to the household accounts." He paused. "Do you understand? I can't possibly give you money."

David nodded. "I want you to remember I was your friend before I knew who you were."

"I'm well aware of that," said Alden, and a look of gratitude came over his face. "Perhaps I can think of another way to help you get the money."

David remained silent. He knew that if it happened at all, it would have to be on Alden's terms.

Harvey Bosch was keeping Natalie waiting and she wondered when and why she had lost her place on his roster of preferred patients.

Harvey never missed a chance to massage an ego, and while his methods were obvious and crude, his practice thrived among people who normally didn't tolerate crudeness.

As a young resident he had saved the life of Cora Sandford's niece who had tried to self-abort, nearly killing herself along with the fetus which had been found (uncannily complete save for the eyes) among the blood-soaked Porthault sheets.

Harvey had not only saved the girl's life, but repaired her perforated uterus and managed to detraumatize her. The child, he lied, was hopelessly defective. He would have been a vegetable had the pregnancy gone to term. It was for the best.

From then on he was the favored ob-gyn man of every woman within the reach of Cora's persuasive voice. He had his office in one of the dark limestone buildings on Park Avenue. You reached his suite by a private elevator whose door sported scenes of nubile maidens dancing in the forest.

Natalie had never liked Harvey Bosch. She suspected he was secretly contemptuous of his patients and probably didn't like babies any better. He was most distant to those who needed his sympathy—menopausal wives about to be divorced and women who ached for babies but could not conceive. He was privy to the most agonizing secrets and used the information to his own advantage. She knew he would be aghast that she had waited almost six months before coming to confirm her pregnancy. What could she say? Harvey, I've never liked you; I had to force myself to come here; I probably won't come again? No. She would thank him as she always did and get away as quickly as possible.

She felt sleepy and clumsy and lacking in energy and was glad there was a car waiting. The off-duty policemen from the village next to Pheasant Hill who moonlighted as chauffeurs always drove her in now.

The waiting room was empty except for an ill-dressed young girl staring off into space. Natalie shrugged and closed her eyes. Almost immediately she thought of Sorbentino. She was no longer able to rely on her contempt for him to keep her sexual feelings under control. She wondered if it were inevitable for a pretty, blond woman of means to end up with such a lover.

Would she continue her clandestine meetings once the baby came? God, no. Sorbentino would go his own way. He had told her so. He

told her many things, talking nonstop at times. Lately he had been
very interested in her growing belly, the spread of her hips, the dark-
ening of her nipples, and the unmistakable line that was beginning
to dissect her body.

"Fascinating," he would say. He often cradled her belly. Kissed
it. Rubbed his penis against it, and she wondered what, if anything, it
would do to the gestating child. She had read that the fetus could hear
everything and "sense" plenty. Could he hear and sense Sorbentino.
Would the child turn crude and arrogant with an overly developed
libido? It amused her that Sorbentino, the least likely candidate,
would become the spiritual father of her unborn child.

"You here to find out?"

Her eyes flew open. It was the girl. "Yes."

"Me, too. How many months have you missed?"

"Four," she lied. She didn't want to have to explain anything.

"Yeah," the girl nodded approvingly. "That's good. They can
still take it if they want to. Not with me."

Take it? The girl was very agitated and couldn't keep her hands
still. "How many months are you?" asked Natalie.

"I think five and a half, but I'm not sure because my period's
always been irregular. It used to come very heavy every three weeks,
so they gave me some shots and for a while it didn't come at all. I
thought it was okay, you know . . . I thought I didn't need to use
anything. But then I started feeling woozy in the mornings and
throwing up . . . and . . . now . . . well, it looks too far gone.
What do you think?" She stood up and pressed her skirt under her
belly to show its true size.

"It's hard to tell," said Natalie with a reassurance she didn't
feel. "Some people get big right away and the baby can be quite
small."

"Yeah," said the girl with relief. "I guess that's true. I didn't
think about that." She waited a moment and stared down at her
hands and twisted a soiled sheet of paper folded several times. "I'm
not sure I want to give it up."

The girl sat down again. She had on a sleeveless cotton shirt and a
full, flowered skirt that hardly closed around her waist. Her shoulders
were lightly tanned with a dusting of freckles which were repeated on
the bridge of her nose making her look younger than she probably

was. Her eyes were very deep set, appearing as two round, reflecting pools cut out of her face. Outside of that her teeth were very bad, some overlapping and in need of care. Her hair was listless and thin. It needed cutting and washing. She stared at everything with the same interest. Narcotics, Natalie decided.

The girl cleared her throat. "I know I don't want them to take it. I'm just about sure on that score."

It sounded as if she was making the decisions as she sat there. "What does the father think?" Natalie knew already the father didn't think much, if anything, but there was little else to say.

"He hasn't been around for a month, but I called his father's office. Strange what you remember when you need to. Dougie used to brag about his father. He always wanted to make believe his father found us in the apartment—which was crummy-looking—how shocked he would be. Not about what we were doing, but about the condition of the apartment. Imagining that scene always made him laugh. He thought it was funny that he spent so much time with me when he could have spent his time in really swell places. He liked to shock me with how rich they all were. He said they were in the stock market, so I called each of those Wall Street offices until I found the one where he worked and I said who I was and that his son, Dougie, had got me pregnant and I didn't have the money to get fixed up. Two days later he sent me fifty dollars in an envelope and told me to come here. That was a couple of weeks ago. He said this doctor would do whatever needed to be done and not to worry about the cost. But that's not exactly what I wanted. I figured if they're rich and everything, I could keep the baby and raise it, and Dougie could come around or not whatever he wanted. I don't think it's right to kill a baby just for nothing, do you?"

"No."

The girl twisted the paper which she had waved around when she spoke.

"Is there anyone to help you? Your mother?"

"I'm not from around here. I came from Michigan eight months ago and worked for the telephone company. I was doing real good, too, on the Teletype—where you type the message instead of speaking it. Businessmen use it a lot calling manufacturers to find out if this or that's been shipped or when it's going to be shipped. Fabrics, boxes, machinery, you name it. But it got boring after a while. You couldn't leave to go to the bathroom without a replacement. Everyone in a line . . . plugging holes . . . plugging lights . . . no windows . . .'' Her voice trailed off. ''My mother didn't want anything to do with me once I left home. She thought I was loose and wild which isn't true. I'm not wild at all.''

Natalie believed her. She didn't look like she had enough energy to be wild. Her fingernails were badly bitten and she was quite pale. Her lips were chapped and peeling. She probably didn't have the money to eat properly, and it looked as if she wasn't sleeping well.

''You really think he'll pay for it, don't you?''

Natalie waited to answer and the girl took her silence for doubt. ''I saw the building where the father works. I went down and had a look at it. It's very big and his name's on the directory. They must have some money. Dougie was just in college and he always had bills rolled up.'' She referred again to the paper in her hand.

''I'm sure he will,'' said Natalie. She wondered what the girl would look like with her hair cut and her teeth fixed.

The nurse came and called the girl in. ''Miss Morgan, go into the first room on your right and put on the gown on the table. Doctor will be with you in a minute.'' The nurse was impersonal but kind. A few minutes later Natalie was called, and she forgot the girl thinking how distasteful it was to have Harvey Bosch examine her. She would look for another doctor after this visit.

Harvey Bosch removed the thin plastic glove which he had used to feel her uterus and tossed it in the wastebasket. ''My congratulations to Alden,'' he said in the high-pitched voice that so irritated her. ''Let's hope, Natalie,'' he paused significantly, ''that this one will stick around the full nine months before it pops.''

He was purposefully trying to humiliate her and she said nothing. ''After you dress, we'll chat in my office,'' he said gaily. ''Sorry, if I kept you waiting. I had a little knocked up bunny to look after.''

He left the room and she began to dress, wondering what she would do with the rest of the afternoon. She had been thinking of buying something for Sara who had twice sent Charlie to play with small presents that had transported Jeremy. There had been a train engineer's cap and a carpenter's apron with ten different pockets which Jeremy wore nonstop every weekend. It made her happy to get Harvey out of her mind by thinking about pleasing Sara with something beautiful and unexpected. She knew Sara would like something extravagant but useful. Perhaps something French. Sara was the best friend she had had in her life. Almost the only friend.

"Everything's normal," said Harvey when she was seated across from him. "You're about twenty-two weeks along." She thought it was odd that he didn't chastise her for not coming earlier. He was playing with a smooth, polished-silver paperweight. "Alden was in to see me," he said suddenly. "He's concerned about the poor record he's had impregnating his wives. He wanted me to take some tests."

She was surprised. She had no idea Alden cared one way or the other, and while she had never used anything to prevent pregnancy, she had taken her infertility to be a matter of infrequency rather than lack on his part. "But that's ridiculous. This is . . . well, I'm pregnant. It's no hallucination."

"Of course, but . . . he wasn't convinced . . . at least then. He wanted to be sure his sperm count was adequate for . . . well, up to the task."

This explained Harvey's manner today. She was under suspicion, and Harvey relished nothing more than using people's intimate secrets to humiliate them. She rose to leave.

"Don't you want to know the outcome of Alden's test?"

"I know what it was," she said and walked out.

The girl was still there, sitting back as if nothing was worth moving for. "Have you had any before?" she asked Natalie who stopped in front of her.

"Any what?"

"Babies."

"Yes. One."

"Do you feel this dragged out? I just can't move."

"Only the first few weeks." Impulsively Natalie added, "Can I drop you off somewhere? I have a car outside." She despised Harvey for referring to the girl as a knocked up bunny. She hoped the nurse reported that she had taken the girl with her.

"All right," said the girl and roused herself with great difficulty. But when she got in the car and Natalie asked where she wanted to go, she looked vague.

"I don't suppose you'd let me ride around wherever you're going?"

The first thing Natalie thought was that she might be a thief. "I'm not going to hit you for money or anything like that," said the girl. "I always liked riding around." She leaned back and closed her eyes and Natalie relaxed in her own corner. "Take us to Bloomingdale's, please," she said. She would buy Sara's present before taking the girl home.

In the housewares department she found what she wanted almost immediately. A set of squat, oversized cups and saucers delicately handpainted with tiny white flowers on a midnight blue background. They could be used for soup or coffee and would look just right in Sara's modern kitchen. She had them wrapped with a card that read, "For my dear friend, Sara. Love, Natalie," and gave the saleswoman the address.

"She's been asleep," said the chauffeur when Natalie got to the car. There was no mistaking his feelings. Natalie shook her gently. She looked much younger asleep, maybe fourteen or fifteen. She could take her home, she thought. To Pheasant Hill. Feed her, give her a good night's sleep, and then bring her back.

"Sorry I conked out on you."

"It's all right. Where do you want to be dropped off?"

The girl seemed to rouse herself from some deep, private reverie. "Oh, yeah . . . sure." She opened her pocketbook and looked through it, carefully placing its contents on the seat between them. There was a half empty packet of Kleenex, a small plastic comb, several bobby pins, a pink wallet stuffed with snapshots, the piece of paper she had held at Harvey's office, and a small brown address book.

The girl picked up the address book. "I don't have the key," she said. "I'm staying with a friend now and she didn't have an extra key. I have to call and see if she's there."

"I'll have to go around the block," said the chauffeur, watching them in the rearview mirror.

Natalie pointed to a phone booth on the corner and told her they would circle the block and pick her up on the way back.

"To the apartment, ma'am?" The chauffeur assumed it was a tactic to get rid of the girl.

"Of course not. Go around the block." She couldn't leave her there.

* * *

"There was no answer," said the girl through the window when the car stopped in front of her. "It's a neighbor's phone. She could be there. She sleeps a lot." She looked up and down the street.

"Would you like me to go with you and wait?" asked Natalie.

"All right." She gave the address as 466 East Third Street.

It was a three-story building sandwiched between two taller ones of once beige brick. Her building had a fake stone veneer that made no attempt at authenticity. The downstairs buzzer was finally answered, and they entered a tiny landing that smelled strongly of urine and garbage. The stench made it impossible to think of anything else.

Her apartment was on the top floor, and the first real shock was the woman who opened the door. She was beyond thin. Her skin had shrunk as if someone had slipped a realistic human mask over a skeleton.

"Jesus, Marcelle, where the hell you been?" The voice was raspy.

"I had to go to the doctor."

The woman looked dazed. "What about the money?" She had the most agonizing look of anxiety on her face. "You said you'd give me the money if I let you stay."

Small beads of perspiration began to form on Marcelle's forehead and upper lip. She looked unnaturally flushed and her pupils were dilated. Natalie hoped it was due to the exertion of climbing the stairs. "I had to take a cab to the doctor."

"You don't have the money?" The woman was suddenly furious. "You don't have the money, you motherfucker? You were shitting me all along?" She went for Marcelle with angry, flailing fists.

"No, wait. Janine, don't . . ."

Natalie positioned herself between them. "I have the money," she said softly, and Janine's fists fell instantly to her sides.

"You do?"

"Yes. How much was it?"

"Five," said Marcelle with contempt.

"You mean five dollars?" Natalie was not convinced she understood.

"Yes."

She pulled five dollars out of her wallet. The woman took it sullenly and headed for the stairs. Meanwhile Marcelle took two dresses out of a closet and slung them over her arm. She was muttering to herself. "I'm not staying another night with a goddam junkie." She stuffed some underwear into her pocketbook and two paperback books which, Natalie noticed, were about childbirth. "Goddam vicious junkie. I'd be better off in the street."

Natalie couldn't get herself to enter the apartment, but saw enough from the door to convince her that Marcelle was right. "Come on," she said to Marcelle, who now had angry tears rolling down her cheeks and all her worldly possessions on her arms.

They rode to the apartment in silence. If Marcelle was surprised by Natalie's circumstances—the chauffeur, the doorman, the marble foyer which was larger than the entire apartment she had just left— she did not show it. She was mildly interested in the large living room overlooking Park Avenue but then fell silent and refused to react to the rest of the extravagant surroundings, as if it were a tiresome joke that had gone on too long. She slumped into a brown velvet wing chair and waited.

"How about a sandwich and some tea?" asked Natalie.

"All right." She didn't seem particularly interested in the food but asked for a Coke instead of the tea.

"What did Dr. Bosch say to you?"

"You mean him back there . . . the baby doctor?"

"Yes."

"He said the family would pay for an abortion, but if I decided to keep the baby, I'd have to pay for it myself."

"Did he say anything else?"

"Yes. He doesn't want to handle the case if I decide to keep it. He said I couldn't afford to pay him and I'd have to go to a clinic. He said I was a foolish girl and at the age when birth defects are sky-high."

"How old are you?"

"Seventeen."

"What are you going to do?"

"I don't know. It's too late to have them take it. He says it's still possible, but I don't think so. Maybe I waited on purpose." It didn't seem to bother her one way or the other. "He said something else that scared me, but I wouldn't let him know it."

"What was that?"

"He said I was small-hipped. That a baby would have a hard time getting through my bony passage." For the first time she looked worried. "Do you think that's true?" She stood up, pulled her skirt around her hips, and presented her backside to Natalie.

"You look all right to me." She looked neither small nor big, and Natalie was furious to think that Harvey had purposely frightened her to accommodate some spoiled brat whose parents were no better than he was.

Marcelle closed her eyes and slept almost instantly, and Natalie's thoughts once again turned to Sorbentino. It had been two weeks since he had called, and she felt a twinge of worry that perhaps he wouldn't call again. She decided to call Cora at the Haas office, thinking she might have been expecting her and had forgotten about the doctor's appointment. Also she would tell her about her stray waif.

Cora made understanding sounds as Natalie told her what she had done, leaving out the part about Harvey Bosch.

"That's admirable, Natalie, providing she doesn't murder you in your bed. Is she on drugs?"

"Of course not."

"Our minister used to send my mother all the unwed mothers in the parish, but none of them would eat properly or take exercise which infuriated mother. They refused to be grateful or take orders. Secretly I was rooting for them since I was too much of a coward to buck the rules. By the way"—Cora's tone turned arch—"you had a mysterious message . . . at least it came on your line."

"Oh . . . from whom?"

"It's not a name, does that make any sense?"

Her heart began to pound. She would see Sorbentino after all. "No."

"Just a number," said Cora. "Well, two numbers. Fifty-first and five sixty-four. Does that make sense? It was a man's voice. Very smooth."

"Sounds like a bookie or someone making a bet." She said her good-byes and went to change her clothes before she remembered the girl and scribbled a note: "Had to go out. See you in an hour or so. Ask Eva (push bell over the fireplace) for help if you need anything. N."

* * *

She hailed a cab and pulled away seconds before another cab, bearing Alden, arrived. He saw her and asked the driver to honk, but the car did not stop and she didn't look back.

He called Cora immediately to ask if she was expecting Natalie. "Natalie couldn't come because she had a little, needy guest," said Cora brightly. "You'll find out about it soon enough. There was a strange message for her, though. Maybe you can figure it out." Cora sounded excited, as if she had stumbled on a secret. Natalie had turned secretive and didn't share anything with Cora anymore. She repeated the numbers to Alden and mentioned that it had been a man's voice.

That the strange message she had delivered to Natalie would end in plain and simple fornication, Cora had no doubt. But who? Sam had no need to be coy or secretive. While some of the details were a mystery to her, she knew that her plan was near fruition. Miraculously, events had conformed to suit her needs. Perhaps the crazy Rosicrucians were right. Could mental energy focused steadfastly on a single objective really bring it about? It seemed so. The message was childishly simple to decipher. She had no doubt that Alden was at that moment rushing to Fifty-first Street to get a good look at his wife's lover.

Alden stiffened, but a surge of gladness went through him. The idea that he could focus his anxiety on something concrete pleased him and his mind became alert and cunning. Five sixty-four and Fifty-first, a message so enticing, it had persuaded his wife to leave a stranger in their home.

"Fifty-first Street," he said when he'd hailed a cab.

"And?"

"I beg your pardon?"

"Fifty-first and what?" asked the driver impatiently.

"Oh . . . anywhere. Make it Fifth." Then he remembered that Natalie's cab had turned south and toward Lexington Avenue when it disappeared. If she were going to the West Side, it would have made a U-turn on Park to Eighty-sixth Street and gone through the park. It had to be East Fifty-first Street. "I'll take Lexington instead," he said.

The Summit Hotel was on the corner where the cab let him out, and he felt decidedly lucky and thoroughly interested in his adventure. His mind was working efficiently.

Everything went well. The man at the desk did not look surprised or curious when he requested the room directly across (which was actually diagonally across) from 564, which, he added casually, belonged to his friend. The clerk stifled a yawn and having collected twenty-two dollars handed him a key.

He could smell her perfume in the air, and for a moment it depressed him. He was sorry it hadn't been more difficult to figure out. His brain and senses were functioning optimally and he wished to give them more intricate clues to solve. As he waited there behind the door, opened a hair in order to hear the slightest movement in the hall, he considered the consequences of what he would find. There was not much to do and his mind was racing.

His thoughts began to drift backward and forward in time. There were moments when he would watch Natalie in the evening as she read a book under soft lamplight and scenes would pass through his mind of everything that was going on inside her. Her belly would grow huge and protruding, out of control, or so it seemed to him.

Then he would remember the details of the other pregnancy—the size of her, the quixotic contractions that occurred during the last few months. What happened to the child when the uterus contracted? Was it pushed into some awkward corner? Into the ribs or the spine? Did it press down on his little chest, crushing tiny riblets? He had heard of babies being born with ribs broken and they blamed it on the birth itself, but he suspected it was the actions of the uterus; and who controlled that but the mother?

When his second wife had borne a child (it had died shortly thereafter), he had been a director of the hospital, and Harvey Bosch had insisted that he don the mask and white gown and join him in the delivery room. His wife was completely awake and normal from the waist up, having had only her lower spine deadened.

That had been years before the natural childbirth craze. Now everybody was clamoring to be let into the delivery room. All those dreary, long-haired young men taking pictures of their wives' vaginas. All those big-breasted women shoving tits into tiny, pursed lips. He had seen the engorged vulva of Samantha's mother when the baby had emerged. He had not meant to see it, but Harvey, sadistic son-of-a-bitch, had placed a mirror so he would not miss anything. The sight of those engorged lips ballooning out was something he would never forget. It looked like an enormous mouth belonging to some Ukrainian peasant made disproportionately chunky by starchy food and hunched-over labor.

Soon after he and Janet were divorced. Thinking of Natalie now, he wondered why in the world he had married again.

His mind turned again to the room across the hall. For a moment he sat back on the floor dazed. The pieces had fit into place so perfectly. Maybe he wasn't actually experiencing it but having a very, very vivid reverie. He marveled that he had such control of his life. But no, it was real. He was in this strange room, and the smell of her perfume was wafting in through the crack in the door.

What would he do to her and to . . . to . . . *him*! Perhaps nothing. Perhaps it would be enough to know.

It was not. He was stretched out on the floor diagonally in relation to the door which was open a crack. He had made the room as dark as possible, and with his nose against the jamb and his eye directly at the crack he could see almost twenty feet down the well-lit hall. When she came out, he saw her perfectly. He saw her face alive and dazzled and it sickened him beyond expectation. He saw the man, but only vaguely. He was watching Natalie as she hurried down the hall.

The force of it hit him. It was, in the worst sense, breathtaking. He had to do something about it or choke with rage. That son-of-a-bitch Harvey had lied to him. It wasn't his sperm that had given her that goddam swollen belly. She had tricked him again. But this time he would get her. The plan to do so flooded into his head so complete, it had a calming effect. He would get her where it would hurt the most.

Dolly and Lucinda were naturally suspicious about Marcelle's sudden appearance. When it became clear that she was no threat to them, they settled into a disgruntled muteness. Mr. Simmons was icily noncommittal except when he had something to report.

"The young lady takes bread and carrots to her room. I've suggested she might eat more at meals if she's hungry, but she says that's not the case."

"Miranda," said Sara softly when she met Marcelle a few days later. She and Natalie looked at each other. Marcelle reminded them of Miranda.

"She doesn't look at all like her," said Natalie.

"No. But that's all I can think of when I see her."

"I suppose I feel the same," said Natalie, frowning. "She's stubborn like Miranda. And full of secret courage. Remember I promised Miranda I would always take care of her . . . oh God, the girls of St. Mildred's."

The first week at Pheasant Hill Marcelle slept most of the time, and then as if she had passed through a stage, she stopped sleeping and took an interest in her surroundings. She shocked them all by speaking fluent French to Cardon. She taught Jeremy the French name for everything in his room, and pretty soon they were greeting each other with *bonjours* and *bonsoirs* and comment-alley-vooz which further mystified Dolly and Lucinda. That she could spout such an elegant language contradicted their original impression that she was hopelessly low class.

"We lived on the border, you know," she explained to Natalie. "There was a French-Canadian woman who took care of me until I was eight while my mother worked."

Natalie took Marcelle for a haircut, and when a dressmaker came to measure her for the plain linen maternity A-lines she needed, she also measured Marcelle.

If Marcelle was pleased to be plucked from her seedy life to plusher shores, she didn't show it. She accepted everything with a polite reserve. The only talk that really interested her was about her growing baby. She read books by the dozen and asked to be taken to bookstores in the area to see what they had on pregnancy and birth.

Marcelle gave them all something to focus on, and the old grudges in the mansion were momentarily forgotten. Being maiden ladies, Dolly and Lucinda were totally absorbed by every detail of the pregnancy.

"He has all his backbone, his brain, his heart, and lungs," she told them with wonder. "His heart's already pumping all his blood and he's no bigger than my hand. In another month my bones will go soft on me. Can you imagine your bones going soft?" Dolly's eyes grew beady with interest. "That's so they'll spread enough to let it out."

Marcelle spent most of her days outdoors. She had a daily swim and helped in the vegetable garden. "If it's all right, I'd like to work in the patch," she would say to Natalie.

Jeremy was the one to most directly benefit from Marcelle's presence. He became her shadow and it seemed they understood each other. She didn't try to get him to like her which immediately intrigued him. "Well, come on if you want to," she'd say on her way to the pool or the vegetable garden.

She never got tired of watching Jeremy, and Mrs. Remington decided to visit her family in England. At first Natalie would tag along with Marcelle and Jeremy when they went to the pool.

"I'm not going to let him drown, you know," said Marcelle as she and Jeremy were leaving one afternoon and Natalie rushed to join them.

"I know you're not," said Natalie and felt an inexplicable sense of relief.

Natalie went into the city two or three times a week and on one of those days visited Rudy Sorbentino. Her need of him increased. The things he said stayed in her mind, making her remember what had been happening when he said them. At times she despaired that he could get her to do the things she did, not the least of which was running to meet him when he called. But beneath the surface static was a definite gladness. Her body had become a source of wonder to her, as if she had discovered new hands and fingers that she hadn't known about. Sometimes she cried convulsively thinking that she had accepted so little all these years. Although she would have never told him so, she was grateful to Rudy. He was the prince that had kissed her awake.

The most remarkable thing that could be traced to Marcelle's presence or at least to her arrival was the change in Alden. His moods were less morose, sometimes even jovial. While he seldom spoke directly to Marcelle, he often spoke of her privately, and it was he who decided that Marcelle should eat with the family, a decision based more on the fact that the dinner table needed livening than not wanting to hurt her feelings.

Also he showed films at night, something that hadn't been done in years. And he invited Marcelle to join them. They now made quite a crowd, which seemed to please him.

Whereas before he had only been politely affectionate with Jeremy, now he spent time with him watching him dive, offering pointers and encouragement. To Natalie's surprise and dismay he began to assert himself in bed as he had not done in almost a year. He often stayed in her bed the entire night and spoke to her in the mornings before Simmons appeared with his tea. If Simmons was surprised, he did not show it, placing the tray discreetly by Alden's side of the bed and leaving the drapes closed. One morning Natalie awoke to find him looking at her with a curious expression.

"I've decided you should have an abortion," he said casually.

She was shocked enough to sit up. "Why?"

"I'm not up to another child. It's senseless. I'm quite sure you're doing it to please me and there's no need. I'll call Harvey later this morning. They need the father's okay, I'm told." There was irony in his voice. Then he swung his legs over the side of the bed and got up. The subject was closed.

"But Alden, you can't decide like that. I have a say in it, and I don't want to have an abortion." She had never considered it and now wondered why. Perhaps she felt she owed him a son. "You don't . . ." She had been about to say, *you don't have a son,* but stopped herself. Strange that in all these years she had never slipped. Since seeing Sam, however, it was all harder to keep straight.

"You mean you won't get rid of it?" Alden seemed genuinely surprised. "That's very disappointing to me, Natalie, and I urge you to reconsider."

The room was overly padded with drapery and carpeting and comforters and puffy furniture, all sounds seemed to get lost. His words didn't sound threatening or sinister, but his eyes were definitely not neutral. They appeared focused and deep and unnaturally bright.

After that conversation, although no one saw the connection, Alden became secretive again, and much of the secretiveness revolved around Jeremy.

Chapter 16

IT WAS EARLY OCTOBER. SARA WAS SUP-
posed to drive out to the lab and pick up
Reynold for the last time. He was healed and could now take care of
himself, climb stairs, drive cars, swing from the rafters if he so
chose, but he didn't have a car and she had promised to come for
him. She only had to stop at the office and cut twenty-two lines out
of her article on Bill Haas.

She had not heard from Bill Waring since that afternoon in his office, and her feelings had settled into a dull persistent ache in her
chest and thighs. The possibility that his desire for her had subsided
or vanished made her feel brittle and hollow. In the back of her mind
she had assumed they would see each other before Reynold was
healed enough to return home permanently. Now that was out of the
question, and she felt hot, salty tears of disappointment ruining her
mascara as she drove to the city. She was lovesick. There was no
other word for it.

When she reached the office, Jane informed her that Tania had
called an editorial meeting for four thirty and she was expressly asked
to attend. She would never make it back in time to pick up Reynold.

"I'm having one of those big days," she said over the phone. "Would you mind terribly if I didn't come tonight? Do you have plenty to read and everything?"

"I have *Jaws* and several issues of *Nature*. I'll probably read *Jaws* and scare the hell out of myself."

"Okay, then, I won't feel guilty," she joked.

"Don't feel guilty," he said seriously. "I'm a big boy."

She hung up the phone and felt freer than she had in months. She had nothing to rush home for. Charlie was going home with Marcelle to spend the night with Jeremy, and Rachel was to visit Penny after school. When the meeting was over, she could do whatever she wanted. It was a feeling she had never had in her married life and it scared her a little. "Earthbound" was the word that came to mind. She was earthbound. For one crummy night she didn't have to rush home and wipe somebody's nose and it scared her. She might take off like a rootless thistle.

At lunch she had two drinks and came back with a headache which annoyed her. A hangover would wipe out the day. She drank two cups of coffee and put ice cubes on her eyes. She worked on her article and attended Tania's meeting. Afterward, at a loss as to what to do with herself, she looked in on Jane and saw her hunched over her massive typewriter as if trying to intimidate it into submission.

"What are you working on so savagely?"

"How the rich entertain." Jane beckoned her in. "Would you believe bogus beef Wellington made from flank steak?"

"No."

"See. You're suckered in too. The rich are cheap. Except when they do it, it's not called cheap. It's called inventive and interesting. Oh, God." She stretched her long legs and sank back into her chair. Sara noticed she was wearing chartreuse wedgies and felt a wave of affection. "Why do we pass on this miserable information?"

Sara looked at her innocently. "How would the rest of us know what to strive for? What to break our backs for?" She slumped into a chair. "What else do they do? Come on, I want to know."

Jane shot her an exasperated look. "They make tablecloths out of old sheets. Not their new Wamsuttas, mind you. They're wash and wear and Bibsy or Fluffy can throw them into the Maytag herself if worse comes to worse. They use the old trousseau ones . . . and here's a direct quote, '. . . the wrinkly Porthaults that no one can be hired to iron anymore.' Enough?''

"Enough. But it doesn't sound so bad to me." Sara looked closely at Jane. She was as white as she had been at the beginning of summer. Pale was a better word for it. And tired. "What doesn't sound good is you." She looked at her friend in earnest. "Didn't you ever want to write a book or something other than . . . well . . . Lists, Lists. Lists. 'Three Ways to a Happier You.'"

"Are you kidding?"

"Then why didn't you? You could have taken a year off to try it. Your reputation is good enough to have come back if you didn't make it."

"Ah, but that's not how one makes it. If you have a failsafe clause, you're sure to use it the minute the going gets rough." She lit a cigarette and took several quick puffs. "One makes it by trying again and again . . . and by having the talent, of course. Besides, I was too happy as a kid. You have to have been really screwed up to be a writer. That's how you get back at your parents but good."

Sara let this go unchallenged. She was used to Jane's outrageous statements. "Don't say that. You have the talent."

Jane sank back, took a strangled breath, and rubbed out her cigarette vigorously. "Yuck." Then she turned serious. "No, I don't. I don't have the knack for the telling detail that makes something instantly alive." She looked mischievously at Sara. "But you do. You have it. You're such a wide-eyed dummy, you write everything you see, picking out everything that doesn't make sense. Look at this! and this! and this! It's all very quiet and sneaky and packs a wallop. You're the one who should be doing a novel. You're a natural."

Sara scrunched up in her chair. "Novels are something that Hemingway does or Fitzgerald or Thomas Hardy. I haven't even worked up to John Cheever. It's not for me. Not Sara from Long Island."

"Hemingway came from Idaho, for godsakes. I would tell you to stop playing Debbie Demure, but I know you're serious and that's too bad. You're wasting terrific talent on shit pieces to fit a formula. Look"—she could see that Sara was not convinced—"do a short story for us. The fiction editor is very democratic. If it's no good, she'll tell you."

"Okay. I'll do a short story."

"When?"

"Soon."

"Now." Jane growled. "It's got to be now."

"What do you mean now?"

"I mean now. Start today."

"Well, I don't know about today. There's . . ."

"Today." Jane was not to be budged.

Sara took a deep breath and smoothed her skirt. "Okay. I don't have to be home today anyway." Halfway out the door she turned back to Jane. "When I was twelve I had a short story published in *The Saturday Evening Post*. They said I wrote with a facility that held their attention," she said dryly.

"So you do," said Jane softly. Then she added, "Write about a dainty, romantic princess trapped inside the body of a broad-shouldered girl from The Bronx." She wrapped herself around her typewriter once again.

"You know such a person?"

"Yeah . . . me."

Sara wanted to say something consoling, but Jane hadn't expressed grief. It did no good to feel sorry for anyone unless you were prepared to find the perfect solution and hand it to them.

She went into the tiny office she used when she worked at the magazine and thought about what Jane had said. The grimy but imposing spires of St. Thomas stared at her moodily through the window. It was five thirty. At home young matrons would be scurrying into Gristede's to buy their chops and steaks for dinner. They'd be flushed from tennis, anxious to get some singles from the cashier to pay the sitter. Perhaps they could sneak a shower. She felt as if she were looking at her life from a great distance.

Three false starts and a sea of crumpled paper were behind her before a real idea began to form. *Natalie*. The mystery of Natalie and her son and Sam Johnson was never far from her thoughts. At times she had the eerie idea that she had stumbled on the information for a good reason that would soon be clear. After all, hadn't they promised to take care of each other when she had left St. Mildred's?

It occurred to Sara with an equal mixture of joy and pain that Natalie and Bill Waring were two of a kind. They sat on some higher ground, making it so damned attractive, picking and choosing someone to invite up. Why did it always have to be her? She sighed and began the story.

> I met her on one of the worst days of my life. It seemed insane that the worst and best thing could happen within hours of each other, but there it was. She wore a ring on her smallest finger which, at eleven, I considered extraordinary. She had the same effect on everyone. You wanted her to like you. You wanted to be important in her life because she was probably the most beautiful person you had ever seen.

When she had finished the paragraph, Sara realized she was crying.

There was a tap on the open door and she looked up to see Bill Waring. He was wearing a lightweight, double-breasted navy blazer and gray slacks. His tie and shirt looked as fresh as if it were eight o'clock in the morning instead of seven at night.

She stared down at her own dress made of fake but convincing suede which was supposed to withstand a day on a camel in the desert and come out shining. It looked terrible. The cuffs were dirty from resting on her desk which had not seen a cleaning lady for two years. Her hair was disheveled, her makeup no longer intact. It seemed fitting that he should see her this way. It showed her how useless it was trying to pretend you were something that you were not. She felt snively and cruddy and wondered just how her ordinary life had become so complicated.

He made no mention of her condition but sat next to her on an old file cabinet and took her hand. She was not surprised. It felt as if they had known each other a long time.

"Jane said I should write a short story," she said idiotically. She might as well have said, "Jane told me to wash my hands before dinner."

"Good for Jane." He began to smile.

"We'll see," she replied testily. How did he and Jane know so much about her.

"What's the story about? Sad, I would say from your general glum look when I came in."

"I was writing about my friend . . . well she wasn't really my friend, but I wanted her to be. We all did. She was incredibly beautiful but . . . uh . . . unpredictable." She was glad that he hadn't gotten to know Natalie.

"Unpredictable? How? With her affection?"

"Yes, exactly. She dabbled in people, and just when you thought she really liked you and were sort of planning your life around her, then she became vague and . . . and distant. As if . . ."—his eyes were level with hers and she couldn't help but look into them—"you had misunderstood everything. It made us miserable. We didn't like ourselves because she didn't like us."

"She could do that to you?" He appeared surprised.

"Especially to me." Both were aware that they were speaking about more than Natalie.

Bill Waring stood up and he was not smiling. Her eyes flickered on and off him in confusion. He was standing against a metal cupboard one leg crossed casually over the other. One shoe on point.

Sara knew instinctively that such revelations were the kiss of death for a man like Bill Waring. He wasn't looking for someone who really needed him. Someone who would look horribly sad and possibly cry and keep on wanting him for years after he had finished wanting them. Bill Waring was looking for someone who didn't need him at all. Someone who would take his beautiful parting memento, something expensive from Tiffany's, and sigh with satisfaction and good will. Even so, she wanted him and steeled herself against the hurt of such a moment.

"Do you still see your friend?"

"Yes. Only now . . . now," she tried to recoup her losses, ". . . I'm stronger." Her entire happiness at that moment depended on him. He was staring at her moodily, his eyes visibly adding it all up. It made her angry. "Don't be distant with me." She was grateful that her voice was strong and did not quiver. "Don't just stand there evaluating everything."

"*Distant?* Oh, my dear." Something inside him gave way. He pulled her to him and began to kiss her over and over, slipping in and out of her mouth. His hands were on her back, on her buttocks. One hand crept up her thigh. "Oh, no," she cried, "don't go there." She was embarrassed by her wetness, but it was too late. He was already there.

"I don't think it's a . . . a good idea," she said trembling, "to well . . . to kiss in the office."

"You're absolutely right. I've never done that in my life," he said tightly and turned his back to her to stare out the window.

"You don't have to say that," she said.

"I'm not saying it for your benefit. It's for my own. I'm trying to remember what I do and what I don't do." He was chagrined. If someone walked in, it would have been awful for her. "How about dinner?" He turned to her with a weak smile and she agreed with relief. Dinner was fine. Dinner was public and would give her a chance to get her bearings. She was even pleased that he was willing to spend some money on her until she remembered that he was rich and bolstered on all sides by expense accounts. Expense account days and expense account nights. She shivered.

Once out on the street she felt more in control. It was a cool autumn night, one of the best that New York has to offer. There was a pinkish glow over everything that was probably caused by some carcinogenic pollutant, but it made the streets look beautiful. When they were well away from the building and ready to cross the street, he got hold of her hand and gently pulled her across. She followed obediently.

When they were seated in the small, underlit restaurant off Fifty-fourth Street, she left him to repair herself in the ladies' room. She studied herself in the mirror and was surprised not to find her same old face looking back. She looked wild-eyed; her face had a luminous recklessness found in pictures of teen-age criminals. She smoothed her hair, rubbed a small, stubby brush over her nose and forehead, washed her hands, and returned to the table.

While he ordered drinks, she looked out into the narrow room. A middle-age couple, the woman overladen with chunky jewelry, were hissing angrily at each other. She felt sorry for them. Bill Waring was still busy with the waiter. She was able to stare at him and was again dazzled by his presence.

Dinner was a blur. A blur of something tricky and French drowning in wine. Had she ordered it? Of course not. He had taken care of everything with a few nods. He was known here. The waiter was used to his language. Had he brought other women? From time to time his thigh brushed against hers, but it was not intentional. He would not touch her in public. She was aware that her thighs ached from being pressed together.

Before dessert she excused herself to call home. It seemed years since she had thought about Rachel or Charlie or Reynold and was suddenly panicked by the notion that she might have to go home before she could kiss him again.

He suggested a phone be brought to the table, but she was horrified. How could she talk to Penny about Rachel? How could she chat idly with Reynold about his health? "I . . . I—no. No," she said firmly. "I'll go to the booth."

Rachel was bubbling over with news about school and told her a joke about a goat. Sara sighed with relief. "Why don't you sleep there." She hadn't planned to say that, but now she wanted to be free.

"I don't want to. I want to wait for you."

"Aren't you tired?"

"I took a long nap when I came in from school. It was so hot there today and the water fountain was out of order. I'm not sleepy at all. Can I just watch Merv Griffin with Penny?"

"Rachel, please sleep there. It's only for one night." Her voice was strained. She saw her freedom slipping away.

"I don't want to, mommy. Don't make me." And then as if she were tuned in to her mother's motives, she added, "I won't. If you don't come, I'll stay up all night."

Sara wanted to scream at her but knew it was hopeless. Even if she insisted, the picture of Rachel stubbornly clinging to the sofa, waiting for her, would ruin the evening. "I'll see you about ten," she said grimly and hung up. She decided not to call Reynold.

"Why does a goat wear a bell?" she asked Bill Waring when she sat down again.

"I don't know."

"Because his horn doesn't work." He laughed more than the joke deserved. She didn't laugh at all. "I can't stay," she said quickly. What could she say? Let's meet again soon? Make love to me, no strings attached? She was too firmly rooted in the past to say anything. The thought of Reynold filled her with remorse. She could see him reading *Jaws* in his innocent single bed. He deserved better. Perhaps Rachel had saved them all.

He was staring at her, and she decided he liked her more since the joke and began to relax. Maybe it was the wine.

"Why are you staring at me?"

"I like the way you look."

She snickered and looked away.

"You ought to be doing something that would bring in some money," he said suddenly. "To make yourself independent."

Why was he bringing that up now? It was the phone call. The phone call meant ties. People to answer to. He didn't like that. "Wouldn't you like money of your own? Not the piddling sums we pay you. I'm talking about substantial amounts."

"Of course. Wouldn't everyone?"

"Do something about it. You could."

She knew better than to ask for reassurance. When he said something, he assumed you understood that he had thought it out. He was not one for idle talk. "You have something in mind?"

"A book."

"A book?"

"Yup."

"A book about what?"

"That's not hard. There are only four or five basic plots."

She thought a moment. "I suppose that's true."

"The idea is not original with me." He sipped his coffee and signaled for the check. "Have you ever heard Gore Vidal on the subject? He says he always writes the same book with different characters. Choose something you feel comfortable with and you're off."

The check came and she took the opportunity not to answer. She couldn't think beyond her need to touch him and of being touched. When they were finally on the street, she searched out his hand. A few steps later he pulled her into the shelter of a small, fake Georgian doorway. He glanced briefly at the name—stenciled in dark blue it said, The Arlington Arms—and kissed her. She would not have thought that he would kiss her on the street. Desire for her had driven him to it.

He hailed a cab, put her in it, and kissed her once more through the window. She gave the driver the address of the parking lot where she had left her car and sank back to remember everything.

Even with all the attention and her genuine devotion to Jeremy, Marcelle was restless and wanted more to do. Also the lack of independence was something she couldn't get used to. A few days after Mrs. Remington returned from her trip to England, she went to Natalie.

"Maybe I could take care of someone's kids around here and do some housekeeping for room and board."

"You can stay here, you know that, Marcelle." Natalie was crestfallen.

"I can't just hang around the house all day. The weather won't stay good much longer. I'll go crazy."

Natalie knew this was true and a few days later, when she spoke to Sara, she knew immediately where Marcelle could go to work. She described the situation to Sara who promised to come right over. She had not done anything about permanent help since Mrs. Ramirez had left, and the housework was piling up.

Natalie was not completely happy about passing Marcelle over to Sara. She was not just another baby-sitter. Natalie felt some pride in her. Rest and exercise and a good haircut had made a big difference in the way she looked. There was a wholesomeness now that went beyond prettiness.

Everyone was disbelieving of how well it worked out. Marcelle and Sara's children were immediately compatible. She was neat, helpful, and not a big talker. When Reynold and Sara went out, she slept over in Rachel's room. Otherwise she returned to Pheasant Hill after dinner. On Mrs. Remington's day off she brought Jeremy to play, but it was never a casual thing. Mr. Simmons drove them both ways. Sara never asked why.

Then there came a day when Alden refused Jeremy permission to go there at all. Also he began to meet the school bus and walked the boy home, unless he was away in which case Mrs. Remington met him. When Natalie questioned him, he said it was precautionary. He also said he had his reasons.

It got worse.

One morning Jeremy whispered to her. "I won't be home on the bus today." He was struggling to put on his jacket on the way to the bus.

"Why not?" asked Natalie. "Going to visit Charlie?"

"Oh, no. Daddy's going to take me. It's a surprise. We're going some place together, the two of us. I'm not to tell you, so don't say I did, will you?"

"No, of course not. Have a lovely time and I'll see you for dinner." She kissed him twice.

"Not for dinner. We won't be home until nighttime."

"Oh? Not until nighttime?"

It troubled her. She waited for the bus anyway until she was sure Jeremy wasn't on it. She waited all evening, willing herself not to lose control and ask Simmons of Alden's whereabouts. At ten o'clock she heard the car in the driveway. Jeremy was carried in and laid on his bed fully clothed. She wanted to go in and see him but was afraid of a scene. She waited until Alden was asleep and then crept in, gently removed Jeremy's shoes, loosened his tiny belt, and whispered in his ear that he was home now and that mommy was close by.

In the weeks that followed Jeremy and his father followed this routine two days a week, and each time it was exactly like the time before. Jeremy was not always sure which days they would be, and he was a little relieved to see Mrs. Remington waiting instead of his father.

"Mrs. Remington," he said one day as they trudged up the driveway, "any volcanoes around here?"

"Volcanoes?" She gave a loud snort. "That's the silliest thing I've ever heard. Worrying about volcanoes when we have real dangers like muggers and thieves and kidnapers." But then she hugged him, sorry that she had brought up the word kidnapers. Would he now ask his father what kidnapers were? She was sure to be scolded about that.

He knew she was afraid he would repeat anything she told him to his parents, but he wouldn't. After all, hadn't his father made him promise not to tell anyone about David? And had he? No. Of course not. He liked going to David's, although he didn't like what went before, the waiting in the park. He also liked the fact that each time he was allowed to take one toy. "You'll build quite a collection and be glad about it when the winter comes," said his father. The image that came to mind was of a squirrel putting nuts away for the cold, and he liked that. He was behaving like a smart squirrel.

*   *   *

It was strange having Reynold home. Counting his hospital stay, he had been away six weeks. While he had spoken to Sara and the children almost every night, psychologically, he seemed to have vanished off the face of the earth. It was a shock for her to find how far she had moved away from him emotionally.

She kept busy. She finished her short story, sent it to *Haute*'s fiction editor, did some free-lance work at home, and waited for her piece on Margaret Martin to actually hit the stands. She also gave thought to Waring's idea that she write a novel. She would surprise him with a complete plot.

Marcelle was growing by leaps and bounds as was Natalie. The doctor said Marcelle had miscalculated and that her baby would probably be born in November. "You'll be flat by Thanksgiving," he reassured her, casting a respectful eye on her enormous belly. Natalie was due not long after.

It was now a week since her dinner with Bill Waring, and Sara found precious few moments when her mind was her own. She found it hard to listen to the children and hard to eat. She toyed with her food and lost four pounds which normally would have been cause for delirium but now went unheralded. This new, reckless Sara felt graceful. She moved differently, and as she and everyone else was well aware, she did most of her moving out of Horse Hollow Estates. Only away from the house was she able to breathe normally. She drove around a lot, turned on the radio loud, emptied her mind, and moved to the music as she drove. She knew this was childish, but it made her happy. She stopped asking herself what a man like Waring, powerful, aloof, astute, endearing, humorous, would want with her. She finally accepted the fact that he *did* want her, and it was wonderful. It was wonderful because she still didn't have to deal with the one thing that would cloud her happiness—*adultery*.

She didn't want to hurt Reynold. Strangely, she didn't think she could, as if she were the only one who could get hurt. But something very strong was pulling at her—a physical pull of such magnitude her limbs literally ached.

That she could weigh eight years of actual plans and dreams and loyalties against this infant emotion that had invaded her heart was alarming. At times she doubted that her heart was involved at all. Bill Waring had reached some other part of her that had nothing to do with her heart. She no longer wanted to be an ordinary woman.

She began going to the office every day, taking advantage of Marcelle while she remained. She didn't see Bill Waring, however, until several days passed. On a Monday he stopped by her office.

"I'm going to Philadelphia on Wednesday," he said. "I'll be back Thursday by dinnertime. Come with me. The train leaves at seven from Penn Station. I'll be the man with a small attaché case and an expectant look on his face." He walked away before she could reply.

She was stunned. She knew exactly what they were going to do in Philadelphia. For the first time in weeks she stopped thinking about making love to Bill Waring. She felt nothing. Neither hunger nor fatigue. She tasted nothing. Her body felt hollow and her hands were always cold.

She made no preparations, but the next night after dinner, with Charlie nodding sleepily as he did his reading on the couch, Sara found herself saying, "I have to go to Philadelphia very early tomorrow, can you wait here until Marcelle comes? I'll be there overnight. There's a big meeting of magazine publishers, and I've been picked to soak up what they have to say about what sells magazines."

"Why you?" asked Reynold.

Why indeed. "I guess they can spare me the most."

The lie came so smoothly it surprised her. She went to inspect her clothes and tried on the hundred-dollar boots she had bought last August. They made her look like one of the musketeers. She knew he would hate them and tossed them into the darkest part of her closet. She pulled out her one Ralph Lauren jacket—"it's a hacking jacket," the saleslady had said, as if anybody knew what the hell a hacking jacket was—with a silk shirt under it she'd look like the snotty girls in the Estée Lauder ads which was probably his type. She'd have to take another top as well, because silk looked terrible after one wearing. A ribbed turtleneck? Maybe she should chuck it all and wear a dress. It was too cold for a dress. And what about shoes? *Shoes!* And . . . oh, no . . . a nightgown . . . underwear. All her decent underwear was dirty. Would Reynold want to know why she was washing all that underwear?

She called Marcelle to make arrangements and then washed her hair. As she lay next to Reynold that night, she began to worry. With a few agile questions he could make mincemeat of her story. What business had she at a publishers' convention? None whatever. Reynold did not ask.

Marcelle's innocent farewell had got to her, too. "Have a nice time," she had said. Sara felt compelled to respond that it was not going to be fun in the least (ha, ha, ha), just a dull convention. As she was falling asleep, she decided not to go. She would be sick in the morning.

She awoke minutes before the alarm at quarter to five and felt okay. She showered and dressed and was ready in time to catch the five thirty-five to Penn Station. Up the long flight of stairs, past the newsdealer and the seedy restaurants, it occurred to her that he might not be there. What would she do? Suppose he was late and missed the train and had to apologize to her. She didn't want to start out as someone who needed an apology.

When she reached the main waiting room, she spotted him. He was wearing a black Borsalino hat with a large brim. It didn't look affected, it looked like the perfect hat to wear on a train. His raincoat was slung over his shoulder and a soft attaché case was being supported by his legs. He was reading the *Times* and didn't look expectant at all. He glanced up when she was still several yards away, and while he didn't rush to meet her, his eyes followed her until she was beside him. She was glad she had come.

It was a place where people kissed hello and good-bye, so no one paid much attention when he wrapped his arms around her. She felt his hands busy under her jacket. They grazed her breasts and slid around her. He was as close to a frenzy as he was likely to get in public. He was not, she was happy to notice, either cool or detached.

"You're stretching my good hacking jacket," she told him smiling.

"I'm happy you came," he said into her ear.

"Yeah, well it wasn't easy. I was going to be very sick this morning." She tried to sound relaxed but knew from his smile that she didn't. "Is this our gate?"

"Yes." He put the paper under his arm and took one of her hands in both of his. "It shouldn't be long now."

"What time do you have to give your speech?"

"At two." That gave them four hours after they arrived. For a full five minutes she was convinced nothing would happen. They would have lunch, he would give his speech, they would depart chaste and unsullied.

* * *

It wasn't like that at all. He had reserved a room for them in the Waterton, an old, elegant hotel filled with antiques, subdued lights, fresh flowers, and polished brass. It looked like a nice ship.

Their room was huge with a king-sized bed of dark, carved mahogany. Off the bedroom was a circular, sun-filled breakfast room. She had insisted on carrying her own small overnight case which she now placed discreetly in the closet. She proceeded to look over everything—the slipcovered glasses, the carafe of ice water, the sterling bucket of ice cubes. She turned the television on and satisfied that it worked, turned it off again. She removed her jacket and hung it up. There was nothing else to do. Before she turned around, she knew he was standing behind her. She could feel his breath on her neck.

It was like dreaming in slow motion. He moved over her quickly on the wide, endless bed, bruising her mouth, sucking impatiently at her breasts, lingering and murmuring into her belly. He rose to look at her. His hair drifted over his brow and gave him a look she wouldn't have imagined, boyish.

He returned to her breasts, taking one into his mouth and then the other. She watched and waited, bursting with attention. His chest was completely smooth, tanned, muscular, and warm. She could feel the heat from it on her bare breasts. She touched it and the warmth of it went through her. Her slim, tan hand fluttered slightly and continued downward. The vision of his cock—rising, swelling, coming toward her—had invaded her thoughts all these weeks. It had thrust and jabbed and throbbed against her over and over, and now here it was within reach, smooth and hard and unbelievably large. She held on to it fiercely.

From time to time he was rough with her and she with him. The waiting now seemed unfair and made them angry and impatient.

There came a moment when he wanted to arrange her on the edge of the bed. She thought of herself as hot wax melted into an odd shape, something out of a Dali painting. She knew what he was about to do and part of her balked. Oh, no. He wasn't going to do that. Not him. He soothed her, patting her stomach gently, and then did what he wanted. She watched tensely as he buried himself between her until she could no longer bear being separated from his erection. She did the same for him and then later they lay end to end. They came often and quickly, unashamedly, making up for lost time.

In between, as they talked, she continued to hold his cock which made him smile.

"How do you feel?" she finally asked him.

"About what?"

"About everything."

"Surprised. Surprised as hell." He didn't elaborate and she didn't ask. He reached for the telephone and ordered a huge breakfast for both of them. They devoured it, speaking hardly at all.

After breakfast he showered and ordered all the local papers—"I'm a news junkie," he explained—and put in a call to his secretary. She lay on the bed watching him. He was meticulously dressed again in a fresh shirt and tie. He looked supremely competent and momentarily out of her reach. She wanted to sit on his lap while he was in his business clothes but restrained herself. She didn't want to screw things up by clinging to him. That's what he liked about her, wasn't it? Her independence.

When he was finished with his call, however, he beckoned to her. "Come here and sit with me," he pulled her onto his lap. "In twenty minutes I have to give my big speech to the association of magazine publishers, so don't arouse me," he told her sternly.

"What are you going to say to the publishers?"

"I'm going to tell them to find someone who can make them happy. That it makes a hell of a difference." She wasn't expecting that and could not speak. What was there to say anyway? When he left, she crawled back into bed and fell instantly asleep.

She awoke to the sensation of him methodically kissing her back, vertebra by vertebra. She let him continue until he was at the lowest one and then she turned around. "I thought I'd better check to see if it was you." He smiled, rose, and removed his tie. There was a magnificently wrapped package on the bed.

"What's that?"

"It's for you."

For some reason that unsettled her. His buying her something was vaguely disturbing. "Why do I get a present? It was a fifty-fifty proposition."

"Because I'm richer."

"Is it a thank-you present?" she asked suspiciously.

"I hadn't thought of it that way."

"How did you think about it?"

"I can't reconstruct the sequence of thoughts and emotions that led up to it, if that's what you want. I can only say that throughout that damn speech all I could think about was you. When I left, I passed a small shop with something in it that I wanted you to have. Open it." He placed the package on her lap.

It was a kimono. A beautiful kimono of lightest silk in all the musky earth tones. It made her look and feel like someone out of Dostoevski. She didn't know exactly how someone out of Dostoevski might feel, but imagined it would be full of life, mellow, encrusted with experience, tumescent, able to sit still for hours. Cautiously happy.

"There." He was obviously pleased. "It's perfect."

"You really thought about me all through your speech?"

She wriggled with pleasure. Nothing had ever felt this sumptuous next to her skin.

"Yup."

"Tell me one thing you thought," she said wistfully.

He stared at the ceiling as if in deep thought. "You didn't tell me you weren't the sort of woman who does this sort of thing. That was a nice surprise." She wasn't sure if he were teasing.

"That would have been stupid. I'm precisely the sort of woman who does this sort of thing, or why would I be here." She paused. "Do all of your other women tell you they're not?"

Again he appeared to be deep in thought. "Uh . . . most of them." Then he burst out laughing and she reached over to pummel him with her fists. He was holding her arms away from him and at the same time trying to nip at her breasts which had burst out of the silk. "Oh, no," she said, "wait . . . wait, I'm kneeling on my beautiful kimono. Wait . . . let me take it off."

"I don't want to wait," he said, stubbornly, straining to make contact with her bobbing breasts, but she could see that he was pleased that she liked her present.

Over dinner, sober and exhausted, she brought up the subject of the book. "I've decided what my book will be about."

"So quickly?"

She didn't like the skeptical sound in his voice but was too excited not to spill it anyway. "It's about a middle-class girl who goes to an elite boarding school and becomes so dissatisfied with middle-class life, she is determined to be someone. She tries to escape, it looks as if she will escape, but in the end she winds up married and in the suburbs just like everybody else.'' She saw right away that he wasn't jumping up and down with admiration.

"Yes?'' He buttered a roll with great care. "What exactly is the story?''

"That's it.''

"That's it? She grows up and marries her college sweetheart and has two kids? She doesn't fulfill any of her childhood dreams?''

"No.'' She tried to sound sure of herself.

"How are you going to fill two hundred and fifty pages?''

"Well . . . her inner feelings about things. You know . . . stream of consciousness.''

"Uh huh.''

"You're not convinced.''

"I won't be the only one. You want to sell two thousand copies and cry for several weeks?''

"No. Yes . . . I don't know. I want to write a book that's good.'' She began to feel that no matter what she said, it wouldn't be the right answer. "Why are you being mean?''

"I'm not being mean. I'm merely trying to give you the benefit of my considerable experience so that you can make an intelligent decision.'' He sipped some wine and took a bite of his salad. "I don't doubt that you could write a very sensitive book about a woman's inner feelings from puberty to menopause, but you should be prepared that it will end up as a curiosity on your book shelf. The realities of publishing are brutal.''

"What are my options?''

"You could better the odds by writing a book with some action, a little suspense, not too many inner feelings, a lot of dialogue, interesting people, some tasteful intercourse.''

"What are you telling me,'' she could feel her face heating up, "that I should sit down and write a piece of junk?''

He continued eating his dinner slowly and deliberately. "What I described is far from junk,'' he continued reasonably. "It demands technical skill, a solid ear for what people really say, a dependable imagination, and no self-indulgence.'' He put down his knife and fork and wiped his mouth and hands. "I'm not saying that you should write such a book, merely laying out the options. It is you who must make the decision.''

She knew he was right. Two or three writers at *Haute* had taken a year off to do a novel only to end up with nothing to show for it but a couple of nice reviews from the *Detroit Free Press* and *The Boston Globe*. She was far too practical for that. "I'm sorry."

"No need to be."

She waited. "If I were to write such a book, I'd need someone guiding me along the way. It would help to have someone telling me what to leave in and what to take out."

"That can be arranged."

"There are people who do that?"

"Not many, but yes, there are some."

"What would I have to do to get one of them?"

"Write a solid outline and three or four sample chapters. About a hundred pages altogether."

"And then?"

"We'd take it to the right people."

"Who's we?"

"I'm using the editorial we. What I mean is I'd introduce you to a responsible agent with some clout, and he'd sell your effort to a responsible editor who would hold your hand while you finished the manuscript."

"Why would she hold my hand? I mean what would be in it for her?"

"Sara, she'd have no choice. If her publishing house paid you thirty thousand dollars advance on a book, a book that hadn't been written, she'd want to make damn sure she wasn't going to get three hundred pages of inner feelings."

"Thirty thousand dollars!" It came out a squeak. "I could get thirty thousand dollars for an outline and three chapters?"

"It's been known to happen."

She was quiet for a long time, mulling over what he'd said. "You should make good use of our relationship," he continued seriously. "It would be foolish not to. Also it would please me to see you financially independent. You'll feel differently about yourself, I promise you."

"But what if I don't have the talent?"

"If you didn't have the talent, why in the world would I have brought it up?"

"Oh, Christ, it sounds like I'm fishing for compliments and I'm not, but I wasn't thinking along those lines and now you've put this whole new thing in my head. And . . . well . . . it's exciting. You have to admit it's exciting.''

He smiled. ''All right, I'll admit it. It's exciting.''

When they were again at Penn Station, he wanted to have a drink before they went their separate ways, but she demurred. The children had not seen her for two days. It would no longer be untroubled pleasure.

He handed her a small slip of paper. ''This is the name of an agent who can help you. When you're ready, just go and see him.''

She wondered if that meant they weren't going to see each other again and a sharp pain pierced her heart. But still she could not ask such a question.

Before she said good-bye, she looked him over closely. She noticed his ears, his lips (thin but not unshapely). He wasn't fat or thin, although his neck was slightly thick, noble, a healthy pink against his shirt.

She waved good-bye to him from her train, touched beyond words that he had waited with her and did not budge until it pulled out. Then she stopped waving and looked straight ahead. She had to compose herself and face her husband.

Chapter 17

AVID DID NOT FEEL GOOD. HE FELT SICK deep inside himself, as if his cells were not regenerating the way cells were supposed to. As if he was growing old prematurely from the inside out. He knew that men failed or succeeded according to their capacity for bold deeds, their capacity to put their lives or their financial security on the line at the time when it would do them the most good. David had come through such testing and won when he had bought out his partners in the advertising business. He had won in a business that was not for the faint-hearted. He was not afraid of bold deeds, but what Alden had asked of him went beyond that. It was reprehensible, it would inflict horrendous anguish. Finally, it was a crime, even though Alden insisted it would never come to that.

Since they had discussed it, David was frightened all the time. The fear seemed to have settled permanently in a place just south of his ribs where it radiated to every nook and cranny of his body so that within minutes he was drenched in sweat that turned cold too soon and left him shivering. His metabolism had been revolutionized by fear. He wondered vaguely if this was a medical oddity and whether it would be of significance in curing low blood pressure—you could scare the patient to death. These thoughts came to him in calmer moments. During other times, when he was numbed by the fear, he was only able to trace the events that had brought him to such a crossroads.

He had stopped running and shaving and changing his clothes every day. His hands trembled when he held a cup of coffee or a glass of whiskey. He didn't look clean or healthy and this pained him.

What pained him more, however, was that his friendship with Miranda, the warmth and camaraderie that had sustained them over the months—some of the happiest in his life—was no longer possible. He still spoke to her on the telephone and occasionally saw her, but he was wary. Wary of that recklessness which had brought them both to this point.

It was not bad luck or a twist of fate or even the malice of Bradley Gifford that was ultimately responsible for their troubles—it was the awful, hidden malice of Miranda toward herself and those closest to her. A malice of which she was totally ignorant.

It wasn't that he didn't care for her anymore or blamed her, but he knew it was hopeless. There was no way to save her. Then it occurred to him that he might be thinking all these things about Miranda because they applied to him as well. Nothing in his background, crazy though it was, should have led him to this. Yet if he didn't do it, all he had worked for would go down the drain.

Quite apart from this was his feeling for Alden who was counting on him. It would hurt him to be let down. It might go beyond that. Alden was counting on him so much that he might refuse to be let down. Maybe it was no longer his choice.

The boy now trusted him. He had helped in the planning of a small bedroom in what had been the dining room. All the toys he had brought each week were there. Three days from now it would be over.

Miranda had been alone for five days without seeing anyone. At first it was welcome. After the last few days at the agency, watching David's face go from disbelieving to somber to haggard, all she had wanted to do was forget the nightmare and wait quietly for the baby.

But now the aloneness had turned creepy. It felt as if she had always been alone. She could not connect one thought to another, which was exactly what she needed to do. She needed to come to some conclusions about her predicament.

The baby would be here in six short weeks. She needed to find out what Sanche was willing to do yet in the next breath she didn't want him to do anything.

"The time for cagey waiting is definitely over," David had said to her in exasperation. She had agreed but was stumped as to what exactly she would ask Sanche to do. Everyone assumed money was the issue. Ask for money. She had heard it from everyone. Even Sue-Ellen, who had pieced together the story and turned indignant and raged for Miranda.

"What a shitheel! He hasn't been to see you? He hasn't set up a trust? What a shitheel!" she muttered over and over, "and you don't get the prize for smartness either."

The weather continued warm well into the fall, but instead of the wistful warmth of Indian summer there was a lingering mugginess. Miranda's head felt stuffy and achy. "It's rhinitis," explained Dean Whitley's nurse, "very common during the last trimester."

The seventh day passed without calls or visitors, and she began making lists of people who might call or write. Dean Whitley had her medical records. If she didn't keep her appointments, he'd call eventually. She wondered if Bradley had reported the latest thing to Barbara Lancia. She hoped he had. She wanted Barbara to realize that she had not taken any part of her dismal advice.

The idea of calling Sanche surfaced now and again, not because she wanted to see him but because there were so few people she knew. She had to maneuver herself into a position of strength once again. But where was she to get that strength when every day she felt less capable of caring for herself?

One morning she woke up and fall was in the air. It gave her new resolve. She would need clothes and a job after the baby came, and she'd better take advantage of her present freedom to get herself ready. Later in the afternoon she walked to Gimbels on Eighty-sixth Street to look at winter coats.

She wanted something beige or camel she told the saleslady, good for going to work everyday. Something simple and classic.

The woman hesitated; whether at the idea of her going back to work or her size and state of dishevelment, Miranda could not tell. She held her head high.

"What size are you when you're not pregnant?"

"Eight or ten. I guess you'd better make it ten."

The woman showed her a chesterfield style with a half belt in back and a camel's hair double breasted with a slightly fitted waist that would not fit past the first two buttons.

"If you could be sure of losing the weight," she mused. Miranda nodded vaguely, completely exhausted. She didn't have the energy to remove the heavy coat. Her hair had been in the same braids for days. The woman had thin features and wore a ladylike knit. She tried not to look directly at Miranda.

"I get tired easily," Miranda apologized.

"Maybe you could come back tonight with your husband. The store's open until eight thirty. You can come back when he gets home from work. Or maybe he could meet you here."

Miranda stared at her hands. "My hands swell so, I can't wear my ring."

"My daughter was the same," clucked the woman sympathetically. "Come back with your husband."

Miranda handed her the coat and fled down the escalator. All she could think about was getting home. As she was nearing the main floor, she noticed a beautiful woman coming toward her. She was so striking, half a dozen people had stopped to stare at her. She was tall, a natural, sunny blonde. Natalie! The name came instantly to mind and her heart began to pound. By the time she reached the main floor, however, the woman had disappeared. Still, the excitement remained with her. She would call Natalie. Natalie would be thrilled to hear from her. She could hardly wait to get home and ran part of the way until a stitch in her side made her double over in pain.

There was an N. Davidson in the Manhattan phone directory, but it was a man. "There's no Natalie here," he said as if he suspected she knew that all along. "Is this a crank call?"

"No," said Miranda quickly and hung up. Natalie's number would be unlisted. She wouldn't even be in New York. She was probably married and living on some vast estate.

That night she dreamt of her baby. It looked the way it did in the photographs of unborn babies with sunken cheeks and hollow eyes. They were both going to view St. Steffan—a relic she had actually seen as a child—and ask for a favor. When she got to the church, however, she pulled back from the tiny sepulchre screaming. St. Steffan, dead hundreds of years, exactly resembled her baby.

In the next few days a change came over Miranda. She was fearful all the time.

She knew it seemed pretentious and silly, but there was no way of making it sound different. She was going to see an agent. Once she got used to the idea, it was kind of exciting, and she walked along Fifth Avenue with the general sensation that her feet weren't quite touching the ground.

Warren Newman's office was on the street floor of a narrow brownstone off Lexington at Eightieth Street. A box of lush, well-tended English ivy spilled out of a huge planter. She breathed deeply to settle her nerves and rang the bell at the iron-grilled door. A buzzer sounded and she walked into a small room with a girl at a typewriter and three or four easy chairs tastefully covered in a blue and white print reminiscent of provincial France. The same print covered the walls up to a low wall of wood paneling painted white. It was a pleasant room furnished with fake but good English antiques. Again she took a deep breath. The girl took her name and disappeared.

"You can go in," she said when she returned. She motioned down a long, dark corridor that led to a back room which was littered with books and manuscripts and papers of every description. Behind a huge oak library table, almost obscured by the bundles around him, was a person she assumed was Warren Newman holding a phone to his ear and a cup of coffee in his hand. He was small and thin with little hair and an esthetic face partly hidden by huge, owlish glasses.

"Why the fuck did you show the book to Harper's in the first place?" he said into the phone. His voice was shrill with frustration. "Look, I'm going to get it back. I don't give a shit how much they scream. They're trying to screw you with ethics, while they get you for nothing. But from now on, God damn it, don't send a manuscript to your mother without having it go through this office. Jesus, what do you think an agent is for? All right, all right, you can thank me later when we get an offer.'' He slammed down the receiver and looked at Sara. ''Who are you?'' His mind was still on the phone conversation.

''Sara Reynolds. Weren't you expecting me?''

He rubbed his chin. ''Yeah, yeah . . . refresh me.''

''Bill Waring said he had spoken to . . .''

''Yeah, yeah. Sure. So what have you got?'' He leaned back, momentarily relaxed and still, and folded his arms as if expecting an entire drama to be performed.

''If you're too busy now . . .''

''I'm always busy. Let's hear what you've got.''

She fingered the manila envelope uneasily. How could she possibly have anything that would interest this impatient, nervous man? ''I had an idea for a novel.'' Her voice seemed to be coming from far away.

''So?''

''The outline is in here. And three chapters.'' It all sounded ridiculous now. Why had she let him talk her into it? ''No one's read it yet, but I thought . . .''

''Okay, okay.'' His voice softened. ''Let me tell you how we work. I don't handle stuff that isn't going to sell. I don't nurse young talent along either. I can't afford to . . . unless, of course, young talent is willing to work seriously toward selling. You get what I'm saying?'' She did not but nodded vigorously. ''There are too many writers who think the world owes them a forum. I don't want to deal with prima donnas or artsy types. We write to sell in this office. If you've got quality stuff that makes sense, I'll get you the most I can and kiss your cheek. If you've got really hot commercial stuff, I'll kiss your ass. Now''—again he leaned back and crossed his arms— ''what've you got?''

''I don't know,'' she said honestly. ''Why don't you read it and I'll know by where you kiss me what I've got.''

He smiled. ''That's good. That's good. You have a sense of humor. Jesus, that's terrific. A writer with a sense of humor.'' He shook his head at the wonder of it. ''Okay, I'll get back to you as soon as I can. Give Mary out there your phone number.'' He was already dialing.

''Is it all right if I leave her two numbers . . . I'm in and out and . . .''

"Yeah, sure. Leave her all the numbers you want." He flashed her a beautiful smile. "Don't worry." He stopped to talk into the phone—"Lena? How the fuck are you? Hold on." He held his hand over the mouthpiece. "When I want to find you, I'll find you."

The next couple of days she was glad to be in her tiny office writing captions for *Accessories. Accessories. Accessories. What Your Mother Never Told You.* The idea of waiting at home for the phone to ring was painful. Even so, she had given his receptionist both numbers and every time her buzzer sounded, her heart jumped.

She had never again discussed the book with Bill Waring, feeling quite rightly that they were too emotionally involved to trade ideas on her project.

"You can trust Warren," he had said when she mentioned that she had seen him.

By the third day she didn't care if Warren Newman called or not. She was sure that he had hated her material and would not ever get in touch with her. On the fourth day she came back from lunch and found a long message at the receptionist's desk.

"The story's okay," it said, "but you're not writing it right. If you'd like to take some suggestions and try again, I'm willing to go along." She felt nervous and upset and waited two hours before returning his call. When she finally got him on the phone, he kept saying, "Who is this? Who? Who?" until she was ready to hang up. She didn't want to explain anymore that she was the girl who had been sent by Bill Waring. She also began to doubt his sanity.

"In the first chapter," he began briskly, "I want you to detail Lucy's loneliness and when she goes home with Thomasina, follow them closely. Show how Thomasina lives. I want details. Microscopic details for about a paragraph or so and maybe one incident to show what a weird wonder she is. Then the friendship means something, you know what I mean? Then you have them hooked." He paused. "You got that?"

"Yes."

"Okay. Now about Lucy. I get the feeling you don't know what Lucy is all about yet and it shows. Sit down and for a couple of days think about what a person like Lucy would order for lunch. Does she sleep in a nightgown or pajamas? You know, stuff like that. When you feel you got a handle on her, then rewrite those two chapters and let's see what you get." She could hear him dragging on a cigarette. "You got that?"

"Yes."

"Good. Get back to me." He was gone.

"How was the lobby decorated?" asked Jane when Sara related the entire episode.

"There was no lobby. He's on the bottom floor of a brownstone and he was in the back room overlooking the garden."

"He's a fag then. He'll level with you. If they're in a high rise on Madison Avenue, they're tough barracudas and lie to everybody. But the fags tell the truth and they're always in brownstones. They like little gardens in the back with cupids pissing into fountains."

"There's a garden, but he was tough. He wasn't a fag. He wants me to redo everything I sent him—should I just give up?"

"Hell, no. If he's willing to look at it, keep going. He must see something there or he'd just send you a nice 'get-lost' note with your manuscript. He's not out to be Mr. Nice Guy, you can be sure."

She suspected Jane was right and revised the chapters, grateful that the anguish over her book was somehow deflecting the anguish over Bill Waring. She saw him regularly now in the office. During the day he came to her office and they went out walking or shopping or for lunch. He never suggested anything more, although he took every opportunity to kiss her in taxicabs and once in the elevator when they were alone.

There were moments, however, when the need to consummate their feelings were unbearable. She knew he felt it even more strongly, because he became tense and sometimes clenched and unclenched his fists. She would have suggested that they go somewhere, but the words wouldn't come. She had been born too long ago for that sort of freedom. It had to come from him.

Perversely, despite her edginess about her manuscript and her affair, at home she felt more bouncy. New sex made her feel as if she could take off in the air, and she flitted about the house like the tooth fairy. Only at night did she get moody. The words of the silliest love songs made sense. When Frank Sinatra sang *My Funny Valentine* on a television special, she had to leave the room.

Reynold, if he noticed the changes, was not the first to react.

Charlie was. Charlie was beset by anxiety. She could tell by his sudden preoccupation with death and other horrors.

"Do they kill the turkey before they take the feathers off or after?" he asked in the supermarket.

"Before."

"Why can't they wait until he dies himself?"

"I don't know."

In the middle of dinner, when she was sure he had nothing more serious on his mind than how to avoid eating his broccoli, he would say, "Do you think bug killer is good?"

"No."

"Neither do I," he was relieved. "Especially that Fly Lure they have on TV."

"What's Fly Lure?"

"It comes with bug killer. Free. For your home."

His anxiety was always there. Spilling over. He had a small part in the Thanksgiving pageant. He was a pilgrim, a catatonic pilgrim except for one line: "On this hill we can build a fort for protection." It was not a difficult line, yet he was uncharacteristically nervous and upset and kept repeating it over and over while alternately snapping his small fingers relentlessly at his sides.

"They could be deaf-mute pilgrims for all the dialogue in the play," said Sara to Reynold, "but he's scared to death. What's wrong with him?" She left the room before he could answer. She knew what was wrong with him.

One day Bill Waring came to her office and closed the door. "Sara," he said, "I won't be satisfied with a sly affair."

She had assumed that was exactly what he would be satisfied with, and for a moment all she could think of was that he really loved her and waves of happiness washed over her.

"What's wrong with a sly affair?" She was trying for humor. What else could she say?

"I want you to be part of my life. I want you close and . . . available. But most of all I don't want you to continue to lie. I don't think lying does much for anyone."

"Oh, I agree, I agree." What he said about lying made sense. She was surprised she hadn't thought about it herself. "No, of course, I can't continue lying."

"Then we must put everything out in the open."

We! It would have been easy to point out to him that there was no we about it. It was she who had to put everything in the open with a decent man who was her husband and the father of her children. A man who had done nothing to make her unhappy. But it would have been childish to point this out to Bill Waring. He knew that the sacrifice was hers. He knew everything. It was not a thoughtless, selfish remark. And he would make it all up to her.

But when it all sank in about two minutes later, she began to tremble. The *open* he was talking about was situated in her kitchen or living room or her bedroom, none of which were really open enough for the confrontation she had in mind. What in the world could she say to Reynold. "I've found someone who doesn't think I should lie anymore, so I have to tell you that I've slept with another man and not only that but he wants me available all the time, so please don't ask me where I'm going because, as you will recall from the beginning of this conversation, he doesn't want me to lie."

That conversation was a turning point. She no longer felt at ease in her own house. She felt most ill at ease in the bedroom. It was obvious she didn't belong there and she began to sleep curled up on the couch, explaining nervously that she had to work late on her outline and didn't want to wake him by coming in. Reynold was always surprised to find her there, and a couple of times he added a blanket to her sleeping body in the early morning when it had turned cold.

On the other hand she relived the lovemaking with Bill Waring so many times, it was like a favorite novel committed to memory. There were wonderful highlights that made her dissolve into obsessive physical need of him, even after having run them through her mind a hundred times. She was disappointed that he had made no move to repeat the closeness they had shared and was wildly relieved when he asked her to come to his house for dinner one day.

"Would you like to come home with me tomorrow night and have dinner? I have a very good cook . . . . a Cuban man."

"That would be terrific," she said, not mentioning that she would have to tell a lie to get there. Happily it was only Marcelle she had to lie to because Reynold had begun working late at the lab and sometimes staying overnight.

* * *

She could never have imagined Bill Waring's house, which was tasteful and elegant with scrolls and fluted columns and cherubim and seraphim all in cast limestone making the entrance a true wonder. A heavy grill arcade came before the main door which was black with a shiny brass knocker. WW Waring, said a small nameplate.

"What's the *W* for?"

"Wadsworth."

"Wow," she said admiringly.

A beautiful, dark small man opened the door. He was wearing a navy suit and a white shirt and string tie. He was not in the least subservient, yet not familiar either. "Good evening, Mrs. Reynolds," he said. "Good evening, Bill." He pronounced it Beel.

She was too surprised to answer. She turned to Beel. "How did he know my name?"

"I told him."

"You told him? You've been talking to him about me?" This seemed too bizarre.

"Let me see," he furrowed his brow, "I believe the exact words were, 'Raymundo, I'll be bringing a Mrs. Reynolds for dinner about seven.' Was I too indiscreet?"

"I'm sorry." Now he had paranoia to add to his list of things he knew about her. She clutched her pocketbook for support. "May I use your telephone?"

"Of course." He ushered her into a small room paneled in reddish leather from floor to ceiling. Two casement windows with diamond-shaped panes were the only interruption. There was a desk with a complicated telephone console. The desk was large, some wormy fruitwood that had been rubbed and polished for about a hundred years. This was not a room for fooling around. Serious thinking was done here. Had he sat here one night and decided that he was going to make her fall in love with him?

She shuddered at the thought and dialed her house. She wanted to talk to the children before they went to bed and make sure Marcelle got some rest. Marcelle was enormous now and should not be on her feet more than necessary. It would not have surprised Sara to see several children march out of Marcelle's gargantuan belly.

"Hello." It was Reynold and for a moment she couldn't speak. "Hello," he said again.

"Hi, sorry. I didn't think you were home. I thought I might have dialed the wrong number."

"Yeah, well, I needed a break. One of the guys brought in his kids today and I started missing Charlie and Rachel. We've been playing hide and seek for the last forty minutes. Marcelle is in no shape to move around. I told her to put her feet up and watch *Beat the Clock.*"

"She doesn't like *Beat the Clock.*" She didn't like the sound of her voice or the conversation. It was the kind of conversation people have when they feel heavyhearted and want to give the opposite impression. It was overly cheerful.

"That's what she said." There was silence. "Where are you, by the way?"

"At work. I'm going to work another hour and have supper with Jane at her place. Okay with you?" Cold, smooth lies.

"I suppose." His tone was guarded.

"Maybe I'll see you before lights out," she said and hung up quickly. Bill was right. Lying was no way to live.

When she returned to the living room, Bill Waring was watching the evening news. He would not ask any questions. In a few minutes Raymundo called them to dinner.

Had she had her mind on nothing but the food, she would have realized how extraordinary it was. Even in her preoccupied state she was impressed. There were delicate crepes filled with a mixture of spicy chunks of lobster, chinese cabbage, and sauteed nuts. After that came crisp lemon sole, shredded zucchini and potatoes, and a beautiful salad.

"This sure beats my usual Wednesday night dinner," she said to Raymundo when he brought the coffee.

Raymundo grinned. "What is Wednesday dinner, hot dogs?" He grinned wider. "All Americans live on hot dogs."

"No hot dogs. On Wednesday I make meatloaf surprise."

"What's the surprise?" asked Bill.

"Huh?"

"In the meatloaf?"

"Oh. The pickle, the pickle. The children are transported each time. Which slice will reveal the pickle? You wouldn't believe the excitement."

Raymundo began to giggle. "You put whole pickle inside?" He was convulsed.

She didn't think it was that funny, but her first instinct was to laugh right along with him. Be nice to the help. Then she thought of all the dinners he had cooked for other women and stopped. He could laugh his Cuban head off all by himself. She would remain sober and disdainful. Had the boss told him to lay it on so thick? If so, she would not deteriorate into a victim. The hell with Raymundo and Bill Waring. Jesus, why did Reynold have to answer the phone?

Her belligerence steadied her and gave her strength and she hung on to it zealously. It helped her to deal with the tour of the house, which was beautiful, and it helped her to deal with his bedroom where they finally ended up. She was interested to see what he would do to her, but not ready to help him.

She sat on the bed and watched him take off what must have been several hundred dollars worth of clothes. There were initials on everything. The Dior *D*. Pierre Cardin's *p*'s and *c*'s. His underwear had dainty pleats and tucks. She loved his clothes. His shirt was ecru— the color of raw silk, reminiscent of dappled sunlight. The sight of his tanned neck, the polished cherrywood of the furniture, the soft textures, reminded her of tinted photographs one might find to illustrate Scott Fitzgerald's stories of rich, bored young men who found life antic at best and not to be taken seriously.

But he was not like that. He was not bored or indolent. Just bemused by it all and very careful to make it interesting for himself.

He made love to her slowly and painstakingly, and she forgot herself completely and melted into him. It was the most she would ever feel. Afterward he held on to her tightly as if to prolong the moment and ward off evil spirits.

"Are the children everything to you."

"Why do you ask?"

"Because the children were the last thing you spoke about before you turned sad and watchful."

He was right. That was the first time she had mentioned her children to him. Then she posed the question to herself. Were the children everything? "I know them so intimately," she began. "I know what scares them and what makes them laugh. When you know someone that well, there's a responsibility to make them happy, to trigger the responses that get the smiles . . . maybe that's love."

She stared at the ceiling fascinated by its seamless perfection. It was an old house. How could he have made everything so perfect? Could he perform the impossible by sheer will? "They care about me, too. They tell me every morning how beautiful I am. When I slip into worn jeans and put a little Erace under my eyes to look better, they tell me I'm beautiful and ask if I'm going to die."

"I find you beautiful," he said simply, "and I, too, want to know if I'm going to lose you."

She rolled over and placed her face into his neck, the space on the back of his neck where class told—either a man had a classy neck or he didn't. He turned and faced her and she found herself looking directly into his eyes. But while her gaze was sober and honest and full of pain as well as happiness, his was only smiling as usual.

"I've got to leave now," she said and rose to dress.

He drove her to her car which was parked under the Metropolitan Museum. When they reached it, he got in beside her, held both her hands and then her face, and kissed her good-bye. She was trembling when she pulled out of the ramp onto Fifth Avenue. She felt as if she had been awakened from a dark, sweet sleep. Every part of her was awake and eager to grow into his image of her. She would write her book and sell it and make him proud. She would bowl him over with talent . . . she would . . . break the news to Reynold.

Miranda was worried about David and was glad when he reluctantly agreed to meet her. He would have preferred a drink but quickly led her to Schrafft's when she told him that liquor went right through the placenta and intoxicated the baby.

"Caffeine isn't great, either," she said removing the bag from her teacup, "but it only makes him a little hyper."

David was not listening. He was shocked at the size of her and by the idea that whatever was in there would have to seek a way out. "Are you going to be all right?" He wanted some reassurance that she was happily settled so he could close off that part of his life. "Are you going to go to California?"

"I don't think so."

"Why?"

"Maybe I don't want to go. He calls everybody darling and sweetheart. It's all so silly."

"Don't worry about that. They all do that."

"I suppose." She didn't want to worry him. It was better if he thought she might eventually go to Sanche. "What about you, David? You've looked better. That son-of-a-bitch Sotheby, when I think of all the boring evenings I sat and listened to him."

David waved his hand in the air as if it didn't matter anymore. The fact that he couldn't tell her certain things created a wall between them, and he found himself wanting to leave. They finished their tea in silence. When they parted, however, they kissed and embraced tightly. Each had the feeling that perhaps they wouldn't see the other for a long time.

Miranda continued to brood about David and wondered if being a homosexual meant always to be subversive and make your life decline. It didn't seem fair. She felt such a pang of sympathy for David who had always been generous and patient with her. Now he needed help and she didn't know how to give it to him. First of all she wanted to advise him to get a better boyfriend.

As she got off the elevator, she noticed the man was coming toward her and holding on to his hand was a small boy. The sight of them so late at night made her uneasy. What he and David did on their own was their business, but to involve a little boy was creepy.

The whole thing was depressing. When she looked down the road at what David's life would be like, she saw no happy endings. He and his friend would never live openly and have a pleasant country cottage and be true companions to each other, so how could it end? Only unhappily. At best it could end unhappily. At worst . . . at worst it could be tragic.

She decided against infecting David with her black thoughts and went immediately to sleep. The next day she spent buying a few groceries and a proper robe to wear at the hospital, as well as two nursing bras which she tried on at home fascinated by the ingenious construction. The baby kicked wildly and she fell into a deep, happy sleep. She felt peaceful and content just to be home with her own things about her. Tomorrow she would get a layette—some undershirts and diapers and those little nightgowns that closed at the bottom like little Swee' Pea wore in the Popeye cartoons.

The small boy walked confidently beside the man, grasping his hand except to tug at his shirt which kept escaping his flannel slacks. He knew his father was happiest when he looked neat and showed no signs of having roughed himself at play. While it was difficult to remain as neat as his father liked, he was determined to try.

He was afraid of his father, but stronger than the fear (which came and went) was sadness. When Jeremy thought about it, the thing his father seemed to be carrying even though you couldn't see it was a heavy sack. Duty. As best as he could understand it, duty was something heavy that had to be with you at all times. He felt sorry for a man who had to carry such a sack with him at all times, although he didn't yet feel sorry for himself. He knew he was strong, although he didn't give that impression. Then, too, he had his mother, a generous compensation for whatever else life might have in store for him. His mother certainly more than made up for his duty, whatever it was.

Because he felt deeply sorry for his father and so grateful for his mother, he decided he would learn to disguise his fear. He would listen without moving any part of his face and fix his gaze steadily on his father's piercing hazel eyes and his rosy cheeks and his long, thin nose. He wanted to show that he was not afraid. That was the least he could do.

Sara wanted to tell Reynold, but the opportunity never presented itself. You had to have the right moment to spill news like that. Reynold was working longer and longer hours and when he was home, quite often she was not.

At the beginning of November her piece on Margaret Martin appeared, and she received twenty-seven letters of congratulations from perfect strangers, four letters of disdain that she should waste her time aggrandizing the crooks that ran this country, and one letter from a woman named Anita Reynolds who asked if they were related.

Although she left several copies of the magazine with the article lying around, she had no knowledge that Reynold read it. By November they were definitely in a mute war. She didn't know exactly when they had stopped talking, but the process by which two people who have shared everything become silent accomplices in silence was complete. They said good morning and good night. They asked each other if they would be home for dinner and if they had responded to this or that invitation. Twice they had gone as a couple to the homes of friends and talked about the school system, how furious they were that Ford had pardoned Nixon, and even laughed unnecessarily loud and long over a silly Polish joke. That night for the first time since she had known him, Reynold drank too much and asked her to drive home.

A week later she opened the *Times* and saw her husband's picture on the first page of the second section. She was so shocked that he hadn't mentioned it to her, that she began to cry.

"The men at the lab," said the story, "are jubilant because they have isolated a heretofore unknown particle." It also said that a team would be meeting their British and French counterparts in Jamaica the following week for a week's symposium to share information. Reynold was going to lead the American group.

"Why didn't you tell me you were going to Jamaica? And what about that picture in the *Times*. You never said anything about that. Why aren't you telling me things?"

"If we're going to have a contest, Sara, about who is not telling things to whom, I believe you would not come up a winner."

She was stunned. Too stunned to take the challenge. "What is that supposed to mean?"

"Come with me to Jamaica," he pleaded suddenly. He, too, did not have the courage to continue.

"All right," she said. She would tell him in Jamaica.

It was a beautiful setting. The hotel had an outdoor pavilion facing the sea where they ate. Every morning Reynold would entice the birds by strewing bread crumbs along the edge of the table. Then he would look out over the water as if looking hard enough would make a distant shore materialize and bring a smile to his face. Aha, there it is! Bali Hi. She was sure the distant shore stood for her willingness to go back to what they had been.

"You know what Jane Seymour says about birds?"

"What?"

"She says the reason birds haven't done much in life is they have one answer to everything. They fly away."

"They don't fly away from their babies." She knew he hadn't meant to be pointed, but the remark stung anyway and made her harden her heart against him. "And they don't fly away from their mates. Sometimes, though, they keep a relaxed distance, but they both are quite sure how far that distance should be." Now he was being pointed.

She couldn't speak.

"What is it that he sees in you?"

Nothing could have prepared her for the fear that overtook her when he finally mentioned Bill Waring. She tried to be angry. "Oh . . . thanks a lot . . . you don't think anyone else finds me attractive?"

Their voices echoed in her ears. It was a lonely conversation. She knew no part of it would satisfy her. She was out alone in unchartered waters and there was no going back.

"Oh, Sara, shut up. That's not what I meant. I mean what does he see in you that makes you feel better. Obviously he's made you feel more like the woman you want to be."

"The woman I *might* be. Ever think of that? Perhaps I'm not just trusty Sara who can make everybody feel good. . . . You want me to be dull and stupid and grow old . . ." She knew she was being childish and spouting nonsense, but her mind was not working. She was running on pure emotion.

"You were never dull or stupid. In fact, when we married, it was I who had to prove myself."

She refused to think of those days. She had to take the conversation to its final outcome. Secretly she kind of agreed with him and was startled by his accurate appraisal of Bill Waring's influence on her. He not only made her feel better, he made her feel exhilarated, as if she could conquer the world . . . in time. But to agree with Reynold would get them nowhere.

"All right," he said, "it sounds as if you've come to some decisions. All right. You've told me. I know. You can relax."

That he could capitulate so easily infuriated her. Why didn't he plead his case? He was going to let her go just like that? Cold son-of-a-bitch.

"That's it?" She couldn't stop herself from asking it. "You're not going to say anything else?" *Aren't you going to plead with me to stay?*

"Isn't that what you wanted?"

"Well, yes . . . but . . . I thought you'd . . . I thought there'd be something else."

He was silent but still faced her. His eyes, usually clear and focused, seemed to be set in an unfamiliar background; they looked strained and cloudy. "You thought I would tell you I loved you . . .

Oh, God . . .'' and then he made a tiny gesture: he brushed his lovely broad forehead with the back of his hand as if to sweep all thought away. Only she knew how unlikely it was that he should make such a gesture of despair. If he hadn't walked away from her at that moment, she would have gone straight into his arms. But this way was better. Once in his arms she would have told him how afraid she was, but that she had to go anyway.

The change in their day-to-day lives was not that great. When they returned from Jamaica, Reynold simply moved into one of the cottages at the lab. He came on the weekends to see the children. He and Sara spoke, shyly at first until they got used to their new status.

When the schoolbus reached his station, his father was already waiting in the Lincoln, and Jeremy realized it was a day when they would go to New York.

"Are you dressed warmly enough? You'll be waiting quite a while before I finish."

Jeremy nodded gravely. He didn't know if he was dressed warmly enough or not. He had found that being afraid made him cold, as did the dark. He could never get used to waiting alone while his father went around and around the track.

They rode in silence and about midway he opened the small, insulated bag that he found on the seat next to him and took out an apple.

"Don't eat it all now," said his father. "Wait until we get there."

"All right." His father thought he'd want to eat at the park while he waited, but that was impossible. The last thing he wanted when he waited was to put food into his stomach.

They passed the cinder path in the park and Jeremy was disappointed to see how dim the light was. It probably was no longer possible to get here in the light. It was November. It would be dark long before his father finished.

A man trotted by on a dirty gray horse and slowed down as if to let Jeremy see the horse, but Jeremy turned deliberately away. He couldn't concentrate on anything but the ordeal ahead of him. He wanted to think of the things that could help him. He could identify almost all of the sounds which was immensely helpful.

There were birds, one owl, the sound of dry leaves caught in a small gust. The squirrels made a terrible racket which had surprised him. Such a big sound to come from such tiny throats. He had been convinced only when he saw their throat muscles moving. The sounds that were the worst were the breathing. It wasn't only his father. There were many runners, each with his own particular breathing. When they went by Jeremy, their breathing was tortured. Some grunted, some wheezed, some sucked their breath in as if they were choking to death. In the beginning he hadn't been able to tell his father from the others; now he could. He knew exactly how his father sounded.

Sometimes the breathing came from behind him, and two or three times he had jumped from his seat, certain he was about to be plucked up and carried off. He felt very light, not quite human, as if any light gust would carry him away. But always it was just runners who were coming from the streets and were already out of breath.

His father had gone around four times, or was it five? If it were five, there was only one to go. It was dark now. The arched lights near where he was sitting were broken, their necks dangling like little dead swans. He couldn't make out anything and had to rely solely on his hearing. When he couldn't see the runners, the breathing didn't sound like breathing and the footsteps not like footsteps. He had to keep reminding himself that nothing was amiss.

When his father passed him for what he thought was the sixth time, he heard breathing alongside him which was strange. Nobody jogged on the uneven ground; they waited until they reached the walk around the reservoir. If someone was breathing so hard beside him, it had to be someone who was either hurt or . . . or . . . very angry. The steps were leaden—thud, thud, thud—and the breathing strangled—a thin whistle and a sigh.

The hairs on his arms stood up and he could feel everything tightening. His scalp, his neck. His legs trembled as they dangled against the bench and felt as if they weren't attached to him. He wanted to rise and run, but how could he run without legs? *Whistle, whistle, sigh. Whistle, whistle, sigh.* He wasn't sure anymore what he heard. There were sounds in front and sounds in back. His father's breathing was different. It was the same sound the dogs made after they ran around the lawn, short and even as if they were saying, *heh, heh, heh.*

Heh, heh, heh. His father was coming around for the last time.

Soon he would take his hand in the dark and say quietly, "All right, son. Let's go."

He held out his hand, searching for the larger hand, but it wasn't there. The *heh, heh, heh* had passed—he heard it passing away from him—but the *whistle, whistle, sigh* was louder than ever . . . in front of him . . . ON HIM!

Something brushed the back of his neck, a flashlight was in his eyes and just as quickly turned off. His ears were stopped with fright, his body trembled with big, explosive beats. His father would not come for him. He had forgotten. Someone would take him away.

Something wet and rough caught his hand and he heard a soft mewling sound.

"Come, Rover," said a voice. It was a dog. A dog licking his hand. He almost cried with relief and rubbed his wet, stinging eyes. Soon after he heard his father for sure. "Come on, son," he said, and they walked hand in hand out of the park and to the car.

"Do you have your lunch bag with you and the toy?"

"Yes, sir," he lied. He had forgotten his bag but would conceal it until they were well under way. He would not want to return there for anything.

In the car his father told him casually that he would not have to wait for him anymore. This was the last time. Jeremy was so relieved, he wrapped his arms around his father's neck impulsively and Alden was surprised.

"Were you so frightened?"

Jeremy nodded, but he could see that his father was disappointed and he added, "Not so frightened. Just sometimes. When I couldn't see." He could have saved himself the trouble of answering. His father was already thinking of something else.

Chapter 18

ELECTION DAY, 1974, DAWNED CRISP AND clear. The sky was a cloudless medium blue and the sun so bright, it made everyone blink.

Natalie awoke at seven forty-five and knew she was already hopelessly late. She buried her head further into the pillow. She had to call at least two hundred people and ask them if they had voted or intended to vote in the congressional election. Depending on their response, she would either thank them for their vote or frighten them politely by reciting the miseries that would befall their district if Bill's opponent were elected. Some of the people would tell her to go fuck herself or to suck their cocks. Some would tell her to tell Bill Haas to go fuck himself. They would refer to him as a "fucking asshole" or a "fucking fag" or a "fucking playboy."

All in all it was an exhausting experience and totally ridiculous. Bill Haas was going to win and everybody was sure of it except Cora, who insisted that nothing was certain but death and that they had conducted this Election Day telephone blitz since she was a young woman. She had commandeered a dozen Junior Leaguers to help from their apartments while she, Natalie, and Letitia spent the day manning the phones at Haas headquarters.

Natalie pulled on heavy, textured tights which she had to struggle to stretch over her sizable stomach. Over them she wore a loose woolen shift. Haas headquarters' only source of warmth was an appliance that resembled a large toaster. Cora would hog it and by the end of the day she'd be numb with cold.

She pulled her hair back in a loose chignon, but it did not have the effect she wanted. Her face had changed little by little over the summer, and now her features were unfamiliar. Cora insisted that meant she was carrying a girl, but she knew it was something else. Sam had changed her face. And Rudy. Both in their way had showed her what she was capable of. She had not seen Rudy for ten days and it had left her restless and jumpy. He decided everything, including where and when he would fuck her.

When she reached the office, she was alarmed to find herself the only one there. Cora had insisted they get started by eight and she was always prompt.

At nine o'clock she finally arrived, looking haggard and gray. Letitia was behind her.

"Are you all right?" asked Natalie.

"Of course. Why shouldn't I be all right?" she asked crossly.

"You look a little tired."

"That's because I *am* tired," she snapped.

Letitia rolled her eyes to the ceiling, and Natalie returned to push the buttons on her telephone zealously.

They worked through the day with nothing but cottage cheese and tea to sustain them. "We'll go home at six," announced Cora in the middle of the afternoon. "That'll give us plenty of time for a nap before the celebration tonight. You are coming to the Hilton, aren't you?" She turned to Natalie.

"I think so. Yes."

"What about Alden?"

"I don't know," she hesitated. She had not seen Alden and had no idea where he was. "I don't know his plans for the day."

Cora smirked. "I'm sure I don't have to tell you, Natalie, that Alden has some dangerous tendencies, dangerous tendencies." She fanned herself with a sheaf of fliers, although it wasn't the least bit warm.

A little after five Natalie's phone rang. "Can you come to the Plaza this evening?" It was Rudy.

Natalie felt some of the tension leave her body. "Not until six."

"All right. I'll be waiting."

She felt more lighthearted than she had all day.

When she arrived at the Plaza, he was waiting for her in the lobby. "I thought we'd have a drink before we went upstairs," he told her. "I'm leaving on the nine o'clock shuttle to Washington."

"Aren't you going to the victory party?" she asked him when they were sipping their drinks at the Oak Bar.

"For what? To watch our boy flash his Harvard grin? I've already seen it."

"He's not all that bad."

"He's not bad at all. Who said he was? I just don't think it's worth going a few miles for one of his smiles. My job's all done." He grinned and led her upstairs.

He surprised her with his lovemaking. He was gentle and patient. He patted her belly lovingly and crooned into it. He spent half an hour between her legs. "Don't worry," he said when she tried to help him enter her, "you can't do much with that belly. It's all right." When she groped for him during each climax, he gave her his hand to hold on to.

Finally he left her on the bed and showered. While she watched, he dressed and packed a few things into a small bag. "This is farewell," he said suddenly. "Old Rudy's bowing out for good."

"But you'll be back?" she said incredulously.

"Nope."

She was stunned. She hadn't expected that. He couldn't mean it. He was making her feel abandoned. Desolate. Fat tears formed in the corners of her eyes and rolled down her cheeks.

He wiped them away tenderly. "I'm going to open a Washington branch. That's really where the action is for a guy like myself. But what about you?" He looked concerned and cupped her face in both his hands. "What's going to happen to you?"

She was suddenly furious with him. She shoved his hands away from her and hoisted herself out of bed, which in her condition took some doing. "Nothing's going to happen to me," she said contemptuously and went into the bathroom slamming the door. She turned on all the water so he couldn't hear her crying, but it was unnecessary. When she came out, he was gone.

It was almost eight when she arrived home. She could see from the street that all the lights were on, making her think they had guests. Perhaps Cora had come over. When she let herself in, however, the apartment was quiet and empty. She went down and then up from room to room and finally found Eva crouched in the kitchen.

"I'm sorry to tell you, missus," Eva looked distressed. "Miss Letitia called from the hospital. Mrs. Sandford had a heart attack and passed away."

Natalie slumped into one of the chairs in her vast living room overlooking the city. She could not have moved if her life depended on it. Eva brought her hot tea and propped her feet on a tiny footstool. Sometime after eleven she came back and found Natalie just as she had left her. "Mr. Haas won, ma'am," she said gently. "I thought you'd like to know." She took the cup from Natalie's lap and helped her up. "Come on," she coaxed, "let me help you into bed."

She crawled into her bed eagerly, hoping for a long, dreamless sleep. She wanted to blot out this day. She thought it was possibly the worst day of her life, but it wasn't. That was coming.

Ironically, once she made the break with Reynold, she saw less of Waring. He left for a week-long trip to Europe and she was left with her remorse and many, many questions. Was she supposed to move freely in and out of his house? It was very definitely *his* house. His and Raymundo's. They would treat her like a guest. And what about her children? Did he want her available only alone or with her children? Did he want Rachel who could be bossy and suspicious? And Charlie who was sometimes clingy and whistled constantly when he was nervous? She knew she could not ask him these questions. They were unanswerable. He would tell her to do whatever made her happy, and right now she didn't exactly know what would make her happy.

There was a sizable hole in her heart for Reynold. Every day the enormity of what she had done grew larger. Her grief and confusion must have been obvious, because for the first time in her young life Rachel was compassionate and generous with Sara. She rubbed her mother's forehead with damp cloths, and she made endless cups of tea which she spilled along the hall each time she brought them to the bedroom.

Sara worked hard on her book, eager to prove that something in her life would reach a fruitful end. She revised the chapters and the outline twice again before Warren Newman was satisfied. During that time he remained reasonable, giving his advice willingly and patiently. She didn't know what to think, but all hopes of fat advance checks faded from her mind.

Five weeks after their initial meeting, after he had read the third version, he called early on a Monday morning. "This time you've got it," he said matter-of-factly, and her insides rearranged themselves in a leap of joy. "Two or three people have expressed interest. I'll Xerox it and send it out."

"How can anyone be interested? You've just read it yourself." Her joy was reduced by half.

"I've been talking you up for weeks. That's my job. It's called creating excitement in the trade." She was used to his sarcasm and knew it didn't reflect his feeling for her work. It simply meant he knew the agenting business all too well.

"How did you know you'd get anything good?"

"I knew. The ones who are going to deliver have a look about them."

"What look?"

"Their eyes are different." She suspected he had made that up as he was talking to her, but she liked to hear it nevertheless. All that work was going to be worth something.

"Are you happy?" asked Jane wistfully when she told her.

"It was my childhood dream," she said and went in search of Bill Waring.

The next ten days were a blur of waiting. She promised herself she would not sit by the phone. She would go about her business. The kids needed sneakers. She owed everyone in the neighborhood a dinner party, but to invite them would be to explain about the separation. No. She would continue to owe them for a few weeks longer.

On a day when she was sure she would go mad with anxiety over the outcome of her book, she called home to find Charlie crying hysterically and Rachel screaming at him to let her have the phone. Where was Marcelle?

"Where is Marcelle?" she asked several times. "Did she take Jeremy home?" In a surprise about-face Alden was now encouraging Jeremy to visit Charlie. "She shouldn't have left you alone. How long have you been alone?"

Rachel finally succeeded in wresting the phone away from Charlie. "Marcelle is gone," she said soberly into the phone. "We were all playing outside and a man came by in a car and told Jeremy to get in it and Jeremy went and that was it. They drove away. But Jeremy was surprised. He hadn't expected the car to take off like that, you could tell. He yelled, 'Hey, wait a minute.' When Marcelle found out about it, she went crazy. Now she's gone to get Jeremy's dad. Do you want me to give Charlie his supper?"

Sara was stunned and confused. "Darling, I'm starting home now. I'll call Penny and ask her to come and sit with you until I get there. Meanwhile give Charlie some gum, it's on the second shelf in the pantry. And please, Rachel, lock all the doors right away. Don't forget. Lock everything until Penny gets there."

When she got home, she forgot everything—the book, Warren Newman, Bill Waring; her heart and lungs felt as if someone had given her a terrific blow. Natalie met her in the driveway with the face of someone who has been made suddenly and irrevocably insane.

"Jeremy's gone," she said in a ghostly vacant voice. "Somebody took him."

Miranda heard the child often, and it surprised her because she had never heard sounds from the other apartments in all the time she'd lived there. By some accoustical law, she decided, his high-pitched little voice was probably carried efficiently through the walls.

David never answered her knocks although he always answered the phone, and while his voice was guarded and nervous, love and concern for her still came through. The biggest difference was that he no longer went out. She didn't hear him in the morning or at night. He told her, however, that his business was definitely on the mend. The agency was going to survive.

One day she stood outside David's door and heard the child inside. She knocked timidly and heard someone (the child?) struggling to open the door.

"Hullo." She was afraid to go in, certain that he had opened the door by mistake and would now make David angry. She had ceased to expect David's life to be accountable, but this seemed perverse in another direction.

"Jeremy," David stood at the entrance to the living room, "you shouldn't have opened the door." He turned to Miranda and took her aside. "This . . . this is my sister's boy," he whispered. "She's leaving her husband and . . . and she's afraid he's going to kidnap the kid."

"What's your name?" Miranda turned to Jeremy.

"Jeremy."

"Where do you live? Do you know your address?"

"Pheasant Hill."

"What a pretty name. Where is that?"

"It's in Ryder's Goose Neck."

"Oh. Do you miss your mommy?"

"No. Yes." He looked to David for assurance. Was it all right to answer all these questions? "My daddy's coming to get me."

"Oh?" She looked at David questioningly, but he merely shrugged.

"What's your daddy's name?"

Jeremy looked surprised. "It's Alden, but I had to think because nobody calls him Alden. Mr. Simmons calls him sir and mommy calls him dear.

"Who's Mr. Simmons?"

"He's the butler."

She raised her eyebrows. "Of course. Who else would he be? I didn't know your sister had married so well," she said to David who appeared extremely uncomfortable.

"She didn't. A salesman actually. The kid has a vivid imagination."

Miranda looked around and realized David could use a break from babysitting and she could use some diversion. "Can he come to my place for a while?"

David looked terrified. "No." He leaped out of his chair as if to physically bar her from taking the boy. Then he tried to smile. "Uh . . . my sister . . . well, I promised her I wouldn't let him out of my sight."

"Why don't you both come?" She looked down at a Monopoly game and a checkers board and tiles. "Let's take these with us."

David looked anguished and then sort of slumped in agreement. "Uh . . . okay. I guess that wouldn't be so terrible."

For the next week Jeremy and David were frequent visitors to her apartment, and twice she coaxed David to actually leave them alone so he could go out and get a change of scenery. She promised to bolt the door and not let Jeremy out of her sight. On one of those days she questioned Jeremy again about his background, and he stuck to his guns about the butler. He even described Mr. Simmons without hesitation and told her about Dolly and Lucinda and Mrs. Remington.

He also told her his last name, and the next day she went to the library and looked up Van Druten in *Who's Who*. There were three of them. An uncle, Milton, a brother, Charles, and Alden, identified as a sportsman and financier. His first marriage had been to Ruth Wilder and his second to a Janet (Taffy) Thornton with a daughter (deceased) resulting from the union. After the entry ''3rd m. 1967 Natalie Hartley Davidson,'' Miranda stopped and read it all through again as if she had missed an important point. Her eyes again arrived at the name, Natalie Hartley Davidson, but her mind, rejecting such a bizarre coincidence, came up blank.

She mulled it all over on the way home, puzzling over David's lies, over his sudden terrible decline. He had assured her that he had raised the money he needed to heal his ailing business, and she wondered why if this were true, he continued to appear so beaten and haggard. But then, entering the lobby and stopping for a moment to adjust her parcels before punching for the elevator, she felt a wetness on her leg, and her mind closed to everything but that sudden eerie itch which is what the blood felt like trickling down her inner thigh.

She was wearing high boots the tops of which stood out slightly from her calf and were now catching drops of blood.

The immediate thing to do seemed to her to lie down, and she placed wads of newspapers under her buttocks in case she bled through to her bed. The trickle stopped, or at least no blood collected under her. There was just the sticky wetness from the initial flow. She would wait to get up and call Dean Whitley.

It was after five and the light was fading when she crawled to the telephone.

''Is it an emergency?'' asked the operator.

''Yes.'' she replied.

In the Alan Gutmacher book on pregnancy there was a list of the seven things that constituted an emergency and bleeding (this was no longer spotting) was at the top of the list. She didn't feel in any danger at the moment, but a gush could come at any time.

"This is Dean Whitley," he returned the call in less than five minutes.

"It's Miranda," she said quietly. "Around four today I began to bleed."

"Yes. Heavily? Was it heavy, more than spotting?"

"Heavy enough to drip down my leg . . . more than spotting."

"Why didn't you call right away?"

"I thought it best to lie down . . . that seemed to stop it."

"Of course. I'd better see you. Where do you live?"

"Eighty-first and Third."

"Take a cab to Lenox Hill hospital. I'm about to make my rounds and I'll examine you in one of the rooms there. Wait for me in the outpatient room and I'll be there." He paused. "It's not necessarily bad news," he added softly, thinking how heartsick she must feel.

He knew he ought not to reassure her. It was against all good medical practice. If you told them nothing was wrong and something went wrong later, they brought it up to you forever after. Still, the thought of her pale and worried was too much to ignore. Maybe nothing was wrong. Or maybe his original hunch had been right.

He saw her right away, huddled in her seat although it wasn't cold in the room. "Come on," he said, leading her to a small cubicle. "Let's take a look."

He spoke a few words to a nurse at the desk and she brought a sheet and draped it on the examining table. "You don't have to take all your clothes off. Just remove your underpants and push your skirt to waist level," said the nurse. "I'd like to put a pillow under you to elevate your hips, we don't have stirrups on this table."

He came in briskly pulling on transparent surgical gloves. "I won't hurt you by inserting a speculum. If nothing's wrong, it would be best not to poke around. What I can do is a superficial examination to see how much bleeding there is likely to be . . . . if it's likely to continue." He felt the cervix which had begun to flatten out but still had a way to go. His glove showed some discoloration. It was not fresh blood. Perhaps it was the end of it.

"It looks good," he told her. "No bleeding now."

He was reluctant to let her go and tried to sound casual when he offered her a ride home. "You should definitely stay in bed for a few days. You shouldn't be on your feet any more than you need to be. Go to the bathroom on your hands and knees."

She wasn't listening to him. The bleeding nagged at her and she wanted more reassurance. "Doesn't the bleeding do something to it? How could it be all right?"

"His heart's strong and steady. He's very energetic, moving around. The bleeding isn't necessarily from the baby. I think it's what we've suspected all along—placenta privae—the placenta growing too close to the cervix. But I don't think it's decisive yet or you'd have gone into labor. Do you have someone to take care of you?"

"No . . . Oh, yes. A friend down the hall. He'd look in on me, I think."

"Do you know him well? Is he a stranger?"

"Definitely better than a stranger," she smiled weakly, thinking of David's complicated life. Still, he would be kind.

"I'll take you home," he said suddenly, "and see that you get into bed."

"You can't make a housecall," she teased him and tugged at his lapel, "the AMA will string you up by your thumbs."

"It'll be our secret." He covered her hand with his for a moment, glad to see her smiling even though it was at his expense.

When she settled herself beside him in the car, the intimacy of it shocked him. He had never been alone with her in any but a public place or professional situation. Now he had to force himself not to touch her.

He liked Miranda's apartment, but the beribboned crib in the corner made him uneasy. There was already a stuffed animal in it and one of those footed sleepers.

"I was serious about the bed rest," he said remembering why he was there. "Have you had your dinner?"

"There's some stuff in the refrigerator." She waved her hand in the direction of the tiny kitchen and gratefully sank into the window seat.

The refrigerator contained a half carton of milk, a container of cottage cheese, and two oranges. "This won't get you through tomorrow," he called out to her. "I'll bring you something on my way to the office tomorrow. I have an hour between the hospital and office hours."

"And you want to spend it pushing a shopping cart?"

"Wait till you see what you get before you canonize me."

He left right away, not trusting himself to sit down, but every day that week he dropped in on her and he found to his amazement that it gave a new purpose to his days. He looked forward to the walk to her apartment which was only seven blocks from his own. He also looked forward to deciding what she might like for dinner. He even looked forward to her wisecracks which were getting a little less personal, or maybe he was getting used to them.

On Wednesday he brought her two books, the poetry of John Donne, a particular favorite of his, and the poems of Edna St. Vincent Millay.

"Pick any day in your life," he said, handing her the Millay book, "and Edna probably wrote a poem about it that will surprise you with how accurately it resembles what you felt. Don't read more than an hour of it though, then you'll be eager to get back to it the next day."

When he arrived on Thursday she had the book on her lap and looked about ready to burst with conversation. "I've found my favorite."

"Your favorite what?" He put some groceries in the refrigerator and came to sit on the floor next to her bed.

"My favorite of her poems. At first I thought it would be the one called 'Thursday.' That's the one where she says if she loves you one day, don't think she's supposed to love you the next day too. But then I realized it scared me. That happened to me too many times. My real favorite is called 'Second Fig.'"

"I was afraid of that," he said mockingly. "Somehow I knew you wouldn't want a solid house built on a rock."

She smiled at him and patted the side of her bed. "Come and see my shining palace built upon the sand." He looked up at her, mentally tracing the outline of her lips. "Dean," she said in perfect innocence, "can you examine me again? Can you tell me if everything's all right?"

His reaction was strong, but he tried to answer calmly. "I . . . I couldn't be impersonal . . . this setting . . . I can't do it. I just can't."

"Oh, God." She couldn't mistake the look in his eyes. "How stupid and insensitive of me." She took his hand in hers and traced the outline of his strong, slim fingers. "You are important to me. I have no one in reserve, you know, waiting in the wings. It's just me and Oscar here." She patted her belly, then took his hand in both of hers and impulsively kissed it and placed it against her cheek. "Please, don't be angry with me. Right now . . . I just don't know what I'm feeling."

He said he understood and left feeling curiously hopeful. He arranged her in her bed and pulled the covers around her. They were on a different footing now than they had been. If it was only gratitude, he'd rather not know it right away. The news would keep. Today he wanted to go home into his narrow bed and dream his dreams.

When she was better and could get around more, he stopped coming on his lunch hour and came in the evenings so he could stay a little longer. She didn't say anything at first, but then she became nervous. "I can get up now and do what I have to," she told him pointedly.

"Are you sending me away?" he asked. "I'll miss coming."

"I'll miss it, too, but I want to be with you wholeheartedly, not just because I need some support. It's just . . . there's been so much . . . let's just wait until the baby comes. That'll be soon, you know."

"I'll be the first to know," he said smiling down at her. He did a little soft shoe step in the hall outside her door. There was hope.

Sara had a great deal of trouble reaching Sam. First she called the theatre, but they were reluctant to give out his number. When she called the third time, they gave her his agent's number, but he, too, would not put her in touch with Sam directly.

"Do you want an interview?"

She decided it would be easier to say she was coming from the magazine. "Yes. But it's a rush thing. We must get in touch with him today."

She had gone to the office purposely for the first time in a week so he could verify everything by calling her back there. She felt uncomfortable being there, as if everything connected with this life was absurd weighed against Jeremy's disappearance.

Her own safety and sanity and the well-being of her children seemed to depend on her putting a distance between herself and Bill Waring.

She tried to think of him as someone in the past. Someone who had helped her know another side of herself but was no longer a flesh and blood occurrence. Bits and pieces of their conversations and lovemaking broke through her general numbness and her heart ached, but she knew the magic was over. Her life had grown suddenly bizarre and unpredictable and Reynold was not around to bolster her. It was as if he, too, had died or been kidnaped.

She told Bill Waring all of this in a trembling voice after an uneaten lunch served impeccably but less jovially by Raymundo in that nearly perfect house. As she spoke, she faced one of his lovely small-paned windows. His breath was warm on her neck. If she turned around, his mouth would be on hers and she'd be lost. But he wouldn't do that to her. Knowing he had all the advantages made him scrupulously fair. She even had a rueful smile because *she* was saying good-bye to *him*, something she would not have predicted. *Raymundo, you grinning idiot, get a load of this.*

"I need you," said Bill Waring, choking it out against her shoulder. It was unexpected. She turned to hold him and felt newly strong. Strong enough to refuse him.

It had been six days since it had happened and Sara didn't like the way it was progressing. The police hadn't been called. Everyone who knew—Marcelle, herself, and the servants—had been sworn to secrecy. Alden, it was reported by a dazed, unseeing Natalie, was handling the details.

It was three o'clock before Sam's call reached her at her desk. "I lied to your agent," she said. "What I've got to talk to you about is far more important. Please. Can we meet?"

"Can't you be more specific over the telephone?" He was more than suspicious. He was annoyed.

"I'm not some kooky, starstruck girl." She reminded him of the evening with Bill and Belinda Haas and he thawed a little. Finally she said, "This concerns Natalie Van Druten."

"Yes?" The voice was low now and interested.

"It concerns her and . . . and . . . someone else. Someone you don't know about. Please, trust me."

"I'll meet you at the Russian Tea Room in half an hour," he said curtly. The story came to mind about the bearer of bad news—she couldn't expect him to be happy to see her.

When she was seated in the restaurant, however, her courage failed her. What right did she have to interfere? It was too late to think about that now: Sam Johnson was striding confidently toward her.

He appeared larger than she had remembered. He was wearing a nubby tweed jacket, no coat, and a heavy, cabled sweater underneath. He ordered white wine for both of them and then folded his arms across his chest to hear what she had to say.

"Did you know that Natalie had a child?" She plunged right in.

"No." He was suspicious again.

"This little boy—it *is* a little boy—" she said gently, "was born on May 19th, 1968, which was only seven months after Natalie was married." She hated the way she sounded, and she could see it didn't enchant him either. But there was no other way. She was building her case, point by point. "Now this little boy—his name is Jeremy—he doesn't look like his parents at all. His hair is curly and very dark and so are his eyes. But it's not just that his eyes are dark, they're especially dark and uniquely shaped. They widen out considerably at the outer corner . . . the way . . . the way yours do." She could see that he had begun to crumple inside but was listening avidly. She also saw, with relief, that he was beginning to believe her. She took a deep breath and continued. "But the thing that really clinched it for me, that gave me the courage to come here and tell you all of this, is his chin. See, he has this tiny crease in his chin just like yours." His strong, dark eyes were filled with pain and supplication. She couldn't look at him, and the worst part was still to come.

"What do you expect me to do about it?" he said finally, almost angrily.

"Right now"—it was difficult for her to speak and she took a huge gulp of her drink—"right now I think you should go to Natalie and stay with her and help her because . . . because . . ." Tears welled up in her eyes and unexpectedly he reached for her hands and held them, stroked them, as if finally he was on her side. "Jeremy was kidnaped," she sobbed, "and no one is doing anything about it."

They sat there for a long time just gripping hands across the table, and then she promised to prepare Natalie and call him back to tell him when and where he should come. He thanked her and kissed her cheek and she fell into a cab and gave Natalie's New York address. Natalie had moved into the city, intuitively feeling that this was the direction where she would most likely see Jeremy again.

Sara had seen the apartment twice, and it impressed and intimidated her much more than Pheasant Hill. There was an air of seriousness and power about it that was unmistakable. It had been in Alden's family for generations, and she was not surprised to hear that it had once been twice as large and contained twenty-three oversized rooms. That seemed perfectly plausible for a man who also kept a tailor in residence at his New Jersey estate during the grouse season so that every guest could have a complete set of shooting clothes.

The apartment had its own elevator which opened into a two-story foyer whose walls were covered with row upon row of Audubon prints in fragile, gilt-edged frames. To the right was a long, stylish, symmetrical room with Georgian moulding on the ceiling and decorated in shades of mint-green.

The room that Sara was most in awe of was a smaller parlor that had been used exclusively by Alden's grandmother and preserved as she left it. It consisted of four huge club chairs upholstered in red silk velvet slightly threadbare at the corners. The paintings were all early Italian Renaissance and Flemish. In the center was an ornate pedestal table holding carved silver boxes; the walls were vermilion silk, the rug green-rose and beige.

It was in this dark, forbidding room that she found Natalie, sitting woodenly at a makeshift altar.

"I've been praying," she said. "I never prayed in my life, not even at St. Mildred's when we spent all those hours in the chapel. And now I find myself praying like a crazy woman. I talk to God all the time. Can you think what that must be like? To be so alone?"

Sara could not. She knew a dozen people who would let her behave as crazily as she needed to and support her bodily or spiritually. Sara had insulated herself against just such aloneness, gathering friends and loved ones like an animal gathers food against the winter snows. The thought of being alone was like an icy arrow in her heart, the same icy arrow of her childhood that could come zinging back at any time. She did not want to end up bitter and finicky like her mother. Nor did she want to follow her father into that other loneliness.

Unlike the isolated woman before her she could turn to Jane, the children, Penny, all the husbands and wives that had traipsed through her living room and talked about babies, breast feeding, diaphragms, and IUDs. Still, as she marshaled her case, she did not feel comforted or safe at all and realized fully for the first time that the main safeguard against aloneness was no longer available to her. She had sent Reynold away.

Natalie had stopped talking and was looking at her questioningly. "You said you wanted to tell me something."

The look on her face was so defiant, Sara thought she might have read her mind. "Why didn't you marry Sam Johnson?" She hadn't expected to come out with it so bluntly and startled herself.

Natalie hesitated only a moment. "You've always thought your earnestness could fix anything. When will you be convinced that it cannot?"

The iciness in her voice made Sara blanch. It was as if they were children again and she was still shy Sara in her too short dress.

"Oh, Natalie, I'm so sorry. I thought I was doing the right thing. I wanted to have someone help you . . ."

"What are you talking about?"

"I've told Sam about Jeremy."

"What have you told him?" Her eyes were neither icy, nor angry as Sara had anticipated.

"That he's . . . that he's probably his son and that he's . . . that he's been taken away."

The next thing Natalie said was so unexpected and spoken so pitiably, that Sara dissolved into tears.

"How did he take the news? The first news?"

"Angry. Angry with himself for not having made you come back." Strengthened by the look of longing in Natalie's eyes, Sara continued. "Natalie, he loves you. And he wants to be with you until Jeremy comes back."

"But don't you see, I can't even think about that until I see Jeremy again. I feel I'll be punished somehow. Do you know what I've been doing the last few months?"

Sara wanted to stop her from speaking. She didn't want to know, sensing it was something horribly private and unlikely. But Natalie was determined to speak.

"I go to hotel rooms and make love to Rudy Sorbentino. He calls me when he wants me and I always go. It has nothing to do with love, mind you. I cringe when I think what I've let him do to me, and not against my will. I wanted it. . . . I could hardly wait to hear from . . ."

"No, please." Sara put her hand to Natalie's lips. "Please see Sam. He has a right after all. It's his son too."

"All right," said Natalie wearily. "But not right now. Give me some time to get used to the idea. You see, I had not counted on seeing him again."

Sara nodded and left for home. Her own children needed her, and she felt like a mother hen who wants her chicks around her. When she reached the house, however, she found Marcelle in labor and had to turn right around and take her to the hospital. Blessed Penny took her children once again so she could wait with Marcelle, who seemed calm and in total control of her labor. She was making funny noises like a little dog panting all the way to the hospital. Also she was staring straight ahead in total concentration, completely oblivious to everything around her.

An hour after they reached the hospital, a gray-haired black nurse came bustling into the waiting room with a broad smile on her face. "Ooooh I got big news for somebody heah." She looked around and seeing only Sara, her smile dimmed. "Where's the daddy?"

"Is it about Marcelle Morgan?"

"Yeah."

"It's only me. I mean I'm here for her."

The nurse was suspicious and some of her ebullience was gone. "Well, she had two of 'em. Two fine little boys." Her eyes began to sparkle again. "Perfect. Beautiful. And she done it all herself. A fine young woman."

Sara dissolved into tears, shaking convulsively. The nurse patted her shoulders and led her quietly to see the babies. Even through her tears and the terrible sorrows of the past few days the sight of those extraordinary infant boys transformed her. She was grinning wildly and would have grabbed them up and hugged them to her had there not been a thick window separating them.

It was ten o'clock when she walked in the door and the telephone was ringing. "Where the hell you been all night?" It was Warren Newman. "I've got some news for you."

"Oh, God, is it good or bad?"

"Not bad."

"You've sold it, is that it? You've sold the book?" Tears of happiness and exhaustion sprang to her eyes.

"Yup. To the Bendel's of the publishing business, Knopf." She was sobbing into the telephone. "Hey, what are you crying about, I haven't told you how much."

"Is it a little or a lot?" she said in between loud, racking sobs.

"It's not little enough for you to carry on like that. It's twenty grand up front, payable in thirds."

"That's wonderful. Thank you. Really. Thank you. You helped me—it wouldn't have worked if you hadn't helped me." For some reason this idea created a new wave of tears.

"You know, it's a funny thing," he said, ignoring her sobs, "authors can't thank you enough when you make a sale. They fall all over themselves. But when the book is finally published, they always feel I didn't get them enough. They're mad as hell."

"I won't. I won't be mad as hell."

"You will," he assured her philosophically, "it never fails."

When she hung up, she dried her tears and tried to think of someone to share her news. Natalie was in no shape to respond to anything. She finally dialed Bill Waring, but not with any confidence. Raymundo answered. "Meester Beel is not at home," he said cheerfully. "Want to leabe message?"

"No. No message."

She went into the kitchen, drank a glass of milk, and tried to relax and get sleepy. It didn't work. She had to talk to someone. What was the good of anything happening if there was no one to tell it to.

Reluctantly, with a lump of fear in her throat, she dialed Reynold's cottage. He answered right away.

"Were you sleeping?"

"No. Is something wrong?"

"No. Nothing . . . well Marcelle had her baby . . . babies—she had twins. Two perfect baby boys."

"My God, twins . . . wow. Is she all right?" She could have kissed him for his extravagant response.

"Yes, fine. She did it all herself, panting away and pushing." There was a long silence and she thought he might have hung up. "Reynold?"

"Yes."

"I sold my book today."

"That's wonderful." He sounded happy but more distant and guarded than he had about Marcelle's news. "When did you find out?"

"Just about ten minutes ago. I didn't have anyone to tell. I hope you don't mind."

"Of course not. I'm delighted for you."

She waited for him to ask her why she didn't tell Bill Waring, but he did not. "Wouldn't you like to know how much I got?"

"Sure."

"Twenty."

"Twenty what?"

"Twenty thousand."

"Sara, that's fantastic." His voice was somewhat less guarded.

"Reynold," she felt tears welling up in her eyes again, "thank you for listening. It's been such a day. I went to see Natalie and she's so distraught over Jeremy. When I got home Marcelle was in labor. I was the only one there for her. The nurse kept asking me where the father was." She couldn't stop crying and Reynold was calling her name, trying to cut through her sobs, but she rambled on, unable to stop. "Then the phone was ringing when I got home. It was my agent. Did you know I have an agent? Doesn't it sound ridiculous? I'm ashamed to say it." She cried louder. When she had some control, she began again, "Reynold, are you coming home this weekend?"

"I think so. Why?"

"Because . . . well . . . so I can tell the children."

"You can tell them I'm coming," he said. "Good night."

After she hung up, she sat for a long time with the open phone in her lap. She had wanted to say different things to him, but now she didn't have the right. She wanted to ask him to help her bear all the awful things that had been happening lately. He had known her so long. He knew everything about her. He knew just what she needed when she was happy and when she was sad. Yet she was the one who had sent him away.

Chapter 19

IT WAS DEFINITELY NOVEMBER WEATHER. THE sun had thinned out and could no longer be counted on to warm. Alden now wore sweat pants under his running shorts and silk-lined mittens.

He began his fourth lap around the reservoir and felt jubilant. Eight miles were now well within his ability, and a new bonus of this prowess was the sudden change in the content of his reveries. They were no longer exclusively filled with past scenes. At times Alden received unmistakable guidance that came in the form of nudges that made him take decisive action in his life. The removal of Jeremy had been orchestrated right here on the track. He had masterminded Natalie's despair so expertly, she was now a virtual stranger.

Many needs had been filled with one stroke. David had his money. Natalie had her anguish. And he had Jeremy. Of course, he hadn't been able to visit David in case he was being followed, but that would come soon.

Having taken all these steps, however, Alden was surprised to still feel a tip, tip, tapping in some inner recess of his consciousness, a warning of something left undone. He had missed something obvious and important, and today he would look for it.

In the next lap he began to feel a total release, and soon his mind gave up its contents and invited him to fill it anew. Without thinking he put David on his mental screen. So . . . the tip, tip, tapping had to do with David? As he watched, David's eyes filled with tears and his face became pale, almost white and twisted in pain. No. It wasn't pain at all, it was fear. He was white with fear. Why was David so frightened? Had he done something wrong and now feared retribution? Perhaps he was thinking of returning the child? Perhaps they had all been separated too long and spirits were low. That settled it. He would visit them and give them a pep talk. He liked the idea of bursting in on them and livening their spirits as George Reems had done to his army of exterminators in Algiers. He would go home and bathe and change, and later after dark he would pay David a visit.

He found Natalie sitting in his grandmother's room, which pleased him. It was almost the exact pose his grandmother took every day and equally unhappy. She appeared so weary and forlorn, he took her hand and urged her to join him for breakfast.

"Come, my dear," he said. "Have something to eat with me. It will make you feel better."

She took his hand obediently, thinking she had never seen this side of him. She wanted to ask if he had heard anything about Jeremy but decided to save the question until later in the day. She allowed herself to ask it once each day, but it would be wasted so early. She felt extremely heavy and limited in her movements. She knew she was totally vulnerable, but still she followed him.

Miranda awoke particularly early that day but remained in bed. She watched all of the *Today* show, including the commercials, with rapt attention. A blond lady novelist overcome with nervousness was being interviewed by Barbara Walters whom Miranda had never liked. But now Barbara was being kind and patient with the novelist and it made Miranda tearful. "I want to be good," she said out loud to the image of Barbara Walters.

When a game show called *Concentration* came up, she continued to watch, miraculously solving the first puzzle with just one eye and a capital *V* showing. It was: "I've got you under my skin." She reached out from her bed and turned up the volume. When there was silence or near silence, too many voices echoed in her head. There was Bob Paxton's voice saying something she had never forgotten: "At school you looked so . . . . so . . . . foreign." Sanche calling her a crazy bitch. Bradley Gifford telling her she was supposed to service him. Barbara Lancia feeding her like an exotic, foreign delicacy to her male friends. Had she missed the point? Had she all along been too vainglorious? That word sprung out at her from the catechism when she was a child. In order to be a child of God, it said, she could not be vain or vainglorious. To her chagrin she found the word perfectly described her innermost feelings—excessive pride and exhilaration in the self. She had meant to shine, and now she considered that perhaps that had been her downfall all along. She had ceased to be a child of God.

Later in the day she roused herself, buttoned up against the cold, and went out to buy a few groceries. She had bled twice since Dean Whitley stopped coming, but each time she waited and the bleeding stopped. Today there was no bleeding, but terror and fear drifted in front of her each moment she wasn't distracted.

When she returned home, she showered, washed her hair, and decided to cook a nice dinner and invite David and Jeremy. She had seen them once or twice during the week, and they both showed the strain of being imprisoned together in David's small apartment. David no longer felt safe coming to her apartment, and he would only let her visit for an hour or two at a time. She would take the dinner to them and perhaps play a game of Monopoly with Jeremy.

They were sitting on the floor, the Monopoly game spread out in front of them, when the door burst open and Alden stood looking down at them with disbelief.

He glared at David. "You've ruined it. My God, you've ruined it!" His eyes were troubled, they seemed to grow larger and deeper. He grabbed Jeremy by one arm and yanked him aside the better to reach David whom he then began to punch as hard and fast as he could, which was awkward because Alden was so tall and David was sitting on the floor.

David struggled to get up, but Alden would not let go of him. His rage gave him tremendous strength, and he picked David up with one arm and threw him against a table. "I told you not to tell anyone."

Each word came out separately. He was breathless. His face was dangerously red.

Miranda, fearful that she would be next, grabbed Jeremy and fled to her own apartment and locked the door. Her heart seemed too large for her chest. It pounded wildly and she was sure she was going to faint. *You've never fainted*, she said to herself, leaning against the closed door. Then she looked down at Jeremy. "Don't worry," she said. "That bad man won't get us."

He looked at her puzzled. "That's not a bad man. That's my father."

She stared at him bewildered. "Your father?"

"Yes. I've never seen him so angry. Do you suppose he'll hurt David?" He looked torn by his loyalties. His broad forehead had tiny creases, his dark eyes were darker. "My father wouldn't hurt anyone unless they deserved it."

"Jeremy," she said trembling, "tell me again, and it must be absolutely true, what is your father's name?"

"Alden Van Druten."

"And your name?"

"Jeremy Davidson Van Druten."

"What's the Davidson for?"

"That's my mom's name . . . before she married my father, she was Natalie Davidson."

My mom's name. My mom's name. Cold air was coming through the window. It had finally turned autumn. *My mom's name.* Through the layers and layers of memory the information raced along. A blond girl. Cool hands folded appraisingly across her chest. Smelling faintly of . . . what? Moss. Fresh water. Natalie Davidson. Oh, my God. So beautiful. So different from herself. *Don't worry, Miranda, I will always take care of you.* It had been said hastily, impatiently, as if having to say it was ridiculous.

She turned the television on loud so Jeremy would be distracted and waited by her own door for sounds, any sounds that the chaos across the hall had ceased. Then she heard his footsteps and could actually hear his breathing. He knocked against the wall, and she heard another door open to search out the source of the thump. Then the elevator whir. The opening and silent closing. She opened her door. Across the hall an elderly woman stepped out timidly in her bathrobe, her face already free of makeup, oiled for the night, her hair in tiny pin curls.

"Did you hear something?" she asked.

"Yes."

"Probably drunk, don't you think? A drunk . . . dreadful . . ." She shook her head and went inside again. Miranda heard several clicks, all her locks. The chain.

She dialed David, but there was no answer. "Stay here, please," she said to Jeremy.

He could smell the carpeting and he could hear a soft thump every few minutes as he drifted in and out of consciousness. The pain in his head and his ankle was making him faint over and over. It felt good, warm, when the blanket of black fell over him. Strange. He had never liked to be too warm, but now he couldn't get enough of it. It was so cold there on the floor. There was a terrible current of air sweeping back and forth across his body, and he began to shiver before he passed out again.

One of the times he came to, he remembered the face. Insanity. There was nothing more powerful or interesting than insanity, and he had seen it. What a pity. He might have been able to stave it off. He had had plenty of time, plenty of warning, yet he had gone along, done nothing. He had felt powerless against that determination. Alden had been determined to carry out his plan.

David tried to go back to a time when he thought well of himself. He had felt best when he began the business, full of hope, bursting with energy. There was nothing that hard work and his faithful brain couldn't accomplish. He had been right. He had made it, but how had it all turned sour? He didn't blame anyone, certain now that the seeds of his future had been planted by himself. "You are the author. It is your script," said the preacher on the radio every Sunday. He had thought it was campy to listen, but now the words haunted him. "What happens to you has first been created in the dark recesses of your imagination. Don't look outside yourself. There is no answer there. Look first inside your own soul." The preacher had also said something else. "Don't entertain doubt as if it were a favored guest. Boot it out and say, 'There's no room for you here!'" Now he understood. He had entertained doubt. He had invited it in.

David began to weep. He was weeping helplessly and painfully into his carpeting when Miranda appeared. It would be so easy to blame her, but hadn't he insisted on being her friend? If she had not come to work for him, his agency would still be thriving. If she had not visited them, he and Jeremy would still be alone and Alden would . . . He had not thought about Alden. My God! He was on his way to kill her.

David's door was slightly ajar, bumping softly against the jamb due to the current from some open window. *The cold crept up on us,* thought Miranda. *It was so warm this morning and now* . . . She opened it timidly. "David . . . David . . ." The room was total chaos and he was lying crazily intertwined with overturned table and chairs, his foot at an odd angle through the leg of a chair. Blood was oozing from his nose which seemed pushed uncomfortably to the side touching the carpeting. His hair was matted at the temples, and at a quick glance he looked like a sleeping child who had played too long and too hard.

She took his head and cradled it in her lap and he stirred.

"He's going to kill his wife," he said.

"Where? . . . Where?" She wanted to tell him that she knew who the wife was, but it seemed pointless. He would think she had gone crazy as everything else had. "Where does she live? Where is he going?"

"I don't know. He never told me that, but Jeremy will know."

She went to get ice for his nose and gave him a glass filled halfway with Scotch.

"The mother doesn't know the boy is here. He was kidnaped."

"Kidnaped? By his own father?"

"Yes. He wanted to punish her for being . . . unfaithful."

"But he . . ." Miranda blushed. She had been about to say that Alden was a homosexual so why should he care, but she couldn't.

"Please go now," said David. "I'll be all right."

"Think, Jeremy." She had returned to her own apartment and was looking for something warm to put on. "What street is the apartment where Daddy and Mommy live."

"Ninety-third. But I don't know the number."

"Haven't you seen it many times? Does it have a canopy?"

"What's a canopy?"

"A thick cloth that comes out on the street. Like we have."

"No. No canopy. Just a lot of brick and a cross on the side of the door." He saw the look of disappointment on her face. "I know something that will help you. There's a doorman and when he smiles, he has a gold tooth right in front."

"What does he look like?"

"Well, he's short and sort of oldish."

She saw he was trying to help her, and she kissed him and told him that he had helped a lot and that he had to stay there for a while by himself but not to worry. If he was tired, he could just go to sleep. She would be back soon.

She had no clothes that fit her and that were also warm, so she struggled into an old pair of wool slacks and strung a rope belt through the gaping waist to hold it together. Over that she wore a loose shirt and a jacket and took a cab to Ninety-third Street to look for a brick building with a cross on the side of the door and a short, sort of oldish man with a gold tooth.

She went up and down the block, certain at times that she had found the building, but there was no doorman to be seen, and she was unable to see any nameplates in the lobby that would help her gain entrance or ask if Natalie lived there. Between Madison and Park there was no building that fit Jeremy's description. She crossed Park Avenue feeling extremely cold and damp. She thought she felt something wet in her pants, but couldn't be sure. She was so cold and nervous she couldn't be sure of anything. Perhaps she was leaking urine? The pad would catch it. She had worn two pads, just in case. She tried not to come down too hard on her feet as she walked. She didn't want to jar anything loose. She didn't want to bleed again. Still, there was no choice. She had to find Natalie.

She had crossed against the light and ran the last few feet to avoid a speeding taxi. On the corner of Park there was a building that wrapped around the block with the entrance on Ninety-third Street. Perhaps that's why Jeremy hadn't known the number. There would be no number on the side entrance. Then she noticed a small enameled plaque on the corner, one facing Park and one facing Ninety-third Street. 131.

She peered inside the lobby and saw a uniformed back facing the elevators. He turned around and came to the door.

"Yes, miss?"

"It's very important that I see Mrs. Van Druten. What is her apartment number?"

Doubt was written all over him. What could she possibly want with Mrs. Van Druten? "I have to announce you."

"Oh, she wouldn't know my name, but you see"—she searched for something to convince him—"I have information about her little boy. You know him. He told me where his mommy lived there was a doorman who smiles a lot and when he does, you can see a gold tooth."

The doorman smiled despite himself and looked more at ease. "Well, she's not here at the moment. Just went out as a matter of fact."

"Alone?"

"Oh, no. With Mr. Van Druten. They both had on exercise suits. He runs, you know. He runs quite a bit." He said it as though she could offer him an explanation. "But he's never taken her with him until tonight."

"Which way did he go? Did they take a cab? Where does he run? Just in the street?"

"He runs in the park. He'll be mugged or killed one night, I'd say. He tells me he carries a gun but that his feet'll save him. He says there's no mugger than can outrun him. I don't know if that's true." He shook his head with real concern. "Give me your name and I'll tell her you was by."

"Oh, no." Miranda was agitated now. "It'll be too late. Never mind."

She found a cab on Park Avenue and asked him to go to the park. "Where does everyone jog?"

"Around the reservoir."

"Take me there."

"I'll take you to the nearest entrance. You have to walk there yourself." He turned around and eyed her skeptically. "You planning to run there now?"

"I'm looking for someone. Please, hurry. It's very important."

"Ummm."

She knew what he was thinking. He thought she was trying to pick someone up. He thought she was a prostitute.

"Look, it's none of my business," he said, "but I wouldn't go into the park tonight. Why don't you let me take you home and you can run in the morning.''

He was gray-haired and his face was creased. Somebody's grandfather no doubt. ''No, please. It's not what you think. I must go to the park.''

He drove to Eighty-sixth Street and stopped on the park side of Fifth Avenue. ''This is as close as I can get to the reservoir. There's a bridle path and beyond that is the track. It's about two miles around. A little less. Are you sure you want to do it, miss?''

She put five dollars in his hand and ran in the direction he had pointed. It was completely dark and all the stars were out. The slight wind had taken away all signs of smog. She began to walk timidly at first on the narrow path. She could see the chain link fence and from time to time rubbed against it as she walked. Her equilibrium was not what it used to be. The bones were spreading.

She didn't know whether to run or just wait for them to reach her. Had it happened? Were they here at all? She felt too chill to keep still and began to move in a cross between a shuffle and a jog. It had been so long since she had been active, her legs felt unsteady and weak. Every so often there was breathing behind her and someone would pass. It was strange. She couldn't hear the footsteps because of her pounding heart, but she could hear breathing, labored breathing which under any other circumstances would have scared her to death. Her uterus kept contracting out of nervousness and fear. A preview of real labor. Real labor. Soon. Soon. How she yearned to see who was attached to that tiny heel. More breathing. Labored. Agonized. Closer and closer and then—THUD! A huge push against her. She screamed.

''Hey, I didn't see you. You can't just stop like that in the middle of the track!'' The voice hurried on.

When her heart had stopped pounding, she realized she was getting wetter and wetter between her legs. Was it urine? Had she peed in fright? She refused to think of anything worse. Not now.

She began again a little faster and then heard another sound that was unlike any of the other sounds she had heard coming. Grunts. Grunts and sobbing. Her heart raced ahead again, so wildly she was sure it could be heard everywhere. But in between the beats, a sob. A wrenching sob and grunt. *Sob, grunt, sob, grunt*. Before she realized it, they were upon her.

She knew it was them and stood in the middle of the path to block them. Natalie came first and Miranda shoved her from the path and hurled herself between them. "Run, Natalie," she screamed. "He's going to kill you. I have Jeremy."

Alden was startled and lost his bearings. He couldn't take any more interference. Any more setbacks. First David had let him down and now, now . . . "What the hell! Natalie, Natalie, come here."

"Here I am," said a voice in the dark. He felt in front of him and caught the roundness of her belly, then before anyone could think or move or run, he put the gun at its center and pulled the trigger.

The sound and sudden stillness calmed him instantly and he felt himself finally at rest. His legs pleasantly tired and eager to stop. All the restlessness was miraculously gone, and he felt as he had long ago before it started. It was the most peaceful moment he had known all his life. Was it a reverie? Perhaps he was still running and had reached some new plateau? That was it! It was too lovely to ever leave. This was the only state in which he wanted to be. He took the gun which was still in his hand and placed it lovingly in his mouth. The second shot was hardly heard at all.

The Maternity Ward
Lenox Hill Hospital
Late November 1974

THE MATERNITY WARD AT LENOX HILL HOS-
pital was not for charity cases. It was a
Park Avenue hospital, an acceptable birthplace for the rich and near
rich whose deliveries were programmed to coincide with a hole in the
doctor's golf schedule. At other maternity wards—Roosevelt or Metropolitan—you could hear yips and screeches of pride and joy in
seven languages any night of the week. The rich, on the other hand,
were virtually catatonic when emotionally overcome, when seeing
their newborns. Conversation was muted. The place was hushed.

Occasionally a premature labor or detached placenta would bring a
Junior Leaguer in bleeding as profusely as her counterpart in Harlem.
In such cases the husband usually cried. When frightened the rich
cried but still didn't make much noise. Characteristically, the comings and goings on the expensive seventh floor with its abstract art
and abstract emotions were as pleasant and predictable as lunch at
Brasserie.

Tonight there were not one but two emergencies, the details of
which had sent the assistant night nurse, Charlene Gibbons, into a
state of nervous excitation.

"There's two of 'em in there. One delivering and one almost dead, getting a transfusion. Intensive Care is full up, so they gave her to us. I'm sure glad to see you, Lena." Charlene couldn't wait to corroborate what she considered juicy and potentially long-lasting drama with her friend Lena, the head night nurse.

"Is the other one pregnant?"

"She had something in there." Charlene was suddenly sober and close to tears.

"What happened?"

"Wait. There's more. One's got a bullet hole right through her. Came right through, baby and all. They did a section, and, you know, that tiny bugger, four and a half pounds, is holding on. I don't know about Mama, though."

Lena put her sweater and bag of knitting under the knee space of the desk at the station and tried not to react or ask any more questions which would be what Charlene wanted. Having whetted her appetite with selected bits, Charlene would now get stingy with her information.

She walked casually to the waiting room and saw a young woman huddled in a raincoat and a man who looked vaguely familiar. She had seen him somewhere. Was it on Johnny Carson or Merv?

"Who's the man with?" she asked Charlene casually.

"He's not your regular street whitey. He's somebody."

"Who?"

"I don't know, but I've seen his face on television."

"What's he doing *here*?"

"Lena, I just repoht the news. Ah don't intehpret de news."

"Shit. I was going to finish my sweater tonight." Lena tried for disinterest. She knew it was the other way around. Charlene's main talent was interpreting and sometimes *inventing* the news on the floor. And when she got going real good, she'd slip into what she called her "nigger jive talk dialect." Charlene had been to Boston University Nursing School and could talk what they referred to as "white folks' English," yet it amused them both to slip into dialect, and they passed what would otherwise have been tedious nights speculating—"Honey, he ain't even been to see de baby. Ah say it ain't hissin' "—about their charges.

Charlene and Lena liked each other. They liked the night shift immensely and worked efficiently as a team even though their outside lives were totally different. Charlene had a family in Queens, Lena lived with her brother in Harlem. The hospital was a good chunk of their lives. They saw it as an adventure with endless twists and turns.

"You ain't gonna finish no sweater tonight, sweetheart. Tonight we gonna be busy." She plucked two charts from her rolling file and placed them on the counter. One was for Miranda Lesley, the other for Natalie Van Druten. "There's big complications." Charlene rolled her eyes to heaven when Lena took the charts and prepared to make rounds. "Oh, yes."

"Charlene, stop farting around. *What* complications? Tell it all, woman."

"Well, the one in Labor Room A is a Van Druten . . . If you read that little book they pass out about the hospital, you know who Van Druten is."

"I ain't read the book. Who is he?"

"He is on de boahd o dis hospital. Dat don mean he wuk heah o nothin' lak dat. It mean money. Van Druten . . . as in Rockefeller . . . as in Vanderbilt . . . Yew know whut ah mean?"

"Is she in labor?"

"Dey tryin' teh git her into labor. Dey wunt dat baby out."

"It's alive, isn't it?" Lena felt uncomfortable.

"I got a beat but it ain't de loudest noise Ah uhver heard in mah life. Ah don know, Lena." Charlene shook her head. "De one in Room B is a spic. She pretty but a spic jes' de same."

"Who's the doctor? Have the doctors been notified?"

"Dey came in together . . . see . . . well . . . dey was in the same accident. Whitley doing it all, cause Harvey Bosch taking his sweet time as always."

"The man in the waiting room," Lena assumed a stern expression, "who's he waiting for?"

"He seems mighty interested in Labor Room A."

"You kidding?"

"No, Ah ain't kiddin', gurl." Having let out more than she intended, Charlene was exasperated. "Enuf funny stuff heah tuh fill a book, why would Ah be kiddin'."

Lena walked stiffly to Room B. She was a large woman and when she turned serious, her back went stiff. The dark-haired girl lying there seemed small and fragile. She couldn't help but notice how pretty the girl was. And how pale. The constant red drips being fed into her arm had done nothing to change the deadly pallor.

"Beautiful or ugly," she said aloud, "ain't gonna mean nothing when you're dead." Lena gave a grunt and entered the room across the hall.

The woman she found in Room A was at term or near term. Her belly was so swollen, you could see networks of veins and capillaries right through her skin. She, too, had an IV, a drug to stimulate contractions. The fair-skinned face on the pillow looked exhausted, but Lena knew this was only the look of sleep. There was a bruise on her left temple, and blood was seeping through a dressing on her left arm and elbow. Lena took the fetal heartbeat and heard the faint but steady tick-tock. "A baby's heart sounds like a cheap watch," she liked to tell the women, and they were shocked when they realized *that* was it. The bare bones facts about birth always shocked the hell out of everyone.

The sight of the two women affected Lena more than she liked to admit. It was one thing to play rough-tough-nurse-that-had-seen-it-all, but another to brush aside the feeling of helplessness. She wanted to help them all. When she had been a little girl, her dreams were all one dream—to become a nurse and bring babies into the world. Right now, four afternoons a week, she was taking the final semester of a midwifery course and would soon qualify to do everything but charge big doctor's fees, as she told Charlene. The state ruling was that there had to be a doctor present even though the midwife delivered the baby, but that was a technicality. She had delivered more babies than anybody would want to know about. Some nurses held a baby back to protect the doctors who were too lazy to show up on time, but she always let them come right out and let the chips fall where they may. The rich got it stuck to them from both ends. They paid a fancy fee, and more often than not all their doctors did was catch the baby when it popped out.

The sight of a woman about to give birth had never failed to stir her. Some of the debutantes had quite a mouth on them when labor got painful. They called her a bitch and a motherfucker when she wouldn't overdose them with medication. But the ones that really irritated her were the know-it-alls who came ready to do battle. They didn't want to be shaved. No enemas. No episiotomies. They were going to do it all by themselves. Sure enough, they were the first to shit all over the bed when the going got rough. Any damn fool maternity nurse knew the baby's head forced you to empty your bowels and caused unnecessary pressure. Still, when they delivered healthy babies, she forgave them. She wanted every woman to leave with her privates intact and a bundle in her arms. And when they didn't, when they quit breathing on her—either one, Mama or baby—it broke her heart. She went again to Room B. This one was in trouble. She would make it a point to sit by her tonight.

"You better make it, you hear, girl?" she said to the motionless figure. "I don't want nobody dying in one of my beds. You got ideas about dying, you wait for the dayshift. Those mothers don't give a shit. We here in the nighttime, we care."

"The one in A I've seen before." Lena handed the folders to Charlene and made notations on a master chart. "She's society. I've seen her in the papers and here. She was at the Christmas party when the big shot shook our hands and called us part of the team." She grunted. "Team, shit." She faced Charlene, ready to do battle. "Charlene, you wrong. The one in B's not a spic. Her last name's Lesley."

"It can be anything you say, but Ah knows a spic when Ah sees one. She shoulda stayed a spic and maybe wouldn't be here bleeding to death."

Lena looked at the two figures in the waiting room. "Those two out in the waiting room is beside themselves wanting to know what's going on, but we got word from upstairs not to answer any questions if reporters come around. Whut you want to do?"

"I'll go out and talk to them."

Sam and Sara stood up when she came through the door. "Please, can you tell us anything?"

"Are you reporters?" Lena stood at her tallest.

"No. Oh, no. We're her friends. Please, you don't have to be specific. Just tell us if they're all right. If . . . they're going to be all right."

Lena softened her expression. "Mrs. Van Druten, she's just asleep. They're trying to induce labor because she was in shock. The baby's a good size, his lungs have what they need to function, so they've decided to induce."

"And Ms. Lesley?" Sara asked.

"I can't say about her. I can't say."

"Do you mind if we stay?"

"You can stay all you want to. And . . . when Mrs. Van Druten wakes up . . . well, maybe she'd like to see you."

They both sat down again to wait.

When Dean Whitley first saw her, pale and still on the operating room table, he was almost convinced she was merely sleeping. He had to force himself to view the wound and stop the liquid flow gushing out of Miranda. He worked feverishly, fully occupied. Maddeningly another part of his brain spun out that stupid religious argument, defended by his best friend in med school, Rosario Cortez— you always save the child, the mother is secondary. It didn't even apply here. Perhaps the child had even saved the mother.

It was a frayed, untidy hole made at close range. The bullet missed her vital organs but took part of the baby with it. He had to do a section. He had to clamp and stitch her body together. And that wasn't the worst of it. She was bleeding from her uterus. Her placenta was torn and gushing. Oh, God, clamps, clamps, clamps. They couldn't get the blood back into her fast enough.

The baby was turned over to a pediatric surgeon and Dean kept a vigil with Miranda. The recovery room was full and he took her into one of the labor rooms. She could not hear him, but he talked to her anyway. He told her that he had been meaning to ask her some questions. He wanted to know if she had enough money. And what was her connection with the Martell agency? Did she still care for the baby's father? And if not, would she please allow him to care for her? He wanted to stay with her until she could hear him, but another of his patients went into labor and he kissed her softly and left.

Sara had received the call about ten P.M. It was a young patrolman named Harold Sadowsky, and he had been so nervous, she had to reassure him that it was all right. Whatever terrible thing he had to tell her, she would handle it.

As it turned out, she could not make sense out of what Harold Sadowsky was saying. No sentence he uttered would stay in her mind to connect to the next, Mrs. Van Druten asked me to call you . . . would know what to do . . . accident . . . another woman . . .

Lesley . . . Miranda—he was looking into her subconscious and pulling out a grab bag of names and horrors—both in hospital . . . not expected to live . . . could you come?

Which one was not expected to live? . . . not sure . . . both in maternity . . . because they were pregnant, he supposed. A third party involved . . . the husband . . . No, not at the hospital . . . straight to the morgue. THE MORGUE! Oh, my God. Head blown off . . . blown his head off.

She knew Harold Sadowsky was not a veteran of relaying bad news or he would never have said, "blown his head off," which would put anyone in shock. He would have said, "died by his own hand" or something similar. He was not through yet. Miss Lesley had tried to tell them about a little boy in her apartment . . . all alone. They didn't want to go there—two men—and scare him. Could she come? Could she make sense of it all? No. Yes. She would come. She would try to make sense of it all.

She had to call Reynold to come and stay with the children, since Marcelle was still in the hospital. He said that he would come, but he did not attempt to comfort her. He was simply indifferent. She could have handled anything else, but his indifference terrified her, and for the first minute she wanted to beg and plead with him not to behave like that.

The young patrolman went with her to get Jeremy, armed with Miranda's handbag and keys, and they all returned to the hospital, including David, whom Jeremy refused to leave. Because of the extraordinary circumstances they had bedded Jeremy down in the children's ward and Sara had promised not to leave without him.

Finally she had the chance to call Sam, who came immediately but was unable to speak a word once he heard and stared mutely at his hands and then the wall for an hour before he said, "Do you think I could see my son?"

Parents wandered through the halls in the children's ward day and night, so no one stopped them. When they came to the room, however, Sara chose to remain outside. After a few moments there were loud, shaking sobs. She heaved a sigh of relief. Jeremy would now have a father whom he would never call sir.

She went upstairs alone and the nurse took her aside. "Mrs. Van Druten has gone into labor and she's coming along quite rapidly. She's conscious and able to respond a little. They expect the baby within half an hour. As for Miss Lesley we can't say. We can't say just yet.''

Natalie's daughter, a seven-pounder, was born at 5:51 A.M., and this time Sara gathered all her courage and pulled the nurse aside. ''If you never do another act of kindness in your life, please let this man visit Mrs. Van Druten and her baby.'' Lena was going to do it anyway, but she didn't mind playing God for a few minutes, hemming and hawing about hospital rules. When she was all alone, Sara called home and told Reynold the news.

''They're both doing fine,'' she said. ''They made it.''

To her relief he didn't sound as indifferent as before. It sounded, in fact, as if he really cared. He even asked her how she felt and if she had gotten any sleep. Maybe he was being kind because he was still half asleep. No. No. Reynold was always clearheaded in the morning. Still, she would not press it. She would just go very slowly and very gently and see if he couldn't find it in his heart to forgive her.

At 5:58, just minutes after baby girl Van Druten was born, unnamed baby boy Lesley died of a bullet wound *in utero*, which had blasted his tiny kidney and knicked his spine. Everyone was amazed at how long he had held on. He should have gone right away, but his perfect little heart had sputtered and kicked and continued to beat long after it had any right to. He opened his eyes once, startling everyone. They were large and beautiful, and it hurt them all to see him staring at them as if maybe they weren't doing their all for him. But it was Lena who really took the brunt of it.

Unnamed Baby Boy was not sitting so well with Lena. To be blasted out of your mother's womb and still hang on so strongly was courageous beyond belief. She had caught a glimpse of him that made her wince. He was perfect, his head round and beautiful, as they sometimes were with Caesarean. But when you looked down, half his side was gone. Just a couple of inches, but it was half of it.

She went and sat by the mother's side and watched the dawn filter through. Absently she searched for Miranda's hand. They always sent her to the mothers who were going home empty-handed. She dreaded it but also dreaded anyone else doing it for fear they would botch it. You had to be gentle but firm. You had to convince them it wasn't their fault. But what in the world would she tell this little pale angel lying here almost gone herself? No, she couldn't be expected to do it. When the mother came to, she would send Charlene in. Charlene would lie through her teeth. Charlene could lie to a dog and tell him wood was meat and have him gobble it down. Charlene would weave her a beautiful story until she was stronger and could handle it.

Having made her decision, Lena brought her attention to the hand she had been holding. It was not as warm as it should be. It was cool and getting cooler. Involuntarily she shook it violently as if to force the blood to heat up. But that was just instinct and she soon placed it back on the bed. Nobody would have to tell this little mama anything. She had gone right off with her baby.